# When FRIENDS Go Bad

Ellie Campbell is a pseudonym for sister writing-duo Pam Burks and Lorraine Campbell. The two sisters were raised in Scotland until they were in their teens, when their parents moved the family down to Sussex. Between them they have had over 140 short stories published in magazines. Pam now lives in Surrey with her husband and three children where she divides her time between writing, family, her allotment, a part-time job and chasing down her writing partner and big sister, Lorraine. After sailing the Caribbean as a charter cook, Lorraine finally settled in Colorado with a husband, three horses and a dog. Their debut novel was *How to Survive Your Sisters*, published by Arrow in 2008.

*Also by Ellie Campbell*

How To Survive Your Sisters

# When Good FRIENDS Go Bad

## ELLIE CAMPBELL

arrow books

Published by Arrow Books 2009

2 4 6 8 10 9 7 5 3 1

Copyright © Pamela Burks and Lorraine Campbell 2009

Pamela Burks and Lorraine Campbell have asserted their right under the Copyright, Designs and Patents Act 1988 to be identified as the authors of this work.

*When Good Friends Go Bad* is a work of fiction. Any resemblance between these fictional characters and actual persons, living or dead, is purely coincidental.

First published in Great Britain in 2009 by
Arrow Books
Random House, 20 Vauxhall Bridge Road,
London SW1V 2SA

www.rbooks.co.uk

Addresses for companies within The Random House Group Limited can be found at:
www.randomhouse.co.uk/offices.htm

The Random House Group Limited Reg. No. 954009

A CIP catalogue record for this book is available from the British library

ISBN 978009951997

The Random House Group Limited supports the Forest Stewardship Council (FSC), the leading international forest certification organisation. All our titles that are printed on Greenpeace approved FSC certified paper carry the FSC logo. Our paper procurement policy can be found at: www.rbooks.co.uk/environment

Typeset by SX Composing DTP, Rayleigh, Essex
Printed and bound in Great Britain by
CPI Bookmarque, Croydon, CR0 4TD

To Esther, Rene and Vic
Our wonderful parents-in-law

# Prologue

SEPTEMBER 1980

A frenzied ferret of a lad with white spiky hair and red-rimmed eyes stood over Jennifer Bedlow and sneered menacingly, his lip curling and chin thrust forward as if daring her to take a whack at it.

'Stupid little first year.'

'First year yourself,' Jen returned sullenly, not certain if he was. He looked big for eleven – but then everyone was bigger than her – and his uniform seemed suspiciously new. No grass stains on the knees of the trousers, no buttons dangling by a thread or snow showers of dandruff marring the blazer's immaculate surface.

Without warning, he gave her a good hard push and bolted before she could respond. Winded, Jen prayed no one had noticed and slipped quietly away from the throng of teenagers amassing beneath the shadows of the nine-foot-high wrought-iron gates.

It was her first day at Ashport-on-Sea Comprehensive, a sprawling grey brick building which loomed sinisterly over the playground, as architecturally exciting as a five-year-old's Lego project with all the razzle-dazzle and appeal of a high-security prison. Charged with the education of over a thousand pupils, its claret-coloured blazers had come to symbolise a scourge of shoplifting, petty crime, violence and vandalism to the quaking

1

neighbourhood. Once ensconced in its listless clutches the most ferocious appetite for learning, ardent dreams of glory or fiery blaze of ambition would shrink and fade in the face of over-crowded classrooms, apathetic teaching and lack of government funding. Of the thirty-eight eleven-year-olds about to join Jen's class, one would try to stab the RE teacher, two would be sent to borstal, three would end up pregnant by fourteen, and four would almost be expelled for an act of arson.

But all this was yet to come . . .

Jen slumped miserably against a wall, already longing for the familiar security of the small village primary school she'd loved for so many years. Nearby another new girl with long neat plaits and a navy tunic reaching well below her knees cowered as three menacing trolls loomed over her with peroxide mullets, inflated chests and crotch-brushing skirts. One of them darted a look Jen's way and she hastily studied her sensible Clarks shoes, kicking some dirt over their gleaming surface.

Suddenly a roly-poly girl with olive skin and a thick mud-brown ponytail planted two sturdy feet in front of Jen.

'Hello, I'm Georgina Giordani Carrington.' She thrust out her hand and in some crazy automatic reflex Jen found she'd opened two fingers to imitate a cutting motion, as if she were being challenged to a paper, scissors, stone contest. She snatched them back as Georgina continued in a posh imperious voice, 'Can I play with you?'

'I'm not playing anything.' Jen blushed furiously, instantly feeling a failure. As if she should be running around organising games of tag, kick-the-can or forty-forty home. But did kids do stuff like that in big school or would that just brand her a hopeless loser? She had no idea. Her mind went into free-fall panic. Why, oh why, hadn't she brought her new and baffling Rubik's cube with her? At least it'd have been something to show everyone.

'Oh.' Georgina shrugged and turned to lean against the wall.

Out of the corner of her eye Jen saw the trolls give the plaited-haired girl a sharp shove then stomp away, cement shaking under their seven-league bovver boots. The girl scuttled over.

'What's a les?' she whispered.

Jen exchanged glances with Georgina, relieved the silence had been broken and yet worried this fragile spirit might attract the bullies' attention to them. Her face was very pale, her jet-black hair massacred by an uneven fringe, and her dazzling blue eyes were framed by fairy-tale lashes.

'They asked if I was a les. I didn't want to say yes or no in case it was like a PLP. When you say no they say "Well, you're not a proper living person" and if you say yes, they say, "Then you're a people's leaning post" and lean on you.' Jen and Georgina looked at her in amusement. 'I'm Rowan by the way,' she breathily added, beaming bravely.

'Well, a les is a lesbian.' Jen had heard the word that summer and turned her widowed father into a stammering wreck by asking about it. Now the ordeal of listening to his excruciating explanation was about to be worth it.

Georgina and Rowan stared blankly at her.

'You know.' Jen gave a look she hoped would say it all. 'A girl who likes other girls.'

'I like other girls,' Rowan ventured timidly.

'So do I,' Georgina asserted.

'Well, I don't mean just likes them, I mean *likes* them, you know.' She flapped her hands, getting as hot and bothered as her dad had been when he tried explaining. It was all more difficult than she'd anticipated. 'Wants to kiss them and things,' she elaborated and found the word he'd told her. 'A female ho-mo-sex-ual.'

'A *homosexual*!' Georgina appeared shocked and their new acquaintance even more puzzled.

For once in her short life Jen actually felt wise beyond her years. She, who, when asked by friends only six months ago if

3

she knew what a period was, had answered with great authority, 'Course I do. It's a full stop, isn't it?'

A ginger-haired girl with a thousand million freckles bounded up to them.

'Are you guys in 1L?' Her accent was American and thrillingly foreign, her metal grin brazenly devoid of the shyness that crippled the English girls with the agony of self-doubt.

'Yes,' they chorused.

'So am I! My name's Nutmeg, but everyone calls me Meg. Come on then,' she chirped. 'We're all meeting up in the back quadrangle next to the huts.'

The three new recruits obediently followed her to a group of their soon-to-be classmates, each looking as awkward and fearful as the next. After all, it was a sharp descent from being kingpins in primary to being squitty little first-years in secondary. Jen was new to the area, as were Georgina, Meg and Rowan, and maybe that was why they were so glad to find each other. But Meg was the one who herded them together, and from that very first greeting Jen knew that not only was she going to like her immensely, but that Meg would be her heroine for life.

She had no idea how often that thought would come back to haunt her.

# Chapter 1

OCTOBER 2008

'Sorry, H, you lost me.' Jen was lining up three sticks of garlic bread on her pregreased baking tray. The lasagne was already bubbling away in a Le Creuset dish, the pasta arranged in precise rows, the cheese sprinkled in a perfectly even layer. 'Start again?'

'Put it this way, treacle,' Helen's husky voice rasped down the phone line, the result of smoking thirty Marlboro a day for the last two decades. 'You were googled. She found you on my website.'

'Googled? Me?' Jen opened the refrigerator, staring blankly at the immaculately organised contents, momentarily forgetting what she was searching for. 'Who googled me? *Why* would someone google me?'

The doorbell rang, there was a scamper of running feet, a quick 'See you tomorrow, Mum' and a slam of the door. Chloe, off to Brownies, with her friend Sophie. She was having a sleepover tonight, Jen remembered belatedly. One less for supper. She sighed heavily. Ollie must have sorted everything, helped her pack her bag, grabbed all the goodbye hugs. They were quite the mutual admiration society, her daughter and her daughter's doting dad.

She should be happy about that. So why so often did she feel superfluous, the piggy in the middle that never manages to catch the ball? In her ear Helen wittered on.

'For your information, technophobe, the whole world's googling each other nowadays. If you didn't act so middle-aged . . .'

'But that's the thing,' Jen protested, tucking the phone beneath her chin. 'We *are* middle-aged. Practically. I'm thirty-eight, you're forty-three. And what my middle-aged brain's having trouble grasping is how could someone find *me* on *your* website? Why do you even have a website? I didn't know you were selling anything?'

Sometimes Helen's high-pitched giggle was contagious, but not today. Not when Jen could hear Ollie bounding down the stairs two at a time.

'Drongo, of course I'm not. I put you down on my Bebo.'

'Bebo? Sounds like a deranged clown.'

Ollie snorted, semi-amused, as he padded towards the tumble dryer bare-chested. 'Helen's on Bebo?' he guessed, raising his eyebrows. 'Now that's sad.'

'Is that Oliver?' Helen's voice took on that reverential funereal tone she reserved for Jen's husband. 'Ask him from me, why's he still hanging around? Has he no pride?'

'Well it's his house and he's paying the mortgage, after all. Be a bit heartless to throw him out in the street, wouldn't it?'

On the other side of the kitchen, the floor disappeared under a deluge of clothes as Ollie rifled through the dryer, tossing clean laundry on to the Italian tiles.

She turned her back on his chaos and found herself staring at the corner of a large manila envelope with a return address that meant it could only be one thing. As usual, Ollie had picked up the post this morning and left it unopened for her to take care of.

'Yeah, well,' Helen responded. 'To get back to Bebo . . . I put you down as my number one best friend, of course.' She sounded peeved. At Jen not appreciating the honour, probably. 'Under your maiden name because . . . well, you know . . . and

6

lo and behold this old classmate of yours contacted me. She signed it *Love and light, Nutmeg.*'

Meg. Oh yes, it would be her. Not sweet, loving Rowan, who'd never wittingly hurt a soul in her whole life and might have been the very person Jen needed to pull her out of her current doldrums. No, because *she'd* vanished off the face of the planet ten years ago. Instead, meddling, mischief-making Meg had tracked her down, without the sense or sensitivity to know that after the Marlow Arms fiasco, Jen never wanted to see anyone from that night again. OK, maybe it was wrong to bear grudges but with everything going on in her life she had the right to be irrational, didn't she?

And now couldn't-she-ever-mind-her-own-business Helen, had opened the door a crack.

*Bugger.*

'So anyway, I emailed her back and . . .'

'Wait, wait.' Jen's temples throbbed. Rising blood pressure, she suspected. Ironic, eh? She'd moved from London almost three years ago partly to be near her ex-flatmate, but these days the woman constantly rattled her nerves.

'Please don't say you gave her my address?' Jen carefully avoided Meg's name. Not that it mattered much any more, but Meg linked to Georgina linked to Starkey and Starkey was taboo in the Stoneman household.

'No . . . though I did pass on your telephone number.' Helen huffily defended the indefensible. 'You need to accept every invitation now. Embrace all offers.'

'Climb every mountain . . . tra la la la,' Jen trilled, as she cut up some tomatoes for the salad.

Ollie was loitering, half listening, drinking milk, not from the bottle the way that had once driven her barmy, but from a glass just as she'd trained him. Was he waiting for her to get off the phone? Would they open that manila envelope together, cooing over it as if it were a newborn bairn?

7

'You know what the matter with you is,' Helen rattled on, in no mood for Jen's silliness. 'You're trying to cope with your problems single-handedly. Not confiding in anyone is making you . . .'

'Please!' Jen yearned to halt Helen's psychoanalysis in its merry tracks. Halt it, turn it round, race it back downhill and straight over a high cliff, watching from the top as it burst into flames. 'Sorry H, this really isn't the time, I've got to go. Speak later?'

Hanging up, she turned to Ollie and was shocked to see he'd not only tidied the floor but folded and stacked the clothes. How long had Helen kept her talking?

He'd covered his rippling six-pack with a slightly frayed sky-blue sports shirt wrinkled from sitting in the dryer. It would have been a moment's work to iron it but, well, that wasn't her problem now, was it? And it wasn't as if anyone else would notice or care when they'd be too busy drooling at how it matched his gorgeous eyes and how his jeans showed off his exquisite bottom. Even the men, damn it. Oliver Stoneman had always been enviably handsome. Nine years married and he still had a perfect body, killer smile and that mop of dirty-blond hair, like a field full of ripened wheat.

*And why shouldn't he look good?* Jen brooded, selecting cutlery to finish setting the table. Unlike most of the Huntsleigh fathers she knew, Ollie was a mere thirty and in his absolute prime. Walking into their local, Ollie drew flirtatious stares like flies to a butcher's, something Jen had first found entertaining, then simply tiresome. Worse, he was entirely oblivious of the fact.

But then again none of the Huntsleigh wives had made her mistake of peering into cradles when seeking their spouses, eloping with what Helen liked to refer to as Jen's 'hoochie-coochie stud boy' – an ill-advised joke of Jen's that hadn't sounded so amusing when Helen blabbed it to Ollie one drunken evening.

Ollie's mobile began to ring. 'Yes, yes,' he said. 'I know. I'll see you there.'

What did he know? Who would he see? And where? At one time she'd have asked him. He was listening now, smiling privately, his mobile clutched to his ear.

She carried two plates to the kitchen table, glimpsing her reflection in the display cabinets as Ollie wandered into the hall, his laughter filtering back. It was so unfair. Most of her life Jen had wanted to appear older. At thirteen she looked eight. At seventeen she could pass for fourteen, but only if she was wearing three-inch platforms. At twenty-five, even with full warpaint, she had to show ID to get served in pubs but now . . .

Father Time had caught up with her. Caught up, overtaken and left her standing. When guys asked Jen her age, no more could she flutter her eyelashes and say in a seductive voice, 'How old do *you* think I am?' and still receive a positive response.

Granted, her ash-blond hair hadn't changed, these days styled in a trim little cap that left her neck exposed and demanded six-weekly visits to the hairdresser. She had her dad's velvet-brown eyes and her Icelandic granny's clear skin and strong cheekbones. A constant running routine kept her slim body toned – essential really, because when barely topping five feet, it took scarily few pounds of belly fat to make her feel like a little round dwarf.

But whence had come that ploughman's furrow between her brows and the completely unmerited laughter lines erupting round her eyes? Let's face it – nothing was *that* funny.

In her velour flared lounging trousers with matching button-down top she looked exactly what she was – how Ollie's youthful metropolitan friends saw her – a dull suburban housewife.

Almost two years before their move, when they lived in the Islington flat they'd bought together when Chloe was eighteen months, she'd been the unwilling eavesdropper on an illuminating conversation at one of those shitty-awful out-of-her-element parties she usually tried to avoid.

The Camberwell flat was filled with Ollie's friends from uni, hip young Londoners chatting about that year's Glastonbury festival. Jen skulked at the top of the stairs behind a giant rubber plant, trying not to feel like everybody's granny. At the time it seemed all she could talk about was Chloe, a subject that inspired glazed boredom in her listeners and even herself sometimes.

'. . . and he's *so* incredibly cute,' a female voice enthused. 'What on earth does he see in *her*?'

'She is attractive in her own way.' The speaker sounded doubtful, like a reluctant defence lawyer who knows her client was seen bludgeoning the victim.

'Maybe it's all that great sexual experience! Older women, younger men, grrrrrr.' The third female gave a tiger roar and giggled.

'You must be joking! I've never seen anyone so uptight. No wonder Ollie works in fucking Outer Mongolia. I heard she trapped him and he only stays because he's besotted with that little girl . . .'

The door to the upstairs bathroom opened and another of the same clique emerged, heading towards Jen, ready to join the gaggle below. Any minute now she'd be seen and caught eavesdropping, however unwillingly.

Nothing else for it. She stood up, marching boldly down the stairs. 'Old Hag coming through,' she declared to their mildly embarrassed faces, and then hid herself amongst the crowd dancing in the living room. She and Ollie, Jen had realised with a shock, were the only married people there. It was then she'd started planting the seeds for change.

Ollie had returned to the kitchen and was staring at the table in evident dismay.

'Almost ready.' Jen picked up the tray of bread, wondering if he'd somehow overheard Helen mention Meg. It was the last thing she needed today of all days, when their divorce nisi was lying forsaken on the table.

But Ollie was already leaping for the door with the alacrity of an overanxious thespian who'd caught his solitary cue. 'I thought you knew I was going out. I was hoping we'd get the chance to catch up first but I'm already miles late. Maybe when I get back?'

'Maybe,' Jen said, feeling stung, knowing that even if he came in early, she'd be in bed asleep – or pretending to be. Damn Helen. Damn Meg. And damn Ollie too. She smiled, too brightly.

When Ollie had left, she threw the unwanted meal in the bin, climbed the stairs and slunk into bed.


'I still don't get it. Why do we have to go there?'

Zeb leaned against the bedroom door jamb, slamming a baseball into his leather catcher's mitt, dark hair shoved under a backward-facing Portland Beavers baseball cap. Ridiculous name for a team, Meg thought, her heart softening at the sight of her son's narrow face, so like her own, and the long eyelashes she would have killed to possess.

'Don't you want to see your Uncle Mace?' She kept her voice cheerful, wrenching free the warped top drawer of the crummy little dresser that she'd rescued from the kerb and repainted. She pulled out bras and panties, throwing them on to a pile of other garments on the bed. 'Visit your mom's old home town, see the school we terrorised when we were just your age? It's an adventure, kiddo.'

'Thought you said it was boring.' He wandered to the bathroom, his voice coming from behind the half-open door as she heard him pee. 'That Ashport place. Like power drills screwing through your skull boring.' The kid watched way too

11

much television. 'You said the school sucked big-time, the teachers were losers and the happiest moment of your entire life history was stepping on to the plane that took you outta there. *And that's why you're lucky to be home-schooled, Zeb,*' he imitated as he flushed the toilet. '*No nasty rules for you. No Little League baseball, no soccer team, no summer camps, no fun.*' He appeared in the doorway, gesturing at his dingy surroundings with an operatic flourish. 'We have our *freedom.*'

'Wash your hands,' she told him, sending him back to the sink with its leaky tap and mould-blackened grout. 'And don't be such a smart-ass. If I miss my old pals, is that such a crime? I haven't seen them for years.'

'Can't be such great pals then, can they? How come they never visit? Or even call?' Always ready with a comeback, Zeb bounded up to sit cross-legged in the centre of the clothes-strewn double bed. Outside a neighbour's beagle barked and howled, chained all day in its weed-infested yard while his owners were out cooking meth or spraying stolen cars or whatever they called work.

'Maybe they email me, clever clogs.' She closed the trailer window, blocking out the noise of the dog and the Hispanic kids next door, screaming and laughing as the eldest dragged the youngest two in a plastic red wagon. 'You don't know everything about your mom.'

'No, but I'd still rather go to Mexico.' Zeb's sneaker knocked a raggedy old concertina file, sending papers all over the crocheted wool cover. 'At least we could swim.'

'Jesus, Zeb,' Meg snapped, on the verge of losing it. 'Cut me a break. You're not the boss of me, not yet anyhow. If I say we're going to England, we're going, mister, and you'd better just start packing. I have important things to do there, if you must know. And Ashport has a beach too.'

*Even if you'd have to be nuts to go in that sewagey water,* she thought.

'I'm done packing ages ago. What's this?' Unchastened, he'd fastened on a scrap of paper. 'I can't read a word of it. Talk about lousy handwriting. It's worse than yours.'

The paper was lined, ripped along the edge. It looked like a torn-out page from a school jotter.

'That is mine,' Meg said, taking it. A memory hit her. Fourteen years old, standing in front of Mr Dugan's English class, reciting a poem she'd written, while behind their hands, Rowan, Jen and Georgina sniggered away.

> 'Rowan is the pretty one
> Who makes the boys look round.
> Georgina is the sensible one
> Feet firmly on the ground.
> Jen is the funny one
> Cracking jokes all day,
> While I am like the butterfly
> Who will one day fly away.

'You didn't know your mom was a poet, did you?'

'That's lucky,' Zeb quipped. 'Cos you might need a new career. Remember when we came back from our last "adventure", old man Bradley at the diner said if we ever take off like that again he wouldn't hold your job open, even if you were Waitress of the Month from January to July.'

But Meg was lost in the memory of that long-ago day. As she'd walked back to take her seat, Georgina had hissed, loud enough for half the class to hear, 'Bloody big-head. Why aren't I the sodding butterfly?'

And Meg had seen Jen and Rowan swap looks. What they couldn't say, wouldn't ever dare say, was, 'Because you're built like a bus, Georgina. You'd never leave the ground.'

Georgina's weight was an unspoken subject.

To her face, anyway.

'Who cares about that dumb-ass Mr Bradley?' Meg reassured her son, a little belatedly. 'It's only a diner.'

Zeb glanced down at the paper again. 'Weren't you as funny as Jen, then?' He sounded disappointed, as if she'd let him down.

Meg pulled a big old suitcase held together with silver duct tape on to the bed. 'Jen could have been a stand-up on *Saturday Night Live*,' she shrugged. 'She had us in stitches most days.' From next to Zeb's left foot, she picked up a cracked old photo of the four of them together on the Ashport promenade. Meg was doing the peace sign above Rowan's head, Georgina was standing sideways on, looking like she'd rather not be there, Jen was stretching her cheeks back so she resembled some creature from a horror movie and Rowan's eyes were half closed, a Buddha-like smile on her lips.

'I was more the . . .' She fumbled for the word. 'Well, I guess the instigator of stuff.' For a brief second she could sense a tiny prickling behind her eyes, before she shoved the scattered documents messily back in their folder.

On the table in the poky dining area, her laptop beckoned. Meg walked over and clicked on the mouse.

It took ages for the refurbished machine to warm up, and irritation flickered as she waited. The computer came from a thrift store, along with almost every possession she and Zeb owned, but at least it worked, not like that crappy CD player she bought last month. Finally, the program began to run – the hourglass icon indicating it was downloading from the server. Apart from a few spam invitations for her to invest large sums of money, ha, there was nothing in her inbox.

Maybe Jen's friend hadn't passed on the message. Or maybe Jen was still sour about Starkey, and Georgina too much of a big shot to return her phone calls or hit the reply on an email? Or were there other reasons for their silence, the thought of which made Meg sick to her stomach? Since their last meeting,

14

she'd honestly thought she'd never see the other girls again. (OK, so they were definitely women, late thirties, but she would forever think of them as girls.) And now here she was, voluntarily opening up the can of worms, getting ready to do a little fishing.

Boy, this trip had better be worth it. Even if she hadn't paid for the tickets, she knew how much things cost in the UK. A year's worth of tips would only go so far before she'd have to start begging Mace or Pop to help her out. If the tests didn't go the way she hoped . . . well, they just had to, that's all. There was more than her life riding on them.

But then again, what had she and Zeb to lose? She swept her gaze around her home, loathing the single wide trailer they'd washed up in, from its Formica kitchen to its fake wood panelling, narrow hallway and ceilings so low Zeb could jump up and touch them. She hated it all: the trailer park, her supposedly temporary job, her whole life.

If only Rowan were around to cast her healing oil on troubled waters, the way she had countless times when things between them were tense. Of the four, she was the only one guaranteed to keep a secret and not pass it on as juicy gossip. Meg had been the worst in that regard but even Jen could accidentally blurt out forbidden information and Georgina often missed the glares and frantic cues shot at her whenever she had put her big foot in it. But Rowan was different, more sensitive.

She and Rowan both had weird parents. Rowan's mother – total wacko, with her beady eyes and wild hair, seeing sin and evil in everything. And Clover and Herb might have been envied by Meg's closest friends, but the other kids at school thought they were odd beyond redemption. Their strange attire, Herb's Frank Zappa moustache. It never paid to stand out in Ashport and Meg's parents were anything but conforming. Clover had even offered the headmaster a toke one memorable sports day to mellow him out. Her 'wanna hit, man?' and his scandalised response had been the stuff school legends are made of. They were lucky Clover wasn't arrested and Meg expelled.

'Wanna hit, man?' became another mocking catchphrase that followed Meg around the playground, just as their classmates, especially the boys, loved to chant at Rowan, 'Yucky da, Taffy, how's your loony mammy?' or their other favourite, 'Rowan was a Welshman, Rowan was a thief . . .' Rowan was too shy to fight back, whereas Meg always had some withering retort to silence their tormentors, usually some sexual insult involving the boys' tiny wienies. But her brash American bravado hid the fact that it took an immense amount of willpower for Meg to go in and fight her way through each day after Clover's faux pas. Few people guessed that secretly she longed to be like everyone else, not some talked-about freak. Rowan was the only person Meg had ever allowed herself to rage and cry in front of. They'd walk for miles along the beach or huddle by the breakwater, smoking a cigarette, sharing their troubles.

Rowan was the dreamer of the group. Never waspish like Meg, nor snobbish or bullying like Georgina nor thoughtlessly eviscerating like Jen's sometimes gut-slicing humour. She'd been the staunchest of friends and ever the mediator, someone to call truce and intervene when the others were ganging up together.

But then again, if it weren't for Rowan, she wouldn't be in this mess. They could all have gone on their merry way, laid the friendship in a deep, deep grave and never had to see each other again.

Finally, Meg fastened the case, slung her carry-on bag over her shoulder and hauled everything to the front door, next to Zeb's backpack.

'Ready?' she asked him. 'Come on Zeb, don't dawdle. The taxi's waiting and you know what the security lines are like.'

'Yeah, well,' Zeb waggled a blue folder he'd picked off the kitchen table, 'you might want to bring these.'

'Shit.' She snatched the tickets from him and shoved them in her black travel wallet. 'Thanks, dude.'

'Yes.' Georgina opened her mouth in an exaggerated fashion and shouted into the elderly man's face. '*That's right. Down near that hole, by the wooden fence. You can tip it out behind the rhododendrons.*'

When she was young, her parents had employed a handyman to do some light maintenance work around their house who supposedly was deaf. Georgina used to turn her back on him and say rude words, like bottom and wee-wee and fart. And then one day her mother asked her if she'd been rude to Dick as he could hear perfectly well with his hearing aid in.

But this chappie didn't seem to comprehend a single word. Communication this morning had been nigh-on impossible, and Georgina was far too stretched to exhaust herself trying to tell him he'd cut the wrong hedge. Where was Aiden when she needed him? She shouldn't have to handle irritations like this overripe, sweat-stained clod in filthy dungarees, grinning inanely as he held out a grimy hand with a barn-load of manure under his fingernails.

Inwardly huffing with annoyance, lady-of-the-manor expression on her face, she dug in her purse for some notes, wondering why her husband had chosen to hire the village idiot. Did he do these things purposely to wind her up? Well, he could darn well unhire him. With what she was paying out, it had to be possible to find a gardener who at least knew his trade, challenged or not.

Sighing, she returned to her huge desk, littered with sketches. Daylight from the floor-to-ceiling bay window streamed on to what she called her 'creative jumble'. She hadn't yet switched on her exorbitantly expensive computer loaded with hi-tech drawing programs. When it came to brain-storming she still preferred paper and pencil.

The phone was ringing again. She listened, willing herself not to answer, six rings, seven, then silence. Five minutes later a tall figure was at the double glass-paned doors to her office, holding out a glass of Perrier with a slice of lime, looking relaxed and ravishingly Byronic in cream chinos and a half-buttoned shirt, a red Kabbalah string tied around his wrist.

'That was Heal's,' he said. 'I told them you were just about there. Couple more weeks at the most.'

'A couple of weeks!' Georgina shrieked at a pitch that almost shattered the bulb in her Tiffany lamp. 'I've barely started the blasted thing.'

'Oh, come on.' He moved over to her, placing the water on the desk and pushing back her hair with a hand chilly from holding the glass. Stooping, he bent to kiss the back of her neck. Despite herself, Georgina felt a familiar thrill of pleasure. 'A few poxy sheets and towels? You could do that in your sleep.'

'But that's exactly it.' Georgina heard her voice grow operatic again as she swatted his chin from her shoulder. 'I don't get any sleep. I'm completely exhausted, lying awake till bloody dawn, worrying about all this.'

'Hmm, I thought I heard you roaming the halls like some poor lost ghost last night.' He opened one of the balls of scrawled-over paper on the desk, revealed a drawing of a butterfly, and crumpled it up again, tossing it into the waste-paper basket in one neat shot. 'Look, Georgie, you don't want to push yourself to a breakdown. We have all those designers on staff, why don't you get one of them to . . .'

'No!' Forcing a smile, she tried to battle her rising hysteria. 'I won't do it. I can't. They're paying for Georgina Giordani and Georgina Giordani it shall be.'

18

Chewing the end of her HB pencil, she experienced a rush of despair, the same terror that hit her at the start of every project, only this time it was worse than ever. No matter that she was a thousand times more successful than that nameless art teacher who'd once sneered at her labours for being 'technically accurate but lacking in soul'. For all that Giordani Designs were rapidly heading towards Laura Ashley status, for all that she had a mini-empire of over a hundred employees in her converted Canary Wharf offices overseeing every aspect of her celebrated lines of clothing, linens, bedspreads, blinds, pillowcases, here she was skulking in her seventeenth-century manor house, relying on her home help to fend off all callers.

Inside her svelte stylish exterior she felt like a big fat fraud. The truth was Georgina Giordani Carrington had run out of ideas. The well was dry. If she was honest, it had never been more than a shallow ditch to begin with.

Back in Ashport everyone knew Rowan was the true artist, who could produce marvels with a piece of chalk and spin fairy tales from a chewed-up stub of crayon. 'Oh, she may have some raw talent, dear,' Georgina's mother would pronounce, rustling *Harpers & Queen* between her bejewelled fingers. 'But you have taste. It's in your breeding. We are related to the Fitzherberts, you know. What you have is simply ingrained, it can't be bought or taught.'

And why was she thinking about Rowan, comparing herself all over again, like she used to so many years ago? Because of that damn Meg, leaving umpteen messages on her answerphone. Well they could jolly well stay unanswered. She pushed the pin back into her long thick hair and smoothed down her Karen Millen smock. Georgina had initially made her name designing extravagant, eye-catching clothes for the plus-sized woman but she no longer had to wear them herself, thank goodness.

Aiden watched her scribble meaningless whorls and circles

on the pad in front of her, his expression veiled behind half-closed eyelids. He walked to the window, gazed out at the debris the gardener had left behind, then turned. 'Well, maybe I'll leave you to it.'

'No. Don't go.' She grabbed his hand as he passed behind the desk, holding it to her shoulder. 'I hate sitting here alone. Can't you stay?'

He wasn't quite pulling away but she could sense his fingers itching to break free. It made her want to cling to him tighter.

'I don't want to hinder the artistic flow,' he said, matter-of-factly. 'You'll be able to concentrate better if I'm not around. I'll be in the drawing room, playing my guitar.'

'Play it in here. It won't bother me, honest. Something soothing. What about that David Gray one that I like? Or a Coldplay song?'

He made a face, shaking his head ruefully, before conceding. 'Oh baby, the things I do for Giordani.'

Half an hour later, she threw the pencil down in disgust.

'This is *such* a waste of time. I might as well give up for the day.'

In a corner of the room, Aiden was sprawled with his legs over the extra-large armchair that was big enough to hold two, fingers picking at the nylon guitar strings as he improvised a nameless blues.

She stared at him, frustrated by his complete absorption while she was ready to tear out her hair.

'Do me a favour, will you?' Her voice croaked harshly and she softened it to a plea. 'How about making me a sundae? To get my creative juices going? Just a couple of scoops of vanilla with a few of those raspberries in the fridge?'

Carefully he put the Gibson on the floor, stood up and stretched. 'I'd love to, Georgie, but no can do.' His eyes met hers and held them with his stare. 'I reckon maybe the freezer's developed some kind of black hole or the midnight bandits are breaking in again. I shoved a couple of tubs of ice cream in there at the weekend and this morning when I went to pull out the butter, it had disappeared.'

Georgina felt sick suddenly, full of shame and self-loathing as she racked her memory. Two whole tubs? Was it possible? Her elbow caught her forgotten glass of water and sent the contents flying over the desk.

'Well, send Max to get some then,' she said through gritted teeth as she mopped up the spill. She could feel hysteria rising again. 'It can't be that hard, can it, to buy some groceries? All I need is a little support, is that too much to ask? Where were you anyway when the gardener was here? Did you even see the mess he made?'

For just an instant her husband's long lean body was completely still, as if he were mentally withdrawing from her crazy rantings. He picked up his guitar by the neck and headed for the door. 'I'll get it myself. Max has enough to do.'

In the doorway he stopped, fixing her with his brown eyes. 'By the way,' he sounded carefully non-committal, 'I didn't want to worry you with this earlier but Meg Lennox called again. Several times. She left an Ashport number on the machine. I didn't answer.'

Georgina found herself doodling a butterfly. It was a nervous habit she'd developed, something she did whenever she was blocked.

'Ashport? Did she say what she wanted?' She kept her eyes lowered.

'Only that it was urgent. "A matter of life and death", apparently.'

Georgina took a moment to shade spots on the wings of the butterfly she'd doodled. The first time she'd heard Nutmeg's voice chirping merrily on the home answerphone, all kinds of unpleasant memories had come flooding back. She'd been filled with righteous indignation for her friend Bella and, remembering other elements of that night at the Marlow Arms, a sense of dread for herself.

'Matter of life and death?' she repeated quietly, almost to herself.

'I guess some things don't change.' She thought she sensed an undercurrent of animosity in his tone, the emphasis on 'some'. 'I'll let you deal with that one, shall I?' he added.

He was cross with her. She just knew it. He'd had enough of her moods and bossiness. Suddenly she was overcome with guilt and fear. 'I'm sorry. I do love you.' It was whispered, part apology, part plea.

'I know.' Lightly he kissed two fingers and planted them on her forehead. 'I'll call Heal's tomorrow.'

As she stared past the rhododendrons towards the massacred hedge, she felt the pencil snap in her hand.

# Chapter 2

By the time the marshal had raised his yellow flag, Jen's heart was climbing into her throat; her palms sweating, adrenalin surging through her veins like a shot of cocaine. Was she petrified? Excited? Out of her bleeding mind? For a few chest-pounding seconds, as the flag quivered in the air, all she could think of was the first time she and Starkey lay on a bed together, his hands fondling her breasts, sliding gently over her navel, flirting with the lace of her skimpy pants until her own hand clamped over his to stop him. Another memory – darker, disturbing – tried to sneak in, but she pushed it away, her clammy fingers tightening over the steering wheel.

She'd been thinking of Starkey a lot lately, not surprising perhaps. Ollie had triggered so many memories of the first boy she'd ever loved. Quite simply Starkey had broken her heart and it had taken years of sleepless nights to accept she was better off without him. So how bloody unfair for these flashbacks to show up today, like a harbinger of doom, as if proof she were facing imminent death.

*Concentrate,* she scolded herself as she focused back on the marshal, the air thick with exhaust fumes and the sound of revving engines. Finally, the flag dropped. Jen rammed her foot down on the accelerator as she lifted the other off the clutch and the car lunged forward, swerving on the tarmac. The cheering crowd was a blur.

What – shit, that was close! – was it Ollie had said? 'Keep your elbows bent and hold the wheel lightly, don't clutch it like you're in the last stage of rigor mortis. All that straight-arm, leaning-back stuff from the movies is so fake – you can't control a car that way.'

And then from the passenger seat his hand had moved to rest heavily on her shoulder, his strong work-blistered fist between hers on the wheel, his manly cheek so close she could feel his breath as he steered them round a practice curve. 'Remember, slow in, fast out. Slow in, fast out.'

'Are we still talking about car racing?' she'd teased.

But Ollie had been serious. 'Stop messing about, Jen. You could get hurt out there.'

A car overtook her on the left, two more on the right. In a flash she forgot everything except that everyone was passing her. She dropped gears straight from fourth to second and jammed the accelerator unmercifully. Too busy smiling at another driver's startled face as she zoomed past, her foot was still floored as the car flew into a curve. There was a bang, the sound of crumpling metal, and a momentous impact that threw her back and forward against her harness.

*Bugger!* She was only at the third corner, the very first lap, and she'd crashed the bleeding car. More of Ollie's instructions filtered into her ringing skull. '*Whatever happens, don't get out until the race is over, or until the marshal tells you to. You'll probably get run over. Unless the thing's about to blow up, of course. If you're hurt – God forbid – or there's smoke coming out of the hood, someone will come to help you.*'

Oh fine! No problem there, then. All she had to do was choose between getting run over or being fried to a sizzle in an explosion of flames. Wonderful options. She was so *so* incredibly glad she'd been talked into this.

She scanned the car anxiously. The bonnet looked like a wrecking ball had hit it but she couldn't see smoke. The marshal came running to the barrier and she gave him a shaky thumbs up. Remembering the protocol, she found the fuel pump and switched it off before staring out in stunned shock, her ears reverberating from the collision.

So much for her moment of glory, such a short time ago. Sitting behind the roll bars on the back of car No. 53 in full get-up, deafened by the roar of engines, breathing in petrol fumes, she'd waved proudly as Ollie drove her round the processional for the Ladies' Race. She imagined with dread how very soon he'd be staring in disbelief at what she'd done to his precious motor.

A pain shot through her knee as she shifted position. Well, at least she wasn't paralysed and her coveralls were reassuringly free of blood . . .

The car shook violently as No. 9 took the corner and put another dent in her Fiat's rear fender. Not fair. Her newly acquired mentor had been quite clear on that point. '*This isn't a banger race, you're not supposed to hit anyone.*'

Right – so where was the black flag then? Apparently that lunatic was getting away scot-free with vehicular assault, and so were the others who evidently found it hard to miss a large non-moving target sticking out alluringly into the track. With only the occasional shuddering sideswipe to occupy her until the race ended, she found herself reliving the unfortunate sequence of events that had brought her to being a punchbag for premenstrually violent speed freaks.

Was it because of her beloved Mini, Mickey Finn? (Jen had decided that if boats were female, cars were definitely male. Noisy, smelly, easily overheated and perpetually full of gas.) She'd arranged to meet her flatmate Helen in a pub on the edge of Hampstead Heath. And, late as usual, she'd driven like a maniac into the car park with a screech of tyres because she was twenty minutes past what Helen had said was the absolute limit she would wait.

As she ran to the pub door, a young man – a kid really, barely drinking age – had held it open, grinning, and said, 'Nice wheelie,' and she'd flashed back, 'Kamikaze parking – it's the latest Olympic event,' and stalked past him.

Later Helen, dressed to score in a shiny new top and scolding Jen for turning up in well-worn jeans and scruffy trainers, suddenly nudged her with a big smirk and said, 'Don't look now, but someone's checking out your booty.' Automatically Jen spun round to find herself staring into very blue eyes and quickly looked away, blushing.

Then, to Helen's great amusement, the blond kid who'd held the door joined them, introducing himself as Ollie. Transfixing Jen and Helen with those incredible eyes, he proceeded to spout forth a load of gibberish in which the words hot saloons, street stox and ladies' night popped out. At first Jen thought he was inviting her to some sort of drinking den – she had a vision of dancing girls, small medieval torture devices and two-for-one Martinis – until her brain took in the words banger and racing cars and everything clicked.

Helen was chortling openly into her glass of Shiraz. At the bar a small group of young men were finding their friend's defection equally hilarious. It appeared to Jen's jaundiced eye as if money was passing hands.

'Nope,' she told the youthful stranger. 'Not interested. If it's all the same to you I'll stick to burning my own clutches.'

'Nonsense,' Helen contradicted, sniggering. 'She's a born racer. A regular Damon Hill, aren't you, Jen?' She nudged her friend again, staring blatantly down at the young man's faded denim jeans, or rather, the bulge by his zipper, and added archly, 'She'd love to see your *hot rod*.'

'And who are you? Her manager or her mother?' Ollie asked

cheekily, earning Helen's undying enmity with one foul slur. Half a pint later, he'd revealed that he was an engineering student, working part-time in construction (which explained the rippling biceps and gym-worthy abs).

'A builder,' Helen sneered, clearly smarting from their opening clash. 'So *you're* one of those vulgar louts that like to harass innocent pedestrians. And tell me, in your experience, has that immortal line "get yer tits out, love" ever, in the whole history of male–female relationships, worked on any woman, anywhere, under any conceivable circumstances?'

Ollie winked at Jen. 'I wouldn't worry,' he said in his best builder's drawl, beer slurping down his chin, which for Helen's sake Jen really shouldn't have found funny. 'We only yell it at the old 'uns to cheer 'em up. I wouldn't take it seriously unless you're walking with a doll like Jen here.'

Pissing off Helen was bad enough, but worse was to come. Not only was this kid at uni but he freely admitted to being a mere twenty years old. A child compared to Jen's mature twenty-eight.

But he *was* determined. Ignoring Helen's open hostility and Jen's threat to charge him babysitting fees, he wouldn't leave until he had a reluctant 'I'll think about it' for an answer.

An amateur stock-car racer, Ollie had entered his girlfriend, Lisa, in a ladies' race – entry fee non-refundable – but since then they'd broken up. Witnessing Mickey Finn do a ninety-degree turn and judder to a halt between two parked cars, he'd had the brilliant idea that Jen should take her place – as a driver, not his girlfriend. And the racetrack, the souped-up Fiat, the chance of accidentally bashing another car and not being arrested, all sounded temptingly dangerous to a confirmed tomboy, especially since her current incarnation as secretary for a shipping agency was sadly lacking in thrills.

Which was why, regardless of all Helen's jibes, she'd found herself burning rubber in the big parade ground of the local

27

military barracks, skidding round corners, under Ollie's tuition, until her head spun.

Who knew how Ollie got permission to practise there, with all the security surrounding the Ulster peace talks. But in those three practice sessions – woefully inadequate, she now realised – she'd learned that few people refused Ollie anything.

It only took a couple of debriefing drinks (not as racy as it sounded – despite Helen's slurs, Jen's briefs stayed up) for Jen to recognise that Ollie was another thing that was temptingly dangerous.

To say she didn't go out with many guys was an understatement, like saying Don Juan was a bit of a lad. Logically she knew that not all men were bastards; Helen had been telling her so ever since they met after the nightmare events surrounding Starkey's abandonment when she'd felt like all the light had gone out of the world, her trust in the male sex irreparably damaged. She'd little interest in giving her phone number to strangers or having some revolting creep maul her in 'payment' for an overpriced dinner, setting them both up for an embarrassing rejection when he expected to come up to her flat afterwards.

In several years only three men had lasted long enough to make it to her bedroom and even then she'd had to force herself to go through the motions, pretending to enjoy the lovemaking while they might as well have dosed her with novocaine for all her body responded. But when Ollie's hand covered hers on the gear shift, she felt parts of her anatomy fizzing that hadn't fizzed in ages.

His childish antics – swinging from his feet on playground monkey bars, dangling Jen squealing over Hampstead Pond, pulling her under a gushing gutter in an unexpected downpour – made her feel like a teenager again, like the light-hearted girl who'd capered around Ashport with Starkey, riding the dodgems when the carnival was in town, spending hours playing shove ha'penny on the crappy slot machines on the decrepit pier.

Better to feel a kid again than a moody cow approaching thirty, a hopeless underachiever who earned peanuts, littered her boyfriend-free bedroom with dirty coffee cups and discarded clothes, and spent her evenings drinking till dawn with her equally dissolute, irresponsible mates.

Helen, Jen's infinitely more sophisticated friend, flatmate and landlady, was the eternal temp, thriving on an endless source of potential boyfriends and fresh scandal. In their shared two-bedroom, fifth-floor flat (the only good thing, Helen said, to come out of her divorce) it was Helen who led the dizzying social life, enjoying steamy sexcapades while Jen was just left with hangovers. That was the status quo, until Ollie disrupted it. However often Jen argued that he wasn't a date, Helen seemed to take his intrusion as a personal insult, until Jen found herself sneaking out to meet Ollie just to avoid Helen's blistering sarcasm.

It was almost worse than her dad had been about Starkey, and at least that was justified, given Jen was still fifteen. From the moment she first met Starkey she imagined him to be the most romantic, tortured, passionate lover her soul could crave, a wounded wolf that only she could touch. And sex – was it ever on their minds, underlying the most innocuous exchange. 'Fancy an ice cream?' SEX. 'Wanna see a flick?' SEX. 'There's a smudge of ketchup on your chin.' SEX, SEX, SEX! If it wasn't for Jen wanting to wait till she'd turned sixteen, they'd have been at it like rabbits from day one.

But sex wasn't part of the deal with Ollie. No messy awkward bedroom encounters to destroy their fun. Nor would this end, like Starkey, in her tears, too many pathetic lonely years of them. No, this – like his car – was destined to be written off the minute the race was over. She would never let him get too close, never risk rocking the equilibrium of her barren life.

But Christ Almighty, how long would she have to sit here? Couldn't somebody win the bloody race by now? Her knee was throbbing and swelling, her eyes watering, her head ached from the noise and the stink of exhaust fumes.

She found herself thinking of a recent pub visit, the jukebox playing 'When a Man Loves a Woman', a song Starkey had loved. Ollie had whirled her round in a jokey dance move and she'd been filled with such a weird mixture of jumbled-up emotions – how could she *ever* have liked anything so corny? – that she'd had to pull free and grab a cigarette from her packet of Silk Cut, puffing away furiously. If her fingers were trembling, it was probably from shame at being seen in public participating in an episode of such horrifying uncool.

On their last encounter prior to today, they'd eaten greasy cheeseburgers at TGI Friday. At the railings by her street door Ollie had bent to kiss her mouth lightly and she'd felt a familiar jolt in the stomach, an unexpected yearning.

Ollie smelled so masculine and yummy, better than any powdered baby, better even than freshly cut grass or autumn woodsmoke, that her traitorous nose wanted to stay glued to his shoulder or nestle into his soft leather jacket like a little fledgling bird.

Anyway, nothing had come of it, whatever ancient instinct her nostrils had been obeying. Before she'd found herself trailing snot marks, she'd pulled her rebellious proboscis away, laughed, patted his cheek and said something like, 'Nice try, sunshine, but I don't do infants.' And he'd shrugged, flipping his blond hair from his eyes, and said, 'I'm falling for you.' To which she'd smartly countered, 'Too bad, kiddo. Hope you find a soft landing,' and skipped hastily through the front door.

Seemed kind of bitchy now, considering she'd just turned his poor Fiat into an origami model, but he hadn't shown any resentment when he'd collected her this afternoon.

Suddenly, the race was over, the tannoy announcing the

winners. Ollie vaulted one-handed over the barrier, his face stricken with concern, as he helped pull Jen and her bad knee out of the car.

'What happened to slow in, fast out?' He scooped her up carefully, his voice gentle and teasing.

'Enough of the sex talk.' She threw her arms around his neck. 'Just get me home, big boy.' And then she succumbed to the delicious sleepiness that crept over her, relaxing into his warm strength.

'I thought you'd take it slowly at first,' he murmured. 'I never dreamed you'd get hurt.' He carried her through the crowd, ignoring her protests she could walk, to the first-aid station to get her knee bandaged. Asking his friend Paul to sort out the wreckage of his car, he then drove her all the way to Muswell Hill, hefted her up five flights of stairs, opened the door, swept past Helen's astonished look of horror and into her bedroom, with Jen giggling as she pointed the way, hiding her face in his shoulder so as not to see Helen's glare.

They fell on the bed together, pools of sweat drenching the back of Ollie's oil-stained vest and dampening his hair. He was breathing hard, the sweat on his impressive muscles glistening.

'Thank God you're such a little thing,' he said. Then he rolled to face her, their mouths met and that was it.

Kaboom!

# Chapter 3

JULY 1998

She recognised Meg right away. Signing the register in the former coaching inn, Jen had just passed over her Visa for processing when she heard the brass bell clang and an unmistakable figure stepped on to the Indian rug in the foyer.

'Meg,' she said, feeling overcome with a sudden shyness. They were virtually strangers now, after all.

For a split second they both stood motionless, the whole foyer between them, brains taking in every detail. Complexion, hairstyle, size, shape, clothes, shoes – Meg was wearing tasselled flip-flops, while Jen had on a brand-new pair of Converse sneakers.

Meg's face was fresh-looking and unlined, beaming from ear to ear, with the same marginally upturned nose and slight overbite that expensive braces had failed to eradicate. Not surprising, given she'd yanked them out as soon as boys began to show interest. But somehow, at twenty-eight, all Meg's features fitted together so much better. Her freckles had faded into a deep tan, her red hair, once a gingery tumble, looked Pre-Raphaelite and romantic, her dandelion-yellow top and fuchsia flares showed off a flat navel complete with ring and butterfly tattoo and the whole hippy ensemble was topped off with a peace-sign medallion and a multicoloured headband worthy of Meg's boho mother.

Impulsively Meg dropped her bags on the floor and ran

across the room. 'Jen!' She threw her arms around her in a bear hug. 'God, it's so great to see you.' She held her at arm's length, grinning. 'You look awesome, dude. Is Rowan here yet? Wasn't this the most excellent idea of hers?'

Jen felt her face go scarlet as she squirmed, horribly aware of being the eye of Meg's hurricane, even though the only witness – the receptionist – was busy with running Jen's card through the machine, apparently unaware that she was witnessing an occasion momentous enough to rival a Beatles reunion.

'Um, yeah, it's great, isn't it?' Jen muttered, dropping her eyes and finding herself stupid and stiffly British. Meg seemed much more American than Jen remembered – after five years at Ashport they'd stopped noticing her residual twang – and, Jen felt guilty wondering this, had she always been so loud?

She tucked a lock of hair behind her ear and gave Meg a weak grin. 'Long time no see,' she managed feebly, racking her brains for something witty or remotely interesting to say.

'We serve food in the bar,' the receptionist told them as she handed Jen back her receipt, 'but we also have a lovely dining room. Our chef is famous ever since those nice folk from Michelin gave us two stars last year. So if you haven't already, we do recommend reservations.'

'We got them already,' Meg stepped up to the desk as Jen scrawled her name, 'under Georgina Carrington. And I've a room booked too, Meg Lennox.' Exuberantly, she squeezed Jen again, one arm around her shoulders. 'Isn't this wild! We're all grown-up.' She laughed from her three-inch advantage. 'If you can call it up.'

She looked as out of place in deepest Wiltshire as her mother Clover had in Ashport all those years ago. Pictures unfolded in Jen's mind like someone flipping through a scrapbook of memories. Always the most flamboyant dresser in their class, Meg had gone full circle from their ra-ra skirt and legwarmer days – Jennifer Beales had a lot to answer for – into the nineties neo-hippy revival.

Details were flooding back. How Meg always told them she was conceived at Woodstock. How Clover and Herb had boasted they'd stayed naked during the whole event and even featured in the famous documentary. Which Jen always thought was another of Meg's stories but when she did the maths, it could have been true, Woodstock being August 1969 and Meg born in May 1970.

Clover claimed Janis Joplin had inspired her singer-songwriter career and Jen recalled that framed photo of Meg's parents at Woodstock, Clover in bell bottoms and a tatty old Afghan coat, Herb bare-chested, wearing a ragged vest and torn jeans, presumably before they stripped it all off and frolicked starkers in that muddy field.

'Are you . . .' Jen started.

'Why didn't . . .' Meg's sentence clashed as they both began talking and then broke off, laughing and apologising.

'You first,' Meg waved.

'No, you.'

'I was just gonna say – why didn't we do this years ago?' Meg continued. 'I meant to write to all you guys. It's just . . . well, you know me, I sucked at English.' She gave an unapologetic shrug.

'Our teacher didn't think so.' Jen shoved her purse into her worn leather handbag. 'You always got far better marks even when you'd scribbled a lot of old rubbish during morning registration and I'd worked on my masterpiece all night. It drove me bonkers.'

Funny how some things stayed with you. Like the image of herself swatting a giggling Meg with her rolled-up notebook, pretending outrage at the sight of another A.

'It was all in the content.' Meg's grin stretched the length of the reception desk as she took a man-style wallet out of her fringed shoulder bag and handed over her Mastercard. 'Lucky for me Dippy Dugan valued imagination over my creative spelling. Made up for the Ds I got from all the other teachers.'

There was another pause as the conversational bucket hit the bottom of that well. Meg twirled her room key round her finger, both of them quietly hoping Rowan and Georgina would appear and help break the ice.

Twelve years had passed since that last fateful escapade in Ashport had got them in trouble with everyone, including the police, and might have meant expulsion if they hadn't just finished their GCSEs. They'd all been pulled out of Ashport anyway. Rowan's mother had dragged her back to Wales, stuck her in some type of Welsh language immersion college where you got reprimanded – Rowan wrote – for talking English during breaktime. Meg's parents had decided Britain was way too uptight and decamped to Seattle to check out the grunge music scene. Jen's father, despite all her tears, hysterics and heartfelt pleas, took them to West Croydon, of all the world's dreary holes, and found Jen her first menial clerking job. Georgina did a term abroad in Switzerland, courtesy of her grandmother, prior to returning to Ashport Comp for her A levels.

'So – I take it the others aren't here yet?' Meg scanned the floral-wallpapered reception area with its fireplace, wing armchairs and framed hunting prints.

'Nope. I already asked.'

'I'm in six,' Meg studied her key, the number burned into a large wooden tag. 'How about you?'

'Four,' Jen said. 'Shall we find our rooms?'

As they lugged bags up the stairs, she too wondered why they'd left it so long. Why hadn't they done anything about meeting again until Rowan's phone call just last week?

They'd sworn undying friendship, even written for a while. Meg sent a few widely spaced postcards, each wackier than the last. Rowan's letters had been full of comical complaints about the nutty teachers chosen by her nutty mother but you could sense the misery beneath her humour. Jen and Georgina's exchanges had lasted the longest, with Georgie sending Jen cigarettes and a weekly two-page missive in her perfectly formed script all through her stint in Switzerland and the Lower Sixth year in Ashport. They'd ended the following October just two months before Jen's whole world was shattered and she no longer cared. About anything.

'Say, babe.' Meg's voice came from the rear, one step behind her on the staircase. 'Are you still cutting your own hair?'

'Only my fringe now. Why, do you think it's too short?' Jen's free hand ran through the curls at the back of her neck, feeling oddly wrong-footed as if she'd been caught out somehow.

'No, it's cool. I dig the Artful Dodger look.' They headed down the hall towards their rooms, Meg's scrutiny taking in Jen's frayed old denim jacket and navy cargo pants. 'Hey,' she made a show of peering into her face. 'Is that *make-up* I see?'

'I've always worn mascara,' Jen reminded her, defensive the way she often had been with Meg, as if not wearing cosmetics as a virtual child had been nerdy in the extreme. 'Even when you knew me. And lipstick and eyeshadow at parties.' She found room four and turned the key in the lock. 'God, how nice is this?'

The room was charmingly quaint, if modest in size: ochre walls, bucolic paintings, an actual four-poster bed and fireplace, exposed ceiling beams and mullioned windows overlooking the yard below.

'Where's the cat?' Meg looked around.

'What cat? Why?'

'I'm looking for a place to swing it. Where's the crapper?'

Further investigation revealed a bathroom with instant-hot

shower squeezed into the dimensions of the average broom cupboard.

'Clever really,' Jen approved.

'We should have shared,' Meg said, when they checked her room, almost identical but with the bathroom down the hall. 'Even a Motel Six would give you two queen beds and your own bathroom. They'd never get away with charging top dollar for a shoebox like this in the States.' She stood on the bedspread and wrapped her leg suggestively round one of the posts. 'But hey, you only live once, right? And look,' she went into a perfect back arch that Jen could only dream of attempting, 'we're all set should we get the urge to do some midnight pole dancing.' She straightened up and jumped off the bed. 'Are you dying for a drink? I am. Let's go to the bar.'

'I can't believe I was actually the first to arrive somewhere,' Jen commented as they went back downstairs. 'Ollie says he's never met anyone who keeps their watch, microwave and every clock they own forty minutes fast and still has to leg it like Red Rum on the home stretch to get to appointments on time.'

'Ollie?' Meg seized on the name, and Jen felt her cheeks flush.

'Just this guy I've been seeing. Nothing serious.' The words cost her a guilty pang as she thought how sweet Ollie had been recently. 'The real bugger,' she went on clumsily, 'is when my flatmate puts all the clocks right without telling me. I'd think she's out to scupper my brilliant career, except I don't have one.'

Was that enough of a diversion? She really didn't feel like telling Meg about Ollie. Not yet. Maybe not ever.

'So, when precisely are you going to marry me?' he'd ask with a grin, as he brought her a mug of tea in bed or wrestled with her in the sheets. And Jen would gaze at the ceiling, finger on chin, pretending to rack her brains. 'Well gee, I don't know. When you've reached puberty, perhaps?'

When he'd first started this nonsense, she'd been clutched with panic. One of many reasons why she rarely allowed her relationships to last more than a few weeks. Ollie was teasing, she reassured herself. He was using her the way she was using him. And what hot-blooded female could boot something so gorgeous and athletically talented out of bed? One day he'd come to his senses. Or she'd come to hers. Until then, the sex was phenomenal, better than she could ever have imagined, and for the first time since Starkey she was actually enjoying herself.

It had barely been four months. Granted, that was a record for her, but surely not reason enough to run, not yet anyway.

'It's hard to envision you with anyone except Starkey, somehow.' Meg trailed her hand idly down the banister, the question plain in her voice. 'The way you two were like soulmates or something, I thought for sure you'd be chained together for life.' Her kohl-painted eyes felt too penetrating. 'Do you ever hear from him?'

'Starkey who?' Strange how his name could still feel like a punch. Jen squinched up her brow comically. 'Oh, that old toerag.' She yawned. 'Classic amnesia case, Dr Lennox. Forgot my phone number, forgot my existence and unless he has positive proof of it being down to alien abduction, he's the last person in the world I'd want to see or hear about again. And who gives a shit? Men are bastards, anyway.'

'Like that, eh? Well, his loss, honey, not yours.' Meg linked her arm through Jen's. 'And exactly how non-serious is this new guy?'

Jen hesitated, but decided she couldn't resist. 'Blimey, I don't know.' She cast her eyes to the ceiling. 'Five or six times a week. Two or three times a night.'

'You lucky, lucky dog.' Meg tugged her towards the red curtain across the entrance to the lounge bar. 'Let's drink to that, shall we? I want to hear all about this stud, every tiny detail.'

'Oh believe me, it's not tiny,' Jen quipped suggestively. She was starting to feel her reserve thawing under Meg's happy-go-lucky nature. 'But I'm having a bit of a flatmate problem. I keep expecting to walk in the kitchen and find the poor sod gutted from sternum to groin while she wipes the bloody blade with a tea towel. Too bad, because he's wonderful really.'

'What?' Meg smirked. 'The thrice-nightly screams of pleasure keeping her awake?'

'Something like that.' Jen didn't want to get into Helen's prejudices. 'Shouldn't we wait at reception? For the others?' She dithered at the threshold to the bar.

'Hey, we're all staying here, aren't we?' Meg towed her through the velvet barrier. 'They won't need bloodhounds to track us down. And how can we miss Georgie with that big lardass.'

'She wasn't that fat!' Jen leapt to her old friend's defence.

'Sez you. Why did they always make her goalie in hockey? No one could get past that porkie pie.' She hooted suddenly, her wicked smile exactly like the old Meg's. 'I'm joking, you know I love her to bits.' She threw herself on a bar stool, clicking her fingers to attract the barman's attention. 'Jim Beam and ginger ale. What you having?'

'White wine please.' Jen sat next to her. 'I haven't seen Georgina since I left Ashport. How about you?'

'Nope. But I heard she's some kinda designer. I ran into Babs Pitstop at Waterloo – remember her?' Jen nodded vaguely as Meg popped a peanut in her mouth. 'I guess they hook up occasionally. I asked about you and Rowan but she said she hadn't seen either of you since fifth year. I thought I was tripping when I got Rowan's note. Did you talk to her?'

'Briefly. She still has that soft sing-song voice, I kept asking her to stop whispering and speak up. She was in the phone box of a café, said she'd got a mountain of things to tell us but she was running out of coins and it could wait till we met.'

'I tried to call her when I first got back to the UK a year ago. But all I got was her crazy mom.'

It was irrational for Jen to feel stabbed, wondering why Meg had tried to reach Rowan instead of her, although she, Jen, had made no effort to contact Meg. But that was the way it had always been. Among little girls you couldn't avoid occasional bitching and jealousy.

Some days one would be your very best friend, some days another. Rowan and Meg often hung out together while Georgina monopolised the horse-mad Jen with her two ponies, boarded at Angela Morgan's equestrian centre. But then Rowan loved horses too, even if she was fearful of riding, and she and Jen spent many happy hours at Angela's long after Georgina got bored and her mares were sold.

When they were only eleven or twelve Georgina liked to invite Rowan alone back to her fancy home to play with her mother's cosmetics. Georgina would style Rowan's black hair as if she were a living doll. And whenever Jen or Meg needed an accomplice for a piece of mischief they naturally gravitated together, Georgina and Rowan being too goody-goody for them at times.

Despite the occasional rocky patches – Meg trying to ostracise Georgina, Georgina trying to ostracise Meg – the miracle was how long and faithfully the four of them had stuck together. Right up until boys got in the way, in fact. Or one boy in particular.

'What did Ma Howard have to say?' Jen asked.

'Zippo. That woman's a total wack job. Wouldn't tell me squat. Obviously still sees me as a real bad influence. Probably strings garlic around Rowan's neck to keep me away.'

'With a cross between each clove to be safe,' Jen laughed. 'Vampire-proof jewellery. Could be a new trend.'

'So how are Clover and Herb, by the way?' Jen asked, while they were on the subject of parents. Meg's parents had insisted on being called by their Christian names. Clover was a hip thirty-four when the girls were all fifteen, Herb four years older. They'd been nothing like anyone else's parents. Jen's dad was quiet, introverted and often bewildered by his single-parent role. Rowan's mum was terrifyingly strict and religious and Georgina's parents were overbearing, obsessed with appearances and, Jen had heard Herb say once, completely up their own arses.

Clover and Herb, by contrast, thought nothing of smoking dope in front of the kids, hanging out with – and openly sleeping with – masses of artists, writers, and musicians. Herb had transitioned from wannabe rock star to guitar technician, session musician and producer of Clover's records. He knew all the famous faces, was in demand for his pitch-perfect ear and virtuoso skills, but was such a pain in the butt no band could put up with him for long. Clover was a one-hit wonder, a female Donovan whose successful single still got airplay but was never followed by another. Meg's first four years, when not on the road, had been spent in some kind of a commune with her aunt. It was the weirdest life Jen could imagine.

In Meg's household everyone argued and talked back, there was none of this children are lesser beings kind of twaddle. You could drink alcohol, stay out all night, have boyfriends over. There was only one rule. Never wake Clover when she was hung-over, no matter how late in the day.

Herb and Clover were far too wrapped up in their own lives to worry much about their two offspring, let alone those offspring's friends, but it was often an eye-opener to visit their chaotic household. And frequently embarrassing. Jen never knew if she'd find Herb walking around naked or bringing a couple of swingers to afternoon tea, or Clover in bed with her astrologer. The biggest, maybe the only, crime in the Lennox world was to be boring.

41

'Loopy as ever. Still living the sixties dream.' Meg snorted into her drink. 'At least they haven't sold out and become realtors or car salesmen like half those baby boomers. Herb's into jazz now, living in New Orleans, but he's so disgusted with the way they treated Clinton after the blow-job scandal, he's talking of leaving the country. Clover's latched on to another new guy, Liver Spot.' She glanced over her shoulder towards the entrance, but the woman walking in was no one they knew.

'Liver Spot? That's his name?' Of course it seemed highly unlikely but you just never knew – Meg had a brother named Mace, a cousin called Tweazle and even an Auntie Sunbeam.

'No, but that's what I call him. He says he's fifty-six but he's closer to seventy I reckon, has these liver spots all over his face. He's like some big deal in the music biz though. He and Clover are planning her . . . uh, let's see . . . thirteenth comeback? What about you, your dad OK?'

'Yeah.' Jen nodded. 'He bought this cottage in Dorset that he's doing up. He's sixty-three. Ambles around in his cardi, a lowslung tool belt, and a pencil behind his ear, looking like a refugee from one of those old BBC sitcoms.'

'Never married again?'

'No, but he's got every woman in the village wanting to mother him and—Oh my God, that's not . . .' Jen dug her old friend in the ribs and Meg's eyes swivelled to follow hers.

They had to look twice to recognise Georgina.

Her eyebrows, always so bushy, were now plucked to perfect arches. Her thick dark-brown hair was cut into fashionable Jennifer Aniston-style layers instead of the curtain she used to tuck behind her ears. Somehow, from being a fat little girl and a shapeless teenage podge, she'd metamorphosed into a voluptuous yet sleekly dramatic woman. A flowing multi-coloured scarf was draped around her neck and she was wearing a long brocade jacket of some silky fabric in a vaguely oriental-inspired design over a shimmering iridescent aquamarine top and matching trousers. But what held Jen and Meg's speechless attention was the slight but distinct bump under her loose-fitting blouse.

Georgina was pregnant!

# Chapter 4

'Jennifer! Nutmeg!' Georgina said in a startled way, as if they'd unwittingly bumped into each other instead of it all being prearranged. 'How *wonderful* to see you.'

Georgina's Mediterranean complexion, inherited from her Italian countess grandmother, had never looked so radiant. 'Does that mean your dad's a *count* then?' their classmates once scoffed, distorting the word count to a vulgar insult. Today she really did look like a countess, rich, glossy, and sporting a flashy diamond ring beside the gold band on her finger.

Her pillarbox-red lipsticked mouth came forward to kiss them both in turn, a perfumed diva to rival Maria Callas.

'Georgina!' Jen felt a surge of emotion that surprised her. 'Wow, this is so great.'

'Hey, lady.' Meg grinned widely as she squeezed the new arrival in a welcoming hug. 'How ya been? I see life's treating you well.' She nodded at the ring. 'Doesn't your hand get tired hauling a rock like that around?'

Georgina laughed. 'Same old Nutmeg. I thought we'd lost you to America for good. Is Rowan here?'

'Nope. Not yet,' Meg replied, moving up to make room for her. Georgina shook her head, bracelets jangling on her wrist.

'Best not. Let's find our table, shall we?' she added commandingly. 'I was worried you might have started without me. Traffic was abysmal.'

It was already seven twenty-seven, Jen realised. They had reservations in the dining room in three minutes' time.

'Blimey.' Jen descended from her perch obediently. 'You've lost . . . er . . . I mean . . . congratulations.' She indicated Georgina's bump. 'Boy or girl, do you know? When's it due?

Georgina went a charming shade of pink. 'January. My husband and I didn't want to know the sex.' She tapped her long nails on the bar. 'Drink up, Nutmeg, or bring that with you, I'm ravenous. Unless,' she paused, looking as if studying their clothes for the first time, 'you were intending changing before dinner?'

Jen looked down at her cargo trousers. 'No, I hadn't thought about it.' She noticed a small greasemark from helping Ollie give Mickey Finn an oil change, but decided to ignore it.

'I think you'll like this place.' Georgina started across the room. 'The maître d's always extremely nice to us.'

Meg threw back her drink in a hurry and grabbed her bag so she could catch up. 'Who'd have guessed you'd be the first one of us to get knocked up? Assuming Rowan doesn't have kids. Wasn't a shotgun wedding, was it?' she suggested flippantly. 'Didja wanna or didja have to?'

Georgina turned her head, looking put out. 'Of course I wanted to. Give me credit for *some* class.'

'Just funning,' Meg said lightly. Unseen by their friend, she crossed her eyes at Jen, who almost laughed out loud. Provoking Georgina had always been one of Meg's favourite pastimes. It was mad to think they'd been separated for over a decade and now here they were obediently trotting after their bossy friend. There was an odd yet amusing familiarity about the way they'd picked up their old roles.

'I can't get over how amazing you look.' Jen gazed up at the towering Georgina, whose face flushed with pleasure.

'Thanks. I thought you might have sprouted a couple of

inches but you're still a shrimp, I see. I always felt such a giant next to you.' Her hands smoothed her belly, and somehow Jen knew she was remembering how large she'd been. 'Still haven't taken to high heels?'

'I can't walk in the things.' Jen had never cared for small talk, especially when the topic was how small she was – unless she was making the jokes. 'Don't you remember me wearing one-inch Cubans when we went to see Ibsen's *Ghosts*? I fell flat on my face in Soho and my knee bled buckets through the whole performance.'

'Not really.' Georgina grimaced. 'School was definitely not the happiest days of my life. I've done my best to forget it.'

That was a conversation-stopper. What were they supposed to talk about for the next twenty-four hours, Jen wondered.

'You don't know what you're missing, Jen.' Meg swayed her hips as they entered the restaurant. 'Nothing like a pair of stilettos to make guys buckle at the knees. Especially when you're wearing nothing *but* stilettos.'

The last line was delivered just as they reached a tall thin man who was presiding over the reservation book. Meg shot him a winning smile and Jen stifled a giggle. Georgina coughed loudly as if it could drown out her friend's indiscretion.

'Good evening, Roger,' she said. 'The fourth of our party's not here yet. Would you be so kind as to show her to our table when she arrives?'

'Of course, Ms Carrington. Now if you'd like to follow Edward,' he said, waving over their waiter.

'Ms Carrington, eh?' Meg said pointedly, as they followed the waiter through the dining room. There were flickering candles on every table – a huge stone hearth cried out for a pair of Irish wolfhounds. The starched white tablecloths stood out brilliantly against the deep red walls and stained walnut beams. The whole room shrieked opulence and history.

'I kept my name when I married.' Georgina lowered herself

into the chair the waiter had deferentially pulled out. She shook out her napkin and placed it on her lap. 'Perhaps we should nibble on some appetisers while we're waiting?' She glanced at the silver watch bracelet on her wrist. 'I'm surprised Rowan's not here yet. Especially since she arranged this. And I really can't stay out late. I'm being picked up later.'

'You aren't staying here then?' Jen asked, taken aback. She'd imagined them chatting till sunup, breakfast with Bloody Marys, a country stroll. And even before Rowan could come bursting through that door, full of apologies and excuses, one of them was abandoning their plan.

'Sorry. I wanted to,' Georgina apologised. 'But I honestly wouldn't be any fun. I'm vomiting night and day, my hormones are haywire, my brain's full of cotton wool and I'm limp with exhaustion. And all this right when Giordani Designs needs every scrap of my energy.' She leaned over and grabbed their hands. 'I was dying to see you all again but this is absolutely the worst time for me to take even a day off. Rowan's timing is terrible, and now . . .' She looked briefly unhappy, then the expression was erased. 'Look, let's order some wine, shall we?' She waved imperiously to the waiter. 'I can only drink a third of a glass but that's no reason why you two should suffer.'

'Works for me.' Meg seized the impressively thick wine list.

'Oh well, that's OK, Georgie,' Jen reassured her. She was disappointed but she could understand, really she could. She'd felt like death warmed over herself the past few days. Perhaps she was coming down with flu, because part of her suddenly wished she was back in London with Ollie, snuggling under the duvet and sleeping for the entire weekend.

'Jiminy Cricket!' Meg exclaimed, flipping pages ever more rapidly. 'How often did you say you eat here, Georgie?' Her finger stabbed an entry. 'Look, here's a real bargain, guys. "An exuberant nose of flowery essences caresses the palate with subtle hints of hot flaky croissants, fruitful citrus orchards and the merest suggestion of roasted hazelnuts and sun-warmed spices . . . blah blah blah . . ." and only a hundred and forty quid a bottle. I bet it's a killer.' She pushed the wine list away. 'I vote for the house Chardonnay. Still a rip-off but at least it's not in triple digits.'

'OK with me,' Jen agreed. 'I drink anything, beer, cider . . . methylated spirits with an oaky hint of paraffin.'

'Let me see that.' Georgina stretched across, not quite so amenable to their wine choice.

The waiter appeared at Meg's shoulder with a bread basket and olive oil, and Georgina took charge. 'Yes,' she jabbed a manicured nail on the parchment, 'I think this. You don't mind, do you, Nutmeg.' It was more statement than question. 'Chardonnay's so *bourgeois*.'

Meg had stuffed a piece of bread in her mouth, preventing her response.

'So, Georgie,' Jen jumped in to keep the peace. 'Giordani Designs. You have your own company? How fantastic! Tell us all about it.'

Behind the leather-clad menu, Meg crossed her eyes again and stuck out her tongue. They needed Rowan to show up, Jen thought, before the sparring started in earnest.

'Well, it's no great shakes really.' Georgina sounded pleased. 'I started in graphic design at university and then I got into textiles. Abstract prints, vivid colours, swishy fabrics. Natural ones like silk, linen and cotton, but you can do tremendous things with Tencel too.' She poured a small amount of oil on her side plate.

'Your outfit's stunning,' Jen said as Meg tossed the menu on the table. 'Did you make that?'

'Actually, yes. I first started sewing up a few pieces for myself because there was nothing around for fatties like me that wasn't hideous or like a Bedouin tent,' Georgina laughed, batting away

Jen's automatic protest at the term. 'Then friends started putting in requests and, well, you know how it goes.

'Needless to say,' there was a silence as she chewed politely at a corner of dark rye, mouth closed, and swallowed, 'this,' she indicated her swollen belly, 'was a complete accident. Here I am, putting together my first collection, and I'm ready to burst into tears or take an axe to anyone who so much as looks at me oddly. It hardly makes for great working relationships – or any other kind, frankly.'

At her right hand, Meg was rolling her bread into little balls and pushing them around the tablecloth. She looked like a black cauldron of simmering resentment. Jen could guess why. Her own heart had stopped momentarily when she'd scanned the list of outrageously priced entrées. But it was a special occasion. So what if she'd be feasting on pot noodles for the rest of the month? Sod the overdraft.

'Once the baby arrives, it'll all be worth it.' Jen tried cheering Georgie. 'Is your husband thrilled?'

'What does it matter? He's not the one who'll have to do the work.' Georgina sounded unexpectedly bitter.

They were all relieved when the wine arrived.

'You could hire a nanny,' Jen suggested, after they'd gone through the ritual of Georgina tasting and approving. 'If you can afford it.'

Obviously she looked as if she could, but you never knew. When they first met her they'd heard a lot about how her grandmother was going to leave her 'oodles' of money, but it would seem callous to ask if the old lady was still alive. Georgina had been very fond of her.

'Sure she can,' Meg answered for her. 'All she's gotta do is quit eating in places like this and go check out McDonald's more often. What I'm wondering is why we couldn't meet in London. The train fare alone cost me hours of shivering in front of a bunch of pervs with pencils, closing in to get the exact dimensions of my crack.' She laughed at their astonished faces, gratified at her ability to shock. 'I model for an art college. Pay's pathetic but it's better than waiting tables.'

'You're not kidding, are you?' Jen marvelled. 'Since when?'

'Six months or so. And why would I kid about it?' Meg emptied her glass of wine in two quick gulps and refilled it.

'I couldn't do it.' Georgina gave an exaggerated shudder. 'Not in a million years. I would die rather than let anyone ogle me in the nude. I don't even like having sex without the lights off.'

'Seriously, what do I care if someone sees my ass – or my tits?' Meg thrust out her chest, hand behind her head in a Marilyn Monroe pose. 'So happens I've real fine nipples, outstanding, some might say.'

'I can't imagine anyone paying to sketch my skinny bod,' Jen reflected. 'Not unless they're practising drawing stick people.'

'Yes, well, not for a million pounds,' Georgina declared. 'It might be sexy and oh so modern—'

'Modern? Are you for real?' Meg interrupted, flabbergasted. 'You reckon Rubens painted from imagination? Get your head out from under your Victorian crinoline, girl.'

'Maybe I am old-fashioned,' Georgina looked unrepentant, 'but I was going to say I think exposing yourself is the definition of crass.'

'Yes, and starving is the definition of futility,' Meg said grimly. 'Holding the same position for hours is damned hard work, nothing sexy about it.'

'Let's agree to disagree,' Georgina conceded graciously. 'And anyway, dinner tonight is on me. No, don't argue,' she held up her hand though no one was, 'I insist. Order whatever you like. It'll be a business expense for Giordani.'

'Oh well, in that case . . .' Meg's good humour was instantly restored. 'Hand over that menu.' She looked up as the waiter loomed again. 'I'll start with the stuffed mushrooms. And,' she smiled at the others, 'shall we share a plate of calamari? I'm famished.'

'I'd be happy to remove this place setting,' the waiter suggested. 'That way you'll have more room.'

'No!' Jen placed a protective hand over it. 'We have one more person coming.' When he left she asked, 'So, Meg, what else are you up to, apart from posing?'

'Yeah, enough about you, Georgie,' Meg tossed her red hair. 'Let's talk about *me* for a minute,' she joked spoofing her old self-obsessed ways. 'I'm an actress, *dahlings*. Can't you tell?'

Hamming it up hugely, she put a finger coquettishly to her cheek, pretending to think. 'So . . . I did some extra work when I was in LA, took a few classes and then enrolled at a drama school in London. My godfather helped a bit with the tuition – he's a movie producer. Schlock low-budget horror things.'

'How can you have a godfather?' Georgina demanded. 'Herb's an atheist and Clover always insisted she was a white witch.'

'Wiccan,' Meg corrected. 'So what? Who says Christianity has the monopoly on godfathers? Anyhow,' she grimaced, 'now I'm thinking I should have stuck to LA or New York. I mean diction is for the birds. Lee Strasberg didn't care if Marlon mumbled, did he?' She stretched for the wine bottle again.

'Listen to the two of you,' Jen moaned, suffering from a mammoth inferiority complex. 'I feel so boring. I'm just a humble old secretary. You'll both be rich and famous soon and I'll still be stuck in a shit job.'

'But you do have a stud-muffin lover,' Meg reminded her. 'Nothing boring about *that*! Three times a night, supposedly,' she told Georgina. 'He sounds scorching. I'll bet he's got a nine-incher.'

'Meg!' Jen slapped the American girl hard on the back, causing wine to shoot out of her nose. 'Behave.'

Even Georgina was laughing as Meg mopped up with her napkin. 'Well?' Georgina questioned. 'Scorching?'

'Definitely, but he is only twenty.' At that moment Jen could have bitten off her tongue. She took an enormous gulp of wine to cover up her slip. Georgina and Meg were staring at her with astonishment mixed with horror (Georgina) and glee (Meg).

'Good for you, honey.' Meg held out her glass to be clinked. 'I'll drink to that.'

'Jennifer Amanda Bedlow.' Georgina closed her mouth with a snap and looked regally disapproving. 'Are you telling me you're involved with a man eight years your junior, a virtual babe in arms?'

'Yes,' Jen stared defiantly, 'and he's at uni. An engineering student.'

'And you say,' Georgina looked primmer than ever, 'that this young man has the most gargantuan willy?'

'I said nothing of the sort!' Jen squawked. 'That was Meg. But since you insist . . . yes, he is quite well . . . built.'

Georgina abruptly threw down her napkin and stood up to summon the waiter. 'Girls!' she said decisively. 'I'd say that calls for champagne!'

# Chapter 5

Where on earth was Rowan? Appetisers a distant memory lingering on their lips and an oily mark on the tablecloth where Meg had dropped a mushroom, they'd given up the wait and were tucking into their main dishes. Jen kept glancing from her rack of lamb towards the door, as if she might still yet appear. Would she be as pretty? More sophisticated? Both Meg and Georgina had changed so dramatically.

It was dark outside and in the windows Jen could see the three of them reflected. Young women in the prime of their life. Older and wiser than the gauche schoolgirls they'd been, and, in her case definitely, more cynical. Only an untouched place setting betrayed the fact that someone was missing.

'Daddy died of a heart attack last year and Mummy lives near Godalming now,' Georgina was telling Meg, bracelets jangling as she leaned forward. 'Has the most darling thatched cottage. She's sixty-two and still extremely active. My brother Lance is a rather well-known barrister . . .' She snapped her fingers. 'Wake up Jennifer. You're miles away.'

'Sorry.' She jumped. 'I spaced out – too much champers.'

Meg stabbed a fork into her risotto. 'Lost in dreams of lover boy?'

'Course not.' But there it was again, that warm feeling. For all her flippancy, Ollie already felt like something she didn't know how she'd survived without.

'So, Meg,' she shook herself, 'what's going on with you? Are you seeing anyone?'

'Different guys. Off and on. All extremely *non-serious* and I'm not mooning over them with soppy smiles like some people.' She tossed her red mane, reminding Jen of a highly strung chestnut Arabian, ready to strike or rear. Next to her, Georgina, making a little castle of her puréed yams, was more like a shiny black Friesian horse, less flighty but not without its own heavy glamour. Which would make Jen – what? The shaggy stubborn little Shetland pony at Angela's that would carry its riders out of the schooling ring no matter how hard they hauled on the reins?

'It can't be serious though, this thing of Jennifer's.' Georgina mashed the castle flat again with her fork. 'I mean, it could never work long-term, could it?'

How odd that Jen should find her certainty offensive when it was exactly what she'd told herself for weeks. She wondered what they'd say if they knew of Ollie's latest proposal, just two days earlier while they were lying under a tree on Primrose Hill that still held the wreckage of their runaway kite. She'd pretended to consider it a huge joke, when he rolled up on to bended knee and jammed the pull top from a Coke can on to her ring finger.

'Veddy nice.' She faked a Yiddish accent as she tilted her hand, admiring it. 'But vot, I'm not good enough for Pepsi?'

'One day it'll be a diamond.' Ollie flopped on to his back. 'Straight up, Jen. I want to marry you.'

'That'll be the day,' she responded chirpily, to hide the tumult of fear and elation inside her. 'Do the words pigs and flying have any hidden subtext for you?'

'Why not?' she asked Georgina now. 'You know nothing about our relationship other than what I've told you tonight. How can you be so certain?'

Georgina looked astonished, unconsciously rotating her diamond ring, as for the first time that evening she struggled to find the words to express herself. 'Well, it's obvious, isn't it? However delightful and sexy he is, how can you possibly relate to a twenty-year-old, socially and intellectually, I mean. Even your musical tastes must differ? I can't imagine what the two of you talk about.' She made this last statement with a nervous laugh as Jen scowled on.

'Who said anything about talking?' Meg jabbed a skinny elbow in Jen's ribs.

'Exactly my point.' Georgina now nodded enthusiastically. 'When you're ready to have children, he'll still be sowing his wild oats.' She sawed into her glazed duck breast with sour cherry reduction, pausing to chew methodically in a way Jen was already beginning to hate. 'When he's in his prime, you'll be an old woman. Absolute recipe for disaster, if you ask me. Men are rotters at the best of times.'

Her mouth curved down cynically and for a brief moment she suddenly looked extremely weary.

'Can we drop the subject?' Jen pleaded, knowing she'd overreacted but unable to joke about this with Meg and Georgina any further. Suddenly she felt moody and depressed, perhaps she was getting a bout of PMT. With a monumental effort she pulled the conversation back to school. 'Hey, remember the way we used to volunteer poor Rowan for science experiments when Mr Isaiah, that teacher with the wonky eye, asked for assistance?'

'Yes, only his name wasn't Isaiah,' Meg laughed. 'We just called him that cos one eye was higher than the other.'

'Was I in that class?' Georgina asked.

'Of course.' Meg played with the wax dripping from the candle and stuck it into the flame. 'God, he was awful. Every experiment went wrong or blew up. And Jen used to goad him by asking, all innocent like, "Do you reckon this one will work, sir?" ' She poured herself and Jen another drink from the rapidly emptying bottle.

Suddenly Jen and Meg were batting names back and forth while Georgina looked bemused.

'. . . when that little nerd with the bottle-thick glasses locked the biology teacher in the cupboard . . .'

'. . . tennis courts flooded so they canoed on them instead . . .'

'. . . detentions all round . . .'

'. . . those rumours about Linda Petroski and six boys in the back of an old Bedford van . . .'

'Linda Petroski was like the biggest liar on earth.' Halfway into their second bottle of wine, Jen was enjoying herself hugely. 'Said she went to the Vatican to meet the Pope, sang backup with the Sex Pistols *and* that she was best friends with Kim Wilde.' Her eyes shone. 'Remember Mr Trance, who used to sneak off with the cutie Canadian commerce teacher?'

'Was he the one who'd have his flies undone and his hand in his packet?' Georgina perked up.

'Packet?' Jen said, puzzled.

'Pardon me, I meant pocket.' Her face turned rapidly crimson.

'Know what you were thinking, honey,' Meg sniggered,

'It really was the most grim establishment.' Georgina regained her dignity. 'Kids throwing chairs. No classroom discipline. Third-rate teachers. Daddy threatened several times to take me away and move me back to private education.'

Yeah, right. Jen could picture Georgina's perfectionist father in his pristine suit, a sneer on his dour face. His sole interaction with his daughter was to criticise and rage if she got less than As. The bastard wouldn't have cared about Georgina's unhappiness and her mother would never have noticed.

No wonder they never wanted to go to Georgie's. Her mother was a snob, unbelievably posh, far too loud and gushing, her lipsticked smile wide and fake. They lived in terror of breakages, spills and mud on her Axminster carpet. The house on its gated estate was half the size, apparently, of their previous home and so crammed with furniture and antiques that it was difficult to move about.

Mrs Carrington had been devastated when the family business collapsed and they'd all moved to Sussex. The woman had never met a Martini she didn't like and she positively doted on Georgina's older brother Lance, but that affection was not extended to her chubby, graceless daughter. Poor Georgie, thrown out of expensive private education into the horrors of Ashport Comp. Her lunchboxes always held lettuce, carrots and apple slices, so she'd spend her pocket money on the school dinner: fried chicken, greasy chips and stodgy, cream-laden puddings.

It was her grandmother on the mother's side, an aristocratic lady who rode to hounds even in her seventies, who'd bought and paid for the ponies. A self-avowed man-hater, she had some feud going with her son-in-law and the rest of the Carrington males, promising Georgina that when she died all her vast wealth would go to her only granddaughter. No wonder Georgina had been such a peculiar mix of vulnerability and surface arrogance.

'The bullying was out of control,' Georgina said now, signalling to the waiter to clear her plate. 'That atrocious punk girl, Yvonne Spitz, her cronies Maureen whatever her name was and Linda Petroski made my life a misery. Pulling off my towel when I was in the showers . . .' She broke off, burying her nose in her water glass.

For a few awkward moments they averted their gaze, not sure how to respond. Then Meg perked up. 'Say, Jen, I'll never forget our first week at school when that big second-year lout made Georgina cry and you went over and started beating up on him.' She began to laugh. 'And he went wailing to the teacher on playground duty, who spun around looking for the bully and there you were, this little shrimp with your fists up.'

Georgina had recovered her composure. 'I do remember Jen fighting a lot. She was a little spitfire.'

'You saved me loads of times too,' Jen reminded Meg. 'What about when Yvonne's gang had me cornered by the tennis courts and said they were going to beat me to a bloody pulp? And you turned on that hose the caretaker had left out and soaked them. They wanted to kill you.'

'They'd have had to catch me first.' Meg's eyes danced in the candlelight with the hint of the wild child she'd been. Jen had always admired her heroic fearlessness, her willingness to tackle situations head on and with a cheerful lack of restraint that somehow persuaded the teachers to let her get away with murder, and meant tough girls like Yvonne rarely chose her as a victim. She could still see Yvonne, Linda and Maureen, the slutty bleached-blond thugs who ruled their playground, mascara running, hair straggling wetly on their skulls and bras visible through soaked shirts. Attacking them with the hose had been one of the greatest triumphs of their school career, even if they'd had to hide for the rest of term.

'If you had a problem, she was the greatest person to confide in,' Meg mused, and they instantly knew who she was talking about.

In the end every conversational byway that evening had led back to Rowan. It felt plain wrong for the three of them to be there without her.

'I always remember her blushing,' said Georgina, daintily dabbing at the corner of her mouth with the linen napkin. 'I've never seen anyone go so scarlet. You couldn't even be jealous of how stunning she was because she wouldn't look a boy in the eye. All that long silky black hair – so wasted on her.' She poured herself more sparkling water, looking like a contented cat, basking in the glow of a perfect life now she'd escaped the horrors of adolescence.

'Speaking of looking at boys, you realise we've been here

hours and you haven't told us one thing about your husband?' Jen declared, just as the waiter came by with the dessert selections. There was a hiatus while they chose.

'What's he like?' she probed as the trolley was wheeled away. She wanted to hear that the fat, lonely, unloved Georgina had found her fairy-tale ending.

'Yeah, Georgie,' there was the faintest hint of slurring in Meg's voice. Her green eyes gleamed as she refilled her wine glass. 'What's the big mystery?'

Georgina threw her hair back, looking distant again. 'No mystery,' she said coolly, and glanced at her watch. 'I just haven't had a chance with all your yakking. And talking of mysteries, Rowan has officially bloody well stood us up.'

'She wouldn't,' Jen said, contradicting the obvious. 'Something must have happened.'

'Does anyone have her cell number?' asked Meg.

'I never thought to ask,' Jen said guiltily. 'She called me from a payphone. Maybe she doesn't have one.'

'She cut off from me before I had the chance,' said Georgina. 'I did a 1471 but the number was withheld.'

'Are you sure we have the right hotel?' Meg's eyelids were looking suspiciously heavy, her head propped on one elbow. 'I can just imagine ditzy old Rowan sitting a hundred miles from here, wondering what happened to the three of us.'

'There's only one Marlow Arms in Warminster,' Georgina said sniffily. 'It was my suggestion anyway and I gave her clear directions.'

'Should we call the hospitals?' Automatically Jen's mind went to motorway pile-ups, flashing police lights, ambulance sirens. 'We don't even know if she's married, she could have changed her name. Did she tell anyone where she was living?'

'Not me,' Georgina said in a let's-calm-down kind of way, picking up a fork as the desserts arrived in front of them. 'But

Rowan always was spacey. I love her to blithery but I can't say this is completely out of character.'

'We did a play at the end of last term about this woman who's in a car crash,' Meg chipped in. 'She comes out of a coma and doesn't remember a thing about her life.'

'Great. How reassuring,' Jen joked, trying to squash her worry. Anything could have happened, it didn't have to be bad. Rowan's car wouldn't start. An unexpected visitor had arrived. She had a conflict in schedules, or simply forgot. Admittedly it was odd she hadn't called the hotel, left them a message, but Rowan *had* always been dreamy. She'd probably turn up tomorrow night, wondering why they weren't there. There was no reason for Jen to have this uneasy feeling about it, no reason at all.

As they traded tastes of each culinary masterpiece – roast caramel pears with mascarpone cheese for Georgina, passion-fruit mousse for Meg and vanilla soufflé for Jen, drizzled with the most delicious chocolate sauce – she still couldn't shake off this strong sense of dread. It was as if . . .

'Oh jeepers!' Georgie squealed uncharacteristically. Her eyes were fixed on a large, imposing figure who had caught Jen's attention when she first walked in. 'I know who that woman is. It's been bothering me all night. She's Bella Stringent!'

'Bella Stringent?' Meg's spine straightened like an interview candidate when her prospective boss arrives, and she swivelled in her chair. 'Where?'

'Who's Bella Stringent?' Jen craned her neck.

'Don't stare. She's just finished Lady Bracknell at the Strand. "A *handbag?*"' Georgina's voice mimicked the aristocratic bellow in a muted fashion. 'They say she's up for an Oscar for that Merchant Ivory film she did.'

'No shit!' Meg took a gulp of wine. For someone who hadn't originally wanted the Sauvignon Blanc she was doing a manly job of destroying the second bottle, especially since Georgina, true to her word, had only tasted a little. 'Should I go over and talk to her? After all we are both in the biz.'

She rose to her feet, staggering drunkenly.

'No!' Both Jen and Georgina sprang up, their chairs skidding backwards.

'People just don't do that over here,' Georgina said hastily, casting an anxious glance around her at the other diners whose peaceful evening they were now interrupting.

'I ain't people.' Meg tossed her red locks, impersonating the dumb blonde from *Singing in the Rain*. Jen grabbed her arm, pinning her to her place. 'How about neither of us will ever speak to you again if you do?'

'Oh well in that case . . .' Meg lurched a little, 'what's to stop me?' To their relief, however, she sat down. 'Who's that little squirt she's with?'

'Search me,' Georgina said a bit too quickly. Jen glanced over but couldn't place him. He was small, middle-aged, with a bulbous nose, sand-coloured wispy hair and a pot belly straining at the belt of his too-tight jeans.

'Bet your life he's some big-shot billionaire.' Meg made as if to rise again. 'Shall I check him out?'

'Sit down you silly moo,' Jen tugged at her arm again.

Meg grinned. 'Gotcha. You *totally* thought I was going to do it, didn't you?' She started laughing and after a second the others joined in.

A little fuzzy from the wine herself, Jen was comforted to know that yes, they were all very much the same. Maybe Georgina was slightly snobbish, maybe Meg was still an instigator, but all that was part of their distinctive personalities. None of her current acquaintances – except Helen, perhaps – had the history she shared with these two, and she'd missed this easy familiarity.

Just as Helen had taken her under her wing in her adult life, the women beside her had seen her through her first teen bra to her first period, had explained to her the mysteries of tampons and French braids, had watched her back through the pits and troughs of adolescence more times than she could remember. Since Jen was only four when her mother died in a car crash, she'd depended on them for all those things a mother might have provided, beginning with sex education (some wildly misleading information there). 'Well, first the boy takes his thingy . . .' 'No, really, you can't get pregnant if you keep your clothes on.' Then there was fashion advice, mostly disastrous, as the merits of frilly pirate shirts over tight leggings, headbands, and legwarmers were earnestly discussed. Social niceties were also included (well, Georgina at least helped her out on basic etiquette). 'If my mother burps/falls over/starts crying pretend you don't notice.' One of them even gave her the recipe for Rice Krispies chocolate squares.

All right, maybe there'd been clashes in the past, maybe there'd be conflicts in the future, but wasn't that always the case once you explored what lay behind people's social masks? Only someone so close could drive you incandescent with rage and yet be forgiven. And only with your best friends could you drop all barriers and truly be yourself, your faults revealed and accepted.

It was the reason their occasional spats sometimes ended in tears and hurt feelings, why there'd even been times when one wasn't speaking to the rest, but for so many years come hell or high water they'd always gravitated back to the friendship that was so much more important than any petty squabbles. And it also made it all the more sad that they'd ever allowed anything to split them up.

Meg was right. It was 'wild' meeting up with them. Now she and Meg were both in London, they could start seeing each other, and Georgina too, when she was up in town. They'd get to meet Ollie and Helen . . . whoa, all right, maybe not the best idea. Georgina wasn't too keen on bossy people – didn't someone say the faults you hate most in other people are the ones you possess yourself? Helen would probably slag off Meg the minute she left and Christ knew what Meg would say to Ollie.

But minor complications aside, they'd all be friends again.

It was only when Georgina had handed over her American Express to pay the bill, to Jen's half-hearted protests and Meg's barely concealed relief, that it dawned on Jen there was still a missing element to the night's tales.

'No, Jennifer, put that away.' Georgina handed back Jen's cash and stood up. 'It's my pleasure but I truthfully have to leave. I'm late as it is.' She'd excused herself earlier to make a call on her mobile.

'Next one's on me,' Meg volunteered. 'If you don't mind pizza in my hovel.'

'Not so fast.' As the waiter returned Georgina's credit card, Jen playfully snatched it up, preventing her escape. 'You haven't told us one single thing about this hubby of yours. Now I'm positive he must be a crack addict or a drug dealer – which is it?'

Then Georgina really did look flustered.

'Neither. He's . . .' she started and suddenly stopped.

Jen saw Meg's eyes widen in astonishment as she looked over Jen's shoulder towards the door. Georgina had stiffened, surprise, anger and, oddest of all, guilt flashing across her face all at once. There was no avoiding it, Jen had to turn to look.

A sledgehammer slammed her in the solar plexus.

His hair was collar-length and wavier, swept back handsomely from his prominent cheekbones. His eyes seemed darker, more velvety-brown than Jen remembered, but still as soulful and unfathomable as those of a Native American shaman. He was broader and more muscular. A man, a grown-up man, no longer the boy she once loved. Recovering from his frozen position in the doorway, he walked over to them and placed a proprietorial hand on Georgina's shoulder, bending to brush her cheek with his lips.

'So this is your *business* meeting,' he said softly. 'I wouldn't have come in, but you were taking ages.'

At first it made no sense. It was like seeing a ghost conjured by a Victorian medium, as if all their reminiscing had acted as an Ouija board, three witches summoning a spirit from the past. How did he . . .? Who told him . . .? But as he straightened up, Jen saw Georgina's face, sort of crumpled in on itself, the swift assessing spark as Meg looked from the other two to Jen, and the sickening knowledge supplied a second blow, crushing her ribcage this time.

Oh God! Meg was standing now and he was kissing her, a big smack on her upturned cheek. Then he let go of her shoulders and it was Jen's turn.

'Come on then, Titch.' He stepped towards her and smiled. 'Give us a hug.'

The arms that encircled Jen's gave out an electrical charge so powerful that if she hadn't been rooted to the floor in shock, she might have been thrown right across the room.

Starkey! Starkey was Georgina's husband. Starkey was the father of Georgina's unborn baby.

And then she knew how deeply she'd been betrayed.

# Chapter 6

It was Clover who first brought Aiden Kenton Starkson into all their lives. She found him working at a petrol station and what caught her attention as she paid was not his long dark hair, pulled back in a ponytail, his discreet gold earring or his Byronic good looks – all the more striking because in those days he only wore black – but the book of e.e. cummings poetry he was poring over. A short conversation revealed that 'Starkey' was a poet, a lover of Kerouac and Yeats, who considered Bob Dylan, Van Morrison and Leonard Cohen to be the greatest writers of any generation. So in typical Clover fashion she brought him home to be her latest collaborator.

Everyone loved Starkey. Herb, who liked to label people in a way that made it hard to tell if he was serious, introduced him as "the coolest cat on the planet" to the stream of artists and performers who flowed through their purple front door, patting Starkey's shoulder in an avuncular way.

Starkey was nineteen, a few months younger than Meg's brother, Mace. Soon he was one of a revolving crowd of characters who regularly shared Clover's candle-lit pot-luck dinners in which brown rice, tofu, almond butter and all kinds of pulses, beans and grains crossed Jen's path for the first time. Only Meg, complaining about all the hangers-on, seemed less than enamoured, declaring herself 'totally bummed' at never seeing her parents without an entourage.

But even she was not immune to Aiden's presence. At fifteen Meg was quite the vamp. She'd lost her virginity the previous year and ever since then had been determinedly stalking any boy who had the fortune – or misfortune – to catch her fancy. She would hover over Starkey while he worked, resting her pointy little chin on his shoulder to see what he was writing, her nubile young breasts in a skimpy top pressing against his back, her ginger curls mixing with his black ones.

She'd laugh too enthusiastically when he spoke, her whole body shaking as if he were the cast of *Blackadder* and *Monty Python* rolled into one. And she'd even rub her toes provocatively up his denim-clad leg whenever they gathered in Clover's incense-scented boudoir, listening to Clover work up chords on the guitar. It was hard to believe that Starkey could resist such an overt seduction.

But he did. His pen never faltered, his dark brows merely wrinkling deeper in concentration as the words flowed out, or he'd casually shift position, moving his leg away, out of invading range, and tuck it under him, never taking his eyes off Clover and her strumming fingers.

Only once when he, Meg and Jen were lying back on the Thai silk pillows of Clover's king-size bed – Meg's parents had separate bedrooms, Clover using hers as studio, sitting room and for all kinds of entertaining – he happened to turn his head and catch Jen staring at him, and a small smile crossed his sensuous mouth as he closed his eye in the faintest of complicit winks.

It was a moment Jen replayed time and time again in long, sleepless nights of restless yearning. For the first time in her young life she was smitten. From then on Starkey was the only one who haunted her dreams.

He called her 'Titch' a name that she would have objected to from anyone else, but from Starkey's mouth it had the same effect as a love sonnet. 'Hey, Titch,' he'd say, 'what's up?' Or 'Hi Titch, how's it hanging?'

To which she never had any good reply, all her brain cells having fled with the onset of first love, taking all her pithy responses with them. She was tongue-tied in his presence, every bit as shy as Rowan. She found it impossible to meet his eyes, her mind would freeze as her face grew hot and not a single coherent sentence would emerge until he'd walked away, leaving her with a sudden influx of snappy comebacks. Soon everybody else was calling her Titch too, and she loved it, because each utterance reminded her of him.

Starkey was an enigma, a mass of contradictions and moods. He could be wildly social, livening up any room he was in, holding court with adults twice his age, or unpredictably silent and withdrawn, emanating loneliness and existential despair to rival any teenage rebel.

Either way he was impossible to ignore. Even Rowan and Georgina fell under his magnetic spell. Rowan decided he was completely 'yummy'. And Georgina swooned, discovering that despite his oddly rough accent, somewhere between East End cockney and South (Sarf) London wide boy, his family were listed in *Burke's Peerage*. In fact he'd dropped out of Eton where he'd been a King's Scholar, on his way to Oxford, until he'd decided the whole scene was unbearably archaic and phoney.

Meg once accused him of being a trust-fund baby, to which he replied equably that the coffers were looking pretty bare and he wasn't pumping petrol because he was getting off on the smell of it.

He had a girlfriend too when they first met him, a voluptuous twenty-year-old Scandinavian called Astrid, with the whitest of white-blond hair, who the four friends were ragingly jealous of, not only because she was older, but also because she managed to be both sexy and ethereal. Next to her they all felt like lumpish, awkward children – which, really, they were.

Astrid came to several of the Lennox parties, a pale sprite smooching with Starkey in the maroon and gold living room painted with astrological symbols. More than once they found her hiding from Herb's wandering hands behind a dust-laden curtain or the life-size African fetish statue sporting a mammoth erection.

Then at one party Starkey's blonde was conspicuously absent. Wandering on her own, carrying a glass of 7 Up with a lemon slice that she hoped made it look like a gin and tonic, Jen passed the open door to Herb's studio and saw Starkey sitting there, picking at the strings of Herb's beloved Stratocaster that none of them were to touch on pain of instant execution. He looked darkly morose, taking long drags on a joint resting between his lips, and Jen, lingering, might have moved on if he hadn't glanced her way and given the tiniest nod, summoning her into the room.

'Meg told me you broke up with Astrid.' Jen never was any good at small talk, so she just said the first thing that came into her head. Starkey looked at her thoughtfully for a second, his dark eyes staring into hers as if waking from a dream.

He played a few notes then said, 'She's better off without me. She wanted the whole hearts and flowers routine, someone who'd call her when he said he would, take her out every Friday, promise to be faithful, say he loved her. I told her when we met I'm bad news. I like my freedom too much,' then he sang, his voice light and ironic, 'but it ain't me, babe,' segueing into a Dylan tune.

'Me too,' said Jen, sitting on a cushion by his feet. 'I like my freedom.' Which was vaguely absurd because firstly, who could be free when you were a schoolgirl and living with your dad, and second, no one had ever shown the slightest interest in taking it away.

But Starkey nodded and simply said, 'Is that so?' The tune he was playing changed. This time Jen recognised it: 'Brown Eyed Girl'. (Since her obsession with Starkey her music repertoire had extended beyond the Pet Shop Boys and Sade.) As a brown-eyed girl herself, she couldn't help a little buzz of pleasure, as if he were personally serenading her. It made her bold enough to reach out her hand towards his fingers that held the joint, feeling very mature and daring.

He shook his head and put the roll-up back in his mouth. 'Don't get started on this shit.' His voice was thick and husky. 'I like you the way you are, sweet and wholesome. How old are you?'

'Almost sixteen,' Jen said with a mix of defiance and disappointment. Clearly he thought of her as a little girl. She stared at him hotly. 'And I'm *not* sweet.'

Starkey grinned, playing the first few bars of 'You're Sixteen You're Beautiful (And You're Mine)'. Then he put down the guitar.

'Let's see about that,' he said, pulling her from her sitting position on the floor towards him. His mouth pressed down on hers, his gentle kiss sucking all the air out of her lungs, the musky taste of marijuana on his lips and tongue. 'Hmmn,' he mused, when he let her go, his eyes burning holes in her tight T-shirt. He brushed her mouth with his for a second time. 'Sugar,' he said. Another kiss. 'And honey.' Kiss. 'And . . .' he kissed her a fifth time, 'could that be golden syrup? You're right,' he said, picking up the guitar again. 'Not sweet at all.'

# Chapter 7

Jen's head swirled, blood pounding in her ears, unable to make sense of the words Starkey was saying, or appreciate the apologetic glances Georgina was casting in her direction, as she picked up the American Express card that had fallen from Jen's numb fingers. Starkey had let go of her but she could still smell his aftershave, still feel his fingers on her arm, his traitorous kiss on her cheek. Georgina looked appalled and abashed, as well she might, the bitch, so close to getting away without Jen discovering her secret.

Meg was already sinking back into her chair, her eyes flitting from one to the other, relishing the drama. She knew. Jen was certain. She'd been too quick to recognise him, surprised but not surprised enough. But how?

Of course. Babs Pitstop. Blabberchops Babs, their old classmate who'd met Meg at Waterloo and filled her in about Georgina. It would explain some of the sly digs Meg had made tonight about Georgina's marriage.

But then why hadn't Meg warned Jen? Why hadn't she come right out and told her? Instead of asking, treacherously, *if she ever heard from him?*

Because, the answer came to her, Meg's mischievous streak had always enjoyed scenes like this. But not at the expense of her best friends, Jen had always thought her better than that. Perhaps Jen wasn't doing her justice, perhaps Meg had been looking for the right way to tell her and then Georgina had arrived and, well, what seems significant and highly crucial to one person doesn't necessarily seem . . .

Traitors, she thought bitterly. They were both traitors.

Starkey's hands had dropped by his sides, his eyes concerned as Meg leaned across the table and shook Jen's arm. 'Are you OK?'

'Jennifer, darling,' Georgina's voice cracked. 'I meant to tell you . . . I wanted to . . .'

'Too bad you didn't follow through,' Starkey said, slipping into the seat beside Jen. 'At least one of us would have been prepared.' His voice was wry and deeper than she remembered. 'Sorry.' This was to Jen and he sounded genuine, she hoped. 'This wasn't planned.'

With difficulty she forced herself to focus. Somehow she was back in her seat, staring at the crumpled napkin in her hand, with Meg, Georgina and Starkey all gazing at her with expressions of varying concern.

'Why couldn't you have waited in the car?' Georgina sounded accusing and almost tearful. 'I told you I'd be right out.'

'I guess I didn't feel like hanging out like some lackey while you dragged out your business meeting.'

'I did not say *business*, Aiden.' She was the only one still standing, ready to bolt. 'You never *ever* listen.'

'I reckon I'd remember if you mentioned these particular guests.' He stretched out his long legs, giving Jen a wry humourless smile with so much history behind it she almost threw up. 'You all right?'

'I'm fine.' Her voice caught and she forced it to behave. 'Why wouldn't I be?'

'Cos you bear an uncanny resemblance to Casper the Friendly Ghost,' Meg suggested. 'Doesn't she, Starkey?'

'No shit.' He looked up at Georgina, dark hair falling over

71

his forehead. 'Guess you kinda forgot to mention our *marital bliss*?' The last two words were drawled with heavy irony.

'Amazingly enough your name didn't come up,' Georgina said sharply. 'We had far better things to talk about,' she added, but her eyes when she stared at Jen were miserable with guilt. 'Should we get you some brandy?'

'No. There's truly nothing wrong with me.' The last thing she wanted was all this concern. 'It's just low blood pressure.' Digging her nails into her palms, Jen forced herself to regain control, when every fibre of her being wanted to jump up screaming; to slap the silly pseudo-sympathetic expression off Meg's face; to kick Starkey in the nuts; to smash the wine bottle over Georgina's head and overturn the table like a petulant teenager. Instead she calmly explained, 'I've had a couple of dizzy spells the last few days. Not been myself.'

'Well, then . . .' Georgina wrung her hands, looking suddenly helpless. 'Perhaps we should go.'

'And perhaps not.' Starkey settled in his chair, his elbow resting on the table. 'I for one would like some coffee. This is turning out to be a helluva night.' He said it softly.

Painfully aware of his presence, so close beside her, Jen was afraid to look up for fear of what she'd see in his eyes.

'I'll get the waiter, shall I?' Meg seemed energised suddenly.

'No, you go, Aiden,' Georgina commanded sharply as she pulled a chair out and sat back down. 'And bring us all some water too. Jennifer and I need a minute to talk.'

*We've nothing to say. I'm going to bed.* Jen tried to force her frozen lips to form the words, but they refused to come, and Starkey was already getting up.

'Yes, your majesty.' He gave an ironic 'see what I have to put up with' bow, that suggested acquiescence only because he felt like it. Taking his own sweet time, he strolled towards the bar, the familiar slouching walk that Jen had forgotten but now seemed emblazoned on her memory as his personal trademark.

He was tall, at least three inches taller than Ollie. Tonight he was wearing jeans, pointed leather boots and what looked like a battered air force jacket, much used and possibly authentic.

Well, of course, the long black coat, the twin of her own, had probably been relegated to the Salvation Army years ago. God, how she'd loved that coat. Striding around Ashport in it, all he'd have needed was a black cowboy hat to look like the silent mysterious hero of a spaghetti Western. She'd even loved how it smelt, a mixture of tobacco, grass and Starkey's own personal warm earthy odour.

How many freezing evenings had he buried their linked hands in its roomy pockets or drawn it around them both as they'd snogged at the bus stop, often letting three buses go by because they didn't want the moment to end? Soft romantic kisses. Wild passionate ones. Starkey used to joke they might as well have their lips permanently welded together. Jen had needed constant applications of lip balm to stop her lips turning into Brillo pads.

But what was the use in remembering all that? He was no Western hero, just the lying cheating sod who'd slouched back in the picture as the father of her so-called friend's unborn child. Nothing could be more final than that.

Their impasse was eventually broken by a booming voice.

'My dahling, I've been admiring that stunning wrap of yours all evening. And that *wonderful* outfit. I simply have to know – wherever did you get it? Who is the designer? I insist you tell me his name forthwith!'

Lady Bracknell herself, Bella Stringent, had launched herself upon them like a thirties ocean liner, all waving flags and popping champagne corks. She grabbed Georgina's hand with her own jewel-encrusted manicured one, giant rings flashing under the chandelier.

For a minute they were all dumbstruck.

Behind Bella arrived her small, sandy-haired, pudgy

73

companion, a cheerful little tugboat to her *Titanic*, holding out his hand to introduce himself.

'Irwin Beidlebaum,' he announced. His accent was thick, his intelligent eyes and energy broadcasting the very essence of a New York Jew. 'Hope we're not intruding.'

Meg gasped, tossing her luxuriant red hair and all but launching herself from her seat in her haste to be first to shake the sacred mitt. 'Not *the* Irwin Beidlebaum?' she said in her most kittenish voice. If he'd worn a ring, she'd probably have knelt down and kissed it.

'I expect so,' he said modestly, pulling chairs from the next table for himself and Bella Stringent.

It was all too much for Jen. She could see Starkey walking back across the room, carrying a tray of glasses.

'Excuse me,' she said politely, staggering to her feet. And then ran to the door labelled Damsel to throw up.

# Chapter 8

She was in there a long, long time. After she'd vomited her entire stomach contents, all that expensive food expelled in sharp, compulsive heaves, she'd rested on the toilet, head in her hands, wanting more than anything in the world not to have to go back out.

Luckily the small though elegantly decorated room had only one cubicle and a lock on the outer door. There was no risk of intrusion when she got up and splashed water over her face, staring bleakly at the dead-eyed, white-faced ghost in the mirror.

What had he seen when he looked at her? The girl he'd first met, the scruffy tomboy who'd played football with her dad? The smitten teenager who'd do anything to impress him? Or Jen, the disillusioned adult, no longer believing the world was an Aladdin's cave of miracles and delights?

As the tap continued to gush unheeded, she remembered how joyfully she'd tried to look sexy for him when they'd started dating. Loose sweatshirts with the neck torn out, drooping to reveal one naked shoulder. Her Saturday job earnings had paid for a tiny leather skirt and a long studded belt that went around her waist twice, fishnet stockings, shortie boots. In the Oxfam shop she'd rooted out a fake leopard-skin handbag, a thigh-skimming petticoat dress, the perfect accoutrements of a teenage girl just discovering her sexual power over men.

She shivered at the thought, resting her forehead on the cold mirror. Her dad always said she was asking for trouble dressing like that and she'd dismissed him as quaintly outdated. 'Men only want one thing' was his litany, said with mild regret for the failings of his own sex. 'I know, I was a lad myself once,' he'd nod soberly as she struggled to imagine him ever being a teenager, chatting up the girls with a Brylcreemed ducktail quiff and pointy winklepicker shoes.

'Look at her, Gordon,' he said once when his old friend, the smiling round-faced foreman of the factory, had stopped by with a bottle of Johnnie Walker. 'She says they all dress like that these days. Her mother would be rolling in her grave if she could see the length of that frock.'

Her father's boss, Mr Gordon Farber, had given her a greasy ingratiating grin. 'Ah well, Derek, old lad, I think you got off easy. At least there's no tattoos or body piercings that I can see, at any rate.'

Her stomach rolled again and she rushed for the toilet, heaving up nothing but bile.

How old and out of touch she'd thought her dad. Almost as bad as Rowan's mum with her favourite oft-recited warnings: 'No man wants to marry soiled goods' and 'They won't buy the cow if they can get the milk for free'. How the four friends had fallen about hysterically as soon as she was out of earshot. Once, when Rowan had left the room, Meg had retorted, 'Yeah, and why stick with a frigid bitch when her milk of human kindness curdled in the udder? No wonder her old man legged it.'

Yet after Starkey's abandonment, all communication cut off as cruelly as if she were a creditor chasing down unpaid bills, Jen had a new insight on Mrs Howard. Left to cope alone, why wouldn't she go insane with grief? Jen herself was almost suicidal after the treachery and awfulness that had befallen her. For long lonely years she'd worn her misery like widow's weeds, black sackcloth accessorised by an invisible force field that shrieked 'keep off'. Should anyone dare approach, a lacerating tongue eviscerated their pathetic chat-up lines.

These days, despite Helen's urging to smarten up, she mostly stuck with jeans and trainers and maybe a nice, not too revealing top. If a man needed to see skin to find her attractive, the hell with him.

Ollie loved her grungy look, he was always telling her so. She tried to focus on Ollie, using him as a beacon to keep the shadows at bay. He wanted to understand her, and he'd been patiently and gradually dismantling the emotional defences she'd spent years building up. But there was no avoiding it, was there? One glimpse of Starkey and it had all come rushing back.

When she came out of the toilet, Meg was waiting in the hall, reapplying her lipstick in the reflection of the round brass door-knob. 'Are you all right? Everyone's worried about you.' She straightened up and squeezed Jen affectionately, ignoring her rigid posture. 'We're in the bar, they're closing the dining room. Here,' she pulled a small bottle out of her fringed bag. 'Rescue Remedy. Put a few drops on your tongue. It's good for emergencies.'

Like a zombie Jen obeyed, tasting only a slight brandy sting. Meg kept up the chatter as she led the way.

'Bella Stringent asked Georgina to design her an outfit for the Tony awards, can you believe it? Next stop, the Oscars! She's up for one, you know.' Her eyes sparkled. 'And Irwin Beidlebaum's a pussycat. I told him I'm an actress. He said next time I'm in something, he might stop by.'

'I'll bet he did.' Jen couldn't help but sound sour, the taste of vomit lingering in her throat despite drinking gallons of tap water. 'Who is this Beetlebum anyway?'

'Hey, where have you been, man?' Meg looked as if Jen had said she'd never heard of Tom Cruise. 'He's only the dude who puts on all those massive musical productions. Mega-big shot.

Ultra-megabucks. Hell, the *New York Times* called him the guy who saved Broadway.'

*Who bloody cares?* Jen wanted to screech. Meg could have been talking Swahili for all her poor beleaguered brain was taking in. 'I thought that was Andrew Lloyd Webber?' she managed.

'Yes, well, *Phantom* was OK,' Meg said dismissively, 'but take it from me, Beetlebum – I mean Beidlebaum's the man. And he thinks he might know my godfather.'

'The schlock horror producer? Fantastic!' Her attempt to mirror Meg's enthusiasm failed. She could visibly see the bumpy return to earth as Meg scanned her face.

'Oh honey, tell me you're not *too* bent out of shape about Starkey and old Georgie-Porgie? I'd never have thought he'd go for her, not in a million years.' Meg stretched a python arm around Jen's neck and affectionately squeezed. 'You were always way too good for that dude. I know you were crazy about him, like light years ago, but this guy you're dating now sounds way more cool. Don't take this wrong but I always thought Starkey was kind of a jerk.'

*Because he picked me over you, you mean?* It was on the tip of her tongue, but Jen held back. It had been tough when her romance with Starkey had caused a rift in the foursome like the San Andreas fault, not immediately visible but it shook their world.

Meg was so crazy jealous that before long she'd even abandoned Rowan.

In a matter of weeks Meg had been sucked into a wilder, more popular crowd, the cool kids who smoked openly in the playground, broke half the school rules, flirted with or cheeked the teaching staff, yet somehow escaped detention. They were the absolute bane of the games mistress, sauntering in at the end of a cross-country run, swigging cans of Coke from a definitely unauthorised stopover at the local sweet shop.

Georgina and Rowan blamed Jen, she just knew it. And looking back she could understand why. Who would have believed that love could be so consuming, so joyful a torment as to make you throw away everything that had once ruled your life? Horses? Forgotten. Friendships? Unimportant. All she wanted was Starkey.

Jen Starkson was scrawled over every one of her textbooks, decorated with hearts and arrows. And when the bell rang, she was on her bike to see him, cycling as fast as her skinny legs could revolve. How bad that she'd turned into one of those godawful girls who discarded their mates at the first whiff of male pheromones.

Starkey had become the oxygen she needed to survive. When he was busy elsewhere she suffocated, unable to breathe, aching with loneliness and loss in the middle of Rowan and Georgina's chatter.

*Upset? About Starkey and Georgina?* She saw Meg's curiosity, tinged perhaps with that most repulsive emotion of all – pity – and knew she had to make her getaway with a remnant of pride. She never could stand people feeling sorry for her or seeing her vulnerable side. Maybe it came of her mother dying when she was too young to remember her and the way grown-ups always treated her when they discovered the fact.

'Oh, puhleeze,' she pasted a huge smile on her face. 'You and Georgie are such drama queens. You actually think I've been crying into my pillow all these years over some spotty lout I had a crush on when I was virtually in nursery?'

Meg grinned appreciatively. 'I don't remember Starkey having spots.'

'That's because they were hidden where the sun don't shine,' Jen lied, shoving Meg with an elbow, a wicked grin playing across her lips.

'Oh ho, so you did get a look at it then?' Meg bumped her

purposely with her shoulder. 'I always figured you for such a good little girlie.'

'Only compared with an old sleazebag like you.'

And pushing and shoving each other like fourteen-year-old lads, they lurched their way back across the bar to the others, the very epitome of high-spirited teasing to anyone looking across the room.

'This is Jennifer.' Meg introduced her to Irwin Beidlebaum and Bella Stringent, as she took the chair nearest the impresario, leaving Jen the space by Georgina. 'She's screwing a schoolboy with a schlong the length of the Empire State Building.'

'Lucky girl,' the Beetlebum approved, eyeing her up and down. 'And lucky man.'

They were all laughing but Jen felt a sharp twist of guilt. He'd been so wonderful with her. That first time they'd fallen into bed together, her knee swollen to the size of a balloon, she'd been so nervous and exhausted from the accident that they hadn't even had sex. They'd spent the ensuing nights just lying in each other's arms, talking, kissing, joking and clowning around until she'd finally relaxed and felt safe with him. And he'd proved the most incredible lover, thoughtful, caring and fantastically exciting. To have him reduced publicly to a mere appendage mortified her. And it was all her fault. Another unfunny joke in the worst possible taste notched up to Jen Big-Mouth Bedlow.

But Irwin Beidlebaum was laughing, tickled by the conversation, the bug-eyed pervert. And how neatly, with one quick quip, Meg had removed her as competition – as if she had remotely wanted to enter. Starkey had positively flinched, his eyes now downcast and glowering.

Penis envy. Meg was brilliant. Men were so predictable. It got to them every time. Wars had been fought over less than this.

'Meg's exaggerating, of course,' she said, winking coquettishly at the Beetlebum, her assumed boldness fuelled by wine, champagne and more wine, and inspired by her fury with Starkey, whose eyes were fastened on her like dark magnets. Meg wasn't the only one who could flirt. If he cared even an iota, she'd use it to make him suffer. 'There's nothing *schoolboy* about the guy.' She felt light-headed suddenly and somehow out of her body. She certainly sounded as if she were channelling Mae West.

'We were concerned you were unwell.' Bella Stringent fixed her with a piercing eye, her voice ringing as if declaiming to the balcony seats.

'Must have been something I ate.' Jen (or was it Mae?) met Bella's gaze head on, so she could avoid her eyes accidentally straying to Starkey or Georgina. Her world had just fallen apart all over again. Why should she be intimidated by fame or weight, however substantial? It was taking every ounce of her willpower just to sit there without fleeing, but she forced herself to summon an extra bout of Mae. 'Evidently the calamari didn't agree with me.'

'Can't abide seafood!' Bella Stringent bellowed. 'I outright refuse to touch prawns or mussels in any form. I detest them like the taxman. All bottom feeders you know.'

A few bar stools swivelled as the occupants turned to see who was making this interesting observation.

'And spotty bottoms at that,' Meg muttered, sotto voce. She and Jen locked eyes before Meg's flicked in Starkey's direction, and suddenly Jen could tell they were both suppressing an insane urge to giggle. Only a momentary spasm on Jen's part, the laugh of a maniac before he shoots himself in the head, but still . . .

Suddenly she felt a marginal release of the pressure that was stifling her lungs. Starkey looked morose, his earlier show of bonhomie completely evaporated. Was she so small-minded that it took him looking like a glowering thundercloud to make her feel ever so faintly mollified?

Apparently, yes. But it wasn't nearly enough.

'But you're all right?' Georgina finally piped up. Sounding relieved she reached for Jen's hand, resting next to her untouched cappuccino. Jen snatched it away as if a flame-thrower had scorched her fingers. She had to quickly cover up by pretending a need to sneeze and fumbling for Kleenex in her handbag, but she could see Georgina wasn't fooled.

Well, and did she want her to be?

Shouldn't she also suffer for being a treacherous cow?

Meg perhaps had an excuse. She'd been in America when Georgina took up with Starkey. And if Babs *had* told her, maybe it was kindness that stopped her spilling the beans. Or perhaps she'd thought it should come from Georgina.

All those years of wishing she could see Starkey one more time, to find out what she longed to know: why he'd abandoned her, where he was now, what he was doing. So many sleepless nights, praying to God they'd stumble upon each other accidentally some day. And now she realised she hadn't really wanted to know. It would have been much better if he'd stayed a mystery, the fabulous boy she'd loved and lost.

Not the sodding bastard who'd shagged around with her best friend.

'But to go back to your work, darling.' Bella had wasted enough time on an unknown and was anxious to return to her own agenda. 'If you design this outfit for me, you'll get enormous exposure. The eyes and cameras of the world will be on your creation, the entire theatrical and film community descending on you. This is merely the tip of the iceberg, my dear. Georgina Giordani – designer to the stars.'

She sketched it in the air over their heads, marquee-size, of course, her flabby upper arms wobbling unmercifully. Meg put a hand up to cover her smirk, her thoughts obvious. *Put her in long sleeves, Georgie. Hide those turkey wings.*

'I'm incredibly flattered.' Georgina sipped at her water,

surprisingly reticent. 'It all sounds like a dream come true. And I would love to oblige. But my business has already grown faster than I could have anticipated. And with a new baby, I'm not even sure how I'd . . .'

'Nonsense!' The prima donna cut her short with a Red Queen chopping motion. 'Women have been sprogging rug rats since the Neanderthal days. *Carpe diem* – seize the day! Hire more people. Be ruthless. Let me tell you, when I was a mere understudy and suddenly the call came to take my place onstage with dear old Larry, well!' She allowed herself a dramatic pause, head turning to make sure all eyes were on her.

'Olivier?' Meg hissed in Beetlebaum's ear.

'None other.' He winked and topped up her glass. They'd been exchanging private snippets of conversation since Jen sat down, and by now Meg was practically on his lap.

'Don't you think I was terrified!' Every sentence of Bella Stringent's seemed to end in an exclamation mark. 'These are the moments on which success or failure is hinged! Of course, I got a standing ovation and never looked back!' she finished modestly.

Jen couldn't take it a moment longer: Starkey sitting by her, silent and brooding as Svengali; Georgina dwarfed by the operatic forcefulness of the theatrical star, their two contrasting perfumes clashing in Jen's suddenly hypersensitive nose; Meg practically sticking her tongue in Beetlebum's ear, flicking her hair and fluttering her spiderlike false eyelashes so persistently it looked as if she were having an epileptic flirting attack. And Beetlebum was lapping it all up, knowing that by all recognised Laws of Attraction he should be at the bottom of the gene pool, having nothing going for him except immense power, unattainable wealth and an open ticket to fame.

'I have to go outside,' she said, abruptly. Her face was almost mummified from trying to look cheerful. Although, frankly, everyone was so caught up in their mini-dramas she could probably have fallen weeping on the tabletop and announced her intention to slit her wrists without an eyebrow being raised. 'Pollute some fresh air,' she added, in case anyone cared. 'I'm gasping for a fag.'

'Dear old Quentin Crisp said exactly the same thing to me, last time we met,' Beetlebum remarked to all, Meg laughing the most, of course.

'Me too.' Starkey leapt up, his chair clattering back as he shoved his hands in his jacket. In a few long strides he was through the bar and across the lobby, so that suddenly Jen was in the awkward position of following him out.

# Chapter 9

Well, she could hardly have stayed, could she? What sort of a fool would she look announcing 'changed my mind, the urge passed' and sitting back down? Never mind the twinge of alarm that passed over Georgina's face, knowing she shouldn't join them because of the baby. And besides, old Bella would never let her escape. *And why shouldn't the great Giordani experience even a fraction of the jealousy and pain that is eating me alive?* Jen thought. She still wanted to know why Georgina had never told her, least of all not tonight.

A flash of foreboding accompanied her exit – did she honestly want to be alone with Starkey? Could she endure his proximity without breaking down? Meg smoked too. She could have saved her, provided an opportune buffer, but oh no, she was far too busy ingratiating herself with the squatty toad in there.

Standing out in the warm night air, she busied herself pulling a cigarette out of her pack, managing with a huge effort to keep her fingers steady as Starkey lit it, cupping his hand over hers and shielding the flame from the gentle July breeze.

'Cheers,' she said, as a memory tugged her painfully, a picture of the way he used to light both cigarettes then hand one to her.

'Quite the scene, eh?' He pulled a small pouch out of his pocket and busied himself rolling a joint. 'A bit too Restoration comedy for my taste. I kept expecting to see a footman rush in wearing a powdered wig.' He licked the top of the Rizla paper, twirled it expertly and stuck it in his mouth.

'Oh I don't know.' Bitterness leaked into her voice. 'It's not every evening you get to meet a star of stage and screen, a legendary impresario, your two long-lost best mates and a fink ex-boyfriend.'

Starkey inhaled deeply, held the smoke in his lungs for a long, long moment and then blew it out.

'Want this?' He held it towards her.

'No.' Her own cigarette was burning her throat. She stubbed it out and ground it under her heel.

'Still sweet,' he said softly, and she knew he was remembering that first kiss. She wanted to run but her feet had grown roots, clutching the gravel of the car park, the way she was clutching on to the last bit of strength that might get her through this. She couldn't see past this moment, only that the future seemed beyond bleak, all the old wounds torn open and freshly raw again.

In the dark, she could see a glowing tip of ash, casting a reddish light on his face as he brought it close.

'Listen, kid, I warned you I was no good.' His voice was pensive. 'I told you I couldn't make anyone happy, not even myself.'

'You also said you weren't the marrying kind,' she snapped, not in the mood for being patronised.

He made a mirthless sound that in no way resembled a chuckle. 'I'm sure Georgina would tell you I was right. Always knew I'd be a rotten husband.'

'Yes, but you still married her, didn't you?' Mae West had gone, just when she needed her most. Now she sounded more like the whining schoolkid she'd been when she first met him.

He shrugged. 'She wanted it.'

'And you didn't?'

He repeated the movement, which she could just see in silhouette, his tall figure outlined against the star-filled sky, broad shoulders, his expression hidden by the darkness. How often had she snuggled into those shoulders, buried her face in the warmth of his chest?

'Maybe by then it didn't matter that much, either way,' he rasped.

'Wow, that must make Georgina feel great.'

'I'm not a nice guy.' He rubbed his nose, sounding rueful. 'You had a lucky escape.'

'Oh yes.' A slight tremor threatened to give her away. 'I feel *so* lucky.'

There was a long silence as he took a few steps away from the dimly lit coaching lamps that hung outside the inn. The marijuana smell drifted back to her as he stood stock still again. Finally, when she could hardly stand it any longer, his voice came out of the darkness.

'I was a bastard to you, I know.' He paused again as if reflecting. 'If it's any consolation . . .'

'It isn't,' she cut in.

'I've never loved anyone the way I loved you.' He'd come back close to her, shoulders hunched, arms folded. She could now see the strain written on his face. 'Probably never will. But you were so young. I couldn't be responsible for myself back then, let alone anyone as bloody amazing as you.'

'Yeah, right,' she said bitterly. 'I was so bloody amazing that you had to do a runner.' Jen found herself shaking, despite the warm night. 'I suppose it'd have been just fine if I'd been a total slut.'

'Better, anyway.' He took another drag and exhaled thoughtfully. 'Sluts I could handle. I was used to them.'

He took a step towards her and then stopped, scuffing his heel on the ground.

'Look, my life's screwed up in more ways than I care to stand here and explain. I'm not asking you to understand. But if it means shit to anyone, I was heartbroken too.'

'You know what?' She pulled another cigarette out of the pack with shaking fingers, just to have something to do. 'It doesn't. Because you had a choice. I didn't.'

'If you believe that then you have no clue what I was going through. I was young too, and stupid with it. Things were getting intense, far too fast. Man, I was such a fuck-up, I couldn't imagine myself ever settling down.'

'Nor could I, for God's sake! I was only sodding sixteen!' Jen burst out incredulously. So much for her cool.

'Whatever. So I was an idiot.' He sent a plume of smoke into the air. 'I had this notion that all nice girls wanted commitment.'

'No, Starkey, what they really want is to be ditched after just over a year,' (fifteen months, two weeks, one day, four hours) 'without even a phone call.' She found she was crumbling the unlit cigarette, paper and tobacco falling to the ground. 'I suppose you thought it'd be *much* more amusing to let me wait for hours at a freezing railway station, watching all the passengers get off the train and the train after that and the train after that? Such a nice cinematic feel, especially since it was pissing down with rain. It may have looked cool in *Casablanca*, but in real life it honestly stinks.'

Starkey had been hooked on those old films. Didn't even care that they were in black and white. Robert Mitchum. Marlon Brando in *The Wild One*, James Dean . . . all the bad boys. Loners who were oh so tough with the dames but couldn't hide their aching hearts. Cuddling together on the single mattress in his dilapidated squat, propped up on pillows, eating pizza and watching their latest rental video on his nineteen-inch screen, she'd thought Starkey was more handsome, more romantic, more *everything* than any of the heroes they were watching.

'I was hurting too.' He muttered it hoarsely into the ground. 'I tried to make myself get on that train but I couldn't. And when I called your house, you'd already left. Yeah, I know I shouldn't have done it like that but why drag it out? I didn't want to see your face when I hurt you. Do you think I haven't gone back over it a million times, wishing it were different?'

'I've got to go, all this fresh air is making me sick.' She couldn't bear to hear one more word.

'You were the best, maybe the only great thing that ever happened to me and I wrecked it. And, brainless bastard that I was,' now his voice sounded as sour as hers as she fled to the porch, 'I managed to convince myself it was the kindest way.' His words followed as Jen tugged at the inn's brass door latch. 'I thought you'd get over me quicker if you knew I was a shit.'

The door flew open, propelled by a pull from inside.

'Fuck,' Starkey swore. Meg stood there, a fallen blossom of faded flower power, hanging on to the wall to support herself. She'd clearly been knocking back the brandy.

'Get over yourself, dude.' Her hair fell messily forward so that only her sharp little nose peeked out as her head rested on her raised arm. 'We always knew you were a shit, di'n' we, Jen?' Beidlebaum appeared behind her, shrugging on his sports jacket. 'Jen's way way happier without you dragging her down, man. Irwin and I are goin' to find a club or a bar to keep on partying. Whaddya think, kids? Are you in?'

'Where's Georgina?' Starkey sounded frustrated, though it was hard to tell whether it was remembering his wife or Meg's interruption that put the edge in his voice.

'Gone, girl, gone.' Meg wobbled as she brandished a brandy snifter, defeating Beidlebaum's attempts to remove it before she spilled the contents over herself or him. 'Bella Stringent took her home. Wants to bug her some more about her Tony rags. Old Georgie said she was feeling bad. Got the pregnancy blues.'

Carrying Starkey's child. The child that could – should, if

dreams and prayers carried any weight – have been hers. Jen's hand went to her belly in an unconscious imitation of Georgina's earlier gesture and then froze in place.

God, how could she have been so thick? Her befuddled mind was battling the booze she'd swallowed earlier, doing sums, counting back, trying to remember exactly how much she'd drunk, almost choking on the memory of her cigarette. It was too early to be sure – but it was the most obvious explanation for the queasy lightheaded feeling that had dogged her this last week, her unusual tiredness and the trouble she was having stuffing her suddenly sensitive breasts into a bra that had mysteriously shrunk? It was ludicrous she hadn't realised earlier. But it hadn't even crossed her mind, probably because it was the last thing on earth she could deal with right now.

'I need to sleep.' She stumbled past Meg, tripping over the Indian rug on her way to the stairs. She felt sick, tired, headachy and outright wretched. Her feisty attitude and spunk had drained, leaving her legs and stomach like jelly. PMT, she tried to tell herself. A familiar misery, like a werewolf howling at the full moon. PMT caused aching breasts, raging hormones and bloating, didn't it? And the sight of Starkey and Georgina would make anyone want to puke.

Everyone had followed her into the lobby, and now she could sense all eyes watching her climb the stairs, Starkey's hot and blazing, she imagined, Meg's undoubtedly seeing double, ole Beetlebum's cool and mildly interested.

To hell with them all. What was the bleeding point in getting close to people? You only ended up regretting letting them in. That traitor Georgina had done well to skulk away, tail between her legs. Jen's head was whirling as she flopped down on the bed. Then moments later she ran to the bathroom to throw up, again.

Tossing and turning in bed that night, Jen replayed the evening's events again and again. Blue eyes popped into her vision, then orbs of a brown so deep they looked black. Ollie and Starkey. Starkey and Ollie. The dark angel. The golden youth.

Eventually, feeling too hyped up and agitated to sleep and in desperate need of someone she could talk to, she pulled on a jumper and padded down the hallway to room six.

Her hand was raised, fist ready, when she heard Meg's distinctive laugh. Then a low rumble, a man talking, the words muffled by the stout wooden door. Again that same flirty giggle.

Feeling like a peeping Thomasina, Jen slunk back to her room. For a long time she sat on the bed, cross-legged, holding her feet and gently rocking.

The clock said two a.m. So what if Meg had a man in there? None of her business if her friend chose to consolidate her exploitation of the spectacularly unattractive Beedle-Butt. Or if she'd picked up a complete stranger in whatever dingy pub or low-rent disco the two – or three if Starkey had gone with them – had stumbled into after Jen went to bed. Or . . . no, it didn't bear thinking about.

Some aspects to Meg would never change. She'd turned her back on her friends before. Why should Jen be surprised if tonight she was again ignoring Jen's pain for her own selfish interests? Heroine for life? She thought back to their first morning at school. Was she ever wrong there.

Betrayal dumped on betrayal, as if everything spinning in the blender of her mind was marshalling itself into one coherent argument for never ever trusting anyone, no matter how often you told yourself that there were good people in this world.

She was lying on her stomach, face pushed into the pillow, when she heard a knock. A sound so soft at first it barely registered, but quickly she was startled. Her heart was thumping so hard it almost drowned out the hoarse whisper that seeped through the door.

'*Jen?*'

91

# Chapter 10

In the king-size cherry sleigh bed, under the thick goose-down duvet with its brilliant vermilion and periwinkle cover patterned in bold designs from Giordani's first-ever bedroom range, Georgina lay waiting for her errant husband. Her forehead and cheeks were damp with cold cream and her swelling body veiled in a lemon brushed-cotton nightgown.

There was an open book in her hand but her eyes weren't taking in a word. All she could visualise was Jennifer's face when Aiden walked through the door and Aiden staring back at her, his expression hungry as a starving Siberian wolf. Why had she ever agreed to meet her old school chums tonight? That life was so far in the past. What had she been thinking? That this little get-together could come and go without Jennifer ever finding out?

Blasted Rowan for arranging this and never turning up.

She returned the book to the nightstand. Where the blazes was Aiden anyway? She didn't dare to imagine, yet she couldn't stop her mind racing. Was he still with Jennifer? Had it been inviting disaster to leave without him?

But what choice had she had, she thought miserably. She couldn't face going back there to break up their tête-à-tête. If Aiden had an ounce of consideration he'd have known what his wife was going through, known that he should have put her first and not left her feeling second-best.

Why, oh why – tears welled in her eyes – had he walked in tonight? Aiden was so perverse, if she'd begged him to come and meet her friends he'd have insisted on staying in the car. What had aroused his curiosity when she'd told him it was just a business meeting? And why, she bit her lip at the injustice, had Jennifer made Georgina feel like she was the baddie? Aiden had ruined that relationship long before Georgina had appeared on the scene. He'd explained how he'd acted like a rat, how unforgivable his behaviour had been. And Georgina had been so hoping that Jen wouldn't despise her, that if by any misfortune she did find out, well, that maybe she'd hate him so much it didn't matter any more or that enough time had passed for her feelings not to be hurt. Yet apparently there was no statute of limitations on boyfriend stealing.

Sleep would be impossible till Aiden got home. Tomorrow she'd search for her tattered old address book and look up Rowan's mother. As long as Rowan wasn't lying in hospital with a couple of broken legs at the very least, Georgina was going to get her number off Mrs Howard and give her a piece of her mind. But even as she thought it she knew her anger was misplaced.

What an awful, awful, night. Once Aiden showed up, the whole evening had fallen apart faster than a piñata at a Mexican birthday party. Jennifer's face had turned white and stricken and she'd refused to speak to her for the rest of the evening.

Nutmeg had acted outrageously, practically jumping Irwin Beidlebaum under Bella Stringent's long regal nose, when it was clear to everyone else that the grand diva and the legendary impresario had more going on than a casual dinner date.

Poor fat Bella. Georgina could identify with the large and not terrifically attractive actress. Overpowering and voluble though she was, however pumped up on artistic acclaim and her own monumental ego, no woman liked to lose a man to a younger woman. No wonder Bella had insisted on driving

Georgina home, pretending to be oblivious to her escort's indiscretion. It was a matter of pride, and her insistence had helped restore a few shreds of Georgina's, even if she was paying the price for her cowardly retreat now.

One thing at least was crystal clear. Whatever she'd had in common with Meg Lennox no longer existed. The girl was impossible. She was argumentative, catty, rude and always looking for opportunities to twist the knife. It was hard to imagine how they could ever have been friends.

Her thoughts were interrupted by a loud clunk, thud and a curse from downstairs. Georgina's scalp tingled as she switched off the fringed lamp, pretending to be asleep as her husband stumbled in. Four fifteen a.m. and Aiden had only just returned.

Her heart pounded as he climbed into bed, smelling of whisky, aftershave and his blasted pot. She flinched as his cold feet touched hers and turned her back, eyes wide open in the darkness, body curled around her growing lump.

What could have kept him out so late? And what on earth could he have found to do until this ungodly hour? Beneath the more obvious odours, she thought she caught the subtler smell of perfume.

And – for tonight's jackpot question – who had he done it with?

It wasn't quite morning when Jen fled the now oppressive Marlow Arms. She crunched across the gravel, duffel bag over her shoulder, towards the trusty Mickey Finn.

Like a hell-bound suicide racer she drove through the sleeping countryside, pushing the poor beleaguered 1200 cc engine into a performance rarely seen on even the German autobahns. She made only one five-minute stop as she reached the edge of London. Amazingly no flashing blue lights appeared in the rear-view mirror, but an inadvertent glimpse of her face

94

made her recoil. Talk about *Night of the Living Dead*, she looked like a blotchy-eyed zombie.

Stumbling through the door of Ollie's rented Bounds Green studio using the key he'd given her for emergencies, she tried not to notice with disappointment the stained carpets and damp-marked ceiling of his rundown student digs. Stepping over mounds of textbooks and half-completed diagrams, she headed for the tiny, mildewed bathroom.

She stared in the mirror and dabbed hopelessly with a sodden tissue at the trails of mascara decorating her cheeks. Splashing water repeatedly on her face, she tried to cool down her telltale red-rimmed eyes. Nothing worked. Giving up, she slipped quietly back into the main room. Slivers of light edged through the ill-fitting curtains. It was, quite frankly, a dump, almost as bad as the dismal hole Jen had rented until Helen stepped in to save her with the offer of a room in her 'kicked-the-cheating-husband-out' bachelorette pad.

Well, at least she knew Helen would stick by her through the hard decisions that lay ahead. Of course Helen would blame Ollie, hating him more than ever, because in her overprotective way she took every slight misunderstanding between him and Jen as a toxic insult meriting the death penalty at least. Helen always meant well, but the thought of her escalating reactions made Jen feel like an underage teen fearful of confronting her mother now that the very worst had happened. What a mess. What a night.

She shivered, easing herself into bed next to Ollie, carefully trying to extricate a corner of the blankets he'd huddled into so as not to wake him. Not carefully enough.

He stirred and yawned. 'What time is it?'

'Late. Or early. Depends on whether you're a morning person or a night owl.' It was feeble but it was the best she could do when her heart was dragging behind her in lead-weighted boots.

'Thought you were spending the weekend with your mates?' He sat up, sexily sleepy-eyed, his hair ruffled and messy as a dozy little boy's. How was she going to break it to him? 'What's with the panda eyes?' His smile was concerned. 'You look like a goth and it's not a look that suits you. Heavy night I take it?' He dropped a kiss on her neck, his voice gentle, as he pulled her down beside him and twined his naked body around hers. The words she needed to say caught in her throat. She blinked her eyes, furiously, willing them not to brim over.

'Hey, are you all right? What happened?'

It was too much. The sympathy totally unravelled her. Jen felt all the tightly coiled emotion rip free from her iron resolve, and tears soaked the pillow in which she'd buried her face.

'I'm sorry.' She mumbled. 'I'm so sorry.'

'Look at me.' He sounded anxious, turning her over to face him. 'What's wrong?'

*What's wrong?* Jen shook her head and sniffed. *I'm pregnant, damn you. I stopped at an all-night chemist. I peed on the stick in the car park because I couldn't take another single second of wondering and hoping I was wrong and still the blue line appeared and now I'm up shit creek without a paddle.* But nothing came. She couldn't voice the words. She thought of Starkey, no longer Starkey, her Starkey, but Georgina's Aiden. She thought of the giggling she'd heard from Meg's room and how, heartbroken and anguished in her solitude, all she'd longed for was to be in Ollie's comforting arms. And then had come that knock on the door . . . She swallowed a lump back down in her throat, feeling absolutely wretched. Just when she'd thought the night couldn't possibly get worse.

Pushing all thoughts aside, she sat up, inhaling deeply. 'Did you mean what you said, you know, at Primrose Hill?' She pushed her knuckles into her corner of her eyes, trying to stem the flow, and looked at him.

'About marrying you?' Startled, he sat upright again, the

sheet dropping from his muscular young chest. 'Sure I meant it. You know I did. Tomorrow if you want.'

With one hand palm out, like a traffic cop, she held him off, needing to speak without the solace he offered and that her body yearned to lean into.

'And you love me? You really, really love me? You're certain?'

'What is this?' he said with a grin. 'A *Cosmo* quiz?' He gathered her into his arms and kissed the tip of her nose. 'Yes, Jen. I really, really, *really* love you. Now and for ever. Till death us do part.'

She felt the brittle tension inside her relax, for the first time in the nightmare hours since Starkey's surprise appearance.

'All right then, yes,' she said. 'The answer's yes, but only if you still want me after I tell you something . . .'

# Chapter 11

OCTOBER 2008

'So how was Brownies last night?' Jen held her nine-year-old daughter's hand as they walked the half-mile downhill through the park to Chloe's primary school. 'What did you do?'

'We learned how to do a reef knot. And we played Sheep Sheep Come Home. The leopards chase and have to catch you.' She tucked her little lime-green scarf into her woollen coat.

'Quite fun, eh?'

'Nah, it was boring,' she yawned. 'I wanna quit.'

'Oh? Oh dear.'

There was a few seconds' silence.

'I dreamt about aliens last night.' Chloe again.

'What type of aliens?'

She did a quick couple of skips to keep up with her marching mother. 'Purple slimy ones and they were attacking us from all around and we had to get away from their testicles coming through the window.'

'I think you mean tentacles.' Jen suppressed a smile as a rather grotesque vision materialised in her head. 'At least I hope you mean tentacles.'

'And then we ran into the cellar and hid behind a big wooden trunk.'

'Mmm. We don't have a cellar – nor a wooden trunk.'

'I know that, durr,' Chloe scoffed. 'Can we get one, though, Mummy, when we move house?'

'*If* we move house,' Jen muttered, thinking back to yesterday evening. The ominous ringing at six o'clock just as she was helping Chloe with her homework. For a moment she feared it was the phone call she'd been dreading ever since Helen passed on her number to Meg, but it was only marginally better – the estate agent finally returning her call.

'Look, Mrs Stoneman.' Mr Hagard's voice oozed practised sincerity. 'We took down their particulars, we made the appointments. We can't physically stick collars round prospective buyers' necks and drag them in.'

'No, but you could at least vet them,' Jen had bristled. 'Our property's been on your books for ages now and I'm sick of people not showing up. I spent the whole day waiting in and half the morning cleaning up.'

Actually not true. As Jen had grown older, she'd also grown neater. Obsessively so. A reaction perhaps to that terrible phase after Chloe was born, when bundles of nappies, bouncing harnesses, drying Babygros and all manner of toys swamped every inch of the Bounds Green studio and cluttered the dinky Islington flat they bought as soon as Ollie graduated and was earning decent wages.

How snowed-under she'd felt. Hopeless against the rising tide of chaos, especially as Chloe cried for the entire first three months. Jen was so lethargic, tearful and exhausted it took a monumental effort to change a nappy or shuffle out of pyjamas before Ollie arrived home from uni. Long crying bouts, irritability, sleepless nights, all classic signs of post-natal depression, and Jen might have been smart enough to self-diagnose, except that her newborn daughter seemed to share the same symptoms.

Chloe came out of the womb protesting and appeared instantly aware of what Jen had feared all through her pregnancy. Nature had made a horrible mistake. She wasn't cut out to be a mother. Even as a child her baby dolls had ended up dismembered or press-ganged as crew for her fantasy pirate ship. Fortunately, Ollie was smitten the first time he laid eyes on Chloe's tiny face and fat little fists. At least one of the pair had innate parenting skills.

But these days 36 Woburn Close was immaculate. Unannounced visitors (Helen/meter readers) could pop in any time to find mirrors and windows polished to a sheen, spiders' webs disintegrated before they could anchor their first threads. Someone could take a good long sniff at the toilet bowls and encounter only a whiff of Ocean Sea Breeze. People could safely eat from her sparkling kitchen floor.

Her mind went back to the argument with the estate agents over the buyers who'd gone AWOL. 'We were supposed to have three appointments,' she'd continued briskly, 'but the only couple who came hadn't put their own place up for sale yet.'

'I'll give Mr and Mrs Burgess a call now, Mrs Stoneman.'

'No.' Jen had mentally counted to ten. 'If they'd any real interest they'd have turned up, wouldn't they?'

She knew she shouldn't be so frustrated with it all. It was nobody's fault that they'd put their own place on the market just as banks were about to collapse around them and shares and property began nosediving. When you compared a few dud potential buyers with redundancies, repossessions and global economic collapse, it should be no big deal.

Nonetheless, the strain was starting to get to her. Since they'd signed on the dotted line, agreeing to Hagard & Whipping's 1.75 per cent sole agency commission, she'd had at least six possible buyers failing to show, two couples putting in offers then withdrawing, others raising their hopes and then it all faded to zilch.

One man drooled over the family room. 'Oh and we can

have a pool table over there, right in the centre,' he gleefully told his wife, who was busy measuring the windowsills for curtains. Another woman insisted on swapping mobile numbers with Jen, cooing, 'It's *exactly* what we've been looking for,' before scooting off never to be seen again. Jen felt like ringing her up a fortnight later, saying, 'Well?'

And chains, the dreaded endless anonymous chains, where at any moment, someone's last-minute decision could knock down the whole skittle set. She wanted it to end. She wanted Chloe to know where her dad was going to be living and for her to know where she and Chloe were going to be living. She wanted them to exchange on this house, so they could start looking for places of their own.

'It's a buyer's market right now,' Mr Hagard pulled Excuse Number Two Hundred and One out of his big fat excuse bag, 'with the housing collapse and no one wanting to move around Christmas.'

'But it's only October.' On a scale of stress factors, selling your house had to rank right up there with divorce and death, especially when your fate was in the hands of a total nitwit.

'It'll take two months minimum to go through,' he countered gloomily.

They'd lowered the price fifteen thousand, then another fifteen and they were considering another fifteen, but not with these agents, not if they were sending any old punters.

'You're not listening to me, Mummy.' Chloe pulled her attention back to the present.

'What . . . pardon? Sorry, what were you saying?' Caught out again.

'You never listen to me.' Since they'd told her Mummy and Daddy would soon be living apart – but we love you, darling, and it's nobody's fault – Chloe had become twice as diligent in cataloguing all Jen's failings. As if she wasn't already keenly aware of most of them.

'No, no, go on. I did hear the last bit, something about . . . wanting something.' It was a good guess. Wasn't Chloe always wanting something?

'Yes.' Chloe eyed her suspiciously. 'I was saying that I need velvet material.'

'Yes, that was right, velvet. Er, what for again?'

'Tudor costumes,' Chloe sighed. 'For school. Do you have any in your shop?'

'I don't know, probably. I'll look, but I . . .' Jen stopped as a loud honking noise resounded from over their heads. They both looked up to see a gaggle of black-headed, white-throated birds soaring downwards in a V formation, resembling a Second World War invasion force as they turned in perfect synchronisation and landed feet first into the nearby lake.

'Are they swans?' Chloe put her hand to her eyes and squinted.

'No, they're geese. Canadian. They're like Tesco – taking over the world.'

Jen dropped her daughter off in the school playground, and watched her run happily over to her squealing friends, before heading to work along the high street. She walked past the old timber-beamed buildings, reflecting on the town she'd chosen for her family.

Huntsleigh, Berkshire. On the exterior everything was lovely. Convenient location close to both M25 and M4 motor-ways, detached houses with spotless double-glazed windows, sweeping driveways, magnificent hills looming above extensive parks and forests, cute little surrounding villages, olde worlde pubs, but – behind those spotless double-glazed windows – there was something missing.

The people here weren't like Londoners. They didn't laugh at the same things; they were snobby and well spoken, not funny and street-smart. The mothers she'd met through Chloe only seemed to care about things like status and shoes, while the fathers were similarly preoccupied with golf and gin. They drove too fast in their flashy petrol-guzzling four-by-fours. She could go on and on but it would only make her seem whiny and ungrateful.

She was the one who'd decided on this move. She'd had such idealistic visions about living in the countryside, buying a big farmhouse with a paddock, a pony and perhaps even goats. They'd have fresh milk in the mornings, bright sunshine every day. She and Ollie could have revived their relationship and run through buttercup-filled meadows hand in hand.

Nothing had turned out as she'd planned: not the big farmhouse (after searching for months, they decided that Chloe, being an only child, shouldn't be too isolated); not the pony and goats (they needed the paddock for that); not even the bright sunshine (this was England after all) – and especially not the relationship-revival fantasy.

If anything the move had killed outright their already flagging marriage, lacking friends and social activity to disguise the fact they'd grown apart.

In fact nothing about leaving Islington had turned out how she'd hoped. It was as if she'd forked greedily into a lovely scrunchy roast potato only to find it was a parsnip – and a rotten one to boot.

Ollie liked the buzz of the city, loved it, truth be told. He had mates scattered all over London, some of whom he'd known nearly all his life. Jen was the one who told him he was being selfish, insisted Chloe couldn't possibly go to the local underachieving secondary school, where the Ofsted report was so scathing they were thinking of replacing all the staff. Helen was living in Huntsleigh by then and raved about it. The fresh air would be so much better for Chloe, Helen said, and honestly should Ollie have the final vote, considering he spent more time working abroad than he did at home?

Besides – Jen had hammered in more points every time her husband returned from Tanzania – it wasn't as if they ever went to art galleries or the theatre, well, hardly ever and there were trains, weren't there?

The sad truth, Jen had to admit as she came to a halt outside the charity-shop door and pulled out a shiny pair of brass keys, was that the disastrous move was *her* fault. She'd dug the grave and when Ollie reluctantly gave the nod, she'd rapidly flung all their beds into it, before he could change his mind.

# Chapter 12

'How much for this, my dear?' Tuesday, two o'clock, and a woman in her eighties handed a Donna Karan black pleat-belted dress over to Jen for inspection.

'I'll just check.' Jen gently fingered the delicate fabric, admiring the nipped-in waist and fine netting around the shoulders. She turned it over and examined the label. 'For you, Mrs Cartwright,' she pulled off the fifteen-pound price tag, 'nine pounds.'

Mrs Cartwright beamed delightedly, rifling through her threadbare old purse. 'I'll take it. Be marvellous for my granddaughter.'

Anamaria sashayed across the carpet, long black hair skimming her slim waist. 'I found these,' she said, showing Walter a dark cloak and an *Addam's Family* wig. 'Will look good in our new display, no?'

'Perfect, my dear.' Walter took it. At an age when most people were retired, the spry bespectacled seventy-year-old ex-navy serviceman and his wife Enid had found their niche managing the hospice charity shop where Jen and the Spanish girl, Anamaria, volunteered. 'Jenny, why don't you stick this on the dummy in the window?'

Usually the part-time helpers came in on alternate days, but with Halloween just around the corner Walter had decided to fight back against the so-called credit crunch and taken it upon himself and his 'valiant team' to cheer up the whole of Huntsleigh with a magnificent window display.

'All hands on deck,' he'd bellowed down the phone to Jen when he'd called her that morning.

'OK, right, where are we?' He consulted his clipboard. 'Three. Ceilings to be festooned with fake cobwebs, spiders hanging by threads. Any spiders, Enid?'

'There was a couple of rubber insects in with a box of farm animals, I think. And a big soft one with all the stuffed toys. It had a leg ripped off though.' Enid, a soft rotund woman who favoured pink, was fussing over a rack of fancy-dress clothes, hanging a home-made lion costume next to a pint-size ballerina's tutu and tiny slippers.

'Doesn't matter. No one's counting. Now for the fake cobwebs – any suggestions?' He tapped his dentures with his pen.

'There's about a yard of black lace in the linen section,' Jen offered, 'And I think they sell fake cobwebby stuff in Poundstretcher.'

'Not in our budget. See what you can do with the lace, will you, love?' He looked at his board again. 'Four. Any yellow or orange clothes pass to Anamaria, as she's offered to be a pumpkin for the day.'

Better her than me, Jen thought. Her mind flashed to a Halloween past where she and Ollie had gone to a party, Jen dressed as Bride of Dracula in a tattered wedding gown with pretend blood oozing from her mouth, Ollie as Dracula, of course. She sighed, focusing on arranging the cloak Anamaria had found around the window dummy's shoulders.

'I can give you some real pumpkins from my allotment,' a grey-haired old man with side whiskers piped up.

'Great. How many?' Walter's pen poised over his clipboard.

'Er . . . four? Would be more, but the wet weather's played havoc with my crop this year.'

'Four's plenty. We can have one on the counter, one on the

stand in the corner and two in the window making eyes at each other.' He winked at his wife. 'You can do the carving, dear.'

'I'd be happy to, love, if you'll take out your teeth and model for me.'

Jen smiled, feeling a pang as she pulled out tablecloths looking for lace. Enid and Walter were like a double act. Constantly bickering but clearly wild about each other. Nothing like her and Ollie, who seemed to have sunk into that most deadly of emotional states – terminal politeness. Not even a spark of good honest hate to put a little zing into their domestic doldrums.

Anamaria was now serving the old man with the allotment. 'So how old do you think I am?' he was asking her.

She screwed up her dark eyes, pretending to ransack her brains. 'Er . . . fifty? Sixty, no?'

'Ach, away with you, I'm ninety-four years young,' he replied in a quavery voice. 'And how long do you think I've been married?'

'Sixty years?' Anamaria guessed again.

'Forty-nine. 'Twas my second wedding.' He chuckled away, enjoying his joke. 'First wife ran off with my regimental sergeant, Nobby, in 1935.'

'I know a Nob,' Mrs Cartwright broke in from the book corner where she'd been rummaging through the Barbara Cartlands. 'Not the same one, I'm sure.'

'I've known lots of Nobs,' said Walter airily. 'In the navy. At least that's what I called them.'

Jen spluttered. Sometimes she couldn't tell whether Walter was being playful or not.

'Nobby Haversham,' Mrs Cartwright went on, 'from my church. He went on that World Wide Web place, got talking to his childhood sweetheart and before you could say Jack Robinson he went and proposed to her.'

'How romantic,' said Enid, carefully wrapping the wool scarf and leather gloves the old man had chosen with tissue paper.

Jen wouldn't have been surprised if she'd added a blast of her ever-to-hand violet eau de toilette.

'Romantic? Weren't romantic.' Mrs Cartwright suddenly turned indignant. 'He's been married to poor old Myrtle since the war.'

'Good grief!' Enid exclaimed. 'He must be a lively one for his age.'

'Well, not the first to do a runner and certainly not the last,' Walter chirped.

'Oh I saw a programme on that,' said Jen. 'Trisha's show. Internet romances.' Everyone looked blank. 'Trisha? She does a kind of chat show on TV. They discuss issues, like a UK Oprah?'

'Who's Oprah?' asked Enid.

Jen gave up and went back to her tablecloths.

'They were a happily married couple, I tell you, until Nobby lost his marbles.' Mrs Cartwright glared. 'What gets into men, I don't know. They say she's shacked up with him in a flat above Waitrose. Myrtle's spitting blood. Years of marriage down the drain. Downright immoral.'

Jen saw Anamaria grin in her direction, tickled by the thought of pensioners' lust, but her response was feeble. The childhood-sweetheart story had struck a chord. All the time she'd wasted mooning over Starkey. The effort she'd made in putting that part of her life behind her. And now Meg's email threatened to stir it all up again.

'I tried to learn the computer myself at night classes,' Enid told Mrs Cartwright, 'but the teacher said my mouse and me were incompatible.'

'Lucky for me, eh?' Walter winked at Jen. 'No Internet romances for her. Still, I feel sorry for the poor old codger.'

Everyone stared at him, Anamaria frozen with her hand in the farm animals box, looking for spiders.

'Sorry for *him*?' Enid arched her brows that were more liner than hair, unlike Anamaria's which were strikingly thick and unplucked. While the twenty-four-year-old Spanish girl didn't even use – or need – make-up and was wearing ripped jeans, the old lady looked ready to foxtrot the afternoon away, face carefully powdered, her wrinkled lips defined by a fresh coat of lipstick and a string of African ruby-red beads accessorising her pink cowl-neck sweater and magenta wool skirt.

'Can't have been easy for him now, can it?' Walter took off his wire-rimmed glasses, polished the lenses with his shirt cuff and put them back on. 'Married to the wrong woman all those years. Never able to forget his one true love. No man breaks up his home for nowt.'

Anamaria was laughing as she carefully placed a plastic arachnid on to its black lace web. 'Oh ho, Walter, *you* are the romantic, I think.'

'Well!' Enid made the word sound like a choir solo. 'And don't you think the silly old fool might have sorted himself out earlier? What took him so long? Who's going to take care of that poor wife he abandoned?'

'Codswallop!' Mrs Cartwright slammed her walking stick into the ground. She looked from Jen to Enid to Walter, shaking her head. 'Downright immoral,' she repeated. 'You young 'uns don't know anything nowadays.'

The whole building shook as the door slammed shut. The whiskered old gentleman startled, shaken out of his daydreams.

'You're right though, Walter, my son.' He pulled a string bag out of his pocket with a trembling white hand and carefully placed his parcel inside. 'Life's too short. Have to grab your happiness where you can.' He nodded courteously at the ladies. 'And good day to you all. I'll drop round those pumpkins tomorrow.'

The shop was busy for the rest of the afternoon. By four thirty Walter's list was almost completed and everyone was occupied with their allotted tasks.

109

'You all right, love?' Enid addressed Jen as they sat on the floor together emptying a box of toys, throwing away the broken ones and putting the rest on to shelves.

'Yes, fine.'

'Just seem a little quiet today.'

'I'm all right,' Jen smiled. 'Honestly.'

'If ever you want to talk, you know. I may not be the world's best listener with my hearing, but I'll nod a lot and make the right noises.'

Jen laughed. 'You're very sweet.'

Enid yawned. 'How about a nice brew and a biccy? I'll make it.'

'No, I will.' Jen stood up and stretched. 'I could do with moving around. Get my circulation going again.'

She walked into the back room, where she found Anamaria sitting at a table making a poster.

'For the window display?' Jen asked as she leant over Anamaria's shoulder.

'No, this is something else. I found a dog yesterday. Running along the road. Starving and so frightened. Maybe someone threw him away, because he is *so* ugly.' She said it affectionately as she pressed hard on the paper with a thick black marker. 'But then if they lost him, they can come here, no?'

'Good idea.' Jen switched on the kettle and pulled out four mugs. 'My daughter Chloe's forever pestering me for a dog.' She emptied the teapot of old tea bags and plonked in three more. 'But I've always said no. One more thing to look after. And think of the mud.'

'You never had a dog when you were a kid?' Anamaria asked. Only she pronounced it 'keed'. She always said 's' with a lisp too – thtarving.

'No. I wanted one. But my dad used to say it was too big a responsibility.'

That's what she'd told Chloe too. And Ollie. Who will end

110

up looking after it? Who'll have to take it for walks? Clean up the mess? I know it won't be either of you, she'd said.

'So you like working here, no?' Anamaria asked.

'It suits. You?'

'Yes, very much.' Anamaria nodded. 'I learn the English, I listen to the jokes and I speak to people. And I don't have to pay for study classes. And you? How long you have been here?'

They'd not had the opportunity to chat. Anamaria was new and more often than not they were on different shifts. How long? Jen closed her eyes as she tried to calculate.

'About ten months now.' Seemed unbelievable. 'We've been in Huntsleigh almost three years.'

Ironically, just as the wheels were set in motion for them all to move, she'd finally found part-time employment she really loved, helping a friend in her photographic studio. It was always the way, wasn't it? Like discovering the single uncrowded beach on the last day of your holiday, or meeting your ideal man the day before he emigrated for good or married someone else. It was interesting, learning shutter stops, lighting and the ins and outs of Photoshop, after all those years of tedious office work, and another thing she found herself uselessly regretting.

Her wages had been essential until Ollie graduated; she'd been able to quit her hated clerical work to take over the childcare the day he brought home his first big pay cheque. Until the photography gig had showed up, just as Chloe started primary school, she hadn't missed the daily grind one jot.

These days Ollie was working for an oil-exploration company for a ridiculously high salary, going abroad for ten-week stretches. If Jen was in a real job they would hardly have seen each other. Better they should both be free on his leave dates, Ollie had reasoned, catch up on weeks of missed intimacy, do things together as a family. And it had been like that, at first.

Besides, local jobs were scarce and Ollie earned more than

enough to support them all comfortably. It would be wicked to take bread from the gaping maws of people who really needed it. But this last year she'd increasingly missed the stimulation of being needed outside the home. And so she'd gone the 'helping a good cause' route.

If taking in pennies for other people's old junk didn't have the same zing as assisting in a photo shoot where she'd met actors, celebrities and even a famous writer or two, to whom could she complain? It was all going to change now anyway, she thought, stirring her tea. As Helen kept reminding her, soon she'd be responsible for putting her own bread on the table.

'You want to start with that lot in the corner, Jenny?' Walter asked an hour later.

'Sure.'

Behind the beaded curtain she untied one of the black bin bags and pulled out a pile of glossy magazines. She idly flicked through the first pages – candid snapshots of celebrities with spots on their faces or, horrors, underarm hair, followed by a feature on things readers wished they'd known in their twenties, thirties and forties. In Jen's case, she pondered, her twenties list would read something like:

Don't marry someone just because you're pregnant.

If you suspect you might have post-natal depression you probably do.

Relationships can be extremely fragile.

She picked up the next magazine, the cover line blaring *When Good Friends Go Bad.* Kneeling, bottom on heels, she scanned the opening lines.

*Lara Smith is only twenty-three but she knows first-hand the pain of deception.*

*'My best friend got pissed one night and confessed she'd slept with not one but two of my boyfriends,' the bubbly air hostess told me at her high-rise flat in Stansted. 'We've been mates since we were six.*

*To be honest, I like her much better than I liked either of them. I don't want to stop seeing her but I can't trust her any more. It's a dilemma.'*

'Oh, now what we have here?' Enid had come into the back room. She pulled a cardboard box towards her and started sifting through unsorted stock alongside Jen. 'Nice set of bedsheets and couple of pillowcases. Look expensive – fancy.'

And familiar, Jen thought, her eyes drawn to the design.

'Jenny,' Walter's voice came from the front of the shop, 'your daughter's on the phone.'

Disbelievingly, she flipped a corner of the top sheet before rising to answer Chloe's call. Just as she'd suspected, the initials GG were emblazoned in one small corner.

Georgina Giordani. How bizarre was that?

# Chapter 13

Helen looked up from her cod and chips, her brightly painted lips, carefully lined to make them appear fuller, pursed in surprise. 'Hasn't called you? Really?' She was displaying an impressive amount of cleavage, the lacy edge of her bra peeping out of her low-cut geometrically patterned wraparound dress.

'Not yet.'

Helen had dropped by the shop as Jen and Walter were cashing up to say someone she knew couldn't make their reservation at Fingers, apparently the best, most overbooked fish restaurant this side of the Thames, and Helen had taken over the slot and needed company. And, much as Jen hadn't really felt like it, she felt even less like spending the night at home after the spat she'd had with first Chloe, then Ollie on the phone.

'Odd,' Helen mused. 'I gave her your phone number, she was so insistent. And I've just forwarded a desperate-sounding email from her on to you this afternoon. Wonder why she hasn't called?'

'Because she's a complete flake.' Jen shuddered as Helen scraped her fork across her plate. Her nerves were extra-sensitive at present. 'We didn't get on that well last time we met. There was no message from her on my voicemail anyway.'

'Talking of messages, I've left you heaps.' Helen's expression was affronted, expecting an explanation.

'My mobile's been playing up,' Jen said guiltily as she toyed with her mushy peas. Helen wanted to help, no doubt about that, but right now she just couldn't face one more piece of unsolicited advice, especially about the Ollie/money/job/sort-your-life-out-and-stop-sticking-your-head-in-the-sand thing.

'On your landline,' Helen countered stonily, then visibly relented. 'And if I can't reach you then nor can the estate agents. Look, love, you can't spend your days just loafing around watching the Trisha Goddard show. I was reading the paper today, repossessions are up by seventy-one per cent and house sales have slumped. Loads of people I know have been made redundant. It's going to affect all of us, you've got to stay on the ball.'

'I know.' She was sick of hearing this. Sick of being told it was time to face hard reality when she wanted to pull the bedclothes over her head and not get up until at least the year 2020.

'How's Chloe handling things?' Helen probed.

'Fine, apart from we're both cross with each other.' Jen squeezed some lemon on her haddock, trying to make it more palatable. Her appetite was down to zero. She seemed to have a lump permanently lodged in her throat. 'Wants to go trick or treating Friday night. And I don't want her to. We drum into them to be wary of strangers and suddenly they're all off ringing any old doorbell.'

'*All* off?' Helen was checking out the other tables for single white males. So often Jen had the uneasy sensation that if the right prospect walked in she could find herself eating alone.

'The whole world apart from Chloe, seemingly.' Jen half-heartedly nibbled at a chip.

'Whatever you do will be wrong round here.' Helen popped a chunk of fish in her mouth, washing it down with wine. 'Huntsleigh folk are schizo about Halloween. The bible-bashers consider it akin to devil worship, old folk huddle indoors fearing eggs'll be chucked at them if they don't cough up, and everyone else considers you a spoilsport if you don't put lit pumpkins in your window, dress as ghouls and send your kids out begging. You have to make your own mind up and stick to your guns.'

'Problem is my guns are firing blanks.'

'What do you mean?'

'Ollie said yes, after I'd said no.'

Helen's face soured with disapproval and Jen immediately regretted her indiscretion. Helen's attitude to Ollie had never really warmed. Heck, she'd never quite forgiven him for the unplanned pregnancy, for marrying Jen when she was most vulnerable, or even for being a smart-arse on the night they'd all met. And now all her reservations were being justified. Although she'd never actually said I told you so, Jen couldn't help but feel it was always on the tip of her tongue.

'To be fair,' she added, backpedalling as hard as she could, 'he hadn't known I'd said no. Chloe didn't tell him. She was playing us off one against the other and now he doesn't want to go back on his word. We had a set-to about it.'

'There you go.' Helen slammed her hand down on the table. 'Exactly the sort of thing Katy Osbourne had to put up with from her ex. He'd let their son buy PlayStation games meant for eighteen-year-olds, knowing she wouldn't let him watch a DVD that was higher than a PG. He'd . . .'

For someone so keen to find her own Mr Right, Helen certainly took pleasure in the faults of others' Mr Wrongs. Jen's mind drifted back to the argument with Ollie. They'd both come close to losing their tempers for the first time since this war of politeness had set in. Ollie had insisted he had as much right to decide what Chloe could or couldn't do, and Jen had responded that he didn't appreciate that you had to give your children firm guidelines and she'd said no first. God, was this how things would be in the future? Always fighting for control?

'Katy had strict bedtimes, he let her daughter go out till all hours.'

She still wasn't sure she should have backed down. But with the two of them ganging up on her like that . . .

'. . . face up to her fears.'

She snapped back to Helen's monologue.

'Because if she didn't, her mediator said, Katy and her husband would always be stuck in the past.'

'Blast!' Jen suddenly put her hand over her mouth in horror. 'Bollocks.'

'What's the matter?'

'Velvet. I forgot to get velvet. Chloe'll be furious!' Another failing to add to her daughter's catalogue. 'It's for tomorrow. I promised her. Oh God.'

'Don't be so hard on yourself.' Helen shook her head. 'You've got a lot on your mind. You know I'm worried about you. I think this divorce may be affecting you terribly in all kinds of ways that you won't admit. Isolating yourself, not answering your phone.' Her voice hushed, her head came forward as if they were MI5 agents exchanging secrets. 'It's not like before, is it? You know, when . . .' Mercifully, Jen thought, Helen caught herself and tried another tack. 'You should try counselling and get Ollie to leave. I just can't fathom . . .'

Jen poked at her haddock and changed the subject. 'Hey, did you know Björk's first job was deworming fish?'

'Worms!' Helen put down her knife and fork, then blinked at Jen. 'Fish have worms?'

'Mostly cod. She used to pick them out with tweezers.'

'I've never heard of such a thing.' Helen looked slightly sick. 'And who would tweezer them out – wouldn't they simply throw the fish away?' Putting her napkin on her unfinished meal, she pushed the plate to one side.

Immediately Jen was swamped with guilt at her own irritability. Poor Helen. Always thinking of Jen's best interests,

117

arranging this nice meal out, giving advice, and how does she repay her concern? Putting her off her fish, that's all. How bad a friend was she?

An image came to her of Helen standing on the doorstep of the Bounds Green studio, holding out a covered dish.

'Heat it in the microwave and tell him you cooked it yourself. That'll impress your new hubby.'

'Oh, Helen.' Jen's red sleep-deprived eyes had filled with tears. With one glance Helen took in Jen's T-shirt, stained with milk and baby sick, her desperate expression, a bawling Chloe on her shoulder.

'Hand her over.' Helen held out her arms. 'Colic?'

'I don't know. She hasn't stopped crying all week. Ollie had to go to the library to finish his coursework. He didn't want to leave but he has classes all afternoon.'

'Give me Chloe and go to bed right now. Don't worry, love. Auntie Helen's here.'

And she had been. For months at least, turning up with meals and groceries until the worst of it was over and Jen could to see a glimmer of light as gradually the smothering gloom began to dissipate. She felt full of self-loathing suddenly. What an ungrateful bitch she'd become.

Helen had already rescued her once before from an era so dark Jen wouldn't allow it wiggle room in her memory banks, and still neither of them could forget how close she'd come to the perilous edge. No wonder Helen felt she had the right to push and interfere. Wasn't it the Chinese who believed if you saved a life, you were responsible for that person for ever?

And yet the weight of obligation was crushing. No matter how many times she had been there for Helen, offering a sympathetic ear when her latest affair went wrong, helping her paint her entire flat, hosting a surprise fortieth birthday party when Helen had felt so low about entering a new decade, Jen could never equal the balance. If it wasn't for the debt she owed her she might have drifted away from Helen years ago, so often it seemed they had nothing in common except the past, that their relationship should long have been outgrown. But Helen wasn't the type to let friendships drift.

Maybe Helen was right. Maybe the divorce *was* affecting Jen more than she'd realised. Or was she just so isolated, stressed and unhappy that she was in danger of turning into a recluse, wanting to tell the whole world to shove it? Jen longed to find a deep hole and bury herself in it, away from well-wishers and enemies alike.

'It was just a talk show, Helen.' She tried to make amends, pushing her own barely touched plate aside. 'I'm sure Björk made the whole thing up. Celebrities say anything for publicity.'

Still it was a relief to notice Helen, irrepressible to the end, archly giving some male the glad eye over Jen's shoulder. Happily, he wandered over to their table, saving Jen from further discussion of her current state.

On leaving they walked to Helen's car.

'Mind if I stop by my house before I drop you off?' Helen remotely flicked the locks. 'I'm popping over to visit my mum and I need to pick up a few bits and bobs.'

Sitting in the car outside Helen's bungalow, Jen listened to the radio while her friend ran inside. A Beatles song ended and a new one began. 'You're Sixteen You're Beautiful (And You're Mine)'.

Jen gulped. Starkey's song, the one he'd sung to her. Of course they played it all the time, it had haunted her for years but still . . . it had to be another sign.

'OK.' Helen was back, throwing a plastic bag in the back seat, and they sped off.

'Do you want to come in?' Jen saw a light on in Chloe's room as they approached the drive.

119

'Mum'll be waiting. And I'm starting a new temp job tomorrow. Health clinic. I'd better be fresh for it if I want to nab myself a handsome young doctor.'

Jen looked up at the window again as Helen turned off the engine. 'Probably Ollie reading Chloe a bedtime story.'

Helen was silent, lips pressed together.

'I can't just kick him out, Helen.' Jen shook her head. 'Besides, it's still his house.'

'Go on, tell me, none of my business. Wait, here!' Helen reached into the back seat and chucked the plastic bag at her. 'For you.'

'What's that?'

'Open it.'

Jen undid the knot and peered inside. Material. Red, gold and green velvet.

'Oh, Helen . . .'

'Curtains from my old flat. I'll be glad to be rid. Now listen, you, get those phones fixed, all right?'

And she was off.

Jen stood in the driveway, watching the rear lights disappear into the distance.

Three signs. Three sodding signs.

Meg's phone call.

Georgina's bedlinen.

Starkey's song.

It seemed the world was conspiring against her. There was a steamroller trundling in her direction and she was the paralysed rabbit caught in its headlights – did steamrollers have headlights? – all right, in its path then, unable to avoid the fatal impact, the engine of fate pushing for the most ill-timed resurgence of a past she'd rather forget.

# Chapter 14

'A lump. What type of lump?' Georgina was in the Canary Wharf offices of Giordani, looking out at the grimy old Thames through floor-to-ceiling windows on a depressingly grey day, even for late October. She'd shut the double doors for a moment's privacy to take Jennifer's call.

'My friend forwarded on an email of hers which Meg headed as urgent,' Jennifer's voice was uncharacteristically flat. 'Shall I read it?'

'Go ahead.' Georgina ignored the whirl of activity on the other side as her employees scurried here and there, answering phones, taking orders and gathering in the banquet-sized conference room for this meeting that Aiden, the bully, had insisted she attend. He'd practically manhandled her into the limo despite all her firmly stated refusals, wailing excuses and pleas of sickness.

Well, too bad, they could all jolly well wait.

'OK. She says, *Hi Jen, your friend seems to have given me the wrong number so I'm emailing. So here's the scoop. I've just gotten to England for some dumb medical tests. They found a lump but I'll tell you about that when I see you. Any chance of hooking up with you and Georgie? This week if poss. Wouldn't ask, hon, but it's pretty crucial. I'm staying at Ashport with Mace, Meg. That's it.*'

'She said a matter of life or death to me.' Georgina gave an

121

exasperated sigh. 'She left a few messages on my voicemail last week. No email though – must have been deleted as spam. I didn't call back. I thought she was just being her usual drama-queen self, and frankly I just can't deal with her right now.'

Perturbed, she paced her huge split-level office, hardly noticing the expensive artwork, the glass and chrome furnishings. How happy she'd been when she'd first bought this building. How tailor-made it had seemed with the cavernous warehouses below, where cartons of her famous clothing and fabrics could be stored and loaded for export, and the gleaming, modern offices above where new and exciting designs would be born daily, nurtured from an initial spark of an idea to their final glorious creation.

Or that was the theory at any rate. Instead the Heal's project was long overdue, suffering from miserably overextended labour pains. If Aiden had his way, she'd be surrounded by doctors sharpening their forceps ready to do some yanking. But creativity didn't work that way.

'Yes, well, it sounds dramatic all right,' Jennifer replied.

'That was all? Didn't she give details?' Georgina glanced with distaste at the portfolio of sketches on her desk. They weren't right. All the yes people would coo over them, applaud her genius, but she, Georgina Giordani Carrington – and possibly the buyers – could call a dog a dog, especially when it was urinating on her lawn.

'I read you the whole thing.' Jennifer sounded remote. Surely after all these years she couldn't still be angry about her and Aiden? Or perhaps she resented being used as Nutmeg's mouthpiece?

'Yes, but what kind of lump? Whereabouts? Neck? Breast? Groin?' Georgina turned her back as Aiden walked into the office, tapped his watch twice and walked out again.

'She didn't say.'

'What size? Pea? Plum? Grapefruit?' She couldn't find her

blasted pen. The fountain pen she took to every meeting, used to sign every contract, the one her father had given her when she graduated. Where on earth could it be? She pushed aside her desk diary and gave a sigh of relief as she uncovered it. Silly to be superstitious but Georgina believed strongly in luck, good or bad.

'How am I supposed to know? And before you ask, no, I have no idea if it's malignant. Or why she isn't getting tested in the States.'

'So you haven't emailed her back? Or telephoned?' Georgina did her best to make it sound neutral. Ten minutes ago when she was flicking through her diary, wondering why Aiden had arranged all these blasted lunch meetings when he *knew* she found the entire public eating thing an absolute ordeal, she'd had quite a shock when her receptionist informed her Jennifer was on the line, experiencing a mixed bag of emotions veering between astonishment, excitement and dread.

'I wanted to talk to you before I contacted her. See what you thought.'

Silence while Georgina took this in. If truth be told, their last meeting ten years ago had been about as jolly as three pit bulls tied together in a sack.

'Bottom line,' Jennifer continued, 'do we agree to meet her or not?'

'What do you think?' Georgina stalled.

'I'd have said no, but the lump has me worried. Of course,' she sounded mildly sarcastic, 'we don't know if it's a pea, a plum or a sodding bloody potato. But on the other hand, what if she's . . .'

'Has she spoken to Rowan?' Georgina interrupted.

'I don't know,' Jennifer replied. 'Did you ever hear from her again?'

'No. I tried tracking her down but I simply couldn't find her. You?'

'I had other things on my mind.'

Georgina didn't respond.

'Sorry, Georgie,' Jennifer continued, 'I can't talk long, the shop's getting busy.'

'You mean we're both shopkeepers, how frightfully funny.' Georgina seized on what she thought might be a small patch of common ground, however weedy. 'We just opened a third Giordani. In Bath. We . . .'

'I don't own it,' Jennifer interjected. 'I work here. Voluntarily. For a charity.'

'Oh? Well done,' Georgina congratulated her. 'We all have to do our bit. So tell me about your life? Do you have children?'

'One child, a little girl.'

'How lovely. And how long married? Who's the lucky chap?'

What a preposterous thing to say, thought Georgina. As if she were likely to know him. She couldn't help but feel ridiculous, too, for being relieved that Jennifer had settled down, as if she was still some threat after all these years. Aiden had never explained his late return that night after the reunion, but she had her suspicions.

'His name's Oliver Stoneman. Ollie. He's an engineer. Actually he's the student I was seeing when . . .'

'The young stud! Really? So you *did* get married. And it all worked out. Goes to show how wrong I was. No one should *ever* listen to me.'

'No, you were right. We're about to divorce,' Jennifer said, sounding even more subdued.

'Oh, I'm sorry.' Worse and worse. Nearing forty and about to be single again, just as her youth had well and truly faded? Georgina couldn't imagine a worse fate. And working for nothing in some second-hand dump, sifting through people's discards. Life could be so cruel.

'So do you want to be part of this or not?' Jen sounded like she couldn't care less one way or the another.

Liam, a young intern with a striking resemblance to Tin Tin, stuck his cockatoo crest nervously through the door. Sent to do Aiden's dirty work and clearly not relishing the job.

'Five minutes,' Georgina mouthed silently, holding up one hand, fingers splayed. Liam nodded and disappeared. 'I don't know. So she's staying in Ashport?'

'So it would seem.'

'Permanently? Or temporary?'

'I don't know.'

'Married?'

'Haven't an earthly.'

'Children?'

'Not a clue. Look, quit with the questions, you know just as much as me now. And my manager needs the phone. I'm going to meet her whatever you decide. Whatever her faults, she was a good friend. I don't see how I can refuse. So are you in or not?'

Georgina walked to the window again, but she was no longer seeing the Thames. She was remembering a younger Georgina, greasy-skinned, grossly overweight, sick with nerves and excitement as she headed out on her first ever date.

Gary Lewis, one of the alpha males in fifth form, had passed a note to her across the canteen.

'Odeon. Six p.m. this Friday. Meet me there?'

Disbelieving, she'd glanced across the chatting heads to Gary's table, where eyes were keenly watching her reaction. When they saw her look, Gary gave a foxy grin and a thumbs up.

'Oh goblins.' She turned away, blushing, unable suddenly to swallow a bite of her sponge pudding. 'Oh crumbs.'

'Let me see that.' Jennifer won the tussle for the note, Rowan and Nutmeg reading over her shoulder.

'Georgie, that's brill. We'll be able to double date,' Jennifer said, the only one with a boyfriend.

'I'll do your make-up,' Rowan offered.

125

Nutmeg was less enthused. 'Gary Lewis is a total prick. I wouldn't fall for it.'

'You're only saying that because he didn't ask you,' Georgina bristled. Now that his acne was almost cleared up, Gary was definitely one of the better-looking boys in their year.

'Are you kidding?' Nutmeg tossed her ginger head scornfully and shook her multitude of bracelets. She'd favoured a Madonna look ever since the Live Aid gig and today the scrunched gelled hair around her forehead was backcombed, piled high and held with tortoiseshell clips while the rest hung loose and messy. 'I wouldn't be seen dead with that immature clown. Anyway Herb got me tickets and backstage passes to Saturday's Stones gig. He's playing with the warm-up band and David Lockhart, the hunkiest guy in the Lower Sixth, is going with me. So there. Herb knows Mick from way back.'

Sometimes she hated Nutmeg.

Still, when Gary blocked Georgina's path after lunch and asked, 'So will you go out with me?' Georgina found her throat too dry to speak and only managed a helpless nod.

She got her mother to drop her two streets from the Odeon so she wouldn't look like a fool arriving with a chaperone. They'd been out shopping that morning and she had on a black crushed-velvet dress with a little white collar that, remembering it now, made her look like an overstuffed maid. Her stockings were white which Rowan said was very mod but made her legs more sausage-like than ever, her black shoes had a half-inch spiky heel which was hard to walk in. Rowan, true to her word, had applied her black eyeliner along with a layering of sage advice.

'Let him pay for the tickets. Boys like that. But bring money just in case he doesn't have enough for yours. He'll probably want to hold your hand as soon as the film starts. If he wants to kiss you, say yes.'

As she approached the cinema she wondered what Jennifer

was doing. Off with Starkey, no doubt. They rarely saw her outside school these days.

She remembered the feel of cold hard bricks as she leaned against a wall, almost too scared and keyed-up to turn the corner. All that stood between her and her first-ever date was one small road. She pictured herself walking to the cinema entrance, finding Gary standing by the edge of the pavement, looking up and down the street for her. Or perhaps he'd be in the queue, waiting for tickets. Yes, that was more likely. Today was the first showing of *Top Gun*, loads of kids she knew would be there. Kids who'd called her fatso or made oinking noises as she passed would see her go up and take Gary's hand. Maybe he'd even kiss her. She took a deep breath, summoned up her courage, and straightened up.

'Wait! Georgie!' There was the sound of running feet and Nutmeg screeched to a breathless halt, wearing leopard-print stretchy jeans and dozens of chain necklaces over a baggy white blouse. 'Don't go.' She was doubled over, panting. 'It's all a big set-up. Gary and his mates are in Wimpy's over the road. They dared him to ask you, they've got a big bet on it but he's going to stand you up. I wormed it out of David when he came to my house.' She stopped wheezing but her artfully dishevelled hair was still damp with sweat. 'All the boys know about it. Some of the girls too,' she added with more truth than tact.

Ashen, Georgina almost collapsed as she sagged against the wall, her legs losing strength. She felt sick . . . mortified . . . shrivelled with horror, sweat breaking out on her brow as the awfulness of the cruel joke overwhelmed her.

'But what . . . what should I do?' Her lower lip wobbled, her whole body trembled as she thought of how they must all be laughing at her. *Stupid fatso. Actually thought a boy might fancy her. Can you imagine it!*

'I'll have to leave school,' she whispered, sinking to the pavement, her knees jellifying. 'I can't go back there. I'll just die.'

'Not so.' Nutmeg pulled her up with all her wiry strength, her fingers emerging from the cut-off tips of her black net gloves. 'Because you're coming to the gig with me. Clover's waiting with the car, the Stones don't come on till nine. I told David to go screw himself. And if old acne-face or anyone says a word about it, you tell them you planned to stand him up all the time. Just say he's not your type and you had a *far* better offer.'

There was a tap on the door and Georgina wrenched her mind back, realising Jennifer was still waiting at the other end of the line for an answer. No one had ever done anything that nice for her before or since. Nutmeg had sacrificed her chances with the school heart-throb to save her from public crucifixion and managed to turn her, albeit temporarily, from an object of derision to the envy of their school as the two of them swanned around the corridors the next day, talking loudly of how Mick had shaken their hands when Herb introduced them in the hospitality suite and how Bill Wyman had asked them if they'd like a Coke.

And now Nutmeg had a lump. Wasn't it time to put old resentments aside?

Her sales director John stuck his head through the door.

'Ready, Georgina? Aiden says you'd better get out there. They're all waiting.'

Sighing, she walked to the desk, picked up the portfolio her design team had produced. Not one in the whole shebang she was mildly enthusiastic about, and yet her entire empire could hardly grind to a halt because she was having the artistic equivalent of writer's block. Or could it? Did she really give a fig?

'Georgina?' She heard Jennifer's voice crackle.

'Yes,' she said at last. 'Yes, I'm in.'

# Chapter 15

'Far out, Georgie. Thought you said a good-size country residence? This is like a goddam stately home!' Meg viewed the expanse of sweeping lawn from the patio doors. 'Where's the lake? No, wait, don't tell me. Behind the gazebo, turn right at the summer house?'

The words were light but the tone subdued as she played with the curtain cord. Only someone who knew her could tell she was still shaken by Georgina's initially frosty reception.

'Fine view from the west wing, eh Carruthers?' Jen joined in. 'Are you taking in lodgers? Because once my pile of old bricks finally sells, Chloe and I would be happy with a room over the stables, honest.'

'Don't be silly,' Georgina laughed, showing an array of perfectly straight, dazzling white teeth. 'It's not nearly that grand. There's no lake or summer house. And the previous owner had the stables converted to garages. It's merely a house, that's all, and rather oversized for the two of us. Although it *is* a Grade II listed building.'

'That's a load off. We'd hate to think you were slumming it, eh, Meg?' Jen prompted. At least complimenting Georgina lavishly on her opulent surroundings provided some distraction from the awkward atmosphere that had marched in with them, somewhat like the stray mutt that had once decided to join Jen and the others carol singing. The black mongrel had run into

129

people's houses just as the quartet struggled through the first bars of 'Good King Wenceslas', causing such havoc and giggling fits that instead of filling their decorated pails with scads of loot, most householders had ejected the tuneless four (plus dog) before they could get out a single note.

Barely half an hour ago she'd almost wondered if Meg would suffer the same fate.

She and Meg had pulled up in their cars at exactly the same time, Jen in her BMW, Meg in a dark blue Punto. They swapped curt embarrassed hellos without the hugs or enthusiasm of a decade earlier and side by side, like adversarial lawyers heading to a mitigation meeting, climbed the flight of stone steps between miniature poplars in gigantic carved marble urns.

'Some place, eh?' Meg was the first to break the excruciating silence, hands shoved into her pockets, shivering a little. She looked a shadow of her former self, her face thin with little lines around her eyes, a downturned droop to that sassy mouth. She was drowning in an oversized old parka and even her red hair seemed to lack its usual verve and vitality. It wasn't hard to believe that she could be seriously ill after all.

'I've never seen anything like it,' Jen said truthfully. 'Lucky Georgina.'

The Jacobean red-brick exterior with rows of windows reflected the light of a late autumn day, the bright russet of the Japanese acacia contrasting with golden-leaved beech trees, laurel hedges, blue pine and magnificent horse chestnuts.

'Should we knock or ring the bell?' Meg indicated a heavy brass knocker on the stout wooden door.

'Ring, I think.' Stepping forward, Jen pressed the button.

Immediately the chimes sounded, Georgina whipped the door open so fast she might have been lurking behind it. She fixed Meg with a basilisk stare, arm out as if barring a vacuum-cleaner salesman from entering, scattering dirt all over her carpet and sucking it up for a cheesy demonstration.

'Before you take one more step, Nutmeg Lennox,' she glowered, 'I think you have incredible gall showing up like this. You've hurt a lot of people with your outrageous behaviour.'

Of course she'd been pregnant last time they saw her, but once again Georgina won the award for most changed. She'd lost so much weight that her face looked almost too gaunt, and those perfect shiny white teeth must have sent at least one dentist's child through university. Her stylish apricot pussy-bow blouse and shimmering brown wide-leg trousers hung loosely on her with barely a suggestion of her former curves, so that, Jen thought wickedly, with that mass of upswept hair adding volume to her head, she was in danger of looking like the stop sign on a lollipop man's pole.

Hearing Georgina's attack, she pretended to stare at the entry to conceal her emotions. Meg's outrageous behaviour? What about Georgina's deception?

Lost for words, Meg's pale sharp face had seemed even whiter. She started to stammer something but Georgina railed on.

'Were you or were you not completely out of order? Stealing Irwin Beidlebaum from under poor Bella's nose, just as they were tweaking the final details on Bella's contract. Not to mention being blotto, incredibly lewd *and* offensive to Jennifer and me.'

Meg looked astounded. 'That was ten years ago! Old Bella's had two sell-out Broadway shows and like twenty lovers since then.'

'True enough,' Georgina continued to bar her entrance, 'but Bella has become a very dear friend. I design all her frocks, we email each other weekly and she most certainly hasn't forgiven you. I mentioned I was seeing you today and she said to be sure I give you a piece of her mind.'

Rather than devastated, Jen thought Meg actually looked relieved. Had she expected worse than this?

So Meg's flirting with the impresario hadn't ended that night. Now she vaguely recalled spotting a photo somewhere of Irwin Beidlebaum at a royal film premiere, and Meg had been with him. At the time Jen was throwing up daily and still adjusting to the notion of bringing new life into the world, so she hadn't given it much thought.

'OK,' Meg said sheepishly, 'you can tell Bella you've said her piece. I admit it – my bad. I was a selfish out-of-control bitch. If it's any consolation, I still feel like a louse about that night. I got so totally hammered.' She twirled a strand of red hair around her finger as her green eyes pleaded like a little girl's, looking so diminished and helpless that Jen suddenly felt sorry for her.

'That's hardly an excuse,' Georgina said sternly.

'What can I say, guys?' A premature firework exploded in the sky as Meg hugged her arms to her body, shivering against the cold wind blowing at her back and through the still open front door. 'That hoity-toity restaurant. Hundreds of dollars for a bottle of plonk. And me flat broke, drama-school reject, even waiters looking down at me – I felt like the hillbilly cousin.' Her ungloved fingers fumbled at her bag zipper, dug in and extracted a lipstick.

'While you, Georgie,' she went on applying a fresh layer without the benefit of a mirror, 'were on top of the world, Bella Stringent grovelling at your feet, the next Vera Wang to be, and like, so obviously rolling in it. It made me feel like such a big fat failure.' She capped the lipstick with a snap.

'Yes, well,' Jen tried to interrupt, realising she needed a wee. 'It's all ancient history now . . .'

'Rolling in it?' Georgina looked offended. 'I was in hock up to my eyebrows, Bella Stringent's Tony awards dress only just saved us. If you imagine I've had it easy . . .'

'Course I don't, Georgie,' Meg cut in, hands spread wide, with a lower voltage version of her old grin. 'Just had a few hang-ups back then. You're looking at the new "evolved",' she waggled two fingers, imitating quotation marks, 'Nutmeg Sunflower Lennox. Nothing like ten years of hard knocks and having your mortality tested to make you see the light.' She included Jen in her smile. 'Hell, I'm thrilled for your success. I'd be wearing Giordani myself if I had the bucks.'

'Good,' Georgina scowled, 'because I've paid for everything in this house with sweat, tears and bloody hard work. The last thing I need is someone coming in, sneering about silver spoons.'

'For Chrissake, Georgie.' By now Jen was hopping from foot to foot, ready to burst. 'Why don't you take her out the back and shoot her? I'm meeting Ollie and Chloe at a fireworks do later and if I have to wait here another five seconds I promise I'm going to wee on your doorstep.'

'Oh sorry. Come in then,' Georgina said ungraciously, shutting the front door finally and leading the way. 'The powder room's the first door to the right.' A woman appeared from a doorway. 'We'll have tea in the drawing room, if you don't mind, Miss Dandridge.'

Meg caught Jen's eye shooting get-a-load-of-old-Georgie glances behind her back. Despite herself, Jen nearly laughed out loud. Powder room. That's what Georgina's mother had called their toilet and probably her mother before that, and it had never failed to get a laugh from her three friends when Georgina had slipped up and said the words too. All of a sudden the knot that had formed in her stomach when she set out this morning eased a little, as she slipped into the downstairs loo that showed no sign of powder whatsoever.

'For pity's sake, Nutmeg,' Georgina said as her housekeeper put the tray on the coffee table and left. 'Stop fidgeting about and sit down. Tell us why you wanted to see us so urgently. What was this matter of life and death? Jennifer said . . .' she hesitated then forged on, 'something about a lump?'

Jen bit her lip. Pea, plum or grapefruit? She felt horribly guilty remembering her ridiculous conversation with Georgina. If Meg were really seriously ill . . .

'I came over here for tests,' Meg tossed her hair as she flopped like a rag doll on to an enormous overstuffed armchair, 'but do you mind if we talk about something else? It makes me too nervous. Until I get the results, I don't think I'm quite ready to share.'

'O . . . K,' Georgina said slowly, and exchanged a bemused glance with Jen. 'What else do you want to talk about?'

Jen was equally taken aback. All this urgency and insistence on meeting up and now Meg said she wasn't 'quite ready to share'?

'Anything! Did you watch the election results on the news? Yay for Obama! We finally elected a black President.' Meg's fingers played with a mammoth crystal dangling from a gold chain around her neck, the mother rock among several chains of crystal beads. 'By the way Georgie, if it makes your friend Bella feel better, tell her Irwin Beidlebaum was a shit to me too. Threw me over after he had his wicked way and not even a sniff at an audition. Instant karma, I guess.'

Add a turban, Jen thought, and she could be a sexy fortune-teller, reading palms on Ashport pier. Her blouse was lilac, long and floaty with transparent batwing sleeves, her wrists and fingers weighted down with bracelets and rings. Lace-up pointy-toe boots and grey tights peeked out from under her ankle-length purple batik skirt. Not a bit like the old flaunt-every-inch-of-flesh Meg.

Nevertheless, in comparison, Jen felt a boring dowdy frump in her kilt-length pleated skirt, court shoes and sage-coloured thin-knit sweater with matching cardigan and a string of pearls inherited from her mother that she'd hardly ever worn. This morning, inserting the matching pearl studs in her ears, she'd thought the sum total was, if not her usual style, at least charmingly retro – the perfect outfit for a sedate afternoon tea with the classy Georgina Giordani. But not now – unless your idea of retro chic was Velma from Scooby-Doo.

'So, Jennifer.' Georgina turned away from Meg, visibly disapproving, and dropped two cubes of sugar into her bone-china tea cup. 'You're getting divorced, you said? What happened? Did he have an affair?'

Jen flinched. Georgie really wasn't interested in small talk with either of them. But resting her saucer back on the table she realised, for the first time in ages, she actually wanted to confide in someone. Neither of them knew Ollie. They had no alliance to him or reason to judge like most of their friends. And, most significantly, they weren't Helen. They would listen unbiased. That was one of the worst things about divorce, she'd discovered. The way people felt they had to take sides.

'No,' Jen said. '*I* did.' For a second she allowed herself to enjoy their looks of shock, and then relented. 'Only joking. But I have admitted adultery, even though it's a lie. We decided to file for the divorce ourselves, without solicitors or anything, save the hassle.' And really why should the lawyers pocket the money when she and Ollie were intelligent, reasonable people and had agreed everything?

'What hassle?' Meg said bluntly, looking dwarfed by the massive armchair as she pulled her feet up under her. 'My Nevada divorce took two weeks and cost us less than six hundred dollars.' She settled herself more comfortably, looking like Alice in Wonderland as she sipped her no-milk, no-sugar tea and balanced the saucer on her knee.

All the furniture seemed to be designed for giants. The big squashy sofa that Jen and Georgina were on would easily seat another three, the yawning gap between them like that separating two warring lovers clinging to opposite sides of their king-size bed. But then again, anything smaller in this room would seem puny, and from the crackling fire to the well-stocked bookshelves the atmosphere was one of pleasure and comfort first, with elegance and function galloping up in a neck-and-neck finish.

'Yes, well, it's not like that here.' Jen shifted her weight against a peach cushion with white stencilled leaves. 'We had five choices.' She used her fingers to count them off. 'One, we cite two years' desertion – doesn't work because he's still in the house. Two, we cite irreconcilable differences and wait for two years' agreed separation and consent, but we didn't want to wait two years.' Nor two seconds, even. Not once Ollie had brought up the subject. 'Three, worse, wait for five years' separation – clearly impossible. Four, we cite unreasonable behaviour and then it will be forever cast in stone that we've been horrid to each other. And five, we opt for adultery and it's all rather quick after that. So we chose five.'

Not that anyone would know. Or at least they wouldn't have if she hadn't unthinkingly told big-mouth Helen, Huntsleigh's unofficial town crier.

'But why should you be the one who's cheated?' Georgina asked, outraged. 'Why not him?' Helen's reaction exactly.

'We tossed a coin. Besides, I don't want everyone wandering around feeling sorry for me.'

'No, instead they're going to assume you're—' Georgina stopped abruptly and got busy stirring her tea.

'A no-good dirty tramp,' Meg finished for her, with a grin.

'I wasn't going to say that,' Georgina said indignantly. 'But, really, wouldn't unreasonable behaviour have been the better option?'

'I know, I know.' Jen rubbed her eyes. 'Bizarre, isn't it? Somehow I don't mind it going down on the court records that

I've been shagging someone senseless behind my husband's back, but God forbid people might think I've been the inciest bit unreasonable.'

Meg and Georgina broke into spontaneous laughter, and after a second Jen laughed too. The atmosphere seemed suddenly more relaxed.

'That is so *you*, Jen,' Meg said, mopping up tea that had spilled over her saucer. 'You always had the oddest logic.'

'Oh no, shagging around is so much better than being unreasonable!' Georgina smiled indulgently. 'So who is this imaginary lover?'

'I don't have to name him actually,' Jen adopted a fake prim tone. 'I see no reason to sully his reputation since he doesn't exist.'

'That's no fun. Mmm. Let's see, who can we come up with for Jen's illicit squeeze?' Meg ran her tongue over her teeth as she thought. 'I know, he's called Leonard Leopald, his friends know him as Lenny. He has a pencil-thin moustache and he's . . .'

'A zoo-keeper!' Georgina broke in. 'Special care of the gorillas.'

Meg threw her an appreciative look. 'Yeah and on full moons he likes to throw back his head, thump his chest and howl. Ow-woooo!'

'And he has a thick bushy mane like a lion.' Georgina's bony shoulders shook.

'And short hairy bandy legs,' Meg sniggered.

'And you don't consider shagging *him* would be unreasonable?' Jen said, deadpan.

They fell about in whoops of laughter. When they finally caught their breath again, Georgina said, 'So why *are* you getting divorced?'

Jen shrugged with feigned indifference. 'Didn't work out. I don't really feel like going into it, either. Anyway,' their concerned expressions demanded a little elaboration, 'the absolute should be through fairly soon and since the respondent – me – won't object, it all looks cut and dried.'

'You might be accused of committing fraud,' Georgina ventured.

'By who?' Jen said, fiddling with the butterfly back of her pearl stud, which was pinching a little. 'Who would know or care besides Ollie and me? It's not like we need documented proof and have to hire a private eye to catch me and my so-called lover boy in the act.'

'I still think it should have been Ollie,' Georgina said. 'What about *your* reputation?'

'What reputation?' Jen laughed. 'Shit, maybe I'm ready to put it about a bit.'

There was a loud explosion that made them all jump – another rocket had gone off, close to the house this time.

As if on cue, Aiden walked in.

# Chapter 16

There were signs of more than one unauthorised firework celebration early the next morning as Jen did her usual two-mile run. The overnight rain still dripped from the trees and soaked the carpet of chilli-red leaves on the ground.

Jen found herself wishing she was back in her warm cosy bed, wrapping the duvet over her head and sleeping till noon.

There were blackened strings of squibs by the lake and fizzled-out bottle rockets in the wet rough grass. On the edge of the thicket she spotted another crazy soul braving the elements, a small dog yapping beside her. Anamaria. She wasn't exactly swinging her hips, rumba rumba, but her walk definitely had a dance-step rhythm. On another day Jen might have veered away to avoid breaking her pace with unscheduled chit-chat, but the going was impossible anyway, with her feet soaked and running shoes caked with mud. She still hesitated in approaching her colleague, however.

Since Chloe was born, her shyness and unwillingness to spontaneously socialise had grown, rather than the reverse. She had a horror of unwittingly inserting herself where she might not be wanted – she'd seen Helen do that often enough. At the school gates the other mothers had already formed their cliques the year before she and Chloe arrived. And although Ollie would sometimes bully her into inviting people over for supper, as soon as he left for work she would gratefully sink back into her reclusive state. Knowing no one really wanted that awkward extra person at their dinner parties, especially one who was married, she always declined invitations made in Ollie's absence. She had a strong idea anyway she probably wouldn't be asked to supper by many of their old friends now they were divorcing.

Her head throbbed. She'd stayed far too late at Georgina's and by the time she'd bolted to the big bonfire party on the common, Ollie and Chloe were nowhere to be seen. Her heart had jumped in panic as she'd searched the crowd, dialling Ollie's mobile repeatedly, as she envisioned screams and fire engines and awful accidents. But his phone went straight to voicemail and fortunately none of the bystanders recounted any horror stories of a little girl who was burnt to a crisp or lost her entire hand and had to be rushed to hospital. So there was nothing to do but go home and wait.

She later learned Chloe had got cold and Mrs Hutton, a schoolfriend's mother – a young, attractive, *divorced* mother – had invited the two of them back for hot chocolate. Chloe was bubbling with the fun of it all when they finally made it back, but the look Ollie gave Jen spoke volumes, all written in fire and brimstone. She hadn't dared say, 'Well, you could have called.'

'*Hola*,' Anamaria greeted her as Jen caught up. 'How are things?'

'Could be better. Is this the dog you found?'

'Yes.' Anamaria bent to pet the peculiar beast, of which terrier was the only discernible strain. 'I call him Feo because he is so ugly. Look!' She wiped the wet rough fringe back from his bulging eyes and lifted up his top lip to show his yellow Dracula teeth and blood-red tongue.

'No one's claimed him then? Are you going to take him to the pound?'

'I will keep him, yes? He's very sweet.' She looked down at him affectionately.

'They're a lot of work,' Jen cautioned. 'Your place will be full

140

of dirt and dog hair.' She realised she didn't even know where Anamaria lived. House? Flat? Married? Single? 'And what will you do with him if you want to go away somewhere? Would you put him in kennels?'

Anamaria shrugged and said nothing. *I sound old,* Jen thought. A neurotic no-fun-at-all housewife. When did that happen? She used to be fun. Could slam schnapps shots with the best of them. Last one off the dance floor. Thought nothing of clubbing till dawn or taking off with Ollie and Chloe for an impromptu camping trip. When did it all change?

The vibrant energetic girl beside her chatted away, telling her about her nine brothers and sisters, all their antics growing up in Barcelona. She had on a wax jacket, her hair wet, ripped jeans as always and thick-soled black boots. God, wouldn't it be great to be twenty-something again? So alive. Living in a foreign country, all that energy and optimism.

But now Anamaria was telling her about a fight with her boyfriend.

'I burnt all his underpants outside on the barbecue,' she said. 'Put them in a big – how you say? Heap? And put a match to them! And I told him you don't ever come back.'

'But why?' Jen asked.

'Why burn his pants?' She tossed her head indignantly. 'Because it made me feel good.'

'No, I meant what did he do?'

'Do?' She looked mystified. 'I told you. He was out all night, he did not come home until six in the morning. Hip, hip, Feo. Come.'

'Oh.' Jen must have missed part of the conversation. 'Well, then good on you.'

Anamaria bent to pat Feo, who chose that moment to pause and cock his leg on a tree.

'Yes, but is a problem,' she said. 'I live in his house. And now I have a dog. No one will rent to me. You are married, yes?'

'Not for much longer.' Anamaria's openness about her relationship suddenly made Jen want to confide in her. 'He's all tetchy this morning because I was out with old schoolmates and missed a fireworks do.'

Anamaria grunted expressively. 'I hated school. The building, the nuns, *todo*, *todo*, *todo*. I used to wait for the younger kids coming home. Steal their sweets.'

'Popular, then?'

'I didn't want to be popular, I wanted to cause trouble. So what are they like? These old friends.'

'Well,' Jen thought for a moment. 'Georgina's extremely successful. And famous. Her company's called Giordani – have you heard of it?'

Anamaria pursed her voluptuous mouth. 'No.'

'Oh, well, anyway, she lives in the most amazing house. A mansion almost.' *And she's married to my old boyfriend.* No, she couldn't say that. It sounded so infantile. 'And she used to be fat but now she's rail-thin and I suppose glamorous, although between you and me, she looked better with a few more pounds on her.'

They both stepped off the path to allow a red-cheeked small boy to whizz by on a bike with rickety stabilisers. 'And Meg . . .' Where to start? 'She's American. She used to like to cause trouble too. You know, *loco* – queues of boyfriends, do anything for a dare. Only these days she wears this big gemstone round her neck, claims to be a "healer" and carries an amethyst and pendulum in what's supposedly her medicine pouch.'

'A healer?' Anamaria frowned. 'What is healer?'

'Faith healer, I suppose.' Jen held her hands stiffly perpendicular to her temples as if giving herself a blessing, feeling mildly silly.

'Ah, *curandero*.'

When Meg told them about her new 'profession' the day before, at first they'd thought she was pulling their legs. But

142

she'd described her skills and beliefs with such passion it was hard to remain sceptical.

'Cosmic energy or something like reiki, I think. She says an angel talks to her. Only Meg's the one who needs healing. She's sick.'

'Sick? How sick?' Anamaria was fascinated. Maybe Jen wasn't so dull after all. This was as good as a soap opera.

'Didn't say exactly. But I think, maybe, *dying*.'

Only she hadn't said that, had she? Or anything specific. She'd talked about how much she missed them, explained how she'd abandoned drama school just weeks after they all last met and then ended up in Las Vegas where anyone could find work.

'That's when I hooked up with my now ex-husband. Champion bull rider,' she related cheerfully. 'He'd just taken second place at the Wrangler National Finals rodeo. I simply flipped over that sweaty cowboy look and that giant silver belt buckle. Smitten by that first Stetson-cocked nod. We went out partying together on the Strip. Ended up in the Wee Kirk o' the Heather wedding chapel to be married by Elvis that very same night.'

'That night?' Georgina exclaimed.

Meg shrugged her thin shoulders. 'Natch, we were both ripped out of our skulls.'

'Your life sounds like a romantic comedy,' Jen marvelled.

'Or a tragedy,' Aiden muttered in a low wry voice, breaking his awkward silence for the first time since he'd walked in.

He didn't look at Jen but she was horribly aware of his presence, the words spoken outside the Marlow Arms ten years ago still hanging invisibly in the air. He'd said little but the necessary greetings, sitting on the arm of the sofa next to Georgina, effectively placing his wife between them.

'Any kids?' Jen tried to concentrate on Meg. Ever since Aiden had showed up, gorgeously casual in his 501 jeans and

Armani sweater, she'd felt like an impostor in front of the one person who knew the true Jen. He was probably in danger of busting a gut from internal laughter, pegging her as an insecure fraud. How she wished she could rip the pearls off her neck, stuff them in her bag.

'A boy. Zeb.' Meg's whole face softened. 'Nine years old. He's the best. Makes all the rest of the bullshit worthwhile.'

'Chloe's nine too. Ollie's and my daughter.' She thought about the night she'd found out. It was even harder to look at Aiden.

And then Georgina had said, 'How lovely.' But it came out weird, her voice all high and bright, as if she were taking part in a Noël Coward play. 'Didn't have any myself but good to keep the world populated.' She plucked at an imaginary piece of fluff on her trousers and Aiden placed his hand, gold band gleaming, on her shoulder.

'But . . .' Jen protested then stopped, confused. Even obsessive tidying-up couldn't eradicate all traces of Chloe. There was always a toy that had slid unnoticed under a chair or a fingerprint on the wall.

'I lost it,' Georgina broke in briskly. 'Happens, you know.' Irritably she shrugged off Aiden's hand. 'You were saying, Nutmeg?'

There was a small pause as Meg blinked, then made her surprising announcement.

'Rowan and I had a pact. When we were in the last year of school, we swore in blood that if anything happened to either of us, we'd take care of each other's kids. I want you to help me find her.'

Shocked, everyone reacted at once.

'You're joking, right?' Jen.

'But that's the most nonsensical . . .' Georgina.

'It's a wind-up, isn't it, Meg?' Aiden said, grinning lazily as he slid off his perch to stand above them all, legs astride, hands on hips. 'You got the wrong day. This is Guy Fawkes Night, not April Fool's.'

'I'm real serious. Rowan totally meant it and so did I.' She said it with finality. The sort of finality of someone making deathbed plans. It stunned them all.

'You're not saying you're . . .' Georgina couldn't voice the last word.

'But why Rowan? What about the bull rider? Shouldn't Zeb be with his dad?' Jen was equally shocked.

'The bull rider's history. We were divorced after a couple of months. I couldn't stand that whole rodeo circuit and he was a mean drunk. A few too many kicks in the head along with the thirty broken bones. The dude existed on painkillers and rye whisky. Man, he was *so* not cut out to be a daddy even if he had given a shit. And Rowan and I had a deal. We swore that we'd never let our kids have the sort of life we had, or worse, end up in an orphanage.'

'An orphanage?' Horrified, Georgina looked as if she were regretting every reproachful word that she'd ever uttered to Meg. 'You weren't orphans!'

'What sort of life? You had the coolest parents in the world,' Aiden objected at the same time as Jen said, 'At sixteen? Why would you even think of that?' And for the first time since he'd walked in they really looked at each other and just as quickly looked back at Meg.

Meg's eyes went to Aiden and Jen in turn.

'You don't have a clue.' Unconsciously her fingers found the turquoise pendant dangling from her neck. 'Herb and Clover weren't noted for their parenting skills. Did you know they used to forget me and accidentally leave me places? No kidding, when I still in diapers at least twice they left me at a truck stop and drove off, each of them thinking the other one had put the car seat in the car . . . that is, if they even bothered with a car seat.' Her mouth quirked wryly. 'Mace was only four or five but if he hadn't yelled blue murder, they'd have ended up in Memphis or Chicago before they noticed I was gone.'

'That's terrible,' Jen said.

'Oh come on,' Aiden scoffed, folding his arms and leaning back against the wall to watch everyone's reactions with bemusement. 'You're exaggerating.'

Meg looked pissed off.

'No, Starkey, I'm not. Think we had a healthy nurturing environment? An orphanage might have been better. I got chocolate chip cookies laced with hash in my Christmas stocking when I was only twelve. Mace and I had to fend for ourselves for days on end when he wasn't even ten yet, because they were out cold or off at some weekend drugfest. Oh yeah, they were heaps of fun.' She leaned forward, her face pinched and intense. 'Herb's shacked up in Phuket with an eighteen-year-old stripper called Imee and Clover's in Acapulco scrabbling to sell timeshares.' Her gimlet stare pierced through him. 'Would you want them taking care of your kid?'

'What about Mace?' interrupted Georgina, shifting in her seat to block Aiden's view of Jen. Jen noticed she wasn't the only one attempting to ignore Aiden, his wife was doing a much better job. Georgina had rebuffed every one of his affectionate touches and now she'd turned her back to him. Perhaps they'd had a fight. Or maybe she just wasn't very loving.

Meg snorted. 'Remember Mace in high school? Blissed out on Ecstasy or acid, doing everything from sniffing glue and household cleaners to swigging Night Nurse. You wouldn't recognise him today. A tax adviser. And his soon-to-be second wife – Evil Plastic Woman I call her – hates my guts.'

Classic Meg, Jen thought, watching her get up restlessly and walk to the window, where she played with the trim of Georgina's floor-length drapes. How often had Meg whispered to them in some steamy café, 'Everybody's looking at us. They *hate* us because we're having so much fun.' Or 'Look at those guys, they *love* us! They think we're *hot*.' It was always love or hate, no notion that the four friends might go unnoticed by most people, no sense of a middle ground when it came to emotion.

'Why did Rowan promise?' Jen questioned, though she could make a likely guess.

Meg rolled her eyes from across the room. 'Are you shittin' me? Her mom was as cuckoo as Joan Crawford and the crazy mother in *Carrie*. Who wouldn't rather be a truck-stop runaway than with that nutty broad?'

Yes, exaggeration was always Meg's thing. Rowan's mum might have been a touch wacko but prone to thrashing her child with coat hangers and crucifixes or stabbing her with scissors, she was not.

'So why didn't she call this Rowan?' Anamaria's well-defined brows frowned in puzzlement, the dog lead in her hand beating time to her squelching steps. She seemed enthralled by Jen's story.

'Because she can't find her.' Jen shivered, inadequately dressed for this slower pace. 'And we all used to be friends. Best friends. Until . . . well, I guess we were drifting apart before this, but something happened.'

The memory gave her chills. Meg showing up at the riding stables, a gigantic joint in the back pocket of her jeans, talking about smoking the peace pipe. The four of them huddled in the hay barn, only Georgina refusing to smoke, fearing the loss of control from getting high. If only they'd all taken that view, because the consequences of that day were so severe that Jen hadn't touched marijuana since.

No one knew which one of them had dropped the not quite spent match or flicked the ember that had started the whole conflagration.

All they knew was that the flames came frighteningly

quickly. As did the fire engines, the police and all the ensuing fury.

It could have all been so much worse. They could have died, horses burned alive, the neighbourhood incinerated. The stable owner, Angela, might have sued them for the damage. But even though only the barn had been lost and no one was hurt, it was quite bad enough.

'After that we all went our separate ways,' Jen told Anamaria. 'Our parents saw to that. Ages ago Rowan contacted us, wanted us to get together, but she never showed. And now Meg claims her *angel* says it's vital we find Rowan. That Rowan needs us and we need her.'

'But do you believe that?' Anamaria said. 'Do you believe there is an angel?'

Jen snorted. 'Meg told us she was a mermaid when she was eleven. Said her tail returned when she went into the sea, but only if it were midnight and a full moon. But, well, last night at least one of us thought we should help her.'

And the most unlikely one of all.

She and Georgina were trying to take it all in when Aiden had gone over to the antique dresser and pulled out a pen and a sheet of embossed paper.

'All right then,' he'd said. 'Let's do it. Where should we start? Meg, how about you ask around Ashport, see if there's anyone there who knows where Rowan moved to? One of my mates used to take art classes with her. I could phone him.'

'Unusual, no?' Anamaria commented. 'The husband will get involved.'

'He's not only doing it for Georgina.' Jen felt obliged to explain. Although it *was* odd, come to think of it. 'Starkey, I mean Aiden, Starkey's what we used to call him, was friendly with Rowan too. We all knew him back then. He's a writer, has published poetry and everything.'

148

'And?' Anamaria gave her a peculiar look.

'And nothing,' Jen said guiltily.

'And nothing? Why, you're as red as that box.' She pointed at a dog litter bin.

'I used to go out with him, that was all,' Jen blurted out. 'And now he's married to Georgina. No big deal.'

'You still feel something? Ah, first love.'

'Not at all,' Jen said stiffly. 'It was just . . . uncomfortable . . . seeing him again.'

For a while the only sound came from woodpigeons cooing in the trees and Feo barking as he splashed happily through the puddles in pursuit of another squirrel.

At least this time she'd been prepared. And Aiden had behaved exactly as she'd expect a nice guy to, the attentive husband, a concerned, interested (but not too interested) friend. He looked great, of course, sleeker, lovely laugh lines round the eyes, not a hint of grey, nothing to suggest he was nearing forty-two. But if she got caught up in this stupid caper of Meg's she'd have to see him again and again. Was she ready for that?

No, she decided. It was time to let those sleeping dogs lie, tuck them in and slip some sleeping tablets into their Winalot if they refused to co-operate.

It made no sense to throw herself in Aiden's path once again. No sense at all.

# Chapter 17

Something was wrong. Very wrong. It was as if Jen had stepped into a game of musical statues with the tape set to pause.

What on earth was going on?

She'd called into the shop and been confronted by Enid standing, freeze-frame, arms stiffly by her sides. Mrs Cartwright stood beside her, mouth agape, and Walter looked even stranger with his right hand raised to his right eyebrow, palm facing downwards in a naval salute.

Jen opened her mouth to speak, but then thought better of it. Her gaze wandered to Enid, whose eyes occasionally flickered to the clock behind Walter's head. She was still wearing her jacket, and in the buttonhole and also, Jen noticed, in the left lapel of Walter's smartest black jacket, were crimson paper flowers – poppies.

Of course, Armistice Day.

Jen quietly closed the door behind her and stood next to Mrs Cartwright, joining the two minutes' silence. Seconds later, Enid gave the nod, Walter muttered, 'Lest we forget,' and they all started going about their business again.

Enid back to putting hats on a tall wooden display stand.

Mrs Cartwright to looking through a rail of dressing gowns.

Walter to manning the ancient till.

'So the hussy said yes, then?' Enid asked. 'We're talking

about old Nobby and his bit on the side.' She winked at Jen. 'Mrs Cartwright's filling us in on all the gory details.'

'She did that.' Mrs Cartwright nodded vigorously. 'Said she'd marry him as soon as the divorce came through. Nobby's letting Myrtle keep the house. Fools imagine love'll pay the bills.'

Walter gave a bark of a laugh. 'Hussy? Bit on the side? Listen to the pair of you. You make the poor old dear sound like an octogenarian Mata Hari! Think she wooed Nobby away with her false teeth and her Zimmer frame?'

'Oh ignore him,' Enid told Mrs Cartwright. 'Sounds like they've made their beds and poor Myrtle's the one out in the cold.'

'Never too late, eh, Jenny?' Walter nudged Jen, who was already busy putting a new batch of videos into alphabetical order.

'Oh, er.' Jen's eyes flicked from Walter to Enid to Mrs Cartwright, recognising when retreat was the better part of valour. 'Oh, er,' she repeated, shoving all the videos on the shelf anyhow. 'I'm sure I hear the kettle.'

Jen was minding the shop alone a couple of hours later when Helen peered round the door.

'What's cooking, good-looking?'

'Helen!' Jen sprang up. 'What's up? Got the day off?'

'No.' she pushed the door open and came in backwards, dragging an extra-large hessian sack across the floor. 'I'm starting a new business.'

'New business?' Jen ran forward to help. 'What happened to the clinic and all those handsome doctors you were supposed to nab?'

Helen flopped into a low wicker basket chair labelled £4.50, relinquishing her burden as if it had taken her last iota of strength. 'They'd been nabbed already.' Her knuckles limply

151

brushed the floor as her head flopped back, the picture of exhaustion. 'All married. I may be many things, but I've a strong sense of sisterhood.'

No guesses which side she'd be on in the Nobby and Myrtle debate. Helen was savagely insistent that husband-stealing was a big no-no – especially by mousy never-say-two-words-to-your-face bookkeepers like the drab little girl who had meekly walked off with Helen's ex-spouse.

Recovering a little, she sat up.

'I've been so busy I haven't had a chance to tell you.' Idly she glanced at the chair's price tag and dropped it back. 'One of the patients, Mrs Mindy, was complaining her house was full of junk. You know I love that clear out the clutter TV programme, so I offered to help. I've been at it all weekend. The woman makes Howard Hughes look like a Zen monk.'

'But what's that got to do with your job?'

'Well, two of Mrs Mindy's friends came in and they both want to hire me. I can always sign on with the agency again if it doesn't work out. Here, give me a hand.' She hoisted herself off the chair. 'I've a heap of stuff in the car.'

She wasn't kidding. Every inch of her Astra estate was full of plastic bags and cardboard boxes. 'Nothing better than chucking out someone else's old tat. You should have seen what I took to the dump. Moth-eaten clothes, old curtains, chewed-up slippers. But I've still got four bags of perfectly good clobber in there.'

'Then why get rid of it?' Jen started carrying boxes to the shop.

'One of my rules,' said Helen, dragging in another bag. 'If you haven't worn it in a year, it's out of there. You have to ask yourself is it essential, do I love it? And believe me there were clothes she hadn't worn in twenty years. Where is everyone? I thought we'd have more help.'

'Walter and Enid are at lunch. My turn next.'

'Good, I was hoping you'd be free. By the way, I saw Ollie in the pub on Sunday. I didn't know he knew Frances Hutton?'

Jen paused, the sharp corners of the box digging into her flesh. She felt her skin chill suddenly. 'She's the mother of one of Chloe's friends. How do you know her?'

'She goes to my gym. We did a pilates class together and she's always on those spinning bikes. Not that she needs toning up, the cow. She and Ollie seemed very chummy.' She quirked her brows, questioningly.

'They could well be,' Jen said flatly. 'None of my business.'

All the same, it was a shock when, later that day, Jen went to pick Chloe up from school and saw Ollie and Mrs Hutton standing together by the gates. Not overly together. He wasn't holding her hand or leaning in to whisper secrets, and when he saw Jen he waved and came towards her.

But they had been talking. And laughing.

It was incredible how much that irked.

'Om . . . om . . . om.'

Meg sat on the floor in yoga pants and a T-shirt, legs crossed in full lotus position, eyes closed, palm of her right hand resting on the palm of her left.

'Om . . . om . . . om. Om . . . om . . . om . . .' On a make-shift shrine in front of her, the elephant god Ganesh sat beside the rose quartz she'd found in Ashport's only New Age store.

*Feel the breath enter, feel the breath leave*, she thought.

She was dreading this whole dumb testing ordeal. She had always hated medical procedures. Even the sight of a doctor's white coat scared her to death. And what would she do if the results were bad? Neither Jen nor Georgina had called her back yet. Why was everything always happening to her? Was all this supposed to be some kind of cosmic lesson? Clover used to say life never hands you more than you can deal with as long as you dose yourself with tranks.

She could hear Mace downstairs rattling around clashing pans.

'Om . . . om . . . om.'

Another smash.

He sounded like a chimpanzee let loose with a giant pair of cymbals. She gave up and went downstairs.

She was bored out of her skull and tired of telling herself this was all part of some great universal plan. There were ghost towns with more life than Armpit Ashport. Especially staying in her brother's semi-detached morgue. 'Meg, I've been calling you. I've cooked supper. You could at least sit down for it.'

'Sure, Pop. Whatever you say.' She surveyed her elder brother, glasses balanced on nose, his once long hair now short back and sides. She kinda missed the Boy George make-up, the crazy pirate outfits, the flamboyant hats that had been part of his wildly camp, New Romantic look in the eighties. Back then he'd been lost and drugged up, but at least he wasn't this stuffy alien she saw in front of her now. Wearing a suit – on a Saturday too. Ugh.

She pulled a cloth pouch from her pocket and extracted cigarette papers and a small cellophane bag.

'And do you mind not rolling up in here? Especially if that's pot. Paula's coming round later. She'll smell it for sure.'

'Whatever you say, bro.' She raised two fingers high in the air in a peace sign. 'Wouldn't want to offend the bitch queen. Don't you ever get high any more? What happened to you?'

'I grew up, Meg, that's what!'

Meg crinkled her nose at the impostor as he stormed off, slamming the door behind him.

She remembered Jen once convincing everyone their RE teacher was an impostor. She'd been off sick for weeks, returning later looking unrecognisably thin and wan. 'Look at how she talks,' Jen would whisper, 'her mouth never went like that, and her eyes used to be green. And she's shorter. I've actually measured myself against her.'

It turned out she was having chemo. Funny, that. A few weeks later her hair had been replaced by a wig and Jen felt terrible, even filched some flowers from Georgina's mother's garden as a gift to make up for her silly jokes.

The two siblings sat opposite each other silently eating dinner. Mace with his head in *The Times*, Meg glazy-eyed, staring at his slight bald patch.

'So who is the man behind that Iron Mask?' Meg said quietly at one point.

'What?' Mace raised his head. He even ate like a Brit, using his knife to squash peas on the back of his fork instead of shovelling them into his mouth like a red-blooded American. She wondered if he stood up when someone played 'God Save The Queen'.

'Nothing.' She kicked off her shoes. He was probably as depressed as she was. Pushing paper round all day in that stuffy office. Paying through the nose for his first wife and kids. Planning a registry-office wedding with his boring fiancée so they could settle down, raise more babies and be boring together.

'Zeb asleep?'

'No, he's playing Pacman on his GameBoy. I asked him to come down, but he's not hungry. Think I'll take him to see the switching on of the Oxford Street Christmas lights tomorrow night.'

'Good idea. Let him take in some London culture.' He propped his chin on his hand, staring. 'Do me a favour, Meg, and tell me what you're up to.'

'Me?' she said in mock surprise.

'Something's going down, what is it?'

'That's for me to know and you to wonder.'

155

'Well, there's the thing,' he nodded soberly, 'I do wonder why you and Zeb are over here with no immediate plans to go home when you can't afford a vacation. I know you home-school Zeb and he seems a bright boy, but isn't there supposed to be some structure, some accountability?'

'Not from me,' she said flippantly. 'You're the one that studied accountability.'

There was the sound of feet on the stairs, effectively ending the conversation, as Zeb bounced down.

'Hey, bud, your appetite come back?'

'Or something,' Zeb grunted, non-committal. He wasn't as bored as Meg had feared. She'd forgotten how novel a foreign country, even a place as tame as Ashport, could be. The differences, the Englishness of it all. He'd gotten a rise out of the scanners in the supermarket that added up your purchases, so all you had to do was take your groceries and the device to the cash register. He was happy spending hours on the penny machines at the amusement arcade, watching Sky movies on TV or playing on Mace's computer.

'Wash your hands before dinner.' Mace fussed over him like the cookie-baking all-American mother they'd never had. 'And get rid of your gum. Sit here. I'll get you a plate. And hold your fork the way I showed you.'

His voice faded out as Meg's eyes rolled heavenward and she began inwardly chanting again. Om. Om. Om.

Later Meg lay in the rust-stained old bath, water slopping over the rim as she heard her future sister-in-law and brother bickering.

Mace was right, she'd already been away too long. Immediate action was called for. She had to get all her ducks in a row in case this whole thing went down badly. And neither Jen nor Georgina had exactly leapt at the chance to shoulder lances and sally forth on Meg's proposed quest.

What the hell had happened to Jen, she mused, as she lathered up her arms. Scruffy, messy, funny Jen. Did marriage in England come with a lobotomy? That suburban-housewife act was almost as shocking as the changes in Georgina. Not to mention her apparent compulsion to tidy up, even in Georgina's already immaculate house. She had wiped down the coffee table with her handkerchief. Meg didn't even own a handkerchief.

She borrowed one of Mace's Bic razors and scraped it slowly down her leg. If she was honest, she knew there was little upside for Jen in joining the search for Rowan. And there was one big downside: Aiden.

She'd seen the shock in Jen's eyes all those years back when Aiden Starkson had walked into that restaurant. She knew her bolt for the restroom had had nothing to do with food poisoning or low blood pressure.

They might have managed to be civilised at Georgie's last week, but it would be only natural for Jen to want to avoid getting involved with Georgie-Porgie if it meant being around Aiden again. Meg wasn't that thrilled about the prospect herself. But she needed Jen's support. If she wouldn't give it, then it was sure as shooting that Georgina wouldn't be lending her assistance, either. Think, Meg, think. She plunged her head underwater and emerged covered in soap bubbles.

Her ears were ringing. No, they weren't. It was her cellphone. Covered in suds, she pulled herself out of the bath and dripped her way over to it.

'Meg?' a voice said. 'It's Jen. What the heck, I'm game . . .'

# Chapter 18

Ashport-on-Sea in winter was not the tourist's beloved Mecca of sticky pink rock, kiss-me-quick hats, fat-lady postcards and a stretch of crowded beach with extremely dubious sand that became an alarming brown when you dug past the first six inches. Instead it was grey, cold and desolate. Any day now the town council would erect a Norwegian fir and string up Christmas lights along the modest high street, but on a chilly Thursday in the second to last week of November, it was as cheerless as an Arctic weather station.

Jen hadn't been back here for twenty-two long years. It felt very odd to be driving around with Georgina and Meg, stopping to stare at the burnt-out old pier which in its heyday had kept them amused for hours, passing the entrance to the street where she and her dad had lived in a grotty little house on an even grottier council estate.

What a tiny insular world it had been. Walking along the high street, they'd even spotted Mr Perkins, their old form teacher, coming towards them, and from long-ingrained habit automatically ducked into WHSmith's to avoid having to say hello. They were skulking behind a display of greeting cards when Meg pointed out that, as intrepid sleuths, they should have collared him and asked about Rowan.

The farm where Georgina had boarded her horses was eerily unchanged. The owner, Angela, lived alone in the house by the entrance to the yard. Her weathered face bore witness to the hard labour of the past decades, but it was as friendly and welcoming as ever. Over stewed tea and stale ginger biscuits she regaled them with stories of their former equine friends, many of them – Jen realised with a jolt – long dead by now. It was almost as shocking to walk along the row of stables and see an old grey muzzle that belonged to Pepper, a giddy young colt when she first knew him, now a sedate pensioner retired to pasture.

She and Rowan had been obsessed with horses, much more so than Georgina if the truth were told. Fearless Jen would persuade Angela to allow her on all the new arrivals to 'ride the buck out of them' while Rowan spent hours in the stables, simply soothing them with her lyrical voice and calming manner. Their favourite had been Murgatroyd, a black Welsh rescue pony who'd been badly treated. Found starving in a barren field, full of lice and ringworm, he was unsurprisingly quite vicious. Even Jen was apprehensive around him but she religiously exercised him and Rowan would spend hours grooming his mane, stroking him and whispering to him. In the end he was as docile as a donkey and they'd both cried the day he was sold to a spoilt little girl who couldn't possibly love him the way they had.

Angela hadn't seen or heard of Rowan since the fire, she said, but they couldn't resist walking around anyway, rediscovering the schooling ring that turned to mud when it rained, the sloping paddock with an assortment of decrepit jumps, the tack room where they'd spent hours soaping bridles, and even one solitary remaining goose. In the old days there'd been a goose, a gander and eventually goslings that Jen and Rowan had pretended to run away from (Georgina being too genuinely petrified) until they grew up so bold no one could enter the yard without the whole flock honking and charging.

Their teeth were chattering, their hands frozen by the time

they finished their tour. Leaving Angela's none the wiser about Rowan, they headed for the nearby library.

'Progress to date?' Georgina said, shuffling papers importantly.

They were sitting in a little café area that Ashport had recently added to its library, espresso coffee being a goldmine compared to the profitless task of lending books for free. They'd ordered a cappuccino, two lattes and three almond croissants, Georgina dithering over the third pastry – she didn't want it, well maybe, no really, she didn't need it, oh crikey, why not.

Nine days had passed since Jen decided for Georgina and herself that they'd join the search. It was Jen's idea to meet on their old turf, make a day trip of it, but now it was increasingly feeling like Georgina was running the show.

'What about the local phone directory?' Jen suggested. 'Look through it for people we knew?'

'Done that,' Meg reported. 'I've trawled through it and called everybody I could think of.'

Georgina perused her list. 'Internet. Any luck there, anyone?' She looked piercingly at Jen, who almost choked on a mouthful of croissant.

'Sorry,' she wheezed as Meg thumped her back. 'Well, I've done my best. I had to get Ollie to give me a refresher course on search engines.' He'd been happy to do it, too. Oh yes, theirs was a *most* civilised divorce. She blinked and looked down at her notepad, feeling like she was reporting at a war conference. 'People Search,' she continued. 'I found Rowan Howard on the electoral rolls. Trouble is I found a boatload of them, scattered countrywide.' She pulled a printed list from her handbag. 'None of them in Ashport, though. It's pretty hard when you haven't a clue where she's living.'

Imperiously Georgina held out her hand. 'Give it here. I'll get Aiden to go through them when I get home. He can at least stir himself to make some phone calls.'

'Yeah, what happened to old Aiden?' Meg yawned, tilting back her chair. She let the front legs return to earth with a thump. 'I thought he'd be here today, he was so hot on helping.'

Jen had thought so too. In fact her nerves had fluttered as she rang Georgina's doorbell this morning, only to fall flat as Georgina came out alone in her military bib coat and curly lambswool hat. Braced as she was for a third encounter, it was as if some of the colour had seeped out of the day. The thought crossed her mind that perhaps Georgina had ordered Aiden not to come. Her attitude towards him seemed so brusque sometimes.

'Man of the moment, my husband. Let's just say his enthusiasm dwindles if not constantly stoked. Likes to set things in motion but not so great at the follow-up,' she added enigmatically. 'And Giordani can't really spare both of us. Our celebrity clients expect at least one of us available in case of crisis.'

'Yeah, let your hubby have the short straw for a change.' Meg unwound her knee-length stripy scarf, the library being centrally heated and positively balmy. 'Right, my turn. I registered on that Friends Reunited website. Guess who the first person I saw was?'

'Jane Rogers.'

'Nope.'

'Peter Martino?' Jen had had a crush on him.

'Guess again.'

'For pity's sake,' Georgina said impatiently, 'just tell us.'

'Frank Benjamin.' Meg sounded triumphant.

The other two stared at her blankly. Then slowly the name clunked a few bells as Jen's memory started connecting. 'Not that guy with the silly laugh who used to fart all the time?'

'Bingo!' Meg scored an imaginary point in the air with an index finger. 'And there was a picture of him too.'

'What did he look like?' Georgina's face suggested an amnesiac checking police photo books in search of a clue.

'Thickened out somewhat and his hair's a touch bouffant, but it was definitely Frank behind those solemn, woe-is-me eyes.'

'He had woe-is-me eyes?' Jen said curiously. 'I don't remember that.'

'No, but he has now. There was a biog with his picture. He's working as a manager in Boots, has two kids, five and eight, and married Isobel Phillips. She was in our year too. Total swot. Became Head Girl in the Upper Sixth after we left. Anyway, apparently she passed away just last month.'

'Oh dear, poor farting Frank.' Georgina bowed her head in reverence. 'Whoever he is. How awful I can't even remember our Head Girl. Maybe I've a block on.'

'Well, what else can we do?' Meg moved on. 'What about Facebook, MySpace and all those sites that say they'll locate a person for free? We should join them all.'

'How about if we . . .' started Jen but was interrupted by Meg, sharply sucking in her breath.

'Oh Christ, I've just had a thought. Rowan, what if she's dead, like Isobel?'

'Dead! What do you mean? Why would she be dead?' Jen frowned, perplexed.

'Because she never turned up,' Meg said excitedly. 'And why not? What if she knew something . . . crashed trying to reach us that night . . . she was asking for help in some way . . .?'

'But . . .' Georgina began.

'What if you have two deaths on your hands?' Meg said it so loudly that everyone in the library café raised their heads, a couple of them suddenly enough to incur whiplash.

The tension broke as Georgina burst out laughing. 'Who are the two deaths? Isobel and Rowan? Meg, you're completely bonkers.'

'And why are they on our hands?' Laughing too, Jen clutched

Georgina's arm with a claw-like grip and transformed her voice into a late-night horror-film narrator. 'Who is the killer stalking the ex-pupils of Ashport Comp? Woo woo woo.'

'Woo, woo, woo? Hilarious, Bedlow.' Meg yawned.

'Could it be,' Jen continued, 'merely an extraordinary twist of fate that in a time span of *only twenty-something years* there's been a horrific spate of one death and one supposed disappearance? Has Rowan Howard . . .'

'Jennifer, be serious now.' Georgina, obviously used to chairing meetings, stopped her before she got too carried away. 'We're wasting time here. Aiden and I have a dinner party tonight.'

'Sorry.' Jen stared down at her notes, wondering why that last sentence jarred. Of course they had dinner parties. Of course she'd say 'Aiden and I' in that possessive way. He was her husband, after all. 'What about Starkey's friend, the one from Rowan's art class?'

Georgina frowned, staring at her own pad. 'I don't think he's phoned him yet. I'll make a note to chase him up on that.'

*I bet you will*, Jen thought, shocked by a sudden vindictive picture of Georgina cracking a whip, harassing and bullying Aiden the way she always used to boss them.

And who was Georgie to snap 'be serious'? Over the past nine days, Jen had been consumed by this search – as if she didn't have enough to do with trying to sell her house, end her marriage, take care of a child, plus fit in a part-time voluntary job. Never mind all the shopping and cleaning to be done. And none of it, not the websites, blogs, Salvation Army, church records, the Mormons – who, according to Meg, had the best genealogy files in the world – had unearthed so much as a hint as to the whereabouts of their missing friend.

It was all a pointless waste of time. A wild goose chase, only this time they were the ones doing the chasing and the geese were miles off laughing up their feathery sleeves. So she couldn't even rustle up a smile when Georgina, getting carried away, suggested checking the names from old passenger ships, and when Meg told them how she'd placed an ad in the local newspaper, entitled 'Desperately Seeking Rowan'.

'I thought it might create a laugh and get us noticed,' she explained gloomily. 'But the only reply was from a mystified Madonna fan. Sorry, Jen,' Meg looked at her sympathetically, 'before, what were you going to say?'

'Oh, nothing, I was just thinking maybe we should go and visit our old school.'

Her words were met with the giddy enthusiasm reserved for snake pits and firing squads. Apparently the prospect of returning to their former seat of learning filled her friends with nothing less than dread.


Ashport Comprehensive was more run-down and sinister-looking than ever, with hardly a blade of grass left on its playing fields (but more than a few clumps appearing in the cracked playground cement). They paused to peer through the railings that stretched along the side.

'Are we going to go in?' Meg clutched the metal bars like a desperate convict serving life.

'Of course,' Jen said just as Georgina responded, 'Do we have to?'

'One of the staff might know something,' Jen said. 'They could have records.'

At the main gates a line of women were queuing to get into the building instead of hiding, as ordered, in their cars, waiting for their kids to emerge. What was going on?

'Ask them what they're all doing here.' Jen prodded Meg forward.

'It's the annual Christmas bazaar.' An old lady with a shopping basket over one arm answered Meg's query. 'Starts at quarter to four.'

'On a Thursday? In November?' Meg sounded surprised.

'They like to do it early. So everybody can buy their presents.'

Jen checked her watch. Three twenty-eight.

'OK, let's do it,' barked Georgina. 'To the back, girls.'

They all shuddered as the bell rang out and kids surged forth noisily. Some things hadn't changed.

'I had a fight in this very playground.' Georgina touched a hand to her throat, looking around her in distaste. 'With that frightfully common girl, Yvonne Spitz. Mr Panser stopped us.'

'Mr Panser?' Meg frowned as they shuffled with the rest of the queue closer to the door.

'Geography teacher. White hairs sprouting from his ears. We called him Pansy Panser. I must have been in the second year,' Georgina reflected. 'She'd been calling me names so I leapt on to her back with a deafening roar to defend my honour.'

Jen caught Meg's eye for a fleeting moment and chewed hard on her left cheek. Georgina leaping on anyone's back at that age without it ending in crushed ribs or even fatality seemed highly unlikely. In all probability Yvonne had jumped on her.

'A crowd of children formed a small circle shouting "Fight, fight, fight",' Georgina stared soulfully into the distance. 'Pansy Panser arrived, everyone dispersed and he took us both into the staffroom and Yvonne said, "I weren't fighting, sir. We was just wrestling a bit for the fun of it. That's right, wonnit, Chubby?"' The weird cockney accent she put on was presumably her idea of working class, nothing like Yvonne's Sussex inflections. She continued grandly, 'And I replied, "Certainly it was, Yvonne," because even though I hated the evil bitch I didn't want to be a grass. And then Mr Panser passed me a paper napkin to wipe my grazed knee and said, "Wait till the bell rings and you can both go to your next class." There was no judgement.' She sounded dreamy, eyes glazed. 'No scolding. Merely the ticking of the wall clock as the minutes passed. The sound of the other

165

children out at play. The distant tinkle of an ice-cream van playing its merry jingle.'

'And you've a block!' Meg was aghast. ''I swear there's FBI dossiers with less detail.'

They were through the doors now, breathing in the familiar school smell of disinfectant and chalk dust.

The crowd surged to the right but Meg grabbed Jen's arm and pulled her the other way.

'Come on,' she said. 'Let's go find our old lockers.'

When they finally made it to the Christmas bazaar the assembly hall looked nothing like it had on those early mornings when the headmaster used to drone at them before class, complaining about pupils running in the corridors or the unauthorised modifications to school uniform. Tables with red and green cloths were set out all around the perimeter with rows of more tables in between. They were laden with everything from mince pies and Christmas cards, to tea towels printed with pictures hand-drawn by the pupils and shop-bought tat.

In the melee they recognised more than one familiar face. Their old games mistress managing the table dedicated to home-made jams and chutneys. The once young and trendy art teacher, now grey and several stones heavier, judging the cake-decorating competition. Enquiries about Rowan, however, met with a total blank.

'I should have brought Zeb,' Meg said, as they passed the Santa Claus onstage and browsed the white elephant stall. 'He might have got a kick out of this.'

They stared at her.

'He's with you? In England? You never said.' Once again Meg had surprised Jen. Did she intentionally forget to tell them things?

'Yeah, well,' Meg's attention was diverted by a giant fruit cake on the next table, proudly displayed on an elevated stand,

166

'who else would I leave him with? Hey, Georgie, how much do you reckon that weighs? Best guess?'

'How many calories is more to the point.' Georgina swept her glance over it, 'I really think we have to go. I told Aiden I'd be home by six.'

'But where's Zeb now?' Jen persisted. 'I'd love to meet him. Maybe you could bring him over to play with Chloe one day.'

'Mace took him to the Science Museum. Hey,' Meg pointed to a little crowd gathered around the tombola. 'Isn't that the old school secretary?' And she was off, weaving through the throng at a run.

By the time the others caught up Meg had ended her conversation and was coming back.

'Big news, girls,' she sang. 'We've had like killer luck!'

'She knows where Rowan is?' Jen gasped.

'Hasn't a clue. Said over a thousand pupils pass through these doors each year,' she affected a prim lecturing tone, 'and they're not obliged to keep records twenty-two years old. But turns out Isobel Phillips loved this place until the day she died. She was very involved with the school after she'd finished uni, even became a member of the board. So farting Frank decided to host a twenty-year reunion in her honour, a kinda memorial party. Everybody she finished school with got invitations, all those they could track down, that is. You must have got one, Georgie. You stayed on.'

Georgina shook her head. 'I throw those things away. Unopened.'

'Whatever. It's on 29th November. Just a week and a bit's time. Isn't that great? What if Rowan's there? Unlikely, I know, but she might have heard about it somehow. And even if she doesn't come, I'll just betcha someone there knows where she is.'

There was little conversation on the drive back, Jen switching on Radio 4 to listen to *PM*, Georgina staring out the window into the darkness as spots of rain hit the windscreen, apparently lost in her own thoughts. But she seemed to rally and shake herself back to reality as they pulled up at what Jen had privately labelled Giordani Manor.

'Ashport's a dump, isn't it?' Her grin was surprising, given her previous silence, and made Jen wonder if she'd imagined the tension in the car, if it had all come from her. 'Even more dismal than I remembered. We can meet in my house again, but it had better be soon if we intend going to that reunion Saturday week. I should get Aiden to sit in.'

And just like that, Jen felt better again. Driving the short distance back to Huntsleigh she found herself singing along with the radio. All in all it had been a fun day. And the reunion was definitely something to look forward to. Something to focus on, a mission to distract her from all the doom and gloom at home.

'Like a virgin . . .' she bawled out and laughed, recollecting Meg's Desperately Seeking fan.

# Chapter 19

Gunfire reverberated through the hall when Jen walked back in the house, throwing her coat on the banister railing.

Ollie was settled on the beige cotton sofa watching *Terminator*, supping lager from a can and eating a large bowl of Chloe's favourite microwave popcorn. Kicked back, relaxed, about as happy as a man could be on a Thursday night alone, so it was a shock when, registering her presence, he snapped to attention, lowered the volume, put the popcorn down and began hunting for a coaster and simultaneously using his sleeve to wipe the damp ring from the coffee table.

Honestly! Anyone would think she was a murderous domineering harpy.

'Don't worry,' she smiled weakly, feeling bad about spoiling his mood. 'Carry on. I can wipe that off in the morning. It's only glass.'

Again, did he have to look so surprised? Just because she'd got a bit tidier over the years, liked things to look nice. It wasn't as if she were *neurotic*.

'OK, thanks,' he said, still staring but relaxing back. 'How was your visit?' he asked, grasping another handful of popcorn. A kernel missed its intended destination and landed on the carpet, but she resisted rushing for the dustpan and brush.

'Fine.' She hated that sofa, she realised now. When she'd first bought the suite Ollie had complained that it was too bland and too narrow to snuggle on, but she'd pushed for its stark clean lines. In the shop its blond wood legs, minimal upholstery and matching glass coffee table had seemed elegant and chic. But the fabric had proved almost impossible to keep clean and once again it seemed she'd sacrificed comfort and even functionality for the sake of appearances.

Ollie was scrutinising her. 'You look happy,' he said, unexpectedly. The thing about blue eyes, when they were the intense blue of her soon-to-be ex's, they made you feel as transparent as that blasted coffee table, as if he could see right through clothes and skin into all her hidden depths.

'Your cheeks are glowing,' he observed. 'Those friends of yours must be doing you good.'

'Probably the sea air.' Now she found herself squirming, wanting to get away from him and his canny insights. 'Is Chloe asleep?'

'Ages ago. We watched a film.' He was still staring at her, damn him. What was he thinking? That 'happy' was so rare for her? Out of the corner of her eye she could see her coat, hanging where she'd thrown it. Better tidy that away, what if buyers showed up tomorrow?

'Wanna sit?' He moved the two cushions which were all the neat-freak Jen would allow, making a space beside him. 'We can watch something else. Shall I get you a beer? I wanted to chat to you anyway, I've been thinking . . .'

*I've been thinking* . . . Why did those words throw her in such a panic? Maybe because last time they preceded him angling for a divorce.

'I need to check the messages first,' she gabbled, launching herself at the phone. 'Did anyone ring?' She was already punching the number for voicemail.

'Helen. Asked if you could call her back sometime. I might have missed a couple of calls though.' Ollie sighed and leaned back, turning up the gunfire again so she had to stick her finger in her ear to hear the announcer say 'Two messages'.

See. Two messages. She felt vindicated. And they could be really, very important. Just because Ollie didn't feel like answering the phone.

'Mrs Stoneman,' the familiar voice was unusually chipper, 'please call me at your earliest convenience. I do believe we have a nibble.'

'It's Mr Hagard,' she yelled over to the mop of dusty-blond hair she could see sticking up above the sofa back. 'He's got a nibble.'

Ollie's head failed to turn. More popcorn fell on the floor. Who cared? Soon she'd be leaving that carpet for good.

The second one was even more gleeful. 'Mrs Stoneman, Mr Stoneman, phone me tomorrow, first thing. I have some excellent . . .' she could almost hear him rubbing his hands together, '. . . news.'

Ollie was asleep the next morning when Jen jumped out of bed at six a.m., unable to wait for daylight. He was making those little puffing sounds that she'd found so cute and adorable when they'd first got together. Now they made her want to stick a pillow over his head.

Maybe they shouldn't be sharing a bed now that the nisi was through. But besides not wanting to upset Chloe, sleeping with Ollie was one of the things she'd find hardest to let go. When his breathing became deep and steady she'd turn towards him, put her arm around his waist, sneak her knee between his thighs and bask in the heat radiating from his body. But what basis was that for a marriage? Wouldn't it be more appropriate to simply buy a hot-water bottle?

She hadn't heard him come to bed and he failed to stir as she put her feet in her slippers and walked to the bathroom. Was he angry with her last night? She couldn't tell any more.

It was half dark when she hit the streets running, then she

had to get Chloe to school. At exactly one minute past nine she was calling the estate agent but there was no sign of Ollie, not even a plate in the sink. He must have gone out for breakfast while she was dropping off Chloe. Anyone would imagine he'd be a bit more interested in this new development, but all he'd said last night was, 'You can sort it out. You're more up on these things than me.'

'Mr and Mrs Radcliffe have put in an offer.'

'What!' Jen clutched at the phone. At last! Thank you God. Thank you Jesus. Mwah. Mwah. She mimed big lip-smacking kisses. I will *never* let you down again.

Mr Hagard sounded exceptionally smug as he named a price that would have seemed ridiculously low a few months ago. 'I know it's not as much as you expected, but Mr and Mrs Radcliffe don't . . .'

'What position are they in?' Jen hated the sycophantic Mr Hagard. Still, if all went well, she wouldn't have to bear him for much longer.

'Only one below them in the chain. It should all tie up nicely. Believe me, Mrs Stoneman, I don't think you're going to get much better in the current climate.'

'What about when the weather warms up?'

'Sorry?'

'Forget it. We'll accept it.'

'Don't you want to consult with your . . . er . . . husband first?'

Sexist pig. Ollie had told her to handle it. And anyway he'd buggered off without his mobile, which was on the table.

'No. *Nor ask my daddy either,*' she added under her breath.

'I see.' On the other end of the line Mr Hagard was tapping his pen against his teeth. 'Well, if Mr Stoneman has any questions, please ask him to give me a buzz, would you?'

'Will do,' she chimed and put the phone down.

Jen spent the afternoon scouring the *Huntsleigh Chronicle* for large flats or perhaps small houses. Now they were under offer, she felt a sudden pressure to buy, but she had no idea what she wanted or what she could really afford. She could rent. But that would mean two sets of removals, two lots of packing and unpacking, two disruptions for Chloe. She closed the paper defeated by the enormity of the decisions still to be made.

And still no sign of Ollie. He knew the estate agent had big news. How inconsiderate to stick her with it all and not even call. All very well to leave her with this kind of stuff when he was away on business, but this was their future at stake now. For all her bravado with Mr Hagard and her anxiousness to get everything settled, what if Ollie didn't believe it was enough?

Chloe entered the kitchen chatting animatedly to a friend on her mobile.

'Daniel thinks he's so well hard, just cos he got a wallet chain and baggy skater trousers for his birthday. Like, wow . . . Becs, tell my mum what he said about your teeth.' She flung the phone at Jen.

'He said I had big sticky-out teeth like a rabbit,' Becs whimpered in her ear.

Chloe took the phone away again.

'He's not exactly fit himself, is he? Minger.'

'Yeah, and rabbits can give a really nasty bite,' Jen volunteered.

'What?' Chloe snorted, unamused, and flounced upstairs.

Another one who wouldn't like this latest development, Jen thought.

The phone rang and she snatched it, expecting Ollie. 'Where the hell have you been?'

'Here,' Georgina said. 'I was calling to invite you over.'


'Don't be worried. This won't hurt a bit.'

'I gotta tell you, honey.' Meg grimaced as a nurse dressed in a smart white tunic drew near. 'Us Lennoxes, we don't do pain. I need the nitrous oxide turned up full blast to get my teeth cleaned.'

'It's just going to be a quick swab.'

'Can I lie down?'

The nurse smiled. 'Yes, if you want.'

Meg winked at Zeb sitting in the chair to her left.

'No need to look like that, kiddo. Bravery doesn't run in our family. Poppa's daddy was the same, they took some blood before he joined the army and he fainted flat out on the floor. Instead of a Purple Heart, they awarded him a white feather.'

'OK,' the nurse said five minutes later. 'All done.'

'That was it?'

'Yes,' the nurse smiled kindly, as she started writing her notes. 'That was it.'

# Chapter 20

Aiden answered the door sporting a just-got-out-of-bed look at five minutes to noon. His dark hair was ruffled, his feet bare and he was wearing an unbuttoned shirt over loose black trousers that might have been pyjamas or part of a karate outfit, it was hard to tell. Anyway he looked unfairly gorgeous.

'Hey, come in.' Sleepily he scratched his chest and yawned. 'Georgina had to pop out, said she won't be long though. Some calamity with one of the shops.'

'On a Sunday?' Feeling shy and horribly ill at ease, she stepped past him into the grand hallway with its elaborately carved Jacobean staircase and tried not to imagine him sweeping her, Rhett Butler-style, into his arms and up its angled corners.

'Yeah, well, when Giordani calls we all jump to it.' He leant forward to kiss Jen on the cheek, his breath warm, his nearness almost suffocating. 'Meg rang to say she'll be late too.'

Bugger Meg, Jen cursed. Why on earth didn't she ring to warn her? Spending time by herself with Georgina would be bad enough. The idea of being alone with Aiden made her feel like a shivering, quivering wreck.

Aiden eyed her with lazy amusement, his long lashes fanning his cheek. 'Make yourself comfortable,' he suggested. 'Our home is your home.'

'Gee thanks!' Did her voice sound as unnatural to him as it

did to her? 'I've always wanted to live in a Grade Two listed manor house.'

'Shall I take your coat?'

'Cheers.' She started to unhook her arms and he came up beside her and helped pull it down from her shoulders.

'And umbrella?' He had her coat over his arm.

'Oh God, yeah, sorry.' She'd forgotten she was still clutching it, even though she'd had to transfer it from one hand to the other to extricate herself from her sleeves. To her horror it was dripping on the floor, probably staining the fine wood. 'Sorry,' she said again, handing it over. He put it in an umbrella stand beside the coat rack and hung her coat over the baluster.

'Don't look so scared, Titch.' He threw her a reassuring smile before leading her down the hall. 'Promise I won't bite.'

You used to, she thought. She'd concocted all kinds of scarf arrangements to hide the marks on her neck.

Her knees were softer than jelly as she entered the drawing room and tried desperately to focus her attention on something other than Aiden. Glancing out the patio doors, she noticed the rain creating circular ripples on a fishpond.

'Do you keep fish in there?' she asked stupidly.

'A few carp I think.' Aiden walked over to look out too, foiling her attempt to put distance between them. 'To tell the truth, I've not checked lately. So you live in Huntsleigh? Incredible, eh, that we both end up in the same corner of England. How long did it take you to drive over?'

'Twenty-five minutes door to door.' Lame, lame, lame. All the history between them and this was the best they could manage? But more unnervingly, their bodies seemed to be having their own much racier conversation. As he angled his broad shoulders towards her, his elbow almost nudging hers, she caught herself twiddling with her hair, licking her suddenly dry lips. She could practically feel magnetic pulses transmitting between them.

'So have you started your Christmas shopping yet?' Could she, if she tried, possibly sound more like a bored-out-of-her-mind hairdresser?

She stopped playing with her hair and instead reached to nervously twist her wedding ring. It wasn't there. She'd taken it off with a bitter-sweet mingling of relief and remorse the day the nisi came through. But now its absence left her feeling naked and vulnerable.

Ollie had lost his wedding ring on their honeymoon in Italy. He hadn't noticed until the last night in Rome. They turned the hotel room upside down searching for it, but they already knew it was futile. It could have been lying in the ruins of Pompeii or on the sandy ground of the Colosseum. Perhaps it was then that their fate was sealed?

Aiden strolled towards the blazing log fire that warmed the panelled room from beneath its ornately etched overmantel. As Jen's chest rose, seeking air, she wondered how long she'd been holding her breath. What a dope she was. She stood in the middle of the room, not wanting to sit down until he did, scared that if she sat first he might cosy up next to her. Not the scene she wanted Georgina to walk into.

'Are you still writing?' she finally said, seizing on a safe topic.

'Yeah, when I can. I'm halfway through a novel. Don't get much chance for it between Giordani and, you know,' he bent down to stab the fire with a poker, hair falling in front of his face, 'taking care of the missus.' He said it ironically. She had a feeling Georgina could be brutally demanding.

'Is this your first book?'

'If you don't count a couple of masterpieces at the back of the cupboard.' He glanced up at her with a grin that made him look nineteen again. 'Weighty pretentious tomes. Useful for doorstops, holding down flapping picnic rugs, that sort of thing.'

'Rubbish. You were so talented. I thought you'd have written at least a dozen hit songs by now. Or your poetry would be a huge success.' How many times had she gone in bookshops checking for his name? So pathetic.

He laughed wryly but she could tell he was pleased. 'Poetry? That's a bigger waste of time than my literary attempts. No one wants to be challenged or think any more. If James Joyce wrote *Ulysses* today they'd dismiss it as the ravings of a madman.'

Privately Jen would agree with them. Mr Dugan had suggested in English class once that they give it a try, and she'd only managed the first page before returning to Dick Francis.

'Anyway, I'm sticking to more commercial ventures these days, if I ever get a chance to finish anything. I keep threatening to rent a cottage somewhere, isolate myself till it's done.' He wandered back to the patio and looked out at the rain. 'The novel I'm writing is a love story. Based in a small town not unlike Ashport. You're in it, you know.'

She almost dropped the Swarovski crystal bird she'd just picked up. Carefully she replaced it on its antique side table.

'Me?' Suddenly she'd forgotten how to breathe again, and she knew her face wasn't just flushed by the fire.

'Don't worry, it's fiction. You won't even recognise yourself.' A blazing log lurched and fell forward, threatening to topple on to the hearth. He padded over and pushed it back in place with the fire tongs.

Where on earth were Meg and Georgina? 'Well, in that case, can you make me a platinum-blonde glam puss with legs up to my armpits and a fiery-red sports car?'

'Yeah, I might.' He seemed to consider it, then smiled. 'If the real thing wasn't s-o-o much better. Amazing eyes, provocative mouth and perfect legs firmly planted on the ground.' He was looking at her in a way that made her spine tingle, his bare feet noiseless as he drew closer. 'No glam puss could hold a candle to you, Titch.'

She gulped, shaken by his compliment. It was so much easier to be enemies.

'Seriously though, I'd love to read it sometime. How does Georgina rate it?' Neat move. Remind him he's a married man. She had to put out this spark between them.

'Oh, you know Georgie.' He pulled his dark brows into a deep brooding V. 'Results person. Won't be impressed until she sees the finished product top of the best-seller lists. Not the type to encourage unrecognised genius. She'd have been the first to tell Vincent Van Gogh to shove a bandage on that ear and go find a proper job.'

There was a short uncomfortable pause. They stared at each other, only a few feet away instead of the several hundred yards that felt like Jen's personal comfort zone with him. She found herself squirming under the intensity of his brown eyes as her fingers fidgeted restlessly with an earring. Aiden was still holding the fire tongs as if he'd spaced out everything except the two of them. She was the first to avert her gaze.

'Sorry to hear about your separation.' His voice, suddenly so deep and smoky now he was talking about her personal life, caught her off guard. 'That guy's a fool. Letting you go.'

'Personally, I think it was a smart move,' she said, edging round the back of the sofa, her own voice light as a tinkle of fairy bells, or so she hoped. 'You know things are gloomy when even the dog's walking around with a miner's lamp.'

Aiden's lips twitched appreciatively. 'Still with the one-liners.' Absently he glanced down, brushing lint off the front of his thigh. 'I love you, Jennifer.'

'I'm sorry. What did you say?' Stricken with shock, Jen stepped back and tripped over a table. Ornaments and photos crashed to the ground, giving her an excuse to hide her burning face as she stammered apologies and bent to pick them up. Dismayed, she noticed that the silver frame of one of the wedding portraits had cracked apart, the glass lying shattered on the carpet, the picture of Georgina smiling up at Aiden sticking half out of the frame.

'Oh bugger. I am so *so* sorry.'

'Don't be.' Relaxed and amused, Aiden squatted down to help her right the table and restore the pieces. 'I said I love your jumper, by the way. It's a good colour on you.'

'Careful.' The mother in her surged forth. 'Broken glass. You'll cut your feet.'

Her jumper. Not Jennifer. Her favourite jumper. All fiery reds and oranges. She'd treasured it for years. The relief was overwhelming, almost as overwhelming as her desire to kick herself until her shins turned blue.

'Thanks,' she mumbled, reaching for an ornament that had rolled under the sofa. 'Ollie,' she stumbled over the name, 'bought it. Surprise. Italy.'

Steady, girl, she told herself, try to at least speak in sentences. She took a deep breath. 'He bought it on our honeymoon. Not that it was much of a honeymoon, I was eight months pregnant at the time.'

She'd started to cry, a few frustrated tears, when she'd tried the jumper on 'just for fun' and it wouldn't go over her bump. As they stepped miserably out into the bright daylight, Ollie had turned and run back. 'Here,' he'd said, a short while later, handing her a gift bag with a flourish. 'You won't always be pregnant. And something that looks this great on you will always be in style.'

'I looked like a bus tipped sideways,' she added now.

That brought a smile to those perfectly formed lips. 'Same old Jen,' Aiden said as he leant over to pick up a fallen china cat, his head so close she could have counted the grey hairs if there'd been any. 'You always could make me laugh. Hang on, don't touch that glass. I'll fetch a broom.'

*Oh yeah, I'm hilarious.* Jen cringed inwardly as he walked out. 'Let's hear it for the funny lady,' she muttered under her breath. 'Well done, Jen, for embarrassing yourself to death.' She returned another wedding picture to its place on the table, this one of

180

Aiden beside Georgina's dad, whose arms appeared glued to his side, Georgina by her mother whose sour expression looked like she'd eaten a pickle. She recognised Georgina's cousin, Liz, in front of them, wearing a revolting pomegranate-red shiny frill-neck bridesmaid dress with a hideous bow.

Good for Georgie. Sweet revenge probably for all the cruel taunts Liz used to bestow upon her. And there too was her much older, moderately handsome brother, pink carnation in his lapel. Georgina used to have such a good relationship with Lance on the few occasions Jen had seen them together, glowing pink when he ruffled her hair or gave her a casual hug. Jen had been quite jealous, because being an only child like Rowan, she would have killed for a brother – if only to be able to beat him up.

Her mind was still reeling from the way she'd misheard Aiden's 'love your jumper' remark. She'd worn this sweater to death in London to lavish compliments, but it had always seemed too loud for tame old Huntsleigh. It had languished untouched in her wardrobe until today when she was digging through nondescript slacks, unremarkable skirts, sedate tops in shades of ecru, cream and navy blue, searching for something to wear with her pushed-to-the-very-last-hanger 501 jeans, not wanting to repeat her previous faux pas of looking middle-aged and boringly suburban.

The problem was she didn't know who she was any more. In Islington Ollie had once described her fashion statement as 'grunge with attitude'. But living in Huntsleigh she'd soon discovered she only had to step outdoors in an oversized hooded sweatshirt and khaki trousers for her neighbours to shake their heads and giggle, 'Goodness, Mrs Stoneman,' as if she were a freak who'd stumbled drunk into the vicar's tea party with a tattoo on her forehead and a piercing in her tongue. And the closer she got to forty, the harder it seemed to find a line between frumpy and mutton dressed as lamb.

She wished that didn't bother her so much, other people's opinions of what was appropriate. Meg would never let anyone alter so much as one dangling earring of her eclectic style, and Georgina had braved much more than subtle disapproval only to emerge a bold butterfly from her plump chrysalis. It was she, Jen, who'd given in to the pressure to conform and in the process lost all sense of identity. She used to have more guts than that.

Aiden came back with a hand-held car vacuum and got to work. Would she ever be able to look at him as '*oh, just some guy I dated*'? A friend? She'd heard of women whose ex-boyfriends, ex-husbands even, were their best pals, confidants for all their problems, drinking mates with the woman's new spouse. But then she and Aiden had only had those fifteen months – sufficient to sear a trail across her psyche but not enough to let the lustre fade – and she'd been so young. So recklessly open with her inexperienced heart.

At least it was far more likely that she and Ollie might become chums after the divorce. It would be a shame to waste all those years and memories. Jen's mind conjured scenarios as Aiden vacuumed and she picked up larger shards of glass: she and Ollie proudly watching Chloe getting married, Jen with her new man at her side; Ollie and her future partner kicking around a football with their future grandchildren; Ollie visiting her in the retirement home, smilingly displaying his third or fourth wife . . .

'Ouch.' She felt a sharp stab of pain and jerked her hand up. 'What happened?'

'Cut myself.' She contorted her face and crooked her finger, trying not to drip blood on the wool rug. 'It's fine, honestly.' Could this day possibly get worse?

'Don't be silly. You need to wash that off and cover it up.'

Aiden grabbed her wrist and pulled her to her feet, leading her through to the kitchen as if she were a foolish child.

'Run it under the tap,' he ordered. 'I'll find the first-aid kit.'

She watched the water in the sink turn red until suddenly he was there beside her again, opening a box, pulling out plasters.

'Now show me.' Gently, he took her hand, the wounded finger extended, and lowered his head towards it. For a second she had a sudden whirling vision of him sucking her finger, vampire-style. But he was unpeeling paper from the plaster, saying in a half-mocking way, 'Don't worry, this shouldn't hurt a bit,' cradling his hand in hers and carefully applying the plaster. It was maximum voltage – no – nuclear fusion, exploding bombs, B52 bombers. His proximity made her head spin, just as it had all those years ago. The world seemed to have shrunk to the touch of his fingers, the shampoo scent of his hair, the racing drumbeat of her heart.

Then she heard a key turn in the front door and with a lurch the room stopped spinning and bumped back down to earth.

# Chapter 21

Meg had finally showed up half an hour after Georgina with some involved story concerning Mace and Zeb and why she was so late.

'Right, any new leads on Rowan?' Jen said, trying to cut short the small talk. She was desperate to escape after her foolishness with Aiden.

'Hope he kept you amused,' Georgina had said, kissing first Jen on the cheek and then Aiden. Oh, she had no idea! Jen hoped her garbled story about her injury and broken glass distracted attention from the guilty beetroot stain of her cheeks.

Now they were having a council of war in the drawing room, papers scattered all over the coffee table. Aiden had showered and dressed in 'more suitable attire', at Georgina's command. The silver frame had been confessed to and graciously dismissed as trivial, and the elderly Miss Dandridge had brought and cleared a light lunch of soup and salad.

But even as she tried to focus on what they were discussing, Jen could still feel the touch of Aiden's warm fingers on her hand, throbbing more than the cut under its plaster. She didn't dare begin to look in his direction. Had he felt even a glimmer of the same sensation? Could the others see how oddly she was acting? It was the worst thing imaginable. She couldn't be still attracted to him. She just couldn't.

'I still believe the reunion's our best bet. Only four days to go. Kismet will bring her to us, I can feel it.' Meg pulled her knees up to her chest and hugged them. Like the others, she was dressed in jeans. But unlike Georgina's own-brand pair, with GG elegantly embellished on the back pocket and a perfectly pressed crease running down the stylish wide-leg cut, Meg's were garishly embroidered flares. Somehow they just made her look so much more at ease, younger even, thought Jen.

'Right on,' Aiden playfully mimicked, stretching out his legs and raising his hands behind his head. 'Good old kismet wants us to party.'

'You're not going.' Georgina rushed in quickly, looking a little white around the lips. 'It's just us girls. We'll need to have our wits about us, not gallivant about for our own amusement.'

Aiden rubbed his mouth, mildly put out. 'Who said anything about gallivanting? I can add the male perspective.'

'Hey, you can leave the men to me,' Meg purred. 'I have my own ways of extracting information.'

'Right,' Aiden quipped. 'If they had a back room and a bed. Which I very much doubt.'

'Are you even listening?' Georgina's voice rose. 'I don't want you there, Aiden. It's going to be enough of an ordeal as it is.'

Aiden rolled his eyes, clearly displeased.

Jen's heart started its slow return to her chest. Aiden at the reunion. It hadn't occurred to her he'd want to come. Nor to Georgina apparently, who was looking sick at the prospect. Somehow Jen knew she didn't want her husband around when people started marvelling at how thin she was, recalling the fat child she'd been. Or puzzling over how she'd ended up with Jen's boyfriend, and thinking how civilised of the three to be out in public together. Nor did Georgina even want to be in the room where Aiden and Jen had once twined around each other at the Valentine's Day dance for fifth and sixth forms.

It was one thing to be civil, even to be united by a quest, but all of them together again at Ashport Comp? That would be entirely too incestuous.

'Well, whether he goes or not,' Jen said, trying to sound like she didn't care either way, 'what did we come up with?'

'I'm about cross-eyed from staring at a computer screen,' Meg said. 'Family-tree sites, Historical Manuscripts Commission, then I became rather caught up with the Beverley family of Tennessee. Real interesting heritage. You can trace the roots right back from—'

'But nothing on Rowan?' Georgina butted in.

'Nah.' She gave a deep sigh. 'I'll keep plugging at the census, but Mace is getting pissed at me for hogging his Dell. What about you, Jen?'

'I went on to the website for the National Statistics Office and ended up in a couple of tracing websites, but then you have start paying. I didn't know if it was worth it. Not with the reunion coming up. Then I started browsing the Scottish Record Office, the National Library of Scotland.'

'But why?' Meg looked deeply perplexed. 'She isn't Scottish.'

Jen shrugged. 'You know what the Internet's like. You get carried away.'

'You can say that again,' Georgina said. 'Between Google, Yahoo and all those people-search sites out there, it would take hours to sift through the rubbish. I got over two million hits for Rowan Howard and not one of them was useful. Somehow ended up watching a roller-skating poodle on YouTube. I even borrowed Meg's idea and had my assistant put a small ad in the Lost and Found section of *Ashport Life*.' She doodled circles on a notepad, while beside her Aiden looked like he was napping. 'But no joy.'

Meg snorted. 'She wasn't a dog, for Pete's sake.'

'No, but she is lost and I thought it might attract attention.'

'Hate to burst your bubble.' Aiden didn't bother opening his eyes, his voice deeply bored. 'But she probably isn't Rowan

186

Howard any more. She's thirty-eight. Don't you reckon she might be married?'

'Shit,' Meg said.

'Well, you do something then, Aiden,' Georgina said, her voice shrill with frustration. 'If you're so clever. If we can't find Rowan Howard, how on earth can we find Rowan No-Name?'

He stretched his long legs in front of him and opened one eye. 'How would I know? This is your "girls" thing, remember?'

Clearly, he was still annoyed at being excluded from the reunion. Not that Jen could blame him. He'd been the first to be enthusiastic about the search, and now he was being elbowed away from their one real lead.

'What about your artist friend?' she asked. 'The one who studied with Rowan?'

'Absolutely nothing,' Georgina said before Aiden could draw breath. 'His old chum is an out-and-out waste of space, wouldn't you say, Aiden?' She didn't wait for a response. 'Aiden called him last week. Still in Ashport but gave up art to fry his brain with alcohol and drugs instead, by the sound of it. The lady who does my laundry has more wits and she's seventy-nine.'

'Seventy-nine!' Meg gasped. 'You have a seventy-nine-year-old woman do your washing?'

'And what's wrong with that?' Georgina sat up straighter. Jen sensed tempers ready to flare.

'It's totally bogus, that's what. You're exploiting a senior citizen.'

'If anyone's being exploited, it's me.' Georgina sounded posh and annoyed. 'Half Aiden's white shirts have turned a ghastly shade of pinky-grey. Besides, she loves doing it, and I pay her eleven pounds an hour.'

'Eleven pounds an hour!' Meg sounded even more shocked. 'That's like throwing money down the drain. Shit, I'd drive over from Ashport to do it for that kinda dough.'

'What, and put an elderly lady out of a job?' Georgina said haughtily. 'I see no reason why people should be treated like useless imbeciles just because they reach a certain age. Mr Worthington, our handyman, is seventy-eight and his wife who cooks for us is a sprightly sixty-five.'

'Don't forget old Max,' Aiden said, sleepily scratching the back of his neck. 'He's Georgina's personal driver.'

'Max is completely different,' Georgina countered edgily. 'He's only fifty-five, not old at all.'

'Don't you guys do anything for yourselves?' Meg looked appalled. 'Why don't you just drive to the office with Aiden?'

'Because,' Georgina said icily, 'Aiden and I don't always work the same hours. I do half my admin in the car and I certainly can't relax with Aiden at the wheel, driving an inch from the bumper in front of him, slamming his brakes on at the last minute. Max is invaluable, I don't know what I'd do without him.'

'Jeez,' Meg sounded disgusted. 'I sure wish I had your worries.'

Abruptly Aiden jumped up, the springs of the sofa vibrating as he vacated his spot next to Jen.

'Am I the only one who thinks this is turning into a colossal waste of energy?' he said, pacing in bare feet. 'What the crap are we doing this for anyway? Some daft childhood promise. Sorry, Meg, but why the heck should my wife justify our lifestyle while none of the rules seem to apply to you? The whole thing's madness. If you're ill, shouldn't you be having chemotherapy instead of cavorting around the countryside?'

'Aiden!'

'Aiden, don't!' Jen and Georgina spoke almost simultaneously. Meg looked stricken, her face, framed by her long red hair, even paler and more pinched than usual.

'Well,' Aiden ran his hands through his dark waves so they stood up wild and untamed, 'it is cancer, isn't it? This lump?'

'Stop it this instant!' Georgina whirled on her husband as if he were a snarling dog she was facing down. 'You're being cruel and insensitive. Apologise to Nutmeg right this minute.'

'Sod that,' he said roughly. 'We're her friends and she could use some home truths. Meg,' he walked over and lightly touched her shoulder. 'I don't want to sound like a brute but if your life's on the line, I'd at least like to know you're seeing a doctor.' His voice had softened. He sounded genuinely concerned now, and Jen thought she saw tears about to well in Meg's eyes.

'Of course I am.' Meg chewed her index finger nervously. 'As a matter of fact I saw another one last week. They haven't called me with the results yet, though.'

'There. Happy?' Georgina asked Aiden. She pushed past him and put her arms around Meg, resting her cheek on top of Meg's head. 'Listen, if it's money you need . . .'

'Do you want to talk about it?' asked Jen gently.

'Not at the moment.' Meg shook her head. 'It's been a stressful week. Can we just focus on Rowan?'

'Fine by me.' Georgina returned to the sofa and picked up her pad. 'But I don't see where else we can look.'

Jen watched her add a pair of ears and a tail to a circle, sparking an idea.

'The cat!' Jen said excitedly. The others looked at her blankly. 'We haven't checked the art connection properly. Rowan was an amazing artist. We could contact galleries and art schools. And her style was so distinctive, all those swirling circles. Remember, the black cat? It was like her trademark.'

'Yes, she even put one on that bright red yacht on a stormy sea that she sold to the Sunshine Bistro.' Georgina leant forward, captivated. 'She was paid twenty pounds for that.'

'A fortune in those days,' added Meg. 'She could have sold dozens by now.'

'Let me fetch my laptop.' Georgina hurried out of the room and came back with a thin silver model. 'OK.' She opened the lid and brought it to life. 'Google. Rowan Howard. Famous artist.'

'If she's so famous, why haven't we heard of her?' Aiden muttered, clearly less enthused. 'We're in galleries often enough.'

'Ssshh.' Georgina flapped her hand at him. 'You're not helping.'

Disgruntled, he flopped into the armchair opposite Jen. Georgie wasn't very nice to him, she thought. You could never really know the true nature of another couple's relationship, but theirs did seem to involve a depressing amount of squabbling.

Meg had got up and was looking over Georgina's shoulder. 'What's that?' She pointed. 'eBay, photographer . . . Howard print sales.'

'Rowan Howard print sales?' Georgina double-clicked on it. 'No, just some silly poster place. *Ugh.*'

'She might have gone to New York,' Jen said. 'Lots of artists do. We shouldn't just stick to the UK.'

'Or she could have drifted off to Denmark in a runaway hot-air balloon.' Aiden yawned. 'Basically, I don't want to be a downer here, but you're searching the entire world for a woman with no last name and no known career.'

'We need drinks,' Georgina said, not looking up. 'Aiden, will you fetch them?'

He slouched to his feet, as Jen glanced up. She couldn't read his expression but for just a second his dark eyes seemed to suck her in.

'Would do but I punched out my timecard when I left the office Friday evening. Enjoy the hunt. I'll send Miss Dandridge in for your drinks.'

And that was the last they saw of him that afternoon. Funny, Jen thought, how she'd wished for him to leave, couldn't wait for him to get out of there. And yet once he was gone she kept glancing at the door wondering if he'd come back, almost hoping he would.

# Chapter 22

'Mrs Stoneman?'

A bear of a man, with shoulders broad enough to fill the entire door, a curly dark beard and wearing a navy raincoat with a tie-up belt, was standing on Jen's doorstep, battered leather briefcase in hand.

'Yes?'

'Mr Moreton. Atkins and Everett, Surveyors.'

'Oh good. Right on time,' she said, ushering him in.

He stepped into the hallway and immediately glanced up. His eagle eyes had spotted the hairline crack in the ceiling.

'Come through, come through.' Jen tried to divert him.

'Can I ask a few questions first?' He stubbornly stayed where he was, unzipped his case and withdrew a sheet of paper and biro. 'They're not strictly necessary but I like to get a sense of the bigger picture, particularly when the buyers have requested a full survey.'

'Sure, fire away.'

'How long have you lived here?'

'Three years.' Long years.

'Do you know when the house was built?'

His tone was very solemn. Maybe surveyors had to be like that, like driving examiners. If they said anything friendly, their comments could be misconstrued and the failed learner might complain they were put off by 'all the chit-chat and flirty smiles', and their failure was nothing whatsoever to do with skidding fifty feet when the instructor whacked the dashboard for the emergency stop.

'It was 1971, I think.' She nodded gravely, to show she understood where he was coming from. 'I can look it up.'

'No need.'

'Would you like some tea?'

'Maybe later. I'll just get on, if you don't mind.'

He disappeared up the stairs and Jen decided to keep herself busy rather than wait dumbly in the hall.

At one point she went into Chloe's bedroom with a basket of clean laundry under her arm, and had started putting her vests and pants away in her chest of drawers when she suddenly realised the surveyor was kneeling down on the floor next to her, holding a yellow and black torch-like thing against the wall, a look of deep concentration on his face.

'What's that?' she asked, quickly shutting the drawer.

'A moisture meter. Checking for damp.'

'Oh, right.'

For one so tall and imposing he was like a tiny mouse, pattering between rooms soundlessly.

She was watching him attempting to lift the carpet extremely carefully when the telephone rang.

'Jen, it's Helen.'

'Oh hi, Helen.' She felt a sudden rush of guilt. 'I'm so sorry I never called you back.' She had meant to. 'But things have been quite hectic really and I lost my mobile with all my numbers in it.' At least she couldn't find it this morning, that counted as lost, didn't it?

'Ollie said you went to Ashport?'

'Yeah.'

'Well, I was a bit surprised, that's all. I thought you hated the place.' Her voice was hushed, thick with meaning. 'After . . . well . . . all your bad memories.'

'I went with some friends. Women I knew at school.'

'So . . . what was it like? Did your old home town look the same?'

'No. Worse actually. Everything just seemed grubbier and poorer.' *And Aiden wasn't there.* God, where did that thought come from?

Hard as it was to admit, returning to Ashport had triggered something secret and dangerous. Every street they'd walked down, every corner they'd turned, seemed to harbour ghosts of the couple they'd been. The little workmen's café that was one of their favourite haunts, the cinema where they'd kiss all through the film, paying no attention to the screen.

How often had she thought and dreamed about him since the trip to Ashport? Her full-blown crush was returning like malaria, the virus mutating to a more deadly form the second time around. Before Ashport, even. Perhaps all the way back to the Marlow Arms. She'd sensed the glimmer of an itch the day she'd first set foot in Georgina's house, had always known how horribly easy it would be to trigger the disease. So that now if she found herself hoping for the sound of her friend's husband's voice or a glimpse of his beautiful face, she had only herself to blame.

Don't be so dramatic, she scolded herself. It wasn't that serious. Nostalgia, that's all it was. She could have him back in her life for a short while in a nice safe role. Put the ghosts to rest. Let the novelty of his reappearance wear off and develop full immunity from the exposure.

'We're trying to trace a friend from school. Long story but . . . well . . . I suppose you could say she's sort of gone missing.'

'Gone missing? What, run away from home?'

'No, of course not. It's just . . .' It wasn't the time to explain the pact, not with the surveyor upstairs. '. . . a long story. So what's up?'

'I've just taken on this new client, Tabitha Titwell. What a name, eh? Drives me to distraction with her inane prattle while I'm trying to clear out her wardrobe. The colour of her venetian blinds, should she paint her walls natural taupe or bleached lichen. And the husband, God help me,' she took a momentary pause for breath. 'The builders found a load of paint pots when they were digging a hole to put in a new patio – said they couldn't lay foundations on all that rubbish so Mr Titwell grabbed a spade and has been spending hours rummaging around down there. All through my consultation he kept popping back in saying he's found another tin of paint. Found another two tins of paint. Any minute I'm expecting the whole house to subside into the foundations. They're off their rockers.'

'They do sound nuts,' Jen offered. 'Maybe he'll strike gold.'

'Gold my fanny!' Helen was in full flow. 'And she's got this most irritating habit of saying "*you said*", "*you said*". Tabitha "you said" Titwell I call her.'

The sound of flushing from the upstairs bathroom momentarily startled Jen, but then she heard the shower, followed by both taps in quick succession. Ah, he must be checking the plumbing system.

'I feel like tipping her into her bin bags along with her bloody clothes,' Helen continued. 'And she has this sister, Tammy, whose bone-idle husband apparently agreed that if his wife stripped the living-room wallpaper, he'd put new wallpaper up, so she went out, bought the wallpaper, stripped the walls and what do you think?'

'The wall collapsed?' Where was that surveyor? His creeping around was starting to creep *her* out. Should she be letting him wander around alone? What if he was a total pervert, at this minute rifling through her intimate things?

'He left the walls bare for, get this – ten years. Isn't that insane!'

'Surveyor's here,' Jen managed to slip in quietly.

'The what?'

'Surveyor.'

He tiptoed past the door.

'We got an offer on the house,' Jen whispered.

'When?'

'Er, a few days ago.'

'Oh. Well, that's great.'

Oh God, she'd upset her again. Should have rung her the moment she got the news, probably. Helen could be so sensitive.

'He's doing a full structural report.'

'Well don't leave him alone for a second,' Helen lectured. 'My friend had a surveyor round and after he left, she found a whole packet of digestive biscuits had disappeared. She was going to do a cheesecake as well.'

'With digestives?'

'Yes, you crumble them up for the base. With butter. Anyway, it's good news that the surveyor's there. Means your buyers mean business. Things could move fast. Have you found a new place yet? Or been to the employment agency? Better get yourself sorted pronto.' Helen's tone had lost all pretence at being hurt and was back on typical bossy form. Jen took a deep breath.

'I know. I will.' She was angry with herself for being so irritated. Of course she ought to be going for interviews. They'd agreed maintenance payments but Ollie wouldn't support her for ever, and she wouldn't want him to. And rather than jaunting to Ashport, a sensible person would have been scouring the estate agents for whatever miserable shack she'd be able to afford with half the proceeds from the sale of the house.

It was just – well, why was Helen's advice always so bleeding *obvious*? As if, without her input, Jen would sit at home in a moronic trance, dimly wondering at the commotion when the new owners moved in their furniture.

'I know you, Jen. You like to procrastinate. Can't turn your

195

back on reality for ever.' Relenting, Helen changed the subject. 'So how about trying out this new wine bar tonight? They have these fantastic karaoke evenings on Wednesdays.'

'Wine bar? For karaoke tonight?' Jen's temples ached at the very thought.

'Full of talent. Both kinds. I'm going to start going every week.'

'Too short notice. I've nothing to wear.' That bit was true. After deciding most of her clothes were drearily surburban, her wardrobe contained almost nothing she felt good in. This morning she'd been so disgusted with the various items she'd tried on and quickly discarded that she'd ended up pulling on a big sloppy sweater of Ollie's over her oldest pair of jeans. It was time for a shopping trip. Oops, hold the horses, no it wasn't. She needed to conserve every penny. God, she wasn't used to this at all. Ollie had always been so generous. Not that she was a wild spender or anything, but it was ages since she'd had to worry about cash flow. 'And besides,' she hurried past the thought, 'the last thing I want to do is go to some pick-up joint. The divorce isn't even absolute.'

'Who said it was a pick-up joint?' Helen sounded indignant. 'It's a laugh, that's all. If you don't get out there, you'll never meet a man.'

'I don't want to meet a man. And if I do,' an image of Aiden sprang up and was quickly banished, 'then I'd prefer it to happen naturally, someone coming into the shop, maybe. Not tramping around wine bars in a low-cut blouse and heels, virtually flashing a sign that says "divorced and desperate".'

'Like me you mean?'

'Not like you. Don't be silly. You're not desperate.'

'Fine,' Helen gave a martyred sigh, thankfully not pursuing the offence, 'if you don't fancy a wine bar, what about a Chinese on Saturday, just the two of us? Before Ollie makes you chop up your joint credit cards.'

'Saturday? Oh I can't. I've got this reunion.'

'Reunion? What reunion?'

'Twenty-year school thing. We only just found out about it last week. We thought it would help us find Rowan. Our missing friend.'

'With these new friends of yours?' She sounded disapproving.

'*Old* friends. Yes.'

'Next week then?'

'I don't know.' She felt a knot form in her stomach, her mind fogged by panic. What *was* she going to do about money? It felt wrong now to go carousing with Helen, spending Ollie's hard-earned income on Martinis and suchlike. 'I'll have to see.'

'Yeah, right. Don't put yourself out,' and she'd slammed down the phone before Jen could react.

Oh God, now she'd done it. Jen cursed herself, dialling the number to call her back.

But she practically jumped out of her skin before she could finish. Mr Moreton was standing right behind her.

'Mrs Stoneman?'

'Mr Moreton. I didn't hear you, erm, hear you come back downstairs.'

'Just to say, almost done. Spot of damp up in the small bedroom, right above the skirting board, and we may have to recommend a specialist to check the timbers, but on the whole everything looks hunky-dory.'

'Great.'

He shifted uneasily from foot to foot. 'Lovely house.'

'Thank you.'

'Much bigger from the inside than the out.'

'Sure is.'

'Deceptive. Like a Tardis.'

'What?'

'Dr Who's Tardis. The old police box.'

He looked down at her, like Shrek's not so green brother, if someone pasted a dark curly wig on Shrek's squashy hairless dome, and added a beard.

'Oh right.'

'And you have super soffits.'

'Well thank you.' She stood up and headed quickly for the hallway. He followed behind. Very close behind.

'Divorce situation, eh?'

'Yes.' So he'd been eavesdropping. The little mouse had big ears.

'Sad state of affairs, isn't it?' Suddenly he held his hand out. 'Name's Bill.'

'Jen.'

So now they were on first-name terms. She felt a touch anxious. Maybe he wasn't a surveyor. She hadn't checked his card. She could be chloroformed, kidnapped and thrown down into a cellar back at his house. And Ollie had gone to London for the day, to catch up on some paperwork at head office.

'Look, would you . . . Do you . . . You wouldn't like to go for a drink one evening . . . with me?' Sweat beaded under his nose and over his temples and he'd moved a step closer to her. His breath smelled like salami. Extremely old salami.

'Um, er, well, you see . . .'

Now, if she said no he might give her a bad structural report. And if she said yes? No, it was too repulsive to contemplate. Heads Mr Moreton wins, tails Jen loses.

'Um,' she repeated and opened the front door as a car pulled into the driveway. A silver Jaguar. And at the wheel was Aiden.

'You see, I have a boyfriend,' Jen beamed. She waved furiously as Aiden switched off the engine. 'Thanks for the offer though.'

Aiden came towards her and she put one arm round his waist and stretched up to peck his cheek. He rested his arm over her shoulders. Just like old times. She was tempted, for good measure, to nestle into his chest. It would be so wonderful to curl into his arms, have him tell her everything was going to be just fine. Easy to see why people waited for the safety net of a new romance before they jumped out of a dead relationship.

But Aiden was Georgina's and everything wouldn't be fine. There was no new romance, just the faded shadow of an old one. The irony of standing here like this, playing the happy couple, was only topped by the timing of his reappearance just as she was losing Ollie. Did someone up there really want her to suffer?

Mr Moreton half smiled, apparently not bothered at losing out on a date one way or the other, and climbed into his car.

'Have a nice day, Bill.' She waved as he reversed out of the drive, not even pausing to nod at her.

'Bye, Bill,' chuckled Aiden as they both watched the car disappear into the distance. He pulled out a joint and lit up, the smoke wafting on the breeze as Jen wondered if the neighbours would notice.

'Thank you.'

'Any time.'

Jen blushed, realising she was still clutching his waist, feeling the ridge of his leather belt under her fingers.

'Oh God,' she groaned, dropping her arm hastily and stepping away. 'Please save me from people like that.'

'Bill hit on you?' He squinted down at her, eyes crinkling with amusement.

'It wasn't just my soffits he was after. I can't bear it. Is this what it's going to be like, being single again?'

He nodded gravely. 'Brace yourself. The word's out. Jennifer Bedlow free again. All kinds of Bills and Bens are on the move, heading in this direction.' He mimed a zombie walk.

'Idiot. Come in, why don't you? Only you'll have to put that out. Can't have my house smelling of dope. I have a daughter, you know.' She gave a false titter to counter her boring rectitude, but Aiden stamped the joint underfoot and followed her inside.

'What are you doing in Huntsleigh, anyhow?' she asked.

'You left your mobile.' He pulled it out of his pocket and handed it over. 'I had an appointment nearby. Said I'd drop it off as it's on the way. How's the injury? Finger OK? No fatal infections?'

She waggled it in the air. 'Right as rain. Fancy a cup of tea or do you have to dash?'

After all, it was only polite to be hospitable, especially after his timely intervention with Barnacle Bill, Mr Rising Damp himself. But the truth was she didn't want to see Aiden go right away. He felt like the only bright spot in an otherwise miserable day, even if the pleasure was borrowed and temporary.

'I can stay for a while. My appointment's not till two.'

He wandered past her into the lounge. 'So tidy! And all these gold sockets – so very kitsch.'

'I'm considering melting them down, I need as much cash as I can muster.' She chuckled to drive away the suggestion of concern that rippled across his face, making sure he knew it was a joke. 'Want me to show you around?'

'Sure.'

She'd done the tour with prospective buyers so many times it had become a habit. You answered the front door and immediately started describing the virtues of the underfloor central-heating system, how the sun always blazed through the French windows, the south-facing garden, how the Neighbourhood Watch was very vigilant, the road extremely quiet but not too quiet to be creepy. 'Move in here, Mr and Mrs Jones,' she'd want to say. 'It's so damn perfect, it's like living in Stepford – only I'm sure your husband would never want to remove your brain, Mrs Jones.'

'What's this in here?' Aiden opened the door to the airing cupboard and peered inside. They'd inspected the downstairs –

cloakroom, toilet, lounge, family room, kitchen and now they were on the first-floor landing. It was only when she saw him nodding solemnly at the neatly folded sheets and towels that she gave herself a metaphorical slap on the forehead. Why on earth had she been boring the pants off him this last quarter of an hour? What a fruitcake he must think her. Not only that, but she'd just realised that ever since they'd walked upstairs she'd been humming, 'But When You Get Behind Closed Doors'. Oh God, she thought, save me from myself.

'Hey, enough of all this. Besides you're too late, it's under offer,' she added smartly, 'and I'm not partial to gazumpers.'

'Actually it's interesting. Gives me new insight.'

Now there was a provocative statement. Suddenly she wished she'd left him outside, snatched back her mobile, forbidden him entrance. Insight into *what?* she wanted to demand. 'So they didn't call you Snoopy Starkson for nothing,' she improvised.

He grinned down at her. 'No, I had to pay big money for the rights to that particular nickname.'

How much happier he seemed today, away from his gothic mansion where he always seemed suitably moody and introspective. But then Aiden always had showed her a side he shared with few people, funny, loving and romantic instead of the cynical bad boy that others saw.

She wondered if he and Georgina laughed and joked the way he used to with her. And how gorgeous he looked, so mature and masculine in his oatmeal cashmere sweater, charcoal jeans, that luscious dark wavy hair.

It wasn't fair. She almost wanted to get up close, peer up that straight nose for stray hairs or search for blackheads on that manly jaw. But she was afraid she wouldn't find anything to repulse. He was nearly perfect apart from one thing – Georgina. Her So-flawless Starkey had become All-too-married Aiden.

The tour continued. She stood in the doorway of the master

201

bedroom while he strolled past their king-size bed and checked out the shower in the en suite. Surely he had no interest in any of it. He was only doing it . . . why? . . . to wind her up?

She couldn't bring herself to follow him in. There was an invisible barrier that she couldn't cross and the photograph of Ollie in cap and gown on the wall, the day he received his degree, stared accusingly across the room.

Aiden stopped to scrutinise it.

'The young stud, eh? Looks like he can handle himself.'

'He can. He's tough. Not that he gets into fights.'

All of a sudden she wanted Aiden to get out of there, to get out of the house. It felt all wrong him being in a place where she and Ollie had once been so intimate, especially given some of the thoughts she was having about Aiden these days. It was like some sordid liaison, even if the truth were much more innocent and unplanned.

Aiden gazed out the window for a few seconds then sauntered back across the room. Casually he leaned his shoulder on the door frame and hooked his thumbs in his waistband.

'OK kid,' he affected a Humphrey Bogart drawl. 'Time to come clean. I've a confession,' she could see the laughter lines crease round his eyes, 'I told a lie. I didn't have an appointment.'

# Chapter 23

Jen was freezing as she jogged across the heath after dropping Chloe off the next morning, her hands slowly turning to blocks of ice, blades of frosted grass sticking up like shards of crystal, making a crunching sound underfoot as she ran.

One thing she liked about Huntsleigh was the variety of landscapes, the remoteness of the heath which in the summer was ablaze with purple heather and wild gorse, the magnificent views of the windy ridge and the peacefulness of the bluebell woods.

She wrapped her scarf tighter round her neck and slowed her pace, worrying about Chloe again. Last night when they were snuggling together watching a Disney rental, Chloe in pyjamas, damp and warm from her bath, Jen had felt her throat constrict at the thought of how she might be affected.

She'd known for some months that Mummy and Daddy were divorcing but up to now it had been purely talk, nothing had changed in her life. Selling the house would make it real. Life was difficult enough for her with Ollie gone for six weeks at a time. Chloe was always so excited to see him when he came home. He always arrived with tanned arms full of presents, like Santa Claus at Christmas ready to devote his entire leave to making them both happy.

But like Christmas, it could never live up to Jen's fantasies of how perfect everything would be as soon as he got home.

All that missing him and breathless anticipation, only to be smacked back to earth by reality.

After the initial gluttony came hard readjustment. Having a man about, interfering, questioning decisions she usually made on her own, creating huge messes with Chloe in some silly game that involved throwing Cheerios around the kitchen, disrupting carefully laid plans with agendas of his own. And then just as she relaxed into the relationship again, started appreciating having him there to share the load, enjoying his energetic vibrant presence, it was time for him to leave and for her and Chloe to begin anew the painful adjustment to his absence.

Eventually she started to resent him being home *and* resent him for going away, silly because he was doing it for the family, building up a nest egg to make up for the years they'd sacrificed while he was studying.

They tried to keep in touch. The business of oil exploration often took him into remote areas, far from civilisation, but there were satellite phones, Skype and email these days. Ollie checked in as often as he could, she and Chloe emailed him, scanned Chloe's paintings to send to Tanzania. But his world was so dissimilar to theirs. It involved work they knew little about, people they'd never met, triumphs and disasters they were at a loss to understand.

And it started to seem too much trouble to fill him in on all he'd missed. It was one thing to excitedly recount an ongoing drama, but too tedious to laboriously type the trivial details of Chloe's homework, or who'd come into the shop that day, in an email that only seemed further evidence of how monotonous and identical her days had become. Or to resurrect some dull little anecdote on his return when the whole episode was cold and buried.

Well, in less than a month it'd be the real Christmas, she thought as she puffed along the footpath, noticing her breath cloud the freezing air. Their last Christmas in the Huntsleigh house, the last time they'd go as a family to the garden centre, bring a tree home on the roof of Ollie's beloved old VW Camper, the last time he'd lift up Chloe so she could put the star on top. The last time they'd exchange smiles as Chloe ripped the paper off the presents they'd bought her.

For so long she'd loathed December, dreaded the memories it brought up, but seeing it through Chloe's joyful eyes had made it tolerable, helped to soften the terrible associations of that awful time.

And then in January a whole new set of problems would emerge. How would they manage custody with Ollie's schedule? How would Chloe adjust? Next year she'd be working towards her SATs, the year following she'd be the same age as Jen had been when she met Meg and the others. Soon there'd be boyfriends, exams, possibly even university and then she'd be gone for good. And what would Jen be left with? Bill, the surveyor, seemed to have revealed to her a whole new void, the life of a divorcee, and she could see it yawning before her feet, dark and bottomless.

No wonder she'd been up at four, hadn't been able to sleep. Aiden kept coming into her dreams, the way he had for all those years until she fully fell in love with Ollie – for good, she'd thought. Even this running couldn't clear her mind. The endorphins were taking far too long to kick in.

So many nights Jen had agonised over Aiden, wondering what she'd done, said or hadn't said, to drive him away, how she could have acted to make it different. If she'd been funnier or less flippant. Was he looking for the silent melancholy type, someone to match his own unspoken agonies of the soul? Or someone more sophisticated, sporting dark lipstick, a cigarette holder? Either way she knew she hadn't been enough. She hadn't measured up. She'd been ready to unravel herself like a pair of old knitted socks, pick up the needles and reinvent herself as a scarf or a bobble hat if that was what he wanted. But she never got the chance to ask.

Now as her legs pumped like pistons in a methodical rhythm, her mind was free to wander territory she'd just as soon not be treading, those barbed-wire fences she'd spent years erecting showing signs of sagging under the recent strain.

She hadn't gone all the way with Starkey until her dad decided to move to West Croydon. Funny how all his attempts to protect her innocence had backfired so radically. When they started going out, after that fateful party, (21st September 1985 at Clover and Herb's, it was etched in her soul and in her diary), Jen had been fifteen and underage. And even when she turned sixteen in January, though she loved Starkey with a passion, the thought of her dad's disappointment had stopped her from crossing that final frontier. She hadn't been a very mature sixteen, hadn't felt quite ready. Some days she thought Chloe at nine had more savvy than Jen did back then.

She'd bolted to Starkey's place in tears the day her dad announced she'd be taking her A levels at a sixth-form college in Croydon. He'd found a factory that was hiring and they'd be out of Ashport as soon as he could rent a house. Turned out he'd been wondering how to break the news for some time, and the fire at the stables not only hurried things along but also justified his decision.

Starkey and a couple of friends were living in a squat, a vacant three-bedroom house with a run-down abandoned feel and a garden full of weeds. They had a squatters' notice stuck to the window, their own lock on the door and the gas and electric switched to their name. But it could barely be called home. There were no curtains, naked light bulbs hung from the ceiling, and the sole furnishings in Starkey's room consisted of a grubby mattress, giant bean bag, portable boombox, 19-inch TV and VCR and a huge poster of Che Guevara.

Starkey answered her frantic knocking at the door. From his

room upstairs, she could hear Springsteen huskily groaning that he was on fire.

'Hey, Titch. What gives?' He'd stared at her with astonishment and concern as she stood in front of him, too tearful to speak. And then he'd led her upstairs, kissed her damp cheeks and red-rimmed eyes, his lips burning wherever they touched flesh. Somehow he seemed to know without her saying a word that the rules had changed. Feverishly they'd undressed each other before tumbling together on his single bed, all caution abandoned as they went all the way for the very first time. Even today she couldn't hear Springsteen sing that song without getting goosebumps.

She'd wept buckets as she lay in his arms after the rapture of their lovemaking had worn off and reality returned. She told him she wasn't going to move, told him she'd get a job and stay in Ashport to be with him. He'd insisted that was a bad idea.

'You don't want to end up like me,' he said, 'qualified for nothing. We've got all our lives to be together.'

After that she was openly rebellious of curfews or restraints. She hated to hurt her dad but she was in the grip of a passion too powerful to withstand, even when she'd been dragged, kicking and screaming, to the grimy brick terraced house he'd rented in Croydon. Her father insisted she got a summer job and contributed to the household. (They'd registered her for college even though her O level results had been disappointing, given the disruptive last year.)

She used her new income to take a train to Ashport every weekend and didn't come back till late Sunday night. She spent whole days with Starkey, lazing in bed till two or three p.m., going out for junk food and cigarettes and coming back to bed again. She didn't look nearly old enough to be able to drink in a pub and none of her friends were around, but she never tired of sitting on his bed that doubled as their sofa, listening to

Starkey play the guitar or slow dancing with him around the zebra-striped bean bag.

By the time she started college her father had unbent enough to suggest that the young man might visit her for a change. Starkey roared up one October Sunday in his Triumph Stag but the visit was not a success. Not with her dad popping his head into her bedroom every five minutes to ask if they'd like a cup of tea, the sound of the opening door making them break apart (once with her bra undone and shoved up under her sweater). Starkey had wanted to drive to the park, but it was pouring with rain and Jen didn't want to get caught in his car with fogged-up windows and some bored policeman peering in to see what they were up to.

But she had a big surprise planned for his second visit.

Her next-door neighbour was holidaying in Majorca, leaving Jen a key to water her plants and feed her cat. An empty house with proper beds, even a multi-jetted jacuzzi – and Starkey coming over for the whole weekend – it was like getting all her birthdays at once. But it hadn't happened that way. Oh no, it hadn't happened that way at all.

She pulled up panting, feeling slightly sick, rested one of her legs on a wooden railing and began to stretch, thinking back to yesterday.

The minute Aiden told Jen he hadn't got an appointment, she became all jumpy and unusually coquettish.

'Then why did you say you had?' She led the way back to the living room, careful not to sashay her hips in Anamaria fashion.

'So I could stop by with your phone. Georgie was working at home today, getting herself in a right old frenzy and it's best to clear out when she gets like that.' He pulled a face as he sat down on the sofa, Jen placing herself in an armchair, a good two feet away. 'Besides, we haven't had a chance to talk, you and I, not really.' His eyes were like melted chocolate, the dark bitter kind, almond-shaped and delicious. Already Jen could feel her pulse race, as if she were on the brink of doing something incredibly dangerous. He was leaning his elbow on the sofa's arm, his hand curling over the edge. All she'd have to do was stretch out her own hand to touch his fingers, or extend her crossed leg to caress his ankle with her foot.

But his next sentence slowed her right down again. 'Listen, Titch, I owe you one for being so nice to Georgie. She's going through a tough time and she really needs a friend right now.' He pinched his lower lip, seemed to hesitate then plunged on. 'If you didn't know her so well I wouldn't tell you this, but she's had some real emotional problems.'

*Haven't we all*, Jen thought. But still the fact that Aiden had chosen to confide in her, of all people, surprised her.

'She has?' she said, baffled as how to react. Should she ask what kind? Or was that too nosy?

Aiden gave an odd laugh, perhaps misreading her confused expression. 'Not what you imagine,' he said, immediately causing Jen to wonder what he imagined she imagined. 'But she's overworked, overstressed and some of her strategies for coping can get a little self-destructive. Under that big front she puts up, she's scarily fragile.'

Jen felt a rush of sympathy for Georgina, mingled with shame at herself. How silly to be concerned, even for a flicker, that Aiden had a less than honourable reason for dropping by. He was a nice guy worried about his wife.

'She was always more vulnerable than she let on,' she acknowledged, wondering what he meant by his reference to Georgina's self-destructive ways of coping. She couldn't ask him, though. It felt too surreal to be having this conversation about her former best friend with her former lover.

'No kidding. Sometimes I think she's driving herself to a nervous breakdown. But she's bloody impossible to argue with. She gets so hysterical.' He broke off, his handsome face clouded. 'Sorry. I won't bore you with my problems.'

'I don't mind,' she said automatically. It was silly. One part of her agreed, thought it was pure nerve for him to discuss his marital woes with her. The wickedest part wanted to laugh in his face, cackle *serves you right, you shit, you'd have been better off with me.* But the part that won felt genuinely sorry that he looked so wretched, that he and Georgie were clearly unhappy.

'It's just, well, a lot of our friends are connected to Georgie through business. And I still feel . . .' He sighed, rubbed his weary face. 'I saw a photo of your daughter upstairs. She looks like you. Very sweet. You know, I envy you.'

'Me?' Jen was staggered. 'Why? I'm a complete failure. Divorced. No job. No life. No money worth speaking of and I'm about to be homeless. I'm not even that good a mother. I forget to bring velvet home.'

Aiden's expression told her she'd baffled him with the velvet comment. But still he said, 'I don't believe that. You were always such a good sport. I'll bet – it's Chloe, right? – I'll bet Chloe has a blast with you. And money never mattered that much to us, did it?' He crossed his ankles and leaned back, shadows under his eyes.

'Yes, well, things do slightly alter when you're approaching forty. We're not kids any more.'

'That's one of my big regrets,' Aiden said slowly. He fiddled with his fingers a bit, stretching them back, examining his nails, avoiding her questioning stare. 'One of many. That we don't have children. Georgina says that Giordani's her baby, but time goes on and that joke starts to wear a little thin. Especially when she's thirty-eight already and we're no closer to starting that family.'

There it was. The thing she'd been wondering about.

'What happened with . . .' She couldn't finish the sentence.

Aiden looked bleak. 'She didn't want it. Not really. It was a horribly difficult time for her. She wasn't that happy about being pregnant in the first place and suddenly there was Bella

Stringent breathing down her neck, making all kinds of demands. It was one of those critical moments. Giordani with the chance to go big-time . . . immense. No wonder it was all too much. She couldn't cope.' He shook his head as if dismissing troubling memories. 'It's ancient history. We can't change the past.'

*This pregnancy couldn't have come at a worse time.* Jen could hear her now. And that was before Bella had commissioned the Tony awards frock. She had a sudden horrible feeling that Aiden was hinting that it hadn't been a miscarriage after all.

She had so many questions but she didn't want to ask them. Not of Aiden. It didn't feel right.

'You could still have children. Lots of women do at Georgie's age and older.'

'That's true.' He smiled wryly. 'If I can just get her to log it into her calendar, we might still get the job done.' She had a feeling he was agreeing only to end the discussion.

'So,' she said, changing the subject, 'is Georgina looking forward to Saturday, did she say what time we were to meet or anything?'

'No, but I'm sure she'll call you.'

'Still reckon there's no hope of finding Rowan?'

'Shit, I don't know. Georgie's been on the blower loads to some guy called Frank. Got him putting posters around Ashport, ads in local papers, bulletins in the school newsletter, you name it. I guess she's hoping the more people hear about it, the more chance there is of Rowan showing. If Georgie enjoys it, it's OK with me.' He paused, a strange smile sending shivers through Jen. 'Hey, remember that time we drove to Worthing in winter because you wanted to swim and the pool in Ashport was closed for repairs? And the heater was broken in the convertible.'

'God yeah! And the soft top had a big rip in it. It was bloody freezing. But the Worthing pool was closed too. So we went on to Gosport to go ice skating and the rink was shutting and they wouldn't let us in.'

'You stamped your feet and said to the guy on the door, "But we've come so far." You were so stiff you could hardly walk.'

Jen smiled at the memory. Instead of splashing in a pool, they'd strolled along the beach, collecting shells and skimming pebbles into the sea. Aiden took off his heavy leather jacket and draped it over her shoulders and then they huddled together under the pier, shivering uncontrollably but just happy to be in each other's company, warmed by their undying love. Undying. *Yeah right.* It was a quick death, quick but not merciful, and the worst thing was Jen hadn't even realised the relationship was sick.

'Somehow, even before I hooked up with Georgina, I've always known I'd meet up with you again,' he said sombrely, 'Even if it was only walking across the street one day.'

A jolt ran through her. She'd told herself the exact same thing.

'Too bad I can never speak to Georgina like this.' He glanced at his watch. 'I ought to be going. Tell you what, give me your mobile number and I'll give you mine. I want you to feel you've at least one friend you can call on. You know, when the pipes burst or the bath taps start to leak.' A roguish dimple appeared at the corner of his mouth. 'I won't have the faintest clue how to fix them but I do know a good plumber.'

'Oh my,' she said mockingly and put a hand to her chest, 'I'm overwhelmed. But it's really not necessary. With Ollie gone so much on business I could actually teach classes in the use and function of the Yellow Pages.' All the same, she found herself stretching for the phone he'd just returned.

'If you ever need anything, seriously . . .' He pulled his BlackBerry from his jacket. 'I want you to contact me. What's your number?'

Was it bad that she handed her phone over so meekly, let

212

him punch in the digits? It was only a phone number, for goodness' sake. Didn't mean that she'd ever use it.

And if she didn't get a move on she'd be late for work. And that *would* be bad. The Huntsleigh Jen was never late.

Anamaria gave Jen a sideways look as they cashed up that afternoon. 'How's that Starkey of yours?'

'What do you mean?' Jen said, mortified. 'Don't say that. Don't ever say that. He's not *my* Starkey.' Maybe she was being paranoid but she knew how quickly rumours could start in a small town like Huntsleigh. The last thing she wanted was for something like that to get back to Ollie or Georgina, or worse, Chloe.

'He's not my Starkey,' she repeated firmly, banging down a bag of change on to the counter.

'*Mierda*!' Anamaria said. 'I was joking. You know, how you say? Idle conversation?' She half-smiled an apology and turned away, but not before Jen realised that her eyes were red. She'd hadn't noticed until now, being too preoccupied by her thoughts. And, for most of the day, Anamaria had been busying herself with completing a jigsaw puzzle. She seemed to make it her life mission that every puzzle sold was intact.

'Is something up, Anamaria ?' Jen closed the till and slipped the key in her purse. 'You look upset.'

'Only that I must go back to Barcelona for a short while. And I don't know what to do with Feo. I have no one to look after him and he cannot come with me.'

'Won't your boyfriend take him?'

'Hah! I would sooner give him to the pound. Let them murder him than keep him with that *cerdo*.' Now she really did look close to tears.

'God, I'm sorry. I didn't mean to snap earlier. About Starkey, I mean. I suppose I'm just oversensitive at the moment. I've been feeling a tad stressed. Need to find a job that actually pays,

213

which won't be easy what with the state the economy's in. Even looks like Woolies is going to be hit.'

'Woolies?'

'Woolworths. The shop. Great pick 'n' mix.'

At least she'd diverted Anamaria to a safe topic. Although, why feel guilty? She honestly believed yesterday's conversation with Aiden had cleared the air, made way for them to go on as rediscovered friends rather than ex-lovers.

As he was leaving he walked over to a photo Jen had taken of Chloe sitting in a deckchair, squinting in bright sunlight, with Prince, the eldest of her grandmother's golden retrievers, resting his head on her lap.

'Chloe, right? And is that your dog?' He smiled, glancing back at her. 'The one with the miner's lamp?'

For a minute she had no earthly idea what he was talking about. Then she realised he was referring to that stupid joke she'd made, about the family dog needing a lamp to wade through the current gloom of her life. He was one of those rare souls who appreciated her wit.

'No, I was just being silly. We don't have pets.'

He examined the photo as though he might be tested on it later.

'Georgie's superexcited about this reunion. It's weird. I can't get her to go anywhere with me but suddenly she's running here there and everywhere over this Rowan search. She's always been an incredible workaholic.' He tilted his head to see the photo at another angle. 'But I suppose Giordani wouldn't be such a big success without her relentless work ethic.'

'Sounds like you had a hand in it too,' she ventured. 'Georgina obviously depends on you.'

'I do my share.' He looked suddenly wistful, still studying Chloe. 'But sometimes I'm not sure the success is worth the sacrifices. I would have loved having a daughter to spoil or a boy to teach football.'

'Chloe plays football,' she blurted and realised it sounded boastful. 'Of course, we're probably well on our way to screwing her up. With the divorce, that is.'

'Nonsense.' He looked at her reassuringly, his hand searing her shoulder in the briefest of touches. 'Kids adapt. They grow up in spite of their parents, not because of them.'

'Yes, well, you and Georgina would probably do a far better job of it than we have.' She said the first words to enter her head, hoping to hide how easily the slightest physical contact with him could throw her off balance.

He was silent.

'Not too late to try,' she added, and immediately regretted the fatuous cliché. Almost insultingly stupid when he'd as good as told her Georgina had no interest in motherhood.

He gave the photo one last lingering look and turned to face her again.

'You know,' he said, 'I didn't come here today to talk about Georgina. There's something else that's been on my mind.'

'Oh?' She kept her hands tucked under her armpits this time, so they wouldn't wilfully, of their own accord, start fiddling with her hair or running up and down her throat. 'What's that?'

His eyes met hers across the room.

'Meg.'

# Chapter 24

'Man on!' one of the spectators shouted. Opposition, Jen presumed, although she couldn't be certain. The pitch might have been floodlit, but her vision was obscured by the heavy mist that blanketed the field.

Why did they have to play these tournaments in midwinter? This one had started at six on a Thursday evening, with a warm-up twenty minutes before.

Jen had been shivering on the sidelines for over an hour, and unlike many of the parents she hadn't even thought to bring a Thermos. And poor Chloe was out there in her flimsy PE gear in this frigid weather. Although the way she was tearing up and down the pitch, long flaxen hair tied back in a ponytail, her fringe masked by a headband, Jen doubted she was feeling the same chill that had by now entered the marrow of her mother's bones.

Suddenly the orange and yellow flag was raised, Ollie indicating one of the opposing school's strikers was too far forward. He was running the line tonight, a task none of the mums fancied, because however often their husbands shuffled salt and pepper pots around the dinner table to demonstrate the offside rule, few were convinced enough of their mastery to dare to put it in practice.

Let's face it, football was Ollie's bag. Oh, she'd knocked a ball around when she was a child, but seldom had it gone in the intended direction. Ollie had bought Chloe a soft toy football before she could toddle on unsteady legs. He was assistant coach to his mate, Saul, whenever his schedule would allow, and was a fundamental player in the pub team, winning most of their games whenever he was home.

In fact, normally, Jen wouldn't attend Chloe's matches if Ollie was back. Not because she didn't *like* experiencing a second Ice Age in glacial temperatures, but rather it was such a great father–daughter bonding experience for them both and she was happy to leave them to it. Only this evening was different. Unloading the dishwasher, she'd opened the drawer in the kitchen and peeked in for the fourteenth time that day.

'*Final and absolute,*' she read over again, '*the said marriage is thereby dissolved.*' She just couldn't comprehend how one little certificate could carry such weight.

So it was over.

They'd lowered the final curtain.

And somehow with that realisation came another feeling, close on the heels of guilt and remorse, the necessity to compete. It was up to Jen to make sure that no longer would Ollie be considered the fun parent, the rule-breaker, and Jen the enforcer, the killjoy who insisted on regular bedtimes, pleases and thank yous, proper food that actually contained nutrition. That was why she'd bundled on her coat, hat and gloves to stand on the south side of the pitch, across from the rival parents on the north side. At first she'd stuck close to Ollie, united front and all, that noticing with a little kick of spite that Frances Hutton had started drifting towards him, seen Jen and swerved to change course. But as the game progressed Jen headed over to the back of the goal to be near as possible to Chloe, to yell out encouragement.

'Hoof it, Hattie!' someone shouted as one of the girls crashed her weight into the ball and it soared high into the air.

'Blue head on it!'

Chloe raced forward and weaved in and out of the other players, ball seemingly stuck to the toe of her right boot as she did all kinds of manoeuvres.

'Tackle, tackle,' a large bull-headed man growled. 'Get in there, Gina.'

'Go for it Chloe!' Jen found herself shouting. 'All the way!'

'Pass, pass!' Someone else yelled.

But it was too late. A hard tackle came in and Chloe stumbled to the frozen ground, clutching her knee. Jen's heart was in her mouth as the players gathered round. Then Chloe was limping towards the side, supported by two of her team-mates, arms over their shoulders, and their coach was jogging to meet them with a first-aid box.

'Chloe!' Jen called, waving and rushing forward. Chloe glanced across at her and half raised a hand, but it was Ollie she hobbled towards.

That stung.

Reaching her daughter's side, she watched as Ollie handed a Gatorade to Chloe who guzzled it down, and saw her wince as Saul examined her knee.

He stood up and patted her shoulder. 'You'll do. Ready to go back in or shall we get a sub?'

'Too right she needs a substitute!' Jen surprised herself by her own vehemence. 'She's hurt. She should sit it out.'

'Mum!' Chloe shot her a look of anguished horror.

Ollie stepped between them, holding up an appeasing hand. 'She's OK,' he said in a soothing voice that only infuriated Jen more.

Helplessly she watched her daughter return to the game, making a brave attempt to conceal her injury. Who would have thought that becoming a parent would have turned her into such a coward? The minute this small fragile creature had been placed in Jen's arms, she'd known the panic of mortality. Chloe was utterly dependent on her. Jen looked in awe at the way the baby's unfocused eyes seemed to widen as her little mouth fastened on to her mother's breast, and felt a deep shuddering fear run through her. What if anything should happen to Jen? Nothing this precious should have to go through life motherless.

And what if anything bad – really bad – happened to Chloe? That was something she was sure her beleaguered heart couldn't survive.

For someone who, throughout her own childhood, revelled in climbing the tallest trees, thought nothing of jumping out of a first-floor window on a dare, it came as a shock to her that as a mother, she was a quaking mass of jelly. For years she and Ollie had battled over Chloe's right to clamber up rocks without a guiding hand, walk along the tops of walls, attempt handstands that might snap her delicate wrists.

It was a side of herself she loathed, knowing that she was turning into one of those creatures she'd always despised, a mother who squawked, 'Be careful,' 'Get down,' 'Don't fall', but she was constantly consumed with fear.

The more anxious she became, the more Ollie seemed to encourage Chloe into riskier and riskier enterprises – not that she needed coaxing. The most extreme example came last year when without checking with Jen, he bought Chloe a dirt bike – with an actual engine – so he could take her scrambling. An embossed gold-trimmed invitation to an early grave if ever one was issued, Jen felt.

The battle over the bike had been fierce. Accusations had flown, hurtful words said that reverberated through both their psyches and had probably launched the demise of their marriage. If divorce hadn't been mentioned, the word had certainly hovered unspoken in the air.

A cheer rang out as someone scored. Chloe seemed to be running normally again, her injury forgotten. The referee looked at his watch and then blew his whistle. Half-time. Jen was relieved. She decided to fetch coffee for Ollie and herself from the drinks machine as a peace offering for their earlier set-to.

Walking over with the two hot plastic cups warming her hands, she saw him laughing with Chloe, who sat cross-legged on her kit bag. Ollie's head jerked to the right, Chloe stood up, bent down and handed him something. Jen's mobile, which she'd left in her bag along with Chloe's fleece.

Ollie glanced at the display, his smile fading. Some sixth sense made Jen hurry faster, the coffee spilling on to her gloves.

He took his coffee from her and handed her the phone. 'Didn't get it in time. Sorry.'

He sounded unconcerned, but Jen had been married to him long enough to notice the tension in his body and know something was wrong.

'Did you see who it was?' Certain she knew, still she had to ask. Not to do so would have been out of character and, hence, suspicious.

'Aiden Starkson.' He looked at her levelly. 'Now there's a blast from the past.'

There was little Ollie didn't know about Aiden. She'd shared too much when they first met, because at the time Ollie had been nothing more than a mate with a useful male perspective she'd found reassuring.

And apart from anything else, in the beginning it had always been an effective excuse for her 'intimacy issues'. The old loved and lost, first cut is the deepest defence. She'd told him everything, every detail, every agony of regret, sometimes laughing about it, drumming up the funniest elements of the whole affair, once – mortifyingly – crying into his T-shirt after copious amounts of vodka. She'd spent the rest of the night retching into the toilet and if Ollie hadn't been holding a washcloth to her head he might have joined her, nauseated as he was by the mere mention of Starkey.

And it would have been far better, if she hadn't got drunk another night, not long after their engagement and revealed the reason for her tearful panda eyes the morning she accepted his proposal – how Georgina had married Aiden, how she thought Meg had known and failed to alert her, the furtive after-midnight tap at her door, and all the other woes that had propelled her flight from the Marlow Arms. Wiser, probably, if she gave up alcohol altogether.

Had Ollie remembered all that when Jen told him on Bonfire Night that she was meeting old friends? He hadn't asked who at the time, but he certainly knew now.

'Georgina must have asked him to call.' She sounded false as a St Trinian's schoolgirl, guilt stamped in large letters on her forehead, just above the scarlet A for adulteress embroidered on her jacket. 'I wonder what she wants? Arrangements about the reunion, I bet.' She drained her coffee and dropped the empty cup in her bag.

'None of my business.' He sounded genuine, but Jen could read the contempt – or was it concern? – in his eyes.

Turning on his heel he walked down the line towards Frances, who greeted him with a touch on the biceps and a smile. Ollie said something and they glanced for a millisecond at Jen, Frances's face conveying a blend of awkwardness, no hard feelings and a soupçon of apology, Ollie's showing nothing at all.

The cold made Jen's eyes sting as she took off her soggy gloves and futilely breathed on her hands.

Frances Hutton was a perfectly nice woman. Extremely nice, she had to admit. Jen had always thought her daughter, Thea, a charming, shy child with impeccable manners. 'Be nice to Thea,' she was always telling Chloe. 'She's new to Huntsleigh. She needs friends.' She'd been thinking for several months that she should invite Frances and Thea over. Now it looked like she'd be serving a big helping of warmed-up ex-husband instead.

The worst thing was, she'd sort of thought she and Frances could be friends. Granted Jen was five years older than the other mother, but she'd sensed a kindred spirit in their brief playground exchanges. She seemed sweet and vaguely dishevelled, one of the few to rush up, out of breath, hair pulled back in an untidy chignon, as the school gates were clanging shut. She wore the kind of clothing Jen had favoured until the disapproving sniffs had steered her towards a more sedate suburban-mother look: cargo pants, fitted T-shirts, Gap zip-ups. She would have felt so much better if Ollie was chatting up an obvious busty blonde or an over-made-up *Desperate Housewife*-style beauty, someone Jen would find easy to loathe. Though for form's sake she was prepared to hate Frances anyway.

Jen could have pegged two loads of washing on the silence that hung in the air during the drive home.

'Careful of the mud,' Jen said as Chloe took her boots off and smashed them against the porch side.

'Can you help me with my shin pads?'

Jen stooped down at the same time as Ollie and they practically banged heads. 'Fine, you do it,' she said. 'Make sure everything goes straight into the machine. I'll run her a bath.'

'How's your knee?' Ollie said, full of concern.

'It's OK, Daddy.' Chloe put her arms around him. Still not too old to hug her daddy, Jen noticed with a pang as she went upstairs. All the other mothers told her that would change. Around twelve, they said. Then you become the enemy. It's nature, they can't help themselves any more than lemmings diving off cliffs.

'Cup of tea?' she asked Ollie later, sticking the kettle under the cold tap. He nodded.

'There's something I've been meaning to tell you.' He took a deep breath. 'Saul suggested I move in with him. Said he wouldn't mind a flatmate. Just until I get myself organised.'

'Oh?' Her back was pressed against the stove as she swivelled to face him. 'What about Chloe?'

'We talked about that. He's cool with her staying over. He has a box room he never uses. Said we could fit a single bed in there. It'll only be temporary. Until I buy a place.'

'Sounds like you've got it all sorted.' She worked hard to keep her voice even, no hint of resentment. 'When?'

'The weekend. No point in waiting, is there?' He met her eyes with a dispassionate blue gaze. 'I'm taking Chloe to Mum's while you're at this reunion. I'll start moving my things after that.'

She was shocked. 'But that's before Christmas. Chloe'll be devastated. And aren't you due back in Tanzania? We told the Radcliffes we'd try to complete after New Year.'

'I'm not going back to Tanzania.' His words hit her like a slap in the face. 'I spoke with the company, told them I couldn't leave my daughter any more. They're shifting the staff around, finding work for me in head office. We'll have to sort things out about Christmas, of course. Maybe I can have her Christmas Eve, take her up to Mum's as usual and you do Christmas Day?'

Jen's mouth hung open, aghast, as the room seemed to tilt, the world overturn so that it wouldn't have been a total shock if a kangaroo popped out of the broom closet. Of course she'd known it would be like this. But not yet. Not so soon.

'At least you'll have me out of your hair.' He was watching the moving-picture show flickering across her face. 'There's a few thousand in the joint account. Why don't you hold on to that? I know it's a bad time to look for work, right before Christmas. I'll cover the mortgage until we complete on this place. And of course I'll be paying maintenance.' He hesitated, looking as if he wanted to say something else.

'Um . . . well . . . thanks.' She swallowed, feeling awkward. 'I'll reimburse you as soon as we get the house money.'

'Whatever.' He looked as unhappy as she felt.

'OK, fine then.' She nodded, searching for words, any words. 'And Saul's a nice guy. You'll have fun, I bet.' She tried to sound upbeat, despite a sudden unexpected tightness in her chest and a hot burning feeling in her throat. 'Couple of giddy bachelors,' she elaborated with forced cheer. 'Parties every night. Black satin sheets and mood lighting, I can just see it.'

'Actually he has a steady girlfriend,' Ollie said witheringly. 'He just proposed. And black satin sheets sounds about as tacky as it gets.' His scorn was evident. 'But yes, he's cool.'

'Won't she mind – the fiancée – having you and Chloe there?'

'If she did, I'm sure he wouldn't have asked me.' He made it sound glaringly obvious. 'Anyway I believe he stays at her flat a lot.'

Great. So Ollie would have Saul's place all to himself. When Chloe wasn't there, of course. Total privacy. How nice for him. Maybe Frances would drop round with casseroles for him the way Helen had brought them to Jen when Chloe was born.

And then another thought spawned and grew, a devil's whisper of temptation she didn't want to listen to but couldn't seem to banish. She too would be on her own. No Chloe. No Ollie. Evening and nights in an empty house. No one to see what she was doing or ask penetrating questions.

Into her weary, muddled mind swam a picture of Aiden's face, handsome, melancholy and full of concern.

'Well, then.' She blinked. 'It sounds absolutely perfect.'

# Chapter 25

Fresh from the shower, a towel wrapped around her wet hair, Meg wandered into the living room, where Mace and Zeb were hunched over a chessboard set up on the coffee table. Zeb frowned in concentration as he held his queen in the air, deliberating over where to position it.

'Who's winning?' she asked. She recognised the pieces, knew the rudiments of the game, but chess had never appealed to her. Forward thinking had never been part of her repertoire.

Zeb looked up. 'I am.'

'Maybe,' Mace said, affectionately swatting the top of his nephew's head. 'If you don't goof it up.' He gave a warning cough as Zeb tentatively touched the piece to a square.

Zeb snatched back his queen as if electrified, a relieved grin on his face.

Meg yawned, sitting down towelling her hair. 'Any messages?'

'Not a thing. All set for this big reunion tomorrow night?'

'Yes. They're going to pick me up in Georgina's car. Have you guys made plans?'

'Mace and Paula are taking me to a movie,' Zeb said. 'Then we're going for pizza.'

Well, that was good. Now she wouldn't have to worry about introducing everyone.

'Shouldn't that be Uncle Mace?' Mace joked. For once, he didn't look quite so much the harried accountant, Meg thought. He'd even relaxed enough to kick off his shoes and take off his tie.

'And Aunt Paula?' Zeb smirked.

'Sure. Why not?'

It was cute to see them together – her brother really seemed to have loosened up around his nephew's youthful energy. It was only when Paula was there, like at yesterday's strained Thanksgiving dinner, that she felt as if someone was running their fingernails down a chalk board. Meg had never met a more uptight conservative Little Miss Prim.

'Tell Mace that story, Mom,' Zeb requested. 'The one about you and Jen setting the stink bomb off in the lunch hall.'

'Oh God, don't.' Meg dropped the towel over her face. 'I have to see those people tomorrow. I don't need any reminders of my wicked ways.'

'Checkmate.' Mace moved his castle with a decisive click. 'See – that's what happens when you don't concentrate.'

'I thought you were excited?' Zeb said, starting to replace the marble chess pieces.

'I was.' Meg began plaiting her long hair into a single braid. 'But then last night I had one of those dreams where you're taking an exam and you realise you played hooky for the whole year and none of the questions make sense. And when I woke up it all came flooding back. All the bitchy things I said and did at school. All the trouble I got into.'

'It didn't seem to bother you at the time.' Mace rubbed the top of his nose where his glasses pinched. He cleared his throat, looking faintly uncomfortable. Meg pulled a face at him.

'Well, Zeb and I have news,' he announced. 'We've found Zeb a tutor. He's going to help get him up to speed. Right, buddy?' He poked Zeb with a toe.

Meg sat bolt upright, her hair swinging over her shoulder. She looked incredulously at Zeb, who flushed but didn't deny it.

'You gotta be kidding me?'

'He's a bright kid. And he's way behind on all the basics. He may be a whizz on the computer but he can't spell, his maths is abysmal and from what I can gather you haven't even begun to touch on science. Paula did some tests with him last night.'

That figured. Paula was a teacher. Meg should have known she had a hand in this.

'He's only nine,' she said. 'How far behind can he be?'

'Plenty. You're not doing him any favours home-schooling, you know. For one thing, how does that fit in with you working? Who takes care of him while you're at the diner?'

'He goes to a neighbour or to his friend Allie's,' Meg said impatiently, annoyed at his interfering and the implication of negligence. 'She's home-schooled too. They have a small farm. They get to feed the chickens and the pigs, grow vegetables, learn math and science in practical ways. Last year he helped Allie's dad install solar panels on the roof. Isn't that more valuable than measuring the square root of some stupid triangle?' If he could only see how free Zeb's life was. No bullies or sadistic teachers harassing him, no peers pushing drugs his way.

'Not if you ever hope to go to college. And he wants to, don't you, Zeb?'

Zeb nodded slowly. 'I guess.' He looked embarrassed. His pale face bore her freckles and his eyelashes were lush and dark. So unfair on a boy.

'This sounds like fun to you?' Meg stared hard at her son.

'I wouldn't mind doing some sums, I guess.' He squirmed. 'Ain't got nothing better to do. There's no kids here for me to play with and it's boring hanging around the house all day.'

'Let me feel your forehead.' Meg was in shock but sort of proud of the kid. 'Do you have a fever?' She placed her hand on Zeb's brow. 'Are you sure you're a Lennox? Herb would be rolling in his grave if he heard you now.'

'He couldn't,' Zeb grinned. 'Pops isn't dead.'

'No, but he might be on his way to an early grave if he hears how you're disgracing the family name.' She grabbed him in a stranglehold from behind and ruffled his hair.

'The idea behind home-schooling, in case you missed the point,' Mace had his disapproving face on again, 'is that you follow some kind of curriculum. You don't spend half the day watching movies with him and the other half goofing off at the park or ignoring him while you're glued to my computer doing God knows what.'

'That's not what we do at all,' Meg snapped, offended.

'It's what you've done since you got here. I've seen those books come out once, twice at the most. I'm surprised you-know-who hasn't put his foot down before about your unorthodox schooling methods.'

She wrapped Zeb's neck in a hug, her hair brushing against his cheek, and met Mace's eyes.

'You-know-who has known for weeks that we're here and hasn't managed so much as a goddamned phone call. So I think it's pretty clear that you-know-who is so far up his you-know-what that he couldn't care less about being any kind of you-know-what to . . .' she hesitated and shot her eyes sideways at Zeb, 'you know.'

'Yes, well.' Mace frowned. 'He doesn't have any choice, does he?'

'Apparently the asshole thinks he does.' Meg let go of Zeb and flopped on the sofa again, picking up the remote control. 'He's trying to wiggle out of the situation as fast as his stoaty little legs will take him.'

'And that's another thing. Would you please cool it on the cuss words around Paula. She doesn't appreciate it at all.'

'No shit,' said Meg, switching the television on.

'What do you think?' Jen asked as she stared woefully in the dressing-table mirror.

'Lipstick's gross. Your dress is yucky and your eyeshadow's too bright.'

'But apart from that?' Jen joked weakly.

'Come here, Mummy.'

Chloe turned on the hairdryer and scrunched and waxed her mother's hair, while Jen sat on a stool next to the bed, putty in her hands.

She was clearly enjoying it, so Jen didn't have the heart to stop her or scream 'ouch' when the pain got too much. It was some kind of divine penance for her sins.

'Do you really think my eyeshadow's too bright?' Jen never knew the correct depth of colour these days, and her make-up bag was embarrassingly outmoded.

'Not really.' Chloe shrugged, adding another great dollop of hair mousse to Jen's already crispy hair. 'But that's what Kelsey's mum says to Kelsey's big sister.'

'That's for school. This is different.'

'But you're going to school.' She began backcombing at great speed. Tears of pain sprang to Jen's eyes.

'As a grown-up, yes.'

'And you've got tangles. You never used to have tangles.'

'I'm growing out my hair. Thought I'd try a new look. You hate this dress then?'

'It's super-dull. Why are you getting dressed so early? It's not even four. Daddy and I aren't going to Nanny's for ages.'

'Because my friend's picking me up at five. Ashport's a long way away.' She was excited, she realised. Who would be there? Would she recognise anyone? Would they recognise her? Twenty years was a long time, twenty-two years for Jen. But biggest question of them all – would she finally reconnect with Rowan?

'Won't Nanny think it strange – you not coming? And you won't get to see Prince. Or Rebel.'

'Another time,' Jen croaked, suddenly overcome, recalling

how inconsolable Ollie's mother had been when she heard their divorce plans. His parents were always so supportive of her and Ollie, never minding that their twenty-year-old son ended up married to a knocked-up woman eight years his senior. His dad had died of a heart attack a few years back and soon Jen feared she'd lose his mother too, along with Ollie's friends and those shared ones in Islington whom she'd have no cause to meet up with any more, or who'd decided to take his side even though no sides had been asked for. You lost so much more than a husband when your marriage ended.

'Right, now,' Chloe said, standing up and opening her mother's wardrobe. 'What dress to wear? Hmm.'

Fifty miles away Georgina was putting the final touches to her make-up, hand shaking as she swept liquid eyeliner across her dark lashes. She was so overcome with dread that she wasn't even sure that she still wanted to go.

Their return to Ashport Comp was summoning memories of the past all too clearly, specifically those of Aiden and Jennifer. They'd been so sweet as a couple, always holding hands, larking about, laughing. When did Aiden ever laugh like that with her? Was it unrealistic to yearn for that kind of closeness with the man you'd married?

He'd come back whistling and happy from Jennifer's house after he'd returned her mobile. Oh, she wasn't stupid, she'd seen the way his admiring eyes followed Jen around a room. And there was definitely an atmosphere when she came home last Sunday to find them alone in the kitchen. Georgina knew the signs. A millisecond too long of eye contact, a prolonged holding of hand in greeting, a tendency to mention their name a little too much.

That was the problem with Jennifer. She was oblivious to how attractive men found her. For all their talk about Rowan's great beauty, really Jennifer was a doll herself, always had been despite that tomboy veneer. Great cheekbones, that gorgeous ash-blond hair with those sultry brown eyes, her petite figure, that vulnerable yet spunky character – men were always drawn to her.

Georgina sighed heavily as she tried to rub off an excess of blusher. She knew she had to trust them. She couldn't keep her husband under lock and key or always in sight. It was only natural he and Jennifer would have things to talk about.

It wouldn't have seemed so difficult to live with if she just felt closer to Aiden herself. When was the last time he had wanted to go out for a romantic dinner? Or had a meaningful conversation with her that didn't revolve around work? She shook her head, reminding herself it was a two-way thing, but wishing all this hadn't been stirred up by Nutmeg's reappearance. She checked her watch. Too late now to back out, she thought, as she hurriedly applied a sheer coat of lipstick and reached for her bag.

'You're going for the full works then?' Aiden asked as she walked into the kitchen looking for her mobile.

She grimaced. Why couldn't he say she looked stunning or simply nice?

'I thought a bit of an effort might be called for,' she said haughtily.

'Mmm.' He wandered round the kitchen, clearly at a loss as to what to do with himself, glowering and glum. Funny, any other time she'd have had to drag him, moody and resentful, to a function like this, and now he was sulking because he'd been excluded.

Maybe she'd been an absolute fool letting Jennifer back in her life again. Asking for trouble, her mother had said, when Georgina had mentioned recent events. Like waving a bottle of whisky at an alcoholic. And why had she? Only because she'd felt so desperately lonely, so in need of a friend.

But what if the remedy proved worse than the disease?

231

She wrapped a red velvet hooded cape around her shoulders. Dramatic but definitely Christmassy, and Georgina had the height and the presence to pull it off. She'd brave it out tonight, she thought. But if Rowan didn't show, maybe it was time to call off this charade.

She saw car headlights sweep across the window. Aiden didn't even look up as she marched grandly past him.

'That'll be Max,' she said, picking up her handbag.

# Chapter 26

The inside of the car was silent when its sleek shape pulled smoothly to a stop in front of the school entrance, the three former pupils lost in their own memories and thoughts. Meg shook herself, jumped out and held the door for Jen just as Max was opening the door for Georgina, the picture of efficiency and dignity with his iron-grey hair and military posture.

All the lights were on in the ground floor of the building, the upper windows dark and lifeless except for a classroom here or there. People, large and small, streamed in from the car park and through the gates as a muffled repetitive bass echoed across the playground.

In the main entrance a huge banner proclaimed 'Ashport Comprehensive remembers Isobel Benjamin' in large letters. A crowd of almost-forty-year-olds, done up to the nines, laughed and chattered their way down the locker-lined corridors, few bearing any resemblance to the fresh-faced teenagers of their youth.

Jen swallowed, suddenly anxious. After more than two decades would Rowan recognise her, and more importantly, would she recognise Rowan? Georgina looked so pale Jen guessed she was wondering the same thing.

Meg grabbed each of them by the elbow and linked their arms, *Wizard of Oz*-style, as the tide pushed them towards the gymnasium. 'Come on, mateys,' she grinned, 'I've got a feeling this is gonna be a whole lotta fun.'

Jen squinted warily at the man approaching in the greeny-brown corduroy jacket as she stood with her food-filled paper plate by the buffet table. Since arriving she'd had several strangers greeting her as if she were a long-lost best mate, laughing uproariously at things she'd done, recounting long-winded stories that failed to register even a faint distant clang. Gratifying though it was to discover she wasn't the nonentity she'd always imagined, it was also slightly worrying to have forgotten her own exploits when they were apparently etched on others' psyches.

Nor did it help that every former classmate asked about Aiden or had some story about the two of them. They'd apparently made quite an impression. 'Lip-locked' one had said. 'Snogging yourselves senseless' someone else had winked. It had become so uncomfortable that Georgina had walked away. Thinking of running after her, Jen had decided against it. Shortly after that Meg had drifted off, and she hadn't seen either of them for almost an hour.

But now, faced with the man in the cord jacket, despite the additional crow's feet and grey peppering the mousy brown hair, something lit a spark in Jen's beleaguered brain, further fuelled by cowboy boots peeking below his jeans, the merest hint of stubble and the shortest of short ponytails.

'Jen Bedlow?'

'Mr Dugan?'

'Tom, please.' He chuckled and pushed his long fringe from his eyes. 'Mr Dugan makes me feel ancient.'

'Tom.' He still had the charming voice, puppy-dog eyes, warm open manner. The young English teacher had been one of the most popular members of staff at Ashport Comprehensive. Friendly and laid-back, he was still able to fire his pupils' imaginations, spicing up lessons by moonwalking past the blackboard or showing films in the auditorium like Derek Jarman's *The Tempest*, which was one of their coursebooks that year. He was quirky, too, fond of belting out folk songs as he strummed a bashed-up old guitar during his lunch breaks.

Jen resisted the urge to sing a bar or two of 'Riding on Your Donkey', one of his old favourites, and instead flashed him a smile.

'Hide me, quick!' He ducked behind a large movable screen disguising a hoarde of stacked chairs.

'Why? Who is it?' Jen gazed around, astonished by his suddenly odd behaviour.

'Linda Petroski,' he whispered hoarsely from his hiding place. 'She's been wittering in my ear for the last twenty minutes. Keeps making inane jokes about the crappy songs I was forced to sing.'

'How hilarious is that?' Jen threw her eyebrows towards the heavens. 'You can come out now. It's safe. You didn't rate those songs, then?' she added as he emerged.

'Hell no.' He breathed a sigh of relief as he gazed at Linda's receding figure disappearing into the throng, clutching a bunch of glittery red balloons. 'Give me U2 or Dire Straits any day. But when I joined the school Risley thrust this ancient scoutmaster's songbook at me. "Get out there, Tom," he boomed. "Stop the kids beating each other up and strum them a tune, Tom."'

'So you soothed the savages.' Jen scooped up some cream cheese with a wedge of cucumber and popped it into her mouth. 'Top marks to you.'

'Thanks, I'm sure. Mmm, what have we here?' He found himself a plate and surveyed the typical cold buffet laid out on trestle tables. 'Quite a spread.' He dipped a carrot baton into a tub of guacamole. 'Someone's worked hard.'

'Rumour has it they were going to do proper school dinners, shepherd's pie, rhubarb crumble and all that jazz, but there was no way of reheating it properly.'

The conversation having dried up between mouthfuls of food, Jen gazed around, searching for familiar faces. There had to be at least a hundred and fifty people here, but she was struggling to spot anyone she actually wanted to talk to.

'I'm surprised you even knew who I am,' she finally said. 'Or did someone split?'

'Well your name badge certainly helps,' Dugan admitted with a broad grin. 'But I've a memory for faces. You were the girl who sneaked the fake vomit into the staff toilet.'

'You remember that!' She almost choked on the breadstick she'd just taken a bite out of. 'Fuck me . . . oh, God, sorry, I mean . . .'

'Hey, relax. As an adult, you're allowed to swear in my presence. I won't give you a detention.' He laughed, his gaze scanning her like a credit-card reader, flashing up 'Approved'.

'An adult? Could have fooled me.' Jen shook her head. This was so weird. Back at school, bantering with one of her favourite teachers – considered quite a heart-throb in his day, though admittedly competition was slim – as an equal. 'I feel about twelve years old, although admittedly it doesn't tally with all these old codgers with beer bellies, balding heads and comb-overs who claim they're from my class. And the men look even worse,' she quipped.

Dugan smiled.

'You're the first teacher I've recognised tonight,' she told him. 'Mind you, I left after the fifth year. Moved away and got some crummy job.'

'Shame.' He leant his hand against a post next to her right ear. 'I had you pegged for sixth form, maybe even university if you ever stopped larking about long enough to study. You were one of the brightest. And your three friends were equally lively.

The frisky four, they called you in the staffroom.'

'They did?' She grinned, pleased. 'Well, I don't know if you heard, but we left under a bit of a cloud. We burned down a barn – accidentally, of course.'

He laughed again. 'A vandal, hey? Well, I'm glad I dropped in. I didn't think wild horses could drag me back here, but I was in the area and curiosity got the better of me. Did you come with anyone?'

'Georgina and Meg. We were really hoping Rowan would be here too, but no joy so far.'

'Oh yes, Rowan Howard.' He sipped at his plastic glass of beer. 'The little Welsh girl. Is she supposed to meet you here, then?'

'No. You see, we've not seen her since we all left school. It's a long story, but basically we're trying to track her down but we're running out of leads, and the reunion was our last hope. Which reminds me, I'm supposed to be on a mission. Listen, do me a favour, Tom.' She chucked her plate in a black bin bag. 'If you hear anything, or anyone mentions Rowan's where-abouts, come and let me know.'

'Sure will. Have fun.' He smiled again, no longer the authority figure but an attractive mature man. With his trim figure and full head of hair, he'd actually aged better than most of the pupils he'd taught

She waved back over her shoulder.

And he had a kind smile.

Meg stood outside the school gates, well away from the huddled group who were cursing the world conspiracy against smokers with blue shivering lips. It was dark, save for a security light about a hundred yards away.

She dug in her purse for a Benson and Hedges packet, extricating a lone roll-up, the last of the small amount of grass she'd wheedled out of one of Herb's old pot-dealing cronies.

Curious to think that to her Oregon pals, tobacco users were a step away from suicidal murderers, alcohol drinkers almost as bad, yet smoking marijuana was A-OK, practically guaranteed you were one of the good guys.

It was two years since she'd touched unhealthy, carcinogenic nicotine, yet all it took was a glass of wine to have her longing for a plain old 'fag'. Addictions die hard.

Tonight's shindig wasn't bad, better than she'd dared hope, with everyone avid to see who'd married who, who'd dumped who, who had the fancy job or failed to live up to their early promise. Some women had gone the whole hog, pulling out their favourite eighties outfits which only made you glad that particular decade was long buried. Meg had dressed simply in a red chiffon button-down maxi dress that skimmed the top of her fringed black suede boots – and thankfully, she thought, pulling it tighter around her shoulders, a decently warm shawl.

Farting Frank, the unofficial host, had asked her to dance as soon as he saw her. And though she'd never liked the guy, she could hardly refuse, all things considered. But then she had to spend the whole of 'Isn't She Lovely' fighting off his clammy hands.

Meg took another drag of her joint and scanned the lonely car park, using every visualisation and manifestation technique she knew to bring Rowan here tonight. She closed her eyes, imagining Rowan leaving a house, getting into her car and finally arriving to find Meg waiting at the kerb. It was so real in her mind, she was almost surprised to find it wasn't true when she opened her eyes and scanned along the empty walkway. Half the night she'd been hallucinating – without any chemical assistance – that everyone with long dark hair was Rowan. She'd even tapped on the shoulders of a few females the right height, apologising when they turned round to look at her in surprise. Hey, someone had to be making an effort, what with

Georgina skulking in a corner and Jen too engrossed in socialising to remember their search.

If they gave up now, where would that leave her? She was fairly certain their briefly rekindled friendship would soon fizzle out, but she was anxious to pretend otherwise for as long as possible. She owed it to Zeb to secure his future. Oh yes, of course she believed in kismet, destiny and all that crap, but in Meg's experience sometimes the universe needed a good hefty nudge to cough up with its bountiful abundance.

It had certainly bestowed plentifully on Georgina, and even Jen seemed comfortably provided for up till now, a lady of leisure for so many years. Was Rowan too living in luxury somewhere, she wondered. Or struggling to make ends meet like Meg? She couldn't wait to discover what she'd been up to all this time. What would she look like? Was she still sweet, still slightly goofy? Why had she let them down that night at the Marlow Arms? OK, maybe she wasn't really considering her as an adoptive mother for Zeb, but more and more she found she really did want to see the Welsh girl again.

She and Rowan had both been outsiders with their 'funny' accents, Meg with her American twang, Rowan with her alien Welsh inflection. It had created a special bond between them. They were constantly teased and laughed at, even by teachers seeking an easy way to ingratiate themselves with the class, nicknamed 'Yank' and 'Taffy', mocked in the dining hall for Meg's tofu wraps and Rowan's home-made table-top-thick brown-bread sandwiches. Rowan's mom was home-grown organic long before it was trendy. She kept bees, kneaded her own bread, fed herself and her daughter from her small vegetable garden and thought that McDonald's was the Devil's work. Not so different really from Meg's Auntie Sunbeam's commune, although bible-bashing Ma Howard would surely have them burned in hell for all that free and easy sex.

Her doobie was scorching her fingers now. She took one last

drag, dropped it on to the floor and ground it into the icy concrete.

Of course, Meg surmised as she turned on her heel and began to walk back along the path, no question Jen was her best bud in lots of ways. She was gutsier than Rowan and had always been way cooler. But when Jen was wrapped up with her precious nags, the Welsh girl would drop everything to hang out with Meg. She could stop by her house, any time any day, and Rowan would be out of that door in seconds, pulling on her anorak with a 'Bye, Mam'.

And it was Rowan who had come through for her that year they were streamed for their final exams. Meg's test results were so bad she was moved down. As if anyone could study for some dumb-ass test with Clover's band rehearsing in the living room till four a.m. and Herb sending Meg scurrying between the kitchen and the makeshift studio for cold beer, Rizlas and a candy-store array of drugs.

Still, Meg had been crushed. To be torn away from her friends, branded a dunce and stuck with the losers in the bottom set had hurt. She didn't know how she could ever face the next term alone. Until Rowan, who'd been sick on the test day, saved her ass. She'd sat the same test the following week and had been put down to the same class. Only Meg suspected that she'd flunked the thing on purpose, given they'd all filled her in on the questions to expect.

Yeah, quite a pal, Rowan.

A better friend than Meg any day.

# Chapter 27

'Ah Miss Bedlow, we mustn't keep meeting like this.' Tom Dugan's voice came from behind Jen's left ear. She'd been studying the old school photos someone had pinned on boards all along the corridor. 'People might talk.'

She turned around. 'Oh, let them,' she quipped back. 'Too late to expel me now.'

'Are you in any of those?' He removed some reading glasses from his inside jacket pocket, placed them on the bridge of his nose and peered closer. 'Where did they all come from?'

'I expect people sent them in or emailed them,' she shrugged. 'Those eighties hairstyles – hilarious, eh?'

'The Maggie Thatcher milk-snatcher years. Power dressing, shoulder pads and Harry Enfield waving his loadsa money about. Who'd guess we'd look back on them as the good old days.' Tom removed his glasses and began walking along the corridor with her towards the gym. 'Are you married, Jen?'

'Yes . . . I mean no. Recently divorced. You?'

'It didn't work out for me either. I'm what you call an incurable romantic. Maybe I never met the right woman,' he said wryly. 'I thought I did once but . . .' He looked suddenly wistful. 'I loved not wisely, but too well. Oh help, do you remember this record?'

Wham's 'Careless Whisper' was playing at top volume.

'God, George Michael. I had such a mammoth crush on him. Broke my heart when it came out he was gay.'

He smiled and held out his elbow. 'Fancy a dance?'

'Oh go on then.'

He led her on to the dance floor, still chatting. 'So the four of you have stayed in touch all this time?'

Jen had to raise her voice to be heard about the din of the music. 'On and off.' It was too much bother to explain.

'I thought you'd be old and frail,' she said as Tom grabbed her right hand with his left and whirled her round. 'Crooked stick, rheumy eyes, Zimmer frame.'

'Hey, I was one of the youngest on the staff, you know,' he laughed as he moved. 'A rookie. This was my first teaching job.'

'No! We must have been a nightmare.'

'Oh, it wasn't so bad.' He swung her back again.

'So you decided not to come in uniform?' he asked, indicating a pair of gymslip-clad women joking with a guy drunkenly displaying the old school tie knotted around his head. 'I reckon you're one of the few that could probably still fit into yours.'

Had she heard right? Was Mr Dugan coming on to her, or was she imagining the little spark between them? Blinking, she averted her eyes from his gaze, pleased by the compliment, yet half expecting to see Georgina and Meg falling about with laughter as they watched her. She was so out of practice – she felt like a sixteen-year-old pretending to be grown-up.

'Just as well I didn't,' she responded, alcoholic courage overcoming embarrassment. 'Everyone's been telling me my skirt was so tiny it looked like a handkerchief.'

'Really?' He raised his eyebrows in devilish fashion. 'We teachers weren't allowed to notice things like that.'

'You mean not unless you were measuring them for detentions?' She batted her eyelids, growing bolder.

'Yes, well, the job had to have some perks.' He grinned at

her. 'Don't mind me, I'm teasing. So, any kids?' He twirled her and pulled her so that her back was against him, rocking from side to side.

She felt her cheeks grow even hotter at his proximity. 'Just Chloe, she's nine.'

He spun her round to face him, no longer in time with the music.

'I can't say I'm terribly sorry you're single again, Jennifer Bedlow.' They'd stopped swaying but his hand still clutched hers. The record came to an end and they broke apart.

Jen's cheeks were still burning two dances later. She'd had a few glasses of wine and her former English teacher was clearly flirting greedily with her. Not only that, she was really quite enjoying it much to the disgust of some white-haired old man who was staring at them disapprovingly over the top of his gold-rimmed spectacles.

The opening notes of 'Karma Chameleon' warbled in the air and Jen had a sudden flashback of dancing to it in her bedroom with Rowan around the age of thirteen, back in the days when they'd attended the weekly disco at the local church hall. Being a musician's daughter, Meg unsurprisingly moved like someone who'd been dancing since a toddler, letting the music carry her away. Georgina found it all too strenuous with the excess weight that she carried. But Rowan and Jen, well, they'd practise for hours so they wouldn't look silly in front of everybody.

'Forward two steps, left foot, back together, side twist, side twist.' Rowan showed her how.

'Isn't it forward back, forward back, side twist, side twist?' Jen had argued.

'That's not the way Boy George did it on *Top of the Pops* the other night.'

'Jenny, Rowan – can I come in?' Jen's dad poked his head round. 'All right, darling? I'm just popping to Sainsbury's. You two OK on your own?'

'Of course, Dad.'

'Don't do anything I wouldn't do.'

'Yes, Mr Bedlow,' Rowan smiled. 'We won't.'

They heard his feet running downstairs and Rowan turned to Jen, her eyes shining. 'Oh, he's so sweet,' she gushed.

'Sweet? My dad? You must be joking.'

Jen was just reaching those dangerous teenage years where sometimes she loved her dad more than anything else in the world and other times she couldn't imagine anyone more dense or annoying.

'I wish my da was still alive. Hey, wouldn't it be the best if your da and my mam fell in love and married!' Rowan linked her little finger to Jen's in their secret handshake, 'I'd be a Bedlow then and we'd be sisters.'

'Yeah, it'd be cool,' Jen had laughed, although thinking the last thing she'd want was Rowan's mum for a stepmother. But they'd gone through a spell of fantasising about the family they could be. Calling each other 'sis', even telling shopkeepers and other strangers they were twins, which was hysterically funny to them both because they looked nothing alike. More than once it had thrown them into such helpless giggles that they'd been sent packing from a shop before they could buy anything at all.

'. . . in time,' Tom was saying.

'Pardon?' Jen looked up at his wistful expression, realising she'd not heard a word he'd said.

'I was saying how it's odd coming to Ashport-on-Sea. A real step back in time.'

'You're right there.'

'Karma Chameleon' had faded out to be replaced by 'All Around the World', an old Lisa Stansfield classic

They danced closer now, humming along, his chin nestling into her hair. It felt good to be in someone's arms. Flattering to have the attention. He was stroking her back. Gentle, little circular movements, but it made her go all a-quiver. She was feeling dangerous tonight. Dangerous and decadent.

The music came to a halt and they pulled apart. It was already approaching ten o'clock, and more people were leaving now than arriving. Jen had to resign herself to the fact that Rowan wasn't going to show.

'Drink?' He led her towards the bar.

'Mmm. Please. White wine.'

Meg trotted over, looking slightly bleary. 'You'll never guess who I just met?'

Jen grinned. 'Tom, remember Meg Lennox? Say hello to Mr Dugan, Meg.'

'Hello, sir.' Meg's mouth tightened in disapproval as she glanced at Jen's hand clutching his elbow.

Tom smiled. 'Hi, Meg. Great to see you again. Can I get you a drink?'

'Jen, guess who I just met,' Meg persisted, ignoring Tom's offer. Jen shrugged, irritated that Meg couldn't take two seconds to be more polite to him. Meg sighed in defeat. 'Gregory Henshaw! He was the one Rowan went out with for a week and then I made out with him a few times because really Rowan hadn't liked him in the first place, but I thought he was quite cute and she didn't mind, so. Anyway, even Georgina admitted to having been on a date with him. He was our shared boyfriend!'

'Ah, high school,' Tom sighed. 'Those were the days.'

'You all got off with him? Where was I?' Jen demanded.

'How would I know?' Meg sounded pissed off. 'Riding your nags? Snogging yourself senseless with Aiden?' It hit Jen like a slap. Meg was only repeating what she'd heard Beryl Johnson say earlier that evening but still, under their current alliance, diplomacy had prevented them all from mentioning that topic until now. She let go of Tom's arm, feeling suddenly under attack.

'Would you like anything?' Tom repeated to Meg missing the tension.

'No ta,' Meg said dismissively.

In silence they watched him approach the person behind the makeshift bar table, pointing to one of the open bottles. Jen grabbed Meg pulling her a few feet away.

'What's up with you?' Jen hissed as glasses were filled and Tom counted out pound coins. 'Why are you being so blinking rude?'

'What's up with me?' Meg hissed back. 'You've been smooching on the dance floor for the last twenty minutes or more. Aren't you a little old to be playing teacher's pet? We're supposed to be . . .'

She broke off. Tom was back, holding a glass of wine out to Jen.

Cautiously Jen took a sip. It was the same vinegary disaster she'd been drinking all evening, Chateau Piss-de-Chat, but after the fourth or fifth glass you no longer shuddered. 'So any leads on Rowan?' she asked, forcing herself to sound casual in front of Tom.

'Nada,' Meg replied. 'How's your search for info going?' She glanced meaningfully from Jen to Tom. 'Hard at it, are you?' she sniped, her voice laden with sarcasm. 'No *worm* unearthed. Oops, I'm sorry, I mean no stone unturned.'

'Exploring every avenue,' Jen answered, waving her glass tipsily and refusing to be baited. She was having too good a time.

'She even sent me out there,' Tom offered, putting an arm over Jen's shoulders. 'Scouring the room for signs of Rowan.'

'Well, she seems to have disappeared off the earth.' Georgina suddenly appeared at Jen's right shoulder. 'Hello, Mr Dugan.'

'Tom,' Jen corrected as Georgina formally shook his hand. 'Mr Dugan makes him feel old.'

'Come on,' Meg grabbed Jen's arm and tugged her forward. 'I need you to sort out the ticket box.'

'What ticket box?'

'It was meant to be your shift,' she said testily. 'It's on the rota chart.'

Baffled, Jen allowed herself to be marched swiftly across the hall, feeling guilty for abandoning Georgina once again. Oh well, Tom would look after her.

'There is no ticket box,' Meg admitted when she finally halted in the girls' toilets. On the wall next to the sink was an extremely inaccurate picture of a penis, below the words 'Mick Morris is a prick'. 'I was just rescuing you from that slimebag Dugan.'

'He's not a slimebag,' Jen said, offended. 'What the hell's up with you tonight? He's actually very nice. I remember us talking once about which teachers we could go for and you said Mr Dugan was at the top of your list.'

'Oh *puleeze*.' Meg's eyes glittered like bottle-green glass through her jet-black kohl eyeliner. 'The dude liked to get high and so did I and that was about all he had going for him.'

'You smoked dope with a teacher?' Jen was shocked.

'Maybe I didn't actually smoke it with him but he bought it from Herb. Quite a few of them did.'

Her pinched little face staring back at Jen in the mirror suddenly looked intense and shrewish. 'I wouldn't care,' her tone hardened now, 'but it seems suddenly you're so hot for him you've forgotten all about why we're here.'

Jen clutched the sink, feeling groggy, her head spinning from the wine and the injustice of the remark. And even if it had been true, so what? If she were just enjoying herself for once . . . How dare Meg criticise her like that? After they'd all gone so far out of their way to help her. And what was it all for, anyway?

'I don't trust Meg,' Aiden had said, the day he'd dropped her phone round. 'She's always been purely out for herself. And this

247

angel-message business, you must know it's bollocks. Been snorting angel dust more likely. What do you think she's up to?'

'She has the pact with Rowan.' Jen frowned, wondering what he was getting at.

'You believe that?'

'You don't?' She was surprised. Hadn't he been the first to suggest they help Meg? What had changed his mind?

'It makes no sense.' He shook his head. 'She's flown thousands of miles so that if her cancer proves fatal someone she hasn't seen for twenty-two years will take her kid. Think about it.'

She did. It sounded ridiculous.

'I don't think that's the whole reason she came.' She felt like a defence lawyer, handed the case with half the files missing on the morning of jury summation. 'She said she was getting medical tests.' *And her angel told her.* Did Jen believe in angels? Evidently Aiden didn't.

'For this so-called lump? What, they don't have oncologists in the States now? Has she told you any more? Like what the results were?'

'Maybe she hasn't got them back yet.' Jen had to admit she thought it odd. Surely it would be criminal to keep people in suspense this long.

'How many weeks can it take,' Aiden echoed her thoughts, 'if it's life-threatening?'

'She'll tell us when she's ready,' Jen had said firmly, dismissing the nagging memory of Meg's many childhood fabrications that had turned out to be untrue.

'I hope so. I don't trust her.' His hand landed warm and heavy on Jen's shoulder, his eyes shone with concern. 'I hate to be the old cynic saying watch your back. But watch your back.'

Now in the toilets, where they used to hide smoking between classes, Meg was staring accusingly at her as if she'd forgotten everything they were doing was all for her. The ungrateful cow.

In a rush it all came back to Jen. How jealous Meg had been of any boy who liked Jen instead of her. How tough she'd made it for her and Aiden when they first got together. Meg could be such fun, it was easy to forget she could also be incredibly self-seeking.

'It's got nothing to do with Rowan, has it?' Jen said. 'You're just rattled because Tom likes me better and you used to have a thing for him.'

'Don't be a moron.' Meg threw her a withering look. 'I'm ticked because this might be our last chance to ferret out any potential trace of Rowan and you're just pissing it away on some creep that Linda Petroski says . . .'

'Linda Petroski?' Jen felt her voice rising with anger as she forced a laugh. 'Linda Petroski, that bottle-blonde, big-bosomed gossip-chops who told us she went to Florida for her holidays and slept with Michael Jackson when everyone knew she was at a caravan site in Cheltenham with her cousin? Linda Petroski, the biggest lying slut in Ashport? She was always a dirty fat fibber.'

Too late she heard the sound of flushing water and watched the door to the last stall open.

'Jen? Jen Bedlow?' Linda Petroski emerged, giving her a welcoming smile. Linda Petroski, boobs now drooped, bleached hair now thinned, and scrawny beyond belief. 'I thought I heard your voice.'

'Linda?' Jen gulped, seeing Meg turn her back, shoulders shaking with laughter. 'How *are* you? You know, you've hardly changed at all!'

# Chapter 28

Ten past eleven and Georgina was sitting on a chair at the far end of the school gym, shoes kicked off, half listening to the results of the Guess Who quiz, when she saw Jennifer and Nutmeg, arm in arm, looking like they'd imbibed a few and giggling like they were both still fifteen.

Seeing Georgie's miserable expression, Nutmeg nudged her in a cheer-up sort of way. 'Was that Mr Panser I saw you with? Looked like you were hitting it off.'

'Looks can be deceiving,' Georgina said flatly. She'd gone to thank him for the way he treated her after the Yvonne Spitz fight and . . . 'He didn't remember me at all.' She lowered her eyes and stared hard at the floor.

'But that's good, surely?' Jennifer sounded confused. 'He's probably thrown by your transformation. Because you look so good now.'

'You mean I didn't look *so good* then?' Georgina raised her eyes to meet her friend's, and suddenly memories long suppressed came charging back. Her sweaty armpits, double chin, trying to run around the playing fields or vault the wooden horse that right now stood in the corner of the gym taunting her. Chubby Carrington, first to be ridiculed, last to have a boyfriend. Oh yes, how true was that song, love really was meant for beauty queens at seventeen. 'Go on then, say it, Jennifer. Because I'm not the big fat cow, lardy legs, buxom buttocks you all, they all, remember me as?'

'No, no of course not.' Georgina caught Jennifer looking to Nutmeg for support.

'You always had a beautiful face,' Nutmeg tried to reassure her. 'And that great olive skin. I was *so* jealous of that, babe.'

Too late. Fat tears rolled down Georgina's cheeks. She could still hear her mother's disdainful voice. *'You're not going to eat that, are you, darling?' 'No dessert for Georgina, she's on a diet.'* The heavy resignation in *'Let's see if they have that in a larger size, shall we?'*

And now her head was crowded with memories of the shouts and taunts that had haunted her days here.

*'Warning, warning. Georgie Porgie approaching pool. Watch out girls, tidal wave coming.'*

*'Heard Chubby Carrington met her soulmate at the zoo. In the hippo pond.'*

*'How do you know if Jumbo George is hiding under your bed? Because your nose is touching the ceiling.'*

'Georgina. What's the matter?' She heard Jennifer's alarmed voice coming from far away. 'Meg, she's crying.'

Would she ever have survived her schooldays if it weren't for her friends? Especially Rowan. Her dad had let her use the small shed at the bottom of the garden as an art studio and Rowan was the only one she'd invite in. They indulged their love of art together, confiding in each other as they painted.

She told Rowan things she didn't even tell Jennifer because she was worried they'd be passed on to Nutmeg, not out of malice but because she couldn't help gossiping, she loved a good story, and Georgina didn't want the bright brash Nutmeg to know what a bowl of shaking jelly they were harbouring in their foursome. But Rowan was a great listener. Not trying to fix things or give advice, just nodding sagely as she applied paint to her canvas. She'd listen for hours as Georgina explained that no matter how hard she tried, her father acted as if she were invisible and her pretty slim tennis-obsessed mother as if she were a cross she had to bear, veering between impatience, irritation and thinly veiled contempt. The only family member who truly showed her affection was her brother Lance, the elder child revered by her parents, but he wasn't home enough to make a difference and she missed him terribly.

'Don't get upset.' Jennifer was shaking her, sounding desperate. 'Everything's OK, honest.'

'No, it's all right. I'm fine,' Georgina wiped away the tears with the back of her hand, feeling her sinuses clog. She rummaged in her handbag, came up devoid of tissues, swallowed and tried to concentrate on the big round clock whose hands had always seemed to stubbornly stick in the agony of gym class.

Jennifer's arm fastened around Georgina's shoulder and Nutmeg shoved what looked like a handful of lavatory paper into her hand.

'It's clean. Blow,' she instructed. 'You're not really upset about Pansy Panser not recognising you, surely? The dude's like older than Moses, he probably doesn't recognise his own face when he shaves.'

'It's not just . . .' Georgina sniffed. 'Of course it'd have been flattering if . . . but . . . oh I don't know, this whole night, it's rather anticlimactic, don't you think? We're still no closer to finding Rowan. We've tried everything. I've even emailed half the galleries in Wales. There's just no place left to look. We have to give up. Then what will happen to us? Will we still see each other? Is this it for our friendship?'

Nutmeg squatted on her heels and held her hand. 'Course not, kiddo.'

'No way,' Jennifer agreed, kissing her cheek. 'In fact, how about you and Meg come for dinner at my place? Say Wednesday? We can crack open some bottles too and celebrate my new-found freedom. And we're not stopping searching for Rowan yet.'

'Though we're running out of places to try.' Georgina

dabbed at her mascara-streaked cheeks then blew her nose, suddenly transforming back to her usual tough, brisk self. No more foolishness, she thought. 'Don't worry, Jennifer, it's the drink talking, I always become emotional after too much wine. Dinner Wednesday sounds marvellous.'

'Great,' said Nutmeg, pulling her to her feet. 'Now let's get you to a restroom. You look like shit, *dahling*.'

'Hi Jen. Meg. Yoohoo. Remember me?'

An hour had elapsed, Jen had enjoyed two more dances with Tom, downed at least three additional glasses of wine, and was now standing next to Meg squinting squiffily at the buxom matron approaching them.

'Yvonne Spitz,' Jen smiled, stepping meaningfully, and perhaps a bit too hard, given the amount she'd drunk, on Meg's toe. 'Yes, of course.'

The tart with no heart. All through school she'd made their lives a misery. From the first day in the playground, when she and her two troll friends had so intimidated Rowan, to every day after that, particularly targeting Georgina who was petrified of them and Jen who refused to suck up like everyone else.

'Look who it isn't,' she'd sneer, banging their locker doors closed just as they were reaching in to pull out their books, flanked on each side by her cronies, Linda Petroski and Maureen Reynolds.

'Taffy, the arty one.'

'You're forgetting the t,' Maureen would scream. 'Crazy as her mammy.'

'And Jumbo, the elephant girl, Jenny Wren, her trained monkey and dippy hippy Meg. I didn't know the lesbo circus was in town. Did anyone bring peanuts?'

And Linda and Maureen would laugh while Meg leaned against her locker, looking bored, Rowan went white, Georgina stared miserably at her sensible lace-up shoes and Jen clenched her fists in fury. Yvonne and her two accomplices had rushed into puberty at an age when their peers were still crayoning in the kiddies' menu at restaurants. They flaunted their extra height, muscle and mammary glands while Jen et al were still wearing vests and Princess knickers. The arrival of Yvonne in a classroom, slinging books on the desk with a thump, chewing gum and commenting rudely on the teacher's hair/clothes/sexual orientation could make the most seasoned educator stammer in fear.

No one would have guessed, staring at the powdered and blue-eye-shadowed woman facing Jen and Meg, that this was the bully who'd sneered at Jen for living on a council estate, stolen their towels when they were in the showers and who'd eternally hung around by the bike sheds, hoping to catch one of them alone. Yvonne Spitz, the adult, looked like Lily Savage on a big night out. Over-made-up, puffy-faced and excessively twinkling with diamanté, she was wearing an expensive-looking strapless sequinned dress and had finished the look with piled-high-to-the-ceiling hair.

'Hey, did you hear Wendy Lugden's a priest now?' Yvonne addressed them both. 'What a hoot, eh, she was the school's biggest scrubber.'

Discretion won over Jen's desire to tell her she'd always thought Yvonne and Linda deserved to share Wendy's title.

'And how about you, Yvonne?' said Meg coolly. 'They let you out of the big house then?'

Yvonne laughed, missing entirely Meg's suggestion that she'd probably done jail time. 'Oh, we're still living in it. No, I'm divorced, divorced and divorced again. My latest beau is a top insurance salesman, took me to Thailand last year on an all-expenses first-class trip. And I've two wonderful children, a boy called Darren and a girl called Pearl. Want to see a photo?'

A plump-faced boy and a curly-haired red-faced girl were smiling inanely by a paddling pool, and Yvonne was in the background in a too-small garish striped bikini, her muffin-top spilling over the waistline.

'Sweet.' Meg made a face, unseen by Yvonne, and passed the photo over to Jen.

'And how's life treating you both?'

'Well, I'm—' Jen began.

'Hey, Meg, remember that Graham Furrow I went out with?' Yvonne interrupted.

'Sure, I do,' said Meg. 'He was—'

'Sexy? I know. Do you think he's here tonight?'

No, but someone *had* mentioned him. Jen saw her chance for revenge.

'You remember Phyllis Ifold?' Another poor sod Yvonne used to bully relentlessly.

'That weed? Yeah, why?' Her peppercorn eyes quickly scanned the hall.

'She's his wife.' Jen took a fortifying gulp from her paper cup and gave a sly wink to a surprised Meg.

'Graham Furrow married Phyllis Ifold? I don't believe it!'

'It was a shock to everyone,' said Jen. 'One minute Phyllis was a lank-haired, big-lipped sort of scruff-bag and then she started working for a fashion mag and became all glamorous. Isn't that right, Meg?'

'Graham was totally besotted,' agreed Meg, catching on.

'How did you find all this out?' Yvonne looked from one to the other, her expression aghast.

'Doreen Mansfield,' Jen informed her. 'She spent half an hour rabbiting on how Phyllis and Graham honeymooned in Mnemba.'

'Mnemba?'

'North-east tip of Zanzibar.'

'And they have four blond-haired, blue-eyed, delightful children,' elaborated, Meg as Jen pretended to concentrate very hard on the bottom of her glass.

'God!'

'Though now she produces blockbuster films,' added Meg. 'They have a swimming pool, large open-plan house and a clear view of the Hollywood sign, so Doreen says.'

'Christ!' Yvonne's face drained of colour. 'You'd never imagine, would you?'

'You never would, Yvonne.' Jen nodded her head. 'You truly never would.'

Meg turned her back, her shoulders shaking.

Yvonne moodily swirled her glass of punch.

'Next you'll be telling me Georgina Carrington's a super-model. Think she's still a chubby-chops?' She leant forward conspiratorially, earning Jen's enmity all over again.

'See for yourself,' said Jen, beckoning Georgie from across the room.

Yvonne stared transfixed as Georgina swanned over, all trace of the evening's earlier blues wiped away. She looked incredible in her emerald-green taffeta dress, the plunging neckline very Sophia Loren, her plum lipstick emphasising the Italian curve of her mouth. For a moment Jen experienced an unaccustomed pang of envy. Who would have thought that out of all of them, Georgina would have turned into such a beauty?

'Georgina? Georgina Carrington?' Words failed Yvonne.

Georgina glanced down her nose with a patrician air worthy of a Roman empress.

'Yvonne. I hardly recognised you. Nice dress.'

Yvonne preened, smoothing it with her hands. 'It ought to be. I paid a fortune for it. Giordani, you know.'

Georgina took a studied sip of wine before she spoke.

'I beg to differ.'

'Sorry?' Yvonne looked radically startled, much like the time in third year Jen had completely lost it and run at her, pulling hair and biting. She'd been well and truly beaten up in return, of course, but Jen had staggered away happy in the knowledge she'd left Yvonne with a black eye and bleeding lip.

'It's a cheap imitation, darling.' Georgina's accent had never sounded so posh. 'Hong Kong knock-off. We had rather a problem with those. Thought we'd rounded them all up but apparently not.'

Georgina's enormous multicarat diamond flashed as she flicked back her hair with one hand and stalked off to find Max.

'Of all the nerve!' Yvonne stared after her. 'What would she know about designer clothes?'

'A lot, I imagine,' Jen answered. 'Georgina *is* Giordani. Georgina *Giordani* Carrington. Designer, owner, the whole shebang.'

'We came here in her company limo,' added Meg. 'That's her chauffeur, Max, she's talking to now. We should probably get going soon.'

At that moment, the look on Yvonne's face was worth the disappointment of not finding Rowan.

Heading over to Georgina, Jen spotted Doreen Mansfield. 'You've heard from Phyllis and she's a famous film producer, living in Beverly Hills married to that sexy Graham Furrow, pass it on . . .' she whispered.

'No she's not. I told you earlier, she works in Tesco, Carlisle.'

'That's not what I told Yvonne Spitz,' Jen said, winking.

'You are awful, Jen Bedlow,' Doreen sniggered.

Jen caught up with Georgina and Meg, radiant in their triumph.

'Elephants never forget, darling,' Georgina said, grinning at Jen.

'Never mess with a monkey,' Jen replied.

They glanced at Meg, knowing what she was about to say.

'Hippies rule!' they shrieked together, throwing their arms around each other and bracing the cold outside, where Max and the car awaited.

# Chapter 29

Jen took another big gasp of breath as she jogged slowly along the top of the ridge. No amount of fresh air was going to beat this hangover, she thought, accepting defeat and resting against a fence. She was at the highest point for miles around, with views right down into central Huntsleigh, the wind whistling through the pines. Bending over to battle her nausea, she spotted someone approaching from one of the tiny tracks that led from the wood below. With a lurch of surprise she recognised Aiden, hair blowing wildly in the breeze, his coat flapping.

'Aiden?' The wind was whipping her own hair in her face, a problem she'd never had when it was shorter.

'So this is how you pass your time,' he said, smiling. 'Are you walking or running?'

'Slow jog till I feel sick, then walking. What are you doing here?'

'I decided to drop by and then I saw a Toyota in your drive and some bloke rummaging around in it. Didn't want to make any embarrassing house calls in case that was the legendary ex.'

'Well it was an ex, but teacher, not husband. It was Tom Dugan, our old English teacher. I drunkenly left my bag at the party and he was kind enough to call this morning to offer to drop it round.'

'Oh, lucky he had your number, eh?' He looked at her imploringly but she chose not to rise to it. 'Quite a habit of yours, leaving things behind.'

'How did you know I was here, though?'

'I followed you. I'm parked back there.' He gestured the way he'd come.

Her mind did a quick calculation. He must have sat outside her house while Tom came back from the car, drank his coffee, accepted her biscuits, chatted about old times and admired her wall lights. God. Was Aiden really waiting all that time *just to see her*?

'OK,' Jen said slowly. Aiden didn't seem to want to offer any further reason for his visit, so she suggested he walk with her.

Aiden squinted down at her, matching his stride with hers.

'How's the hangover?'

'I only had a few glasses of wine. And some punch. So did Georgina send you to check up on me, then?' Silly, but she was actually disappointed. Seeing him magically appear like that had been the stuff of her fantasies for years. Would she ever get over those days of longing for just such an encounter? Only in none of those fantasies had he been a married man.

'No, actually. I came of my own accord, believe it or not. So who's this Dugan chap? Sounds like he's going out of his way to please you?' He arched a brow.

'He's just a . . . a friend, I guess. We had fun last night and he's nice. And it was nice of him to bring my bag round. It's what *friends* do. I get the impression he's actually a little lonely.'

'Wasn't lonely at the party, though, from what Georgina was saying about you two dancing all night.' He made it a statement, his dark eyes fixing on her face as she swept her hair out of her stinging eyes.

'I suppose he wasn't.' She tossed her head, inwardly pleased he was taking an interest, wanting to push his buttons a bit.

'I'm sorry, Jen. We weren't gossiping about you. We feel

protective towards you, that's all. Don't want you taken advantage of.'

'Me, taken advantage of? Does Georgie think she's my mum now or what?'

'Her words, not mine. Georgina said that the four of you always looked out for each other. Has all these wonderful stories about you jumping into battle for her whenever she was threatened.' He shoved his gloveless hands in his coat pockets. 'Actually that's why I wanted to speak to you. She seemed upset last night. I couldn't understand half what she was babbling on about.' He paused, deep in thought, and Jen cursed herself for thinking Aiden had stalked her out of jealousy. 'Was she picked on a lot?' he said finally.

'We all were. Well, really just the usual playground taunts but Georgina probably got it most because of her size – you know how kids are.' She felt uncomfortable, almost disloyal, discussing his wife's old weight problem. 'And I think it all came flooding back at the reunion, she got very upset at one point. But after that she seemed to be having a good time. I thought she enjoyed herself.'

'Probably just the drink talking,' Aiden replied, stopping on the lee side of a giant elm. 'She was in a weird mood but that's not so unusual these days. If you're sure she's OK, I won't bother you again.'

'You're not bothering me.'

They fell awkwardly silent, so when Jen spotted Feo trotting on the path as it dipped ahead of them, and Anamaria's mauve ski hat with the pixie bobbles appearing over the rise of the hill, she was half relieved but equally panicked at the prospect of Anamaria meeting Aiden. There was no guessing what she'd say.

'Listen we . . . I . . . I ought to get back.' She pivoted on her heel, dragging him with her. 'I don't think we should be discussing Georgina like this. She wouldn't like it.'

She glanced behind her. Anamaria was drawing nearer, her fur-trimmed boots apparently sprouting wings. 'Quick, over here!'

She grabbed Aiden's arm, pulling him hastily down a steep narrow path.

'Hey!' he protested. 'Where's the fire?'

'It's . . . it's my boss!'

'Your boss?' Automatically Aiden's head swerved round. 'I thought you did voluntary work.'

'Yes, but with some very peculiar people.' Jen stepped over a log, rapidly increasing the distance between them and their pursuer.

'She's your boss?' Aiden whispered as he carefully studied the Spanish girl through a gap in a thicket. 'Cute, cute, cute.'

'As a viper.' Jen kicked a branch away. 'And wildly eccentric. Trying to dump her dog on everyone.'

They both watched through the thicket. Feo raced over to a rook, causing it to take flight. Anamaria had stayed on the main path. Perhaps she hadn't seen Jen.

'That scrawny thing's a dog?' Aiden asked. 'Looks like someone's hairpiece come to life.'

As they returned in Aiden's car, Jen was horrified to see Ollie's orange camper van in the driveway. Just what she needed. Worse, Ollie was outside, with a hammer in his hand, doing something to their front door.

'Oops,' Aiden said, seeing her can't-we-just-reverse-fast expression. 'Is that him?'

'Yes, but it doesn't matter, does it? We are divorced.'

'Yes, but he does have a bloody big hammer,' Aiden jested as he switched off the engine.

Stepping out the car, Jen's skin prickled under Ollie's gaze, her heart aching as she saw what he was putting up.

'Nice wreath,' Aiden said lightly as Ollie walked towards

them. He wasn't wearing a jacket, of course. Only a regular cotton shirt when she and Aiden and anyone with a grain of sense were bundled under more layers than a polar explorer.

'Thanks.' Ollie's eyes were unusually cold for a man who made friends every time he poked his nose outdoors. It was obvious he knew who was on his doorstep, even if they'd never met before.

The two of them sized each other up like master swordsmen about to duel for a lady's honour, a slight smile creasing Aiden's well-formed lips, Ollie's face devoid of welcome. He was quite a bit shorter than Aiden, by about five inches, but still a muscular powerhouse compared to Aiden's lanky slender frame. Jen felt ridiculously proud that Aiden could see her ex-husband was handsome, clever and worth showing off, certainly no wimp or geek to be trifled with. Maybe she herself wasn't a veritable supermodel, but let it be noted her standards were high. (Take *that*, Mr 'Cute Cute Cute'.)

Politely Ollie held out his hand. 'Aiden Starkson, I assume?'

'You guessed it.' Aiden shook hands, smiling cheerfully.

'Reunion a success then, was it?' Ollie looked from one to the other.

'Great!' Her voice was too high. 'You're back early. I wasn't expecting you till this afternoon.'

'Obviously.' His tone was even, but Jen felt a sting of anger. How dare he assume whatever it was he was assuming. Why couldn't she have male friends?

'Well, I'd better get back to my wife.' Aiden bent to kiss Jen on the cheek.

'Yes, maybe you'd better.' Hostility crackled in the air as Ollie spoke. The back of Jen's neck grew hot as she prepared to crawl under a rock. And she'd thought it was bad in her teens when her dad would emerge to chat to her friends and embarrass her something rotten with his silly sayings.

'Was that really necessary?' she hissed as Aiden drove away.

'You mean our ill-timed intrusion?' Ollie's eyes were veiled. 'Sorry, but Chloe was anxious to get home, show you what she and Mum made us.' He gestured at the wreath. 'Extremely appropriate, I'd say.'

'So who was he?' enquired Anamaria as they sat down over a sandwich in the back room of the shop the next afternoon.

'Who was who?' Damn, she thought she'd got away with it. Anamaria had evidently been waiting to get Jen on her own.

'I saw you up on the heath. Both of you, disappearing off into the mists like big yetis.'

'Oh that, er, yes, well, that was Aiden.'

'Aiden, you say.' Her eyes stayed glued to the table where she'd set out another jigsaw puzzle. Jen thought it was a Constable painting, but she couldn't be entirely certain as it had come with no box. 'The one that is the husband of your best friend, yes?'

'I've barely seen her in the last twenty years.'

'Whatever.' She plonked the four blue corners of the puzzle on to a tray and began looking for edge pieces. 'The man that means nothing to you, but yet your face turns cherry whenever you speak about him.'

Jen put on a snooty voice. 'I've no idea what you're talking about.'

Saved by her mobile.

'So how was the reunion then?' Helen trilled, sounding remarkably happy considering that the last time they'd spoken she'd ended up slamming down the phone.

'Better than expected.' She turned her back on Anamaria. 'Helen, I so apologise about the other . . .'

'No matter.' One thing about Helen, she didn't hang on to grievances. Give her some time to cool down and she'd act like nothing had happened. 'What are you doing tonight? Fancy Malaysian?'

'Oh Helen, I can't. I need to spend some quality time with Chloe. I've not seen her all weekend.'

'I thought Ollie would be stepping up to the plate.'

'He had her Saturday. And she's going to his on Wednesday.'

Anamaria's head was bent examining the puzzle pieces, but Jen could practically see her ears flapping.

'Wednesday then? If you don't fancy the karaoke at that new wine bar I mentioned, we could grab a pizza, open some wine, watch a slushy film.'

'I can't do that either,' Jen gulped. She had a feeling this wasn't going to go well. Helen's resilience could only stretch so far.

'Oh?'

'It's, well, I'm really really sorry, Helen, but . . .' she flinched, hardly daring to say the words. 'I'm having friends round.'

'*I'm* a friend,' Helen said pointedly.

'I know. But . . .'

'Don't tell me. Ex-classmates and I'm not invited.'

'It's not that . . .'

'Don't worry, I can take a hint.' Slam.

Damn, she thought too late, why hadn't she made something up? A parent—teacher conference. An evening class in Mandarin Chinese. Helen was just too used to her lack of social life, to Jen being available whenever she chose to call.

'Just a friend.' Jen saw Anamaria watching.

'You were telling me about your other *friend*. This Aiden.' The girl was relentless.

'His mum's died,' Jen said hopefully. It was true. Happened when he was a kid, but all the same.

'Why is he coming to visit you?'

'We bumped into each other.'

'*Dios mio*! What a coincidence.'

'Georgina sent him.'

'And he dropped everything on a Sunday morning to *please*

her?' Her tone was sarcastic, her expression disbelieving. 'He is a very good little boy, no? Or is it possible he still feels for you?'

'He has friendly feelings. More like a big brother.' Jen didn't need a mirror to realise she was puce again. 'He came to tell me she's broken a leg.' Bugger. Why did she say that? Anamaria was getting her all confused. Only when it might have helped with Helen had her inventiveness failed her.

'Who? His deceased mother? What, after the rigor mortis set in?' She added another jigsaw piece along the side. 'Liar, liar, pants on fire.'

'I'm not. Don't be silly.'

'Are you meeting him up there a lot?'

Jen swallowed. 'It's the first time.'

'Are you sure?' Her coal-black eyes turned to menacing slits.

'Sure I'm sure,' Jen said more forcefully. Searching for a change of subject, inspiration struck. 'Anamaria, I've been thinking. It's going to be lonely with Ollie gone and Chloe staying over with him, so how about I take Feo? *Only* until you get back, though.'

Anamaria's expression instantly changed from frowning to smiling.

'You will? *Estupendo!*' Anamaria hugged her, then noticing a customer waiting by the till, she went to the front of the shop.

Jen gulped. *Now what had she got herself into?*

# Chapter 30

Monday evening. Chloe was on the phone to Ollie. So bizarre to think that he was only a mile away, his second night in Saul's house, yet Jen felt he'd never been so far from her – not even in Tanzania – and the distance seemed to be rapidly increasing.

Chloe was bubbling with excitement. 'We're getting a dog. Yes, a real one. Mum told me. No, I'm not sure what kind. Maybe a cuddly little puppy.'

'It isn't a puppy,' Jen said but it went unheard. 'And it definitely ain't cuddly.' She'd been having misgivings since the moment she'd suggested this to Anamaria. Probably she ought to have told Ollie first, but Chloe had been so full of stories of all, the things she and Daddy had done at Grandma's that somehow it had just slipped out. After all, she had to know sometime. Anamaria was leaving on Wednesday.

'Course I'm not fibbing. Mum, he wants to talk to you.' Chloe held out the phone.

'A dog, eh?' Ollie didn't sound nearly as excited as his daughter.

'Temporarily only. I'm helping out a friend.'

A sound resembling a cat being strangled permeated the air.

'Is that Chloe on the violin?' he asked.

'Yes, well, at least she's practising.'

'I thought we weren't going to do this,' Ollie said flatly, with just a hint of accusation.

'Do what?'

'You know. The divorced thing. Who can spoil Chloe the most, get the nicest Christmas present, best holiday. The tug-of-war syndrome.'

'We aren't. I wouldn't!'

'No?' He clearly didn't believe her. 'All these years we wanted a dog and you were against it. I'm gone five minutes and suddenly it's time to get Chloe a pet. You know, Jen, I'd never guess you'd stoop so low.'

She put the phone down feeling abused and misunderstood. Bugger Ollie. That did it. Feo was definitely staying.

'Lace is in right now. Off-the-shoulder tops. Tiered ruffle dresses. Over-the-knee boots. And, oh yes, ripped jeans are coming back.' Chloe riffled through the Monsoon sales rack. Jen's eyes met the sales assistant's above Chloe's head. The girl, in her early twenties at the most, shrugged. 'What can I say,' she yawned. 'Kid's right.'

'How do you know all this?' Jen had just bought her daughter a new pair of trousers, a T-shirt and a hooded sweatshirt top. 'I can't get you out of jeans and hoodies.'

Chloe pushed out her lower lip like a pouting French actress. 'I stay in touch,' she said airily. 'Kelsey's sister likes fashion mags.'

It was Tuesday evening. The last splurge before the belt-tightening began in earnest. Jen had spent the morning at the charity shop, the afternoon looking through the papers, circling potential jobs. There were scarily few of them in Huntsleigh, and nothing that appealed. But could she afford to be picky when travelling up to London was out of the question for as long as Chloe finished school at three thirty? Why, oh why, hadn't she taken those evening classes after all, worked to get some more qualifications? Even a few computer courses would have helped.

Somehow, after picking up a small number of essentials for Chloe they'd been drawn to the '70% Off' sale sign across the street.

'Well I'm not buying anything off the shoulder,' Jen said decidedly. 'I already went through that once.'

'Oh I don't mean for mums.' Chloe burst her tiny bubble of confidence without even trying. 'But this colour would look good on you.' She held out a light green sweetheart-neck blouse, too summery for the season, which was undoubtedly why it was on the rack.

'Maybe, but are you sure it's my style?' Doubtfully Jen fingered the material. Lace sleeves, she noted. Did that make it trendy? 'I suppose I'll need work gear when I get a job.' She tried to forget the fact that most of her clothes were eminently suitable for any job that wasn't in high fashion or down a sewer.

'How about this?' She held up a white T-shirt. Chloe wrinkled her nose. 'Bo-o-ring.' She started yanking clothes from the rail as if Jen were some poor unfortunate fashion victim and Chloe a junior Trinny or Susannah blessed with a huge TV makeover budget.

'This is well nice. And this. And try this on. It's dead cheap, Mum. Seventy per cent off. Think of all the money you're saving.'

Money she ought not to be spending at all, she thought. She fingered the last item, a slinky satin dress of the kind she hadn't worn in years. She could almost hear Ollie wolf-whistle.

'Great for Christmas parties,' the assistant offered, more interested now.

'I doubt there'll be any this Christmas,' Jen said involuntarily, then could have bitten her tongue out, not wanting to inflict her pessimism on Chloe. She gave a heavy sigh.

'OK,' she said. 'Which way is the changing room?'

*

On Wednesday Chloe took her pyjamas and clean clothes to school for her first sleepover at Saul's. Jen was irrationally nervous about Meg and Georgina's imminent arrival.

After a mad cleaning frenzy she'd worried it might all be too immaculate, so scattered some magazines on to the coffee table before deciding they looked out of place and tidying them away again.

How sterile it looked. Why had she never noticed before? Georgina had managed a blend of style and comfort that appeared effortless, to the manor born – or hired a great interior decorator.

Jen looked around, thinking she'd seen hotel rooms with more personality. All their old Islington clutter, Chloe's first masterpieces, Jen's photos, the trinkets and souvenirs from the early years of their marriage lay packed in boxes in the attic or had gone to the charity shop.

She'd always believed this a triumph. Goodbye dust collectors, hello gleaming surfaces. But since she rarely had visitors, really why did it matter? And Ollie wasn't one of these neurotic husbands who objected to a little squalor. When she first moved in with him, they'd existed for a whole year without owning a Hoover.

Meg looked slightly shocked as she came through the door. 'Jesus! White carpet.' Georgina followed her in, smiling politely and nodding approvingly. Jen suspected this was entirely put on.

'It's cream.' Jen squirmed. 'It came with the house.'

'It's like I'm walking through a deep freeze.' Meg prowled around, inspecting her surroundings. 'Where's the colour, the muck, the reality, man?'

'I hope you left it at the door when you wiped your feet,' Jen retaliated, feeling childishly stung.

'White represents the energy of metal in the five-element system of feng shui,' Meg pronounced. 'This house is completely out of balance. You need to put in some reds and oranges, moderate it with fire.'

'Well, I think it's terrific. Very modern and so, so, uh . . . clean,' Georgina soothed.

'Great. Because it's just about sold.' The hell with feng shui, Jen thought.

'Well then, let's drink to Jen's new life.' Meg held up a bottle. 'I've brought wine.' She put it on the worktop and instantly recoiled. 'Crap, what's that? A giant guinea pig?'

Jen followed her gaze. Feo had emerged from the basket in which he'd been sulking since a tearful Anamaria had dropped him off that afternoon. In all her childhood longings for a pet – dog, cat, even a white mouse – never had she imagined a Feo. In size he was somewhere between a cairn and a chihuahua, with an air that suggested he fondly believed himself to be a Great Dane. His back was long, his legs mere stumps and his coarse shaggy coat might have been cute if it wasn't so sparse, failing to hide his bulging eyes. But here he was, strutting up, convinced that new visitors meant worship and food treats.

'That's Feo.' Jen still couldn't believe she'd let the creature in her house. Muddy paws aside, you only had to look at the mutt and a few hundred more dog hairs would launch themselves into orbit. 'I'm taking care of him for a friend.'

'Oh, isn't he, he's very . . . What an interesting name,' Georgina fudged.

'Means ugly.'

'Very appropriate,' she said smoothly.

And suddenly everyone was laughing and Jen's attack of nerves melted away.

Two hours later the remains of their takeaway lay alongside three almost empty wine bottles. Someone should really clear that mess, Jen thought fuzzily. But blowed if she could be arsed.

'So what shall we do now?' said Georgina, her unfocused eyes resting on Jen. Like the wine bottles the three women sat side by side on the floor, slouched against the beige sofa.

'Sleep,' said Jen, holding her head.

'You can sleep when you're dead. Hey, I know,' Meg turned to her, 'what about the truth game?'

'Truth game?' Georgina squeaked.

'People ask all sorts of personal questions and you have to answer with the total truth.'

'Oh, yeah.' Jen wiggled her toes in her socks. 'We played it once at the shipping agency I worked in. One of the partners told a filing clerk that he fancied her.'

'And?'

'She said he made her physically sick. She got laid off two weeks later.'

Georgina slapped her hand down hard on the armrest. 'Let's play it. You go first, Nutmeg.'

'Jennifer Bedlow,' Meg started. 'What truthfully happened between you and Dastardly Dugan the other night? Did he or did he not try to jump your bones? I saw you two come into the gym together and then start dancing all smoochie-smoo.'

Jen blew a raspberry. 'No, he was the perfect gentleman. My turn. Nutmeg Lennox, do you really have an angel sitting on your shoulder?'

'Not on my shoulder. But . . .' She jumped in hastily as the other two whooped. 'I do have an angel guide.'

'Does she know you're atheist?' Georgina sniggered from the other side of Jen.

'What does she do?' Jen was trying to maintain an expression of sincere interest on her face while ripples of mirth ran around inside her chest.

'It's a he.'

'Figures,' Georgina muttered, blowing a lock of hair from her face.

'Probably called Charlie,' whispered Jen in her ear. 'No wait, Charlie wasn't an angel, was he?'

'He sends me messages from the other side,' Meg added.

'Other side of what? The psycho ward?' Jen had to force

271

herself not to glance at Georgina when she muttered this or she knew they'd both be lost.

'The spirit world, where else?' Meg closed her eyes for a second.

'And how many spirits are usually involved?' asked Georgina.

'How did you meet her, I mean him?' Jen rushed in.

'I studied reiki.' Meg turned her head so that her nose was inches from Jen's. 'Energy healing. And massage. And one day I was working on a friend and there was this glow by the ceiling.'

'It's called a light bulb,' Georgina whispered in Jen's opposite ear. Jen, struggling to contain herself, let out an unintentional snort.

'No, it fucking wasn't.' Meg had heard. 'It was my angel.' She feigned outrage.

'Weren't you scared?' Jen bit her cheek.

'Nah,' Meg said dismissively. 'I have this indescribable feeling of serenity when he appears. Isn't it someone else's turn?'

'No. It's interesting. Does he speak?' Jen waved her glass at Georgina, who topped it up.

'Yes, but only I can hear him. In my head. He sends me messages for people.'

'And have you any messages from us?' Jen squinted at the lampshade above her head, squeezing her lids tighter to see if she could turn the glow into an angel.

'From you?' Meg said, confused. 'But you're both alive.'

'Oh, you have to be dead?' Jen couldn't help it. The laughter she'd been holding back erupted.

'You bet your sweet ass you do.' Meg grabbed a cushion from the sofa and started bashing them as Jen and Georgina fell about helplessly. 'And he says you're a pair of lowlife bozos who can go to hell.'

'Very angelic,' Georgina hooted, dodging another blow from Meg.

'Right, you next.' Meg picked up her glass again and leaned over Jen to look at Georgina. 'Georgina Giordani Carrington,' she slurred, 'who made the first move – you or Starkey?'

Georgina and Jen both froze. Jen felt her sweat prickle under her armpits, her mouth suddenly dry. She couldn't look at Georgina but she could feel the horrible tension emanating from both of them. Luckily the phone rang, giving Jen an excuse to leap for it.

'Hello? Oh hello there, Tom.' Mistake. Big mistake.

Meg and Georgina broke into deafening cheers and catcalls, rolling up their sleeves and kissing their arms with loud slurping noises.

'Sorry? Oh that. It's the TV. Some nature show. About shrieking gannets.' Furiously she flapped her hand for silence.

'Hope I'm not catching you at a bad time,' Tom said cheerfully, as the din abated. 'Just wanted to tell you how much I enjoyed the other evening.'

'Me too.' She was scarlet to her roots under two pairs of avidly curious eyes.

'Maybe we can do it again sometime?'

'Maybe. Uh,' she glanced at the eavesdroppers, 'this isn't the best time for me to talk. I've got friends for dinner.'

'Talking of friends, I was wondering if you're still searching for Rowan Howard?'

'Uh, yes.' She gave a significant look at Meg and Georgina.

'Well, it's a long shot but it occurred to me you could try contacting Gwyneth Minksheaf. If you haven't already, that is?'

'Gwyneth Minksheaf?' The hairs on Jen's arms rose one by one.

'Yes, she and Rowan were soloists in the school choir – always chit-chatting. And I seem to remember the two mothers were close, too. Both being from Wales.'

'That's a great idea. I can't believe we forgot about her. Thank you, Tom.' Saying goodbye, she hung up. 'Ladies, we have a lead. Tom's just remembered Rowan was in choir with Gwyneth Minksheaf.'

'Gwyneth Minksheaf?' Georgina looked bewildered.

'We used to call her Blodwyn,' Meg reminded her. 'Blodwyn Mineshaft – a total dweeb.'

Jen groaned. 'I spent years trying to erase the girl from my mind.'

Now Georgina looked even more bewildered.

'In second year,' Meg explained, 'Jen telephoned Kevin Matthews, faking a terrible Welsh accent, and said, "Hello Kevin, boyo. It's Gwyneth here. I really love you."'

'I've always felt bad about that,' Jen confessed.

'Doesn't sound so awful,' said Georgina.

'No,' Jen agreed, 'but Meg egged me on. I ended up saying I'd strip naked for him on his birthday.'

Meg grinned. 'Let's ring her now,' she said, leaping to her feet. 'Where's your computer, Jen?' Her beady eyes caught sight of Chloe's laptop on the dining table. Purposefully she settled in front of the screen and began tapping.

'Let's stick to southern England, shall we? Minksheaf's an unusual name.' Meg scrolled down, as the other two huddled behind her.

'There's only ten of them. We'll call three each. Now.'

'Three times three is nine,' Jen protested. 'And I'm not doing it.'

'I'll do the extra one. Oh come on, you party poopers. How are we ever going to find Rowan if we don't explore *every* avenue?' She grabbed the phone and began pressing numbers. 'It's ringing . . . Hello, Mrs Minksheaf? No, I'm not selling anything, ma'am. I'm looking for a Gwyneth Minksheaf . . . no, no, sure, right . . . Thanks.' She hung up. 'Darn, and they were tucked up in bed. Your turn, Jen.' Meg held out the phone.

'I'm not bloody doing it!'

Meg flapped her elbows like a bird. 'Chicken, chicken. Cluck, cluck.'

'Give it here.' Jen began dialling. 'Cluck bloody cluck yourself.'

'I beg your pardon?' A startled voice spoke in her ear.

'Hello, Mr Mineshaf— Minksheaf?'

'Yes.'

'This is an old friend of Gwyneth's.'

'I think you have the wrong number.'

'I do? So sorry. Goodbye.' She put the phone down, deflated. 'Over to you, Georgina. Eight to go.'

'Never mind who I am, young man.' Georgina was on her second phone call. 'Write this down. Have you a pencil? Social Services. Capital S, Capital S. Now off you pop to bed and don't forget to brush your teeth.'

She replaced the receiver and shook her head. 'Only eleven and at home alone at this time of night. Probably watching all sorts on television. Some parents!'

Meg took the phone. 'You're too much, Georgie.' She was still laughing as her call was answered. 'Miss Minksheaf? Mrs Minksheaf, hello, my name is Meg and I wondered if you know a Gwyneth Minksheaf, she used to attend . . .'

'Yes I do that,' Mrs Minksheaf said in a thick Welsh accent.

'You do?' Meg's eyes widened.

'She's my daughter. Is this urgent?' Gwyneth's mother sounded elderly, shaky voice.

'Erm, yes, it's very urgent. A mutual friend of ours has died and there's a funeral tomorrow. Do you have her cell number? Oh thanks so much, yeah it was real sad.' She gave a little sniff indicating to Jen to fetch her paper and pen, and scribbled down the number before thanking her and hanging up. She turned to the others. 'Right, who wants to do the honours?' They both pointed at Meg. Sighing, she dialled the number she'd just jotted down.

'Gwyneth, hi. It's Meg Lennox. From Ashport Comp . . . Yes, the American. Yes, ages. I'm afraid I had to tell your mum somebody died to get your number . . . No, nobody did. Well apart from Isobel Benjamin. Farting Frank's wife.' She chuckled. 'He probably . . . About a month ago, I think.' She looked helplessly at the other two. 'They had a memorial . . . I don't know . . . Oh Gwyneth, I'm sorry, I had no idea you were friends. Yes, it was lovely, lots of people came to pay respects. Anyway, the reason I'm calling is I was hoping you might be in touch with Rowan Howard? Oh, did she? Where? Oh, I see . . . Georgina? Yeah, we still speak . . . Yes, she is, to that guy Jen went out with.' She gave Georgina and Jen a quick apologetic smile. 'What's that? Jen?' Her grin stretched wider. 'Yeah. Yeah I know. Oh, that's wicked. Yeah, some people, eh? Right, well then, see you around maybe.'

Meg danced triumphant in front of them, forcing them to follow as she capered into Jen's kitchen. 'Want the news? Gwyneth was broken-hearted Isobel died, happy to hear I'm back in the country and said she'd always hated Jen since she played that practical joke. It went round the school that she was a stripper and she's had therapy ever since.'

'No!' Jen screamed in embarrassment. She grabbed the percolator and began scooping in spoons of coffee.

'OK, so I lied about the therapy. Apparently her mum told her Rowan had gotten into some kind of trouble.'

'What kind of trouble?' Jen's hand jerked, promptly spilling coffee on to the counter.

'She doesn't know but she thinks the whole family moved to Totnes. In Devon.' Her eyes twinkled. 'Let's go there. This weekend. We're on to something, I can feel it in my bones.'

'I don't know,' Georgina said. 'It's an exceedingly long way. And it means more time off.'

'So what? You're the boss,' Meg argued.

'I'll have to get Ollie to take Chloe,' Jen reflected. 'But what shall I do about the damned dog?' She took a step and a sudden dampness seeped into her sock. 'What the . . . ?'

There was a dubious puddle on the Italian tiles. All eyes went from it to Feo, who put his tail down and skulked shamefaced back to his dog bed.

Gleefully Meg slapped Jen on the back.

'Don't worry, dude. Your house won't stay white for long.'

# Chapter 31

For the second time that week Jen woke with an aching head. To think she'd thought her partying days behind her. There was life in the old dog yet, she mused, pulling herself out of bed and dragging on clothes. And talking of old dogs, there was another puddle in the hall. Cursing Anamaria, she opened the back door and let Feo into the garden.

The house seemed strangely empty. No Chloe to take to school, no Ollie reading the newspaper. She sat at the kitchen table drinking tea, while the radio blared, feeling apathetic and unmotivated. She wasn't scheduled to work today. Perhaps a bath would pep her up.

She was adding more cold water to the steaming tub when she heard the phone. By the time she found it – oops, so it wasn't always Ollie who failed to return it to its cradle – it had stopped ringing.

Returning to the bathroom, she checked the water temperature then pressed 1571 to retrieve her messages.

She was affronted by Helen's huffy voice. 'I know you're probably *much* too busy but we switched our wine-bar evening to tonight if you're interested.'

Interested? In her current state a root-canal treatment sounded more appealing, but Helen's tone made it clear she was feeling neglected, and rightfully so. Jen stepped into the oval bath and punched in 14713.

'Hello?' Helen sounded posher than usual.

'Hi, it's Jen. I'm in the bath.'

'Hello?' Confusing. Another voice, a man's, his line buzzing strangely. Did Helen have someone staying over?

Bugger. It wasn't Helen at all. It was Aiden. And Georgina. On different extensions. Instantly she became hyper-aware of her nakedness, the noise of water slopping.

'I've got it, Aiden. It's Jennifer. Calling from the bath, lucky duck. What can I do for you? You must have second sight.'

'Umm, why?' Jen's tired brain creaked into gear. She'd redialled the last number that had called her. Clearly it hadn't been Helen and evidently Georgina knew nothing about it. Which left . . . There was a click on the line and the buzzing stopped. Aiden.

'Because I'm not in the office, obviously,' Georgina said gaily. 'Too incapacitated after that vast amount of wine last night.'

'Oh, right . . . I was just going to leave you a message.' Her mind scrabbled about for an excuse to have been calling. 'About Totnes.'

'You *are* a mind-reader. I was just going to email my secretary to look for accommodation. Would you and Nutmeg like twin beds or would you prefer your own rooms? I hope you don't mind but I have this thing about sharing. I'm an atrocious snorer, Aiden will testify.'

'I thought you were too busy. I haven't even asked Ollie yet. If he'll take Chloe, that is.'

'Aiden talked me into it. Said I need a break. You know,' she quickly changed the subject, 'about Tom Dugan, well . . . I've been meaning to say I hope you didn't think I was gossiping. Aiden said he saw you? I hadn't realised he'd say something, it was totally out of place of him.' Georgina sounded oddly defiant.

'No, no. It's not a problem. Honestly.' So Aiden told

279

Georgina that he'd been round. There was nothing to hide, to feel awkward about. Stupid Anamaria with her filthy mind.

But then what about this phone call?

'He told me you seemed put out, and I was concerned, that's all, about you getting involved with someone so soon after Ollie. Has he contacted you again?'

Had Aiden contacted her? Jen gulped. 'No, God no.' A shiver ran down her spine. 'It was just the one time and I was surprised to see him to be honest, but . . .'

'Because I know Nutmeg and I were being frightfully silly last night, but it does seem as if he's taken rather a shine to you. If he asks you out, do you think you'll see him again?'

'Of course not! Oh dear heavens, Georgina! How could you think . . .' The phone nearly slipped into the water, she was so appalled. She just managed to capture it with one hand. Horrified, Jen realised that she'd been thinking of Aiden while Georgina had been talking about Tom. 'I mean you're right, about it being too soon. I just don't think I'm ready,' she said, wanting to drown herself.

'You could do worse though. Never know, you might have some fun,' she tittered. 'Trust me, I may not always be right, but I'm never wrong. Better than some ghastly vulture anyway.'

'Vulture?' She was still so bothered and confused she could hardly take anything in.

'I was speaking to my production manager, Eleanor Appleby, about that very thing this morning. She said as soon as she got divorced she had all these married men crawling out of the woodwork, waiting to swoop like vultures.'

'My woodwork's vulture-free, thank goodness.' Jen made a shaky comeback. 'Was she tempted?'

'Not in the least. She's a clever cookie, Eleanor. She told me she always knew that if they could do the dirty on their wives, they'd do it to her sooner or later. About this weekend,' she rolled on smoothly, 'I was thinking, shall we take the limo? It's a lot more comfortable and Max is a terrific . . .'

'No! Are you joking? Who takes their chauffeur on a girls' weekend? Don't you ever drive?' Thank Christ for a change of topic.

'I passed my test,' Georgina said haughtily, 'I just don't care for motorways.'

'Don't care for them?'

'OK, I'm frightened of them. There. I'm afraid I'm going to drift to the centre or hit my brakes suddenly and cause a horrific crash. It's got worse over the years.'

'Oh, I'm sorry. Well, don't worry about it. Meg and I will drive.'

Boy, was she glad when that phone call was over! Ducking her head under the soapy water, Jen sat up again, cursing her stupidity. How could she have got it so wrong? Mixing up Tom and Aiden. Of course Georgina wasn't encouraging Jen to go out with her husband in that cosy tone.

Stupid, stupid mistake! And it would have been a hundred times worse if Georgina had caught it.

Or had she?

That story about Eleanor and the vultures – was it a warning? A shot across the bows?

And, even more pertinent, why had Aiden hidden the fact he'd called, and what had he been calling about?

Jen's day didn't improve. That afternoon she tackled the laundry basket. She pulled a load out of the dryer, folded a couple of Ollie's T-shirts, went to his wardrobe and gasped with shock.

She knew he'd moved out, knew he'd packed some clothes that weekend and that he would be collecting the rest one day, but she wasn't prepared for the emptiness that confronted her.

Nothing was in there. Not a tie, a shoe, or a single belt. He'd

281

even taken those woollen walking socks that she'd bought him for his birthday a few years back and he'd never once worn. There was only a big vacant space and several abandoned wire hangers. He must have picked it all up on Tuesday, when she was at work or out with Chloe.

A cold sweat washed over her, prickles running up and down her back. The end of her marriage. Reality had hit all right. With a big hard smack across the top of her head.

No more would his clothes hang in his wardrobe or lie strewn around the bedroom floor for her to gather and wash. No more would he come in from football covered in mud and drop everything on the bathroom floor. And no more would those shaving foams, razors and male deodorants clutter the bathroom.

Strangely, the relief she'd expected, the freedom that she'd thought would send her high as a hot-air balloon, failed to arrive. She dropped on to the bed and began to cry. She didn't cry herself a river, she cried herself a torrent, a Noah-worthy flood. Her pillow was soaked, her nostrils bubbled, her eyes swelled. She hadn't wept so much since Chloe was three days old, all the progesterone had left her body and Ollie had disappeared to fetch them both a bacon sandwich from the hospital canteen.

The storm had abated to a mild squall when the phone rang. She picked it up from the nightstand on what used to be Ollie's side of the bed, loathing herself for the knee-jerk thought that it might be Aiden again.

'Jen?'

'Tom?' She blew her nose into a sodden tissue.

'Are you all right? You sound like you've a cold.' Tom was cheerfully sympathetic.

'Oh just a sniffle.'

'I thought perhaps you might have dinner with me? On Saturday? If you're free?'

'Oh Tom, I'm sorry. I'm going away for the weekend. To Totnes.' She wasn't sure how she felt, it seemed much too soon to be going out to dinner with a stranger, but at the same time it was mildly enticing.

'Totnes?' He sounded enthusiastic. 'One of my favourite haunts. First visit?'

'Yes. I'm going with Georgina and Meg. It's to do with the search.'

'How about when you get back? Any day next week work for you?'

She hesitated, remembering Georgina's admonition to have some fun. Tormented by two unavailable men, did she really want to throw a third into the equation? But Tom was available and reasonably attractive with a generous share of charisma. She had to admit she'd enjoyed their little flirtation. Could he be what the doctor ordered? A diversion away from the heartbreak hotel?

'That'd be great, Tom. Why don't you call me?' she said.

Jen found Helen perched at the end of the bar, clutching a garish-looking cocktail. 'My my, to what do I owe the pleasure?' Helen said, barely looking up to greet her. 'New friends left town?'

OK, she probably deserved that. As often as she'd tried to avoid Helen in the past, rarely had more than a week gone by without her reluctantly knuckling under and agreeing to some outing. But recently she'd been genuinely too wrapped up in her own life to have time for her old friend. No wonder Helen felt neglected. Jen plonked a wrapped package in front of her, a peace offering she'd found at the charity shop.

'Not exactly. And I can't stay long, I'm afraid. The girl across the road's babysitting. Thought I'd see what this place was all about.' Jen grabbed a vacant stool. 'Wasn't there meant to be a gang of you?'

'They may still turn up.' Helen pulled Jen's stool next to her and half smiled. Someone was attempting a poor rendition of Slade's 'Merry Christmas Everybody' on the karaoke. 'So, dinner party a rip-roaring success? Hors d'oeuvres OK?'

'It wasn't a dinner party. It was a council of war. We're still trying to look for . . .'

'Yeah, your old classmate.' Helen ripped the paper off the present. 'And the reunion came to zilch.'

'Actually, yes,' Jen said, surprised. 'How did you know?'

'Ollie told me.' She pulled out a china pig wearing dungarees and carrying a pitchfork. Helen hoarded a huge pig collection, mugs, plates, cushions, you name it, she had a pig-decorated version of it. 'Thanks. I know just the place for this.' She sounded pleasantly surprised, even a little touched.

'Ollie?' Jen was confused.

'I was passing the school at pick-up time yesterday – saw him chatting up Goldilocks.'

'Goldilocks?'

'Hair like spun gold.' Helen clapped as the Slade song ended. 'Or was that Rapunzel? Frances Hutton.'

'How did he look?'

'I'd have to say . . .' she paused, seeming to consider, '. . . happy. In fact he was laughing – quite a lot in fact.'

'Laughing?'

'Yes, you remember. You open your mouth and go ha ha ha.' She broke out into a mock trill of laughter.

'Good for him.' Jen felt a chip of ice lodge in her heart.

'Yeah, and it's about time you got your old laughter muscle working again too.'

*Who says I haven't?* The words rose in her throat and she squashed them back down, unsaid. She was here to mend fences, not set them aflame. No point in rubbing in all the hilarity she'd been sharing with Meg and Georgina.

'Especially if you're hoping for a new relationship. Men don't go for mopey.' Helen shuddered, stirring her brightly coloured cocktail with its glass rod. 'It's not like it was in our twenties. The good ones are married and the others only interested in younger models. There's hardly anyone available but anoraks and geeks and there's even a queue for them. Can't remember when I last went out with anyone worthwhile. You'll see.' She flicked Jen a knowing glance under mascara-heavy eyelashes.

'Ye-es. You're probably right. Although talking of that, someone did ask me out.'

Helen's interest was sparked now, but she looked like she was chewing on a bitter olive. 'Who?'

'No one special,' Jen muttered, already wishing she'd kept her big mouth shut. Not only was she guilty of having a dinner date when Helen had declared it impossible, she'd failed to fill her in on Tom sooner. But really, why should she be made to feel like a miserable worm because a man showed interest, an event incompatible with Helen's predictions of doom and gloom? Sometimes it felt as if Helen preferred it when Jen was in the same sinking boat, with Helen holding the bailing bucket. Why couldn't she be happy for the good moments too? 'My old English teacher.' She felt obliged to downplay it, felt like saying he was twenty stone, bald with bad breath. 'Mr Dugan. I'm not that bothered, but . . .'

Helen slumped over her drink again.

'Oh well, that's good,' she said flatly.

Jen felt sorry for her suddenly. Where were the rest of the crowd she was supposed to meet? Had everyone stood her up?

She signalled to the barman.

'OK if I stay for a drink?'

'Hey, listen,' Helen said as Jen drained her gin and tonic, 'why don't we go for that meal on Saturday?' She stood up suddenly and waved. Two women in high heels and full warpaint spotted her and started heading over.

Oh shit. Would this never end? It was like one of those nightmares where you were running in quicksand, sinking deeper with every step.

'Saturday? Oh, er, you see, I can't. I'm away for the weekend. But as soon as I get back, we should . . .'

'Don't do me any favours.' Helen pursed her lips and rummaged in her handbag, looking for God knew what. 'You know, I'll see you when I see you.' Her tone held no promise of future meetings.

'Actually,' said Jen, taking a deep breath, knowing she had little option but to ask, 'I was wondering if . . . if you'd do me a big favour? Could you look after my dog?'

Helen's jaw fell. She looked truly flabbergasted and not just at Jen's sheer nerve.

'Dog? *You* have a *dog*?' She made it sound like Jen had tattooed her forehead. 'Since when?'

'Since yesterday.' Jen smiled weakly as Helen's friends came up to them.

Helen shook her head. 'You know what, Jen, I think I'm beginning to get a glimpse of Ollie's perspective.'

# Chapter 32

'I spy with my little eye something beginning with M.'

'Motorway?' Jen moved into the fast lane. Friday night and they were heading down the M4 on their way to Devon.

'No.' Georgina shook her head.

'Mutt?' Meg pushed Feo from her lap, where he'd climbed up to get a better view out of the window. 'What is this hairball doing with us anyway?'

' I couldn't find anyone to look after him. Mat?' Jen niftily overtook a lumbering articulated lorry.

'Nup.'

'Mummy?' Meg pointed at Jen.

'No.'

'Moron?' Jen jerked her thumb back at Meg.

'No,' Georgina said again.

'Mr Dugan?' Meg's attempt.

'He's not in the car,' Jen protested.

'No, but you've got a photo of him in your purse. She sleeps with it under her pillow, Georgie.'

'Ha, ha. Map?'

'Correct.'

'But Georgina, we already had that one.'

'Oh did we? Pardon me, I wasn't listening,' Georgina said absently. She'd been attached to her BlackBerry the whole trip, emailing last-minute instructions to the office.

It had been a long journey and it had reminded Jen of their old geography field trips, particularly after the first hour had been spent in full singsong, led by Meg's rendition of 'She'll Be Coming Round the Mountain' and rounded off by Jen's finale of 'There's a Worm at the Bottom of the Garden and His Name Is Wiggly Woo' in silly accents.

Jen felt liberated, suddenly reconnected in spirit with the carefree girl she'd once been. They'd laughed till their sides ached, sung till they were hoarse and conversation hadn't once run dry.

Before Meg and Georgina erupted back into her middle-aged, middle-class routine, she'd lost herself in conformist, conservative Huntsleigh hell. But no more. She'd buy herself a pair of tangerine flares, perhaps even dye her hair a vibrant red. From now on she intended to enjoy her life seeking out glorious silliness. To think she used to reproach Ollie for acting the fool. How could she have forgotten how much fun it was?

Life was a marathon, she decided. Equal start as innocent babies, every tiny step garnering applause. Then school begins, the clapping fades and the race gets tougher. You hit the wild ups and downs of your hormone-fuelled teens and race in and out of love and jobs in your twenties, cruising along with energy to spare. Life develops a steady rhythm until one day you've passed the landmarks of adulthood – marriage, kids – tiring but slogging on. Then, about the forty mark, desperation sets in. Divorce. Redundancy. Friends dropping off. Middle-aged spread. Menopause. Parents falter. Deaths occur. You look awful, feel worse, you've hit the wall and you're afraid you'll reach your limit long before you can call it quits.

But if you push through, Jen thought gleefully, you might just get a second wind. Find new running buddies, regain enthusiasm, and with encouragement and sustenance from your cheering squad actually have fun on the way to the finish. Where, with luck, you could get a great send-off like Isobel Benjamin. A big party. Admiring speeches. And at least a hundred and fifty people raving about how wonderful you'd been.

'Which way? Which way?'

'Right. Go right. Follow that Range Rover.' Jen was directing Meg around the Totnes one-way system.

'And then where? Tell me quickly, because I need notice. Listen, they're honking. They think my driving sucks.'

'Because it does.' Georgina turned to survey the queue of traffic behind.

'Why are they up my butt and flashing wildly?'

'They want you to move faster?' suggested Jen. 'You're going awfully slowly.'

'Look, I can handle five lanes of LA rush-hour traffic any day. It's this dumb stick shift where the door should be that has me freaked. At least I didn't claim a freeway phobia like you, Georgie.'

'We all have our weaknesses,' Georgina countered. 'Motorways are mine.'

True to her word Jen and Meg had shared the wheel of Jen's BMW, one hundred and ten miles each. But the second they left the M5, Meg's confidence had evaporated, everyone screaming as she headed the wrong direction round her first roundabout, crunching gears, the car lurching spasmodically.

'Right here.' Jen leaned over from the back seat, chin close to Meg's shoulder, a printed email clutched in her hand. 'It looks like we're getting near the centre. Now start looking for parking. Georgina's secretary says here that it can be rarer than hen's teeth.'

It was. They circled for ever before seeing a Mini pull out of a Mini-sized space just one street from the B & B. Meg pulled in, reversed out, pulled in again, reversed out and eventually turned the engine off, with one tyre on the pavement and the boot sticking at an angle into the road. As they dragged their wheeled suitcases uphill to their lodging, Georgina complained with every step that she'd have strong words with her assistant when she got back about her choice of accommodation.

Feo was straining on his lead, eyes bugging, red tongue sticking out, in an apparent attempt at self-strangulation.

'I need to walk him,' Jen said. 'As soon as we've got settled. Wouldn't want Meg to step on anything nasty in the night. What about you two?'

'Bed,' Georgina groaned, ringing the bell. 'I'm exhausted.'

When Jen got back, Georgina was sequestered in her room, presumably asleep, and Meg was on the phone to Zeb, clucking away, while the final of *I'm A Celebrity . . . Get Me Out of Here!* played noisily on a small TV.

She thought of calling Chloe at Ollie's, but it was long past her bedtime. They'd dilly-dallied for ages over dinner at the Moto service station. When Meg finally hung up, Jen was already under the covers.

'We really should get Chloe and Zeb together,' she said sleepily, turning off the light. 'What about next week?'

'Maybe.' Meg's words were muffled by her pillow. 'But Mace has Zeb's time pretty much tied up what with this private tutor, and now he's got him taking violin and swimming lessons too. I'm beat. Goodnight.'

'Goodnight,' Jen responded, her eyes closing even as her brain wrestled wearily with questions and the realisation that it was odd they'd still not met Zeb.

When Meg and Jen knocked on Georgina's door next morning, they found her sitting at the foot of the queen-sized bed, eyes glued to a repeat of some old TV game show fronted by Dale Winton.

'Is this piffle really on every Saturday morning?' she called to

Jen as she nosily opened a door to check out the en-suite facilities. Georgina's room was quite a bit larger and nicer than her and Meg's, no surprise. 'Two families against each other. It's hardly even-stevens, one's a van driver and the other's a podiatrist.'

'So what's wrong with van drivers?' Jen closed the door again.

'Nothing. I didn't mean . . . I just meant . . .'

'That they were thicker than foot doctors?' Jen suggested, walking to the window.

On the bed beside Georgina, Meg was paying them no attention. She was flopped, face down, looking through a sea of leaflets she'd found in the entrance hall last night.

'Well, clearly doctors have to be clever. Look, I like van drivers, I have friends who are van drivers.'

'Yes, my dad . . .'

Georgina winced. 'Oh yes, I forgot.'

'Thought you might have.' Jen stared into the street below, listening to the seagulls screaming. 'Did you know we're only thirty minutes from a load of beaches here? If you don't mind sitting on them in all your winter woollies.'

'Shall we watch a film?' Georgina was flicking through the channels. 'This is so decadent, I never get a chance to laze like this.'

'No way, dudes.' Meg rolled over on to her side, waving a fistful of brochures like a winning poker hand. 'We've no time to waste. Look at all these groovy events. There's a veggie festival, wisdom scrolls, Henry Helminger's open healing weekend . . . oh, but you had to book for that. How about this, Wild Food Forage and Feast?'

'Perhaps we should forage in the breakfast room,' Jen said. 'What wild food could they possibly find in winter? Slugs and beetles?'

'And excuse my ignorance,' Georgina lay back on her elbows,

remote in hand, 'but how is foraging for slugs and beetles going to help us find Rowan?'

'Forget it anyway, it was over in October.' Meg scanned another leaflet. 'Hey, what about Touching the Energy of the Bone? Now that does sound interesting.'

'You would want to do the bone thing, Nutmeg.' Georgina reluctantly switched off the TV. 'It's probably some dirty-haired sackcloth-attired yobbo wanting you to manipulate his extremities.'

'Georgina! How *very* dare you!' Jen chuckled in a bad imitation of Catherine Tate.

'Sounds good to me,' Meg tittered. 'Come on you old knuckleheads, time for a quick bite of brekkie and then let's find the castle.'

Before Jen could say 'Let's storm the battlements' she'd headed out the door and was halfway down the stairs.

Totnes was charming, quaint and, being an Elizabethan town, jammed with olde worlde pubs, antique dealers and quirky gift shops.

'Now this is my kind of scene,' Meg said, as they threaded their way through cobbled streets cluttered with organic bakeries, craft studios and New Age cafés. 'I could set up a store doing my healing and angel readings. It's got that vibe.'

'What vibe?' Jen said, pulling Feo away from a lamppost.

'Good energy, dude. Can't you feel it?'

'Can you actually make money from that kind of thing?' Georgina asked.

'Enough to get by on.'

It did look a cool place to live, Jen supposed, positively heaving with history but trendy and alive at the same time. Eat your heart out, horrible old Huntsleigh. All manner of people were lounging around enjoying the pale sunshine, tourists and locals, young and old. Asian monks wandered past in dark red robes, a couple of young hippy guys with shabby clothes were idly strumming guitars on a park bench, watched by three girls with crushed-velvet dresses and long hennaed hair.

They paused to watch a middle-aged black woman with an Afro weave brightly coloured string into a blond child's hair. Even in midwinter the town was lively, eclectic, buzzing.

'Too many bohos,' Georgina sniffed. 'Half look like they could use a good bath. And I've never seen so many white people with dreadlocks. How do they comb their hair?'

'They don't, Georgie,' Meg said as they started up the short but steep castle path. 'You of all people should know, being the famous fashion icon.'

She said the words with a grin and a little show-off twirl. Last night, as she'd clambered into the car, Georgina had surprised them both with bulging paper carriers stamped Giordani. 'Samples,' she had said deprecatingly to their effusive thanks, as they rummaged through their bags in delight. 'We always have oodles lying around.' But to Jen and Meg, both wearing their brand-new clobber today, Christmas had come early this year.

'Far out!' Meg panted, as they stopped to admire the view. They were inside the thirteenth-century Norman motte and bailey castle ruins, on the second tier, having ascended the treacherous narrow spiral steps, and were now looking down at the River Dart and a view of the town. 'If I ever get married a second time, it'll be in a place like this. That or on a beach in Hawaii. So romantic.' She clasped her hands together and held them to her breast.

'Where did you and Ollie marry?' Georgina asked Jen. She had pulled off one of her high-heeled ankle boots and was sitting on cold stone, rubbing her feet. Not the most practical sightseeing shoes, Jen thought.

'Local registry office. Just his parents, my dad, Helen, a couple of other friends. I was eight months pregnant so wasn't anything special.' She grinned at Meg. 'Not an Elvis in sight.'

'Wasn't much of an Elvis,' Meg said. 'Bad wig, didn't look anything like him. Or much of a marriage. The asshole.' She launched a pebble off the parapet.

Jen swallowed. If Meg didn't ask, she had to.

'What about you and Aiden, Georgie?' It felt odd calling him by his real name.

'Dinky little church. It was very beautiful, very old, traditional.'

'You always said you were going to float down the aisle, the virgin bride, all in white with little freesias in your hair.'

'I did have freesias in my hair, but my gown was ivory. I didn't do the white bit.' Georgina slid her boot on again and did up the zip.

'Or the virgin bit?' suggested Meg.

Georgina quirked her brows but didn't comment.

'Right, girls,' Meg said. 'That's the whole of Totnes spread before you. How many houses do you think there are? How long to systematically search each one?'

'Hundreds. And years,' Jen said, dismally surveying the surrounding area. 'It's a needle in a bloody haystack.'

'So what's our plan?' Meg asked cheerily, looking from one to the other. 'We do have a plan, don't we?'

'Perhaps we could ask around the pubs?' Jen ventured, wishing they'd thought this through sooner, now the enormity of their task was apparent. Why hadn't they discussed what they were actually going to do?

'That's a start, I guess.' Meg tucked her cold hands in the sleeves of her jacket and shivered. 'Because if we came all the way down here without a clue where to begin our search, I for one intend to break out the Martinis and get very heavily slammed.'

'You don't have to.' Georgina produced three cardboard folders from her giant handbag. 'I've got it covered. I had a copy of the Totnes phone book couriered to me at the office and my assistant Lucy called every Howard in it, looking for Rowan's mum or anyone who might know her. No luck yet, but we've eliminated all but five. No answer when Lucy called. My thought is to drive round to those addresses and see what we can find out. Anyone we can't talk to today we'll pencil in for tomorrow. Then we'll split up. Jen can try all the art galleries and art-supply shops for leads to Rowan. I'll look for places that sell wool and yarn – remember Mrs Howard used to knit all Rowan's sweaters, those big awful clunky things? And Meg can ask in the health-food shops and check out the churches.'

She handed a folder each to her stunned companions.

'I've been racking my brain and I'm almost sure Ma Howard was Apostolic, but Pentecostal is probably the closest. Oh, and I found an old photo, not a very good one, half Rowan's head is missing but you can see her mum in the background hanging up the washing. And ta da,' she produced her last photocopy with a flourish, 'one of our clever computer chappies did an age progression of what Rowan might look like now.'

'Oh my god.' Jen snatched it from her and found herself looking at Rowan's blue eyes, staring back at her from a mature face with impossibly high cheekbones, a pouting full-lipped mouth and the faintest suggestion of crow's feet and forehead lines. It was surreal and not, she thought, all that convincing. The nose didn't look quite right and nor did the hair, which the computer wizard had replaced with a flirty shoulder-length style and a long fringe swept off to one side. It looked more like a cross between Angelina Jolie and Cameron Diaz than their long-lost friend.

'Far out, Georgie.' Meg was flicking the pages of her folder with an expression approaching awe. 'I feel like I just got enlisted in Mission Impossible. This isn't going to self-destruct in thirty seconds, is it?'

'No, but we'd better get a move on. We've only got the weekend. Chop chop.' Georgina clapped her hands decisively like a nursery-school teacher. 'Time is a-wasting.'

# Chapter 33

It was dark at five o'clock when they called an end to the day's search. There were carol singers standing in the square under a Christmas tree, belting out 'Deck the Halls' while dressed in Victorian costumes. Jen was throwing some change into their donation bucket when she spotted Meg and Georgina approaching from opposite corners. One look at their faces told the story.

'No luck?'

Meg shook her head.

'Just more blisters,' Georgina said, slumping on to a bench. 'I'm exhausted. Still have three addresses for tomorrow, though, where no one was in.'

'They do have some way cool shops.' Meg caught their expressions and backtracked. 'Not that I had a minute to check them out. Oh look, roast chestnuts. Let's get some.'

They bought a paper poke between them and fumbled with the shells, which were almost too hot to peel.

'If you want my opinion,' Jen said, 'it's time to follow Meg's suggestion. Let's get slammed.'

Three hours later they were sitting in their fourth pub, rubbing their bellies (except for Georgina, who seemed to have iron willpower and nibbled where the other two gorged). Their enquiries about Mrs Howard had been sidetracked by the enticing steaming plates of hearty pub food that kept being carried past them. They eventually relented and ordered some for themselves and settled in.

Feet up on a stool, huddled next to a crackling fire, Meg was telling them about one of her lovers. 'His name was Iggy. A Rasta dude, white mother, black father and like the sexiest man alive. I should have stayed with him. I think he could have been the only man I've truly loved.'

'Where did you meet him?' Jen surreptitiously undid the top button of her jeans.

'Jamaica. I spent the summer there before I went to LA to try acting. I was working in a hotel, he was tending bar and we rented a cottage on the beach in this funky little place called Orchard Road.'

'I used to love that Leo Sayer song about Orchard Road,' Georgina commented. 'How did it go again?'

'Haven't a clue.' Meg replied with a half-hearted lift of her shoulders, noticeably disappointed her one true love story took second billing to an old eighties song.

'I think it was something like . . .' Jen paused a moment. 'Yeah, I've got it now. Da da trundle . . .'

'Something about whistle-blowing,' Georgina warbled. 'And turning around and . . .'

They carried on singing for a short while until they realised it wasn't 'Orchard Road' any more but 'I Can't Stop Loving You', and sat in puzzled silence.

'Anyway, who cares.' Jen pondered a moment. 'What happened with the Jamaican? Did you ever see him again?'

'One postcard and that was it.' Meg tucked her knee up under her chin. She eyed Georgina, who'd been lost in her own thoughts, and casually threw a wrecking ball into the relaxed atmosphere. 'So, Georgie. Truth game. You never did answer last time. How did you and Aiden get together?'

Damn Meg, thought Jen. Why did she have to spoil things again? Georgina immediately blushed scarlet and started fidgeting in her chair. Jen almost stood up, thinking about going to the bar to buy the next round, but decided to stay. No matter how awkward this was, she wanted to hear.

'It was just . . . well, you know . . . one of those things. He was there in a pub one summer evening when I was on break from uni and of course the friends I was with knew him. For a while we were simply part of the same crowd and then, well, a few years later it was New Year's Eve and we were both a little tipsy and . . . it happened. It took me completely by surprise. You know when we first hung out together, all he talked about was you, Jen,' Georgina said earnestly, her scarlet face now calmed. 'About what a tremendous girl you were, how much he'd liked you, what an idiot he was.'

She was wrong. She didn't want to hear this. It hurt more than she'd expected. She took a sip of wine, struggling with her churning emotions. Jealousy. Resentment. Regret. Anger. All so bloody understandable if it weren't Aiden and Georgie. Two lonely people. The slow beginning. The innocuous friendship turning to something else . . .

'I used to tell him to call you if he truly felt that way,' Georgina forged on, 'that even if he'd done something frightful, you might forgive him. But he always said it was too late.' She looked horribly awkward. 'Of course if you'd been around he wouldn't have looked twice at me.'

'Rot!' Jen attempted a jovial laugh. 'Who wouldn't go barmy over you, Georgie? You've got the class, the breeding, all the right gubbins.'

'If you mean he went for the money,' Georgina replied stiffly, 'it wasn't like that. Starting Giordani took every penny we possessed.'

Damn. Now she'd offended her. And she honestly hadn't meant to. But then if Georgina wanted to be touchy and oversensitive, too bad. After all, she'd ended up with Aiden. Won the precious prize.

Georgina's eyes caught hers and suddenly Jen was positive she had more to say and equally positive she couldn't listen to another word. Didn't want to hear the sordid details of how Aiden had swept her off her feet and about how her toes curled as he kissed her softly on her rosebud lips and how terrible she'd felt knowing he was Jen's boyfriend first but they just couldn't help themselves. So it was almost a relief when Meg said, 'So, Jen. About this divorce. If he didn't cheat and you didn't cheat, what went wrong?'

'We were miserable,' Jen said simply. 'We should never have got married probably. But I was pregnant.'

'Well, not everybody's ecstatic all the time,' Georgina admonished. 'You have to work at marriage.'

Instantly Jen wanted to punch her lights out. How dare she say that! Stupid smug privileged Georgina, married to the man that destiny had surely meant as Jen's soulmate.

'We did work at it,' she seethed through clenched teeth. 'But when does it stop being work and when does it become a life sentence?'

'Who suggested divorce?' Meg asked, sleepily smiling in a catlike way, her slender fingers playing with the crystal around her neck.

'Ollie. He tricked me, started by saying, "You're not happy, are you?" And I gave some smart-arse answer like "Happy, what's that? Oh yes, I vaguely remember the concept." And then I went, "This is marriage, matey. Happiness doesn't come into it."'

But they had been happy once, she reflected. She'd loved the way he used to serenade her with tuneless love songs from the shower while she brushed her teeth. They used to mock-tango around the kitchen, Ollie dipping her, while more than once dinner burned on the stove top or smoke oozed unnoticed out of the oven. There'd been bike rides with Chloe in a little seat behind him, camping trips, with and without Chloe, and blissful Sundays just wandering around the London parks followed by lazy lunchtimes at the pub. They used to laugh, joke, talk about things.

'Romantic, huh?' Meg remarked drily. 'Did you have to be so brutal?'

'Truth is, I wasn't taking him seriously. I kind of imagined he was going to suggest we all needed a holiday or at worst counselling, and I couldn't be fagged. I mean he's great, Ollie, but I think we just slowly fell out of love. If we were ever truly in love, it happened so fast with the pregnancy and all. But anyway, silly me, I was still completely gob-smacked when he told me it wasn't enough for him and he wanted out.'

In a way, she reflected, hearing Ollie say it aloud had almost been a relief. Like the death of a terminally sick pet that you can't bear to put down.

It was as if she'd always known that day would come. It had taken its own sweet time, tried to lull her into feeling safe, whistling gaily, eyes averted and hands behind its back, but suddenly the cloak had been pulled aside, the sword revealed.

Georgina and Meg's expressions suggested they were taking this all too seriously. As if it were some kind of big deal.

'But are you sure you don't still feel something?' Georgina's eyes were huge, her voice solicitous. 'Couldn't you work it out somehow?'

'It's too late.' She said it with finality. She had to keep some pride! 'He was too young when we married. It wasn't fair to him – or to me. Almost ten years married,' she tried to throw in a joke, to show them it wasn't a major tragedy, 'and he still doesn't know I take milk in my coffee. If you ask me, that's *grounds* for divorce right there.'

'But what did you say? When he asked for the divorce?'

Georgina looked appalled at her flippancy, while Meg groaned at her pun.

'"Fine with me." Then I asked if he wanted Lurpak butter or St Ivel's Gold because I was doing my shopping list. I think he expected more discussion but I grabbed the car keys and drove to Morrisons.' It still made her cringe to think of it. She bent over to stroke Feo who was sitting beside her on the corner seat, wheezing through his pug nose in an asthmatic way.

'You were in shock, probably,' Meg reassured her. 'I dated this actor for almost a year, crazy about the dude, and when he ditched me I blurted out, "You mean no more Malibu beach parties?"'

Alas, Georgina wasn't finished. 'Couldn't you—'

'No,' Jen interrupted sharply. 'I couldn't.' She stared hard at the window, turning her head away from the others. As much as part of her didn't blame Ollie at all – who would want to live with a moody uptight cow? – another more visceral, primitive side considered itself deeply betrayed.

'Have you thought it through?' Georgina asked practically. 'For example, what will you do about custody? Split the week?'

'We haven't sorted all the details.' Jen suffered an unexpected thud of alarm. 'I was thinking he'd have Chloe every second weekend or something.'

'Wouldn't work that way in the US, hon,' Meg informed her. 'Among most of my friends the men share custody, kids are with them half the week, with their mother the other half. Can't move to another state without a huge legal battle, need your ex's written consent to go abroad on vacation. Real pain in the ass, I'm glad I don't have to go through that with Zeb.'

'Yes, well, in England,' Georgina intervened, saving Jen from her momentary panic, 'the wisdom is that children need one real home so they can go to school from the same residence every day, not be shuttled back and forth like wrongly

301

addressed parcels. With most divorced couples I know, the father gets them every second weekend, Friday to Sunday.'

'Hardly seems fair,' Meg observed, her fourth bourbon making her argumentative. 'Assuming having tits makes you a better parent.'

'So does Zeb's father have a say in his upbringing?' Georgina challenged. 'The silver-buckled bull rider?'

'Wait a minute.' Jen had had enough of this bickering. 'I never got my shot at the truth game.' She gazed at Georgina, gratified to see she looked nervous. 'Remember those plimsolls that got nicked from Gayle Honeybreath's locker?'

'Gayle?' Georgina frowned.

'Honeybourne, but we called her Honeybreath.' Jen narrowed her eyes. 'Gayle and her mates frogmarched me to my locker and I, in all innocence opened it up, and there were Gayle's plimsolls. I put it to you, Georgina Giordani Carrington, that you stole those plimsolls and then planted them on me.'

'I didn't.'

'Yes you did.'

'No I didn't.'

'Did.'

'Didn't.'

There was a pause. Abruptly both Georgina's arms flew up in the air, palms out in submission. 'All right. Yes. It's a fair cop. I took them.'

'I knew it. I knew it.' Jen bounced in triumph. 'But why? And why plant them on me? Everyone called me a tea leaf after that.'

Georgina looked shamefaced. 'I loved those plimsolls of Gayle's. They had sweet little stars all over them.'

'But why plant them on me?' Jen repeated, bemused.

'Gayle knew I liked them because I'd told her and I deduced that once she discovered they'd gone missing, I'd be her first suspect. I never dreamed she'd search your locker first.'

A kind of strangulated sound seeped over from Meg's direction. She had her head down and she was shaking. For a brief moment Jen thought she could be choking and tried desperately to recall the Heimlich manoeuvre. But when Meg lifted her head, she was giggling helplessly.

'What? What is it?' The relief of her being OK made Jen grin as well.

'I . . . can't . . .'

'What? What?' Georgina's shoulders started juddering as she became infected by her laughter.

'I . . . I . . .'

'Come on, tell.'

'I split. I told Gayle Honeybreath.'

'You? Why?' Jen's smile faded as her mind reached across the vast chasm of time, attempting to unscramble the events of a quarter-century ago.

'Well, I don't know, Bedlow,' Meg said, unrepentant. 'I was . . . what? . . . eleven? Who knows why anyone does anything at that age?'

'Do you remember our SOS signal?' Georgina was still grinning happily. She shoved aside a couple of soggy beer mats and knocked on the wooden table in front of her, paused, knocked, paused, knocked. 'It meant danger, danger, or urgent, come quick. Like that time we had a party in your house, Jen, with a bottle of vodka and cigarettes my parents had bought in duty-free and Rowan was in the phone box and saw your dad heading home . . .'

'I never did anything to you.' Jen's eyes were fixed on Meg. 'We were supposed to be best friends.'

'Oh for Pete's sake, Jen.' Meg rose to her feet. 'It wasn't me who took the dumb things or stuck them in your locker. I'm going to the bar. Anyone want anything?'

Georgina and Jen shook their heads. It was irrational, Jen knew. Why did Meg's confession bother her more than

Georgie's? Because her heroine had wanted to cause her trouble?

She watched the American woman feed coins into the jukebox, tossing her hair and grinning at a man who joined her. At thirty-eight, especially from a few yards away, she could almost have passed for twenty with her skinny jean-clad legs, her wild red hair. She had an ageless quality, a mixture of innocent waif and wilful sexuality, that reminded Jen of Sissy Spacek. Only Meg saved her great performances for real life.

As if sensing her watchers, Meg turned towards their corner and put her thumb in the air.

'Girls, I scored big-time. Guess what I found out?' she said, rejoining them as 'When You Believe' boomed into the atmosphere.

'Mrs Howard's address?'

'No.'

'That bloke's phone number?' Jen nodded at the man at the jukebox.

Meg ignored them. 'There's a farmers' market. First Sunday of each month. Tomorrow. Why don't we swing by? Rowan's mom loved that kind of stuff. I'll bet my entire collection of Clover albums she'll be there.'

# Chapter 34

'Well, darlings, I think I'll turn in now.' Georgina stood up, sleek and glamorous in an expensive-looking black silk negligee and wrap. 'Talk to you in the morning.'

'See ya,' Jen said. She'd returned to their room from the shower down the hall, washbag in hand, and found Georgina chatting to an almost-naked Meg, who was sitting at the mirror brushing her long red hair, only a tiny thong preserving her modesty.

Georgina looked stunning with her long slender legs and perfect flat stomach just showing through the flimsy material. Not as fine-boned as Meg, but still . . . marriage had obviously done a lot more for her than it had for Jen. No wonder she and Aiden were going strong while Ollie had fled for the hills.

Suddenly feeling as sexy as an old bog brush in her flannelette pyjamas, she hastened into bed.

'Shower hot?' Meg asked, subdued.

'Yes.'

'Good. My turn then.' She walked out, towel around her.

Georgina's mobile rang as she headed out the room and she glanced at the name that appeared. 'That's Aiden,' she said, turning slightly pink. 'Hi, darling, just a sec.' She waved the tips of her fingers. 'See you tomorrow, Jen. Farmers' market first thing.'

As the door closed, Jen noticed Georgina's laptop open on

Meg's bed. Should she take it back to her? It was displaying a Yahoo account and involuntarily her eyes slid over the names, looking for Aiden Starkson. Perhaps he emailed Georgie daily, the way Ollie had done, whenever possible, when he was in Tanzania. But of course that was silly. They spent every day together, not only living but working together. And if he did, it wouldn't mean anything. It could be love letters or business documents. And she would never stoop so low as to read them and find out.

But the name she was searching for wasn't there.

The first entry on the inbox page was a message from I.G. Beidlebaum.

Why would Georgina . . . ? Jen looked again. Of course, it was Meg's account. Meg must have borrowed the laptop to check her messages. But Irwin Beidlebaum?

So she was still in contact with the guy?

Even though she'd said that whole thing was over years ago?

The curiosity was unbearable. The message had already been read.

She guessed that Meg would be another five minutes at least. Feeling wicked as an industrial spy, only without the mini camera, she double-clicked quickly on the heading Re: Test Results.

'Game over,' she read. 'I'm guessing it's no surprise to you. No more bullshit, doll, you've had a good run but every show has its final curtain. Prefer to keep it out of the press but either way you've had your last dime. Say hi to the kid.'

Now what was that all about? Irwin was paying Meg money? And what did he want to keep from the press? Could she be blackmailing him?

She heard a toilet flush, a door close, steps coming down the hall, and clicked to go back to Inbox.

Nothing happened. The screen had frozen, leaving Irwin's email up there for the world to see. The steps stopped, paused, moved on again. As the door handle jiggled, she hit the button repeatedly and this time the screen reverted to the inbox. Leaping into bed, in one smooth movement she pulled the blankets over her shoulders, face pressed into the pillow pretending to be asleep. Steps crossed the room, she heard Meg at the computer, shutting it down.

'Jen?' she whispered tentatively. 'Are you asleep?'

Desperate as she was to know the whole story, it would look too suspicious to pop her head up now, admit she was awake. Meg might guess. Realise she was the despicable sort of snoop you can't trust alone for a second. Meg sighed and the bedside light went off.

It was hard to sleep, her mind flitting from Meg and Irwin to Georgina and Aiden and, yes, even Ollie, thanks to that stupid truth game stirring everything up again. Her throat felt achy when she thought of him. She kept twisting and turning in the strange bed, banging the lumpy pillow and listening to the sound of Meg's deep breathing and Feo snoring at the foot of her bed.

Somehow seeing Georgina wearing that classy wrap and negligee on a common-or-garden girls' weekend had opened a window on to her relationship with Aiden that she'd have much preferred to have kept boarded up with thick wooden planks. Jen couldn't prevent herself from continual thoughts of Georgina as a secret sex fiend, Aiden relishing peeling off those layers of silk to get to that smooth olive skin.

Well, of course, she knew they slept together. But she'd done her best to barricade the topic from her mind. It was like that old cliché of your parents having sex – *ugh*!

Flopping from her back to her stomach, Jen felt sorry for Ollie all over again. It had been years since she'd gone to bed in anything more lust-inspiring than a T-shirt and knickers – and that was just her heat-of-the-summer gear. In winter she wore flannelette pyjamas, woolly socks, and sometimes even a sweatshirt on particularly cold nights when he insisted on cracking open the window for fresh air.

In the early days Ollie used to laugh, saying it was like watching a kid get dressed to play in a snowstorm, and what was the point when they'd only be taking it all off again right away. He was always warm, as opposed to Jen, who spent the winter huddling over radiators and donning heavy fleeces. It was one of the things she'd loved about him, his good-natured willingness to be used as a hot-water bottle for frozen feet – like having a wood-burning stove waiting for her when she'd jump shivering into bed.

Unwilling to follow that line of reflection, she turned her brain to the puzzle of Beidlebaum and Meg. *Re test results.* What did it mean? Did it have something to do with the cancer? Had Meg somehow persuaded Irwin to pay for her medical treatment? But then why would the press give a damn about that – except that they were always avid quest for celebrity titbits? *Hello!* had done a two-page spread on his wedding to the latest Mrs B, she'd flicked idly through it in the dentist's waiting room, and sometime ex-girlfriend, fling, whatever, Meg Lennox had certainly not been mentioned among the guests. No, she'd definitely made it sound as if Irwin was long gone from her life.

But this email told a different story.

Would she ever be able to read what was going on in that mind of Meg's? Ever be able to trust her, separate the kernels of truth from the chaff of deception? Aiden was right, Meg was up to something, keeping secrets.

She was amazed at how disappointed she felt. Everything with Meg was lies and double-dealing, her friendship as much an illusion as the other tales she spun. A funfair with a row of distorting mirrors – entertaining at first, but silly and tiresome the longer you stick around.

At eleven thirty she could stand it no longer. As she sat up,

Feo wriggled to the top of the bed and started licking her face, making little insistent whines. She pulled a sweater over her pyjamas, socks, put on boots, jacket and grabbed his lead.

Downstairs a bell jangled, the front door clicked shut. She looked out of the landing window into the street below.

Under the lamp post decorated with fairy lights she saw a figure bundled up in coat and hat, collar up, click-clacking on heels down the street. A few steps from the B & B the figure glanced back and Jen caught a glimpse of its profile.

Georgina.

Hurrying down the stairs with Feo leading the way, she hastened to open the front door.

She was just in time to see Georgina turning the corner at the end of the road. Where on earth was she going so late? Jen speeded up, breaking into a run, dragging behind her the reluctant dog whose intent seemed to be to mark every lamp post. Jen was a sprinter, but Feo was a distinct handicap and Georgina had a head start. By the time she reached the corner Georgina had vanished into the night.

She slowed down as her steps took her past some kind of sleazy late-night venue. A man in a leather jacket was smoking by the door, watching her with a hard stare. It didn't look like the kind of place Georgina would frequent, a cocktail lounge with a neon silhouette of a bunny girl flashing a sign that said 'After Hours'. What else would be open this time of night? Georgina wasn't the clubbing sort, she'd been the first to suggest an early night. Could she not sleep? Was she meeting someone? Had she doubled back to get the car? All Jen knew was that she didn't like being out here alone at night.

It was all too much suddenly. First Meg, then Georgina. All these secrets. Maybe it would turn out to be nothing, but the truth was the only person you could really trust in this life was yourself. Adoring husbands suddenly told you they hated their lives and you. Best friends showed up married to your one true love. Nice middle-aged men turned out to be rapists. Kids walked into classrooms spraying bullets. Innocent victims were shot on the Underground or were murdered by their next-door neighbours. It was a truly terrible world. You only had to watch TV or read the newspapers to know that nothing was sacred and no one was safe.

The leather-jacketed man stubbed out his cigarette, his eyes cold and unfriendly. She turned on her heel and retreated, scared suddenly, almost expecting to feel a hand grab her arm, horribly aware of her half-dressed state. Now she really regretted her impulsive exit. The streets were empty. Feo would be no protection at all. Next time she'd lock him in the bathroom, where if he did mess at least she could clean it up. It wasn't worth exposing herself to danger, even if Totnes seemed so quaint and friendly in daylight.

She'd lost Georgina, anyway. Whatever she was up to, it was unlikely to involve this seedy club. True, you never knew what strange things people might do, but it was hard to believe the fastidious Georgina would be seen in such a dump.

They'd been having such a great time too, she thought, as Feo, despite her urging, took his own sweet time sniffing and weeing on every interesting smell on the way back to the B & B. The trip to Ashport. The reunion. This jaunt down to Totnes, laughing and joking. It had felt just like old times. Like when the four of them were at school, watching each other's backs, defending each other to the hilt. But that was then and this was now. Why kid yourself those loyalties still held true when it was a dog-eat-dog world and the people closest to you were as likely as not just waiting to plunge in the dagger?

One thing was sure, though, both her friends were proving full of surprises tonight.

# Chapter 35

The strain of too many untold secrets seemed to taint the atmosphere as they wandered through the farmers' market. The jollity of the previous day had evaporated, like the sunshine from the grey overcast sky. Meg was moody, Georgina looked sallow and drawn and Jen, tired after her restless night, struggled to regain a balanced perspective and not walk around in a mammoth sulk. Things felt less sinister in daytime. She'd decided to wait for her friends to confide their secrets, even if she did feel like the only spy left out of a worldwide conspiracy.

Sampling goat's cheese on crackers and home-made cider, they strolled between the stalls selling grass-fed bison meat, organic jams and chutneys, baskets of Jerusalem artichokes, sweet potatoes, Brussels sprouts, celeriac, winter squash, curly kale, dried-flower arrangements, varnished gourds and Advent wreaths.

'I'm not nearly ready for Christmas,' Georgina complained. Her eyes looked slightly red. She'd announced at breakfast she was coming down with flu, hardly touching the huge fry-up that the others put away.

'I love that crusty home-made bread.' Meg skipped past the naked organic hens to a plate of bread samples. 'Yum,' she said, chewing.

'How did everyone sleep?' Jen asked brightly, in possibly her third attempt to draw out Georgie. No point in probing Meg.

She'd only give away that she'd peeked at her email, just as bad as reading a diary. And besides, would she believe a word Meg said?

'Like a log,' Georgina said. 'I was out the moment my head touched the pillow.'

'So-so,' said Meg, who as far as Jen could tell had snored all night long.

'Well I kept waking up.' Jen gave a sly glance at Georgina, who was intently studying some Norfolk pines in pots. 'Hearing doors opening and closing. Footsteps and weird noises.'

'The woo-woo ghostly kind?' asked Meg. 'Because I sensed a strange vibe . . .'

'Oh look,' said Georgina. 'A cooking demonstration.' And she walked away.

In the food area between the Fairtrade coffee and fresh roasting corn on the cob, a woman was demonstrating a recipe for curried squash soup. The smell of frying onions wafted in the air and a small group had gathered to watch.

About to follow Georgina, Jen felt Meg grab her jacket to stop her progress.

'She threw up last night,' Meg hissed. 'Did you hear her?'

'No. Are you sure it wasn't your ghost?' Jen knew she sounded chilly but she couldn't help it. School was supposed to be over but Meg was still telling tales. She broke free and walked over to join the crowd.

'. . . a wonderful winter recipe,' the demonstrator was saying. 'You can add meat to make it more substantial and it also freezes very well.'

A woman walked past with a poodle and Feo lunged at it, barking, making frantic vertical leaps. With an apologetic smile Jen picked up the annoying little canine, grateful he wasn't a Rottweiler.

'I never know what to do with squash,' Georgina told Jen as she arrived beside her, Meg close behind. 'My gardener grows those butternut things but I always end up throwing them out. They seem like such a mystery.'

'Loads of things are mysteries to me.' A gypsy selling lucky white heather approached her and Jen waved her away. 'Seems like everyone's hiding stuff or . . .'

'It's her!' Meg gave out a sudden whoop. 'I know it's her!'

'Who?' asked Jen.

'Over there. In the boots.' She waggled a finger at a woman in a long bottle-green coat and outsize wellingtons. 'Look. I'd recognise that walk and those slumped shoulders anywhere. Jesus, am I good or what? I told you she'd be here.' She began kissing her fingers, 'Thank you, angel guide. Thank you, spirits.'

'Go on then.' Georgina pushed Jen forward.

'Why me?' Jen dug in her heels. Now that they'd found Mrs Howard she felt anxious suddenly, not at all keen on being the one to approach her.

'She liked you best. Thought Meg was evil and that I treated Rowan like a slave. Quick. Run or you'll lose her.'

Mouth dry, Jen galloped along the line of market stalls, the others running behind her.

'Mrs Howard?' She tapped the woman on the shoulder.

Jesus, it was her. Meg was right. The frown lines between the brows and down the sides of her thin miserable-looking mouth had deepened to chiselled canyons, and much of her craggy face was obscured by a knitted hat, but it was definitely her.

'Yes?' The woman squinted at her suspiciously, watchful eyes flickering.

'I'm Jennifer, Rowan's old school friend.' There was a long moment's pause, during which first Meg and then Georgina caught up. 'Jenny? Oh yes, I remember you.' If anything her face became more disapproving. 'Your skirt was like a handkerchief.'

'Kids, eh.' Jen shrugged and smiled as if she'd complimented her.

Mrs Howard looked her up and down, and then did the same to the two women behind her. 'Well then, I'll be off.' She matched her actions to her words.

'Mrs Howard,' this time Georgina leapt in, 'wait. It's me, Georgina. Georgina Carrington. So splendid to see you again!' She threw her arms around Mrs Howard as if she was welcoming a long-lost child. Startled, Rowan's mother froze, her whole body rigid against Georgina's merciless squeezing.

'Georgina? Miss High and Mighty?' Her eyes glowered. 'You made my girl timid. Lording it over her with your hoity-toity English ways.'

Georgina's arms fell away, thrown by the hostile response. 'I – I didn't mean to,' she stammered.

'Rowan wasn't timid.' Meg, who'd been hanging back behind Jen, stepped forward now. 'Just a little shy. We'd love to see her again, Mrs H.'

The Welsh woman scowled, glaring from one to another.

'Look,' Jen pleaded, 'we were wondering if you could tell us how to contact Rowan. Does she live around here?'

Mrs Howard pulled her coat together with one hand, basket over her arm, and regarded them all with a hunted expression.

'No, no she doesn't.'

'Then where is she?' Meg asked with her best coaxing smile. 'Thing is, we need to know. It's a matter of life and death.'

At that Mrs Howard stared at her, eyes widening, head shaking. 'I've got to go.'

'No, really,' Georgina gave a withering look at Meg, 'it's nothing sinister. But we, well, we had a reunion at the school and the three of us without Rowan – why, it's like eggs without bacon.'

Not the best simile, Jen thought. Mrs Howard had been vegan.

'She's gone.' The old lady's tone changed, becoming harsh and forceful.

'Where?'

'Moved. To China, near Peking.'

'Beijing now,' corrected Georgina.

'Could we have the address?' said Meg. 'Not that we're likely to visit any time soon, but we could write.'

'I don't know.'

'What? You don't know her address?' Georgina looked confused.

'Well of course I know her address.' Mrs Howard sounded as icy as the Totnes streets. 'But she doesn't want me giving it out to all and sundry. Besides she's moving again, now, as we speak. Trying Shanghai.'

'What does she do? Workwise?' Jen had to ask.

'She's er . . . um . . . a physiotherapist.'

'A physio, wow. How superb!' gushed Georgina.

'What about her paintings?' Meg asked, slightly bewildered.

'She gave that up ages ago. Childish nonsense. No money in it. No, she's a physio all right. Looks into people's minds and tries to cure phobias.'

'You mean a *psychotherapist*?' Jen said.

'Uh huh. She had to learn hypnotism and all sorts. Look, away with you.' She flapped her fingerless gloves at them, shooing them off. 'I can't be doing with this. I've two cats at home needing fed.'

'Mrs Howard,' Jen grabbed her arm, 'You don't understand. We *need* her address. We really do.'

'I haven't got it. Not on me,' she said sharply, shrugging her off. 'I've got to go.'

'But . . . please, stop. If you . . .' Suddenly Jen was frantic. This was their last chance. They might never bump into Mrs Howard again.

'Now listen,' Georgina held out one of her business cards, 'if you hear from her any time soon, please, give her my details. It has my work address, email and here,' she scribbled something on the back. 'My mobile. Please ask her to call.'

'Yes. All right. All right.' Mrs Howard stuck it in her coat pocket. 'I have to run.' She scowled down at her feet in their wellingtons and muttered unconvincingly, 'Lovely to see you again.'

'That's that then,' Georgina said as they trudged back to their bed and breakfast.

'Told you,' Meg said. 'She *hates* us.'

'You might be right,' Jen agreed. 'She couldn't get away fast enough.'

'China,' Georgina groaned. 'I'll never have time to visit.'

'And I'll never have the dough,' added Meg.

Jen was quiet, thinking a little trip to Shanghai might clear out some cobwebs. If she could save up the cash, that is – ugh, her mind closed once again to the money thing.

'It's me she hates the most,' Georgina groaned. 'Calling me Miss High and Mighty. I'm not high and mighty, am I?'

Jen and Meg swapped quick glances.

'I saw that . . . what?'

'Just,' began Meg, 'sometimes you come across, well . . . a little, er . . .' She looked across at Jen for help.

'Judgemental,' said Jen diplomatically.

'Or patronising.'

'Or snobby. I know you're not really,' Jen rushed to reassure her, 'I mean sometimes it's just the way you talk, your accent and everything, but then there are things you say that sound just like your mum.' She declined from mentioning her earlier van-driver comment.

'Patronising, judgemental, snobby.' Georgina looked miserable. 'No, go on, don't hold back. Hit me.'

'OK,' Meg took her at her word. 'Just yesterday, you called those people bohos, then in the bed and breakfast you sneered at the avocado suite.'

'I thought it was hideous too.' Jen felt she had to defend her a little.

To their utmost horror, Georgina suddenly put her hands to her face and turned away, shoulders shaking.

'Georgina, don't.' Jen put her arm around her. 'We only said that because you asked.'

'So if I asked you to shoot me, would you do it?' Georgina extracted a tissue from her sleeve and wiped her nose.

'Er, no,' said Jen.

'Yes,' said Meg, 'say you were dying of some incurable disease.'

She managed a weak smile. 'Well, that's reassuring. Oh don't mind me. It's not either of you. It's just . . . I'm not at my best today.' She forced a jolly tone. 'Quite an eccentric, Rowan's mother, don't you think?'

Jen snorted derisively. 'Brilliant observation, Sherlock. I'll bet if you looked up "eccentric" in the dictionary, there'd be a picture of Ma Howard and her broomstick.'

'Not to mention she was lying through her teeth,' Meg chipped in.

'How could you tell?' Jen stopped in her tracks.

'Because one, Rowan told me her mum was highly allergic to cats.' She was interrupted by the ringing of a mobile phone.

'Excuse me.' Georgina pulled it out of her handbag and flipped it open. 'Aiden?' they heard her say.

'And two,' Meg continued, as Georgina walked a short distance away, phone to her ear, 'never try to bullshit a bull-shitter. I can spot when someone's lying from three hundred miles away. I swear, if Rowan *was* buried in some unmarked grave, I'd notch Ma Howard as the prime suspect!'

'Why on earth do you think she married him?' Meg asked Jen as they watched Georgina's train pull away from Totnes railway station. Het up and frazzled, she was hell-bent for London to sort out some office crisis, refusing their suggestion that all three drive back early. 'Don't cut your trip short too,' she'd insisted. 'The train's twice as fast.' So they'd packed, checked out of the B & B and Georgie was on a train home.

'What do you mean?'

'Georgina and Aiden, dude. They seem such an odd couple. She's got class, talent – and money now. And Aiden, well . . .' She didn't finish the sentence. 'They seem like totally ill-matched.'

'Why does anyone marry anyone?' Jen said repressively. It was no more than she'd asked herself a dozen times, but she didn't like Meg's implied criticism that Aiden, gorgeous, sexy, kind, talented Aiden somehow didn't measure up. 'Why did you marry the bull rider? Why did I marry Ollie?'

'Well, tequila slammers did it for me. And pregnancy aside, we all know what you saw in Ollie.' She gave a lascivious grin. 'Besides, they're still together. My marriage only lasted five minutes and now you and Ollie are divorced, over, done, end of story.'

'I know, I know.' She was aware that she sounded irritated, but she didn't care for how Meg was saying it, in a sort of jokey casual way. She certainly didn't consider the failure of her marriage to be one big funny hilarious joke. Not yet and maybe not ever.

They made their way back to the car park, Meg sliding into the driver's seat.

'So where now?' Meg asked.

'Home,' Jen decided. 'We're packed. Everything's in the boot and we've done all we can here. I don't really care to hang around shopping, do you?'

'No, I'm good.' Meg clipped up her seat belt and returned to her subject. 'Not to mention all Starkey ever cared about was music and writing. And sex,' she looked to Jen for confirmation. 'Am I right? And suddenly he's shacked up with

318

Miss Prissy Drawers, acting like Georgina's flunkey, and she's running the whole show. So I'm guessing there has to be *a ton* of money involved. How much do you think that business is worth? Do they own it together?'

'I've no idea,' Jen said huffily, as the engine purred into life. 'And stop talking about Starkey as if he's some kind of gigolo. What's he ever done to you?'

'Nothing.' Meg pulled out, horn blaring, without indicating. 'But why are you so damn quick to defend him? He acted like an asshole to you.'

'He was young.'

'Sure, but he still dumped you without even bothering to explain. And married one of your closest friends.'

'Georgie hadn't seen me for years.' Jen drew a face on the steamed-up window. It was ironic that by defending Aiden she was forced to defend Georgina as well. 'I don't know if you can call that close friends.' Still, she couldn't help thinking that if anyone should have been sensitive to the situation, it was Georgina. You didn't expect the same level of delicacy from men.

Totnes receded into the distance as they cruised along the road. From nowhere, Meg said, 'You know they had a humdinger of a fight last night. She was practically screaming at him when I came back from the shower. And I'm positive she went out after we were in bed. I heard her coming back in and when I went to the loo, she was throwing up in her bathroom.'

'You said already.'

'You want to know what I think?'

'Not really.'

Meg looked at her in surprise and Jen kept her face stony. 'I don't really care for gossip,' she said loftily. 'Or people telling lies.'

'Lies?' Meg wrinkled her nose. 'You mean like telling Yvonne Spitz that Graham Furrow married Phyllis Ifold, that kind of lie?'

Jen felt her temper rise. She was ready to have it out with Meg, once and for all.

'That was just a bit of fun and you know it. No, I mean . . .' She cursed as her phone started to ring, snatching it up from beside the gearstick.

'Jen,' Ollie said in a calming tone that immediately got her heart racing, 'it's Chloe. Now she's totally fine, so don't freak out but . . .'

# Chapter 36

Jen stood outside Saul's ground-floor flat, jiggling the set of car keys in her hand. When her first two rings went unanswered she put her hand on the buzzer and kept it there.

Finally it opened. Ollie was in front of her, beaming away, and immediately her back bristled.

'Jen, you're early.'

'I got here as soon as I could.'

'I told you not to hurry. Chloe's . . .'

'Mummee!' Chloe squeezed past Ollie and raced towards her.

'Darling!' Jen gasped as she caught sight of her daughter's thin wiry wrist held in a sling – in a cast. Jen dropped to the ground and flung her arms around her.

'Ouch!' Chloe squealed.

'Oh God, sorry.' Jen recoiled. 'Does it hurt?'

'Not much. The doctor gave me a sticker and some red liquorice shoelaces for being brave. Look, he signed the plaster as well.'

Ollie had explained on the phone it was a bike accident, but he never said how bad. Never said it was . . .

'Broken?' She glared at him.

'A greenstick fracture,' he said simply.

'Isn't that the same as a break? How the hell could you let . . .' She paused as she caught Chloe's expression. 'Sweetheart, can you fetch your things?'

'But Mu-um . . .' she wailed, looking beseechingly at her dad.

'We've just rented a DVD,' explained Ollie.

'Can't I finish it, Mummy?' Chloe pleaded. 'Or you could come in and watch it with us? It's got Johnny Depp starring. Saul's got Quality Street.'

'Johnny Depp *and* Quality Street, whit whoo!' Jen tried not to be the big black raincloud at her daughter's parade but inwardly she was incensed. 'I hope it's a PG.' It was a jab at Ollie, the irresponsible parent.

'No, it's Spawn of Satan meets Freddy on Elm Street.' Ollie gave her a vicious smile. 'You can come in, you know.' He held the door open, glancing at a figure walking through the hall. 'Oy, Saul. Here. Meet my wife – er . . . ex-wife,' he quickly corrected.

'I know him,' she hissed. 'Who do you think takes Chloe to football when you're away?'

'Hi, there.' Saul came to the doorstep and held out his hand, the one without the lager in it. His hair was carrot, a riot of springy curls over an amiable squashy face. This was the first time she'd met him away from the football field and, to her jaded eyes, hypersensitive and on full mother alert, his entire appearance shrieked loafer, deadbeat, slob, from his holey-kneed tracksuit bottoms to his old striped shirt with half the buttons missing, exposing a large amount of curly ginger chest hair. Was that even decent in front of a child not your own?

She shuddered, imagining what the rest of his bachelor pad looked like – probably hadn't been cleaned in years, sofa with springs sticking out, futon on the disgusting carpet.

'Good to see you again.' He gulped from his can. 'Heard loads about you.'

'All bad, I bet.' Jen was only too aware how Ollie would have described her – moody, uptight, critical bitch would probably cover it – but had to shake hands.

'Come in.' Saul scratched his chest sleepily. 'We're getting a Chinese takeaway.'

Well, at least they weren't cooking in what she already pictured as a rat-infested haven for bacteria. She wanted to tell Chloe to be sure to wash her hands.

'Or I'll just drop Chloe back later?' Ollie suggested.

'What time later?' She fidgeted anxiously, hardly paying attention. She was too busy imagining the potential photos in the forthcoming custody battle if she were forced to pull Chloe away from this pit of neglect. Saul's kitchen – mice nibbling pizza crusts left on the counters, ants marching over unwashed plates. Main exhibits would be Chloe's plaster cast and Saul's presumably filthy sleeping bag. And she'd be the picture of perfect parenthood, wearing a little Jaeger suit, in velvet perhaps.

'When the film's over?' Ollie gave her a strange look. Saul poked Chloe in the ribs making her giggle. *Get your filthy paws off my daughter*, she wanted to shriek.

She began shaking her head, suddenly feeling ganged-up against. 'I'm tired, very tired. I'll call you.'

'How was your weekend away? Did you find what you were looking for?'

'Did I find . . .' She backed away. 'No. I'll speak to you later.'

By the time she got home she was in a foul mood, dropping her bag and Feo's lead on the floor, stooping to pick up the letters on the mat. More Christmas cards. The guilt trips were on a faster, more convenient schedule than the Huntsleigh-to-London commuter trains. She hadn't been able to bring herself to send any yet, and each one that arrived addressed to 'Jen and Ollie' or 'Ollie, Jen and Chloe', came with a little stab to the heart. What was she supposed to do? Tell everyone, 'I'm not buying cards this year as my money's going for goats in Africa'? Or bury their new marital status in the midst of one of those round-robin letters everyone hates? '*Our new refrigerator has twice the freezer capacity of the old one, though since Ollie's divorced me he'll no longer be dipping into it. More excitingly, Chloe's showing great promise after her initial struggles with science . . .*'

She put the kettle on and opened the first envelope with a small kitchen knife.

'Happy Christmas,' it read. 'Your Saturday newspaper girl.'

She put it to one side and slit open another and another, still fuming at Ollie. How dare he! He knew she was picking up Chloe, why hadn't she simply marched in there and demanded her daughter come home?

Because she'd have been unpopular. Probably have had to drag Chloe screaming, broken arm and all, into the car.

The last envelope contained a letter rather than a card. By the time she'd finished reading it she was livid beyond belief. She flicked through her mobile and pressed a number.

'She's still watching *Charlie and the Chocolate Factory*.' Ollie sounded like he was eating. Chomping on his chow mein, no doubt. 'It won't be over for at least another hour.'

'I wasn't calling about that,' Jen blustered. 'Hagard's written to me . . . us. The Radcliffes haven't got their lease extension sorted and their buyers are now saying they're not signing contracts until it's done.'

'If only the law was like Scotland.' Now he sounded like he was slurping beer, not a care in the world. He was such a kid sometimes. It infuriated her when she had so much on her mind she could hardly think straight. She should never have left this weekend. If she'd stayed home Chloe would still be in one piece. And maybe the house sale wouldn't be in danger of falling apart. The Radcliffes' buyers could drop out. The market could tank still further and then where would they be? Stuck in some kind of housing purgatory? She couldn't take this limbo. She was desperate to move on.

'Why does everyone keep saying that? We don't live in sodding Scotland, so who cares what their bloody laws are!'

'I'll talk to Hagard tomorrow. He seemed to have his act together last time I spoke.'

'And when was that?' Her voice lashed sarcasm. 'Because he's bleeding useless now.'

'Jen,' Ollie said edgily, 'what's going on? Why are you so angry? I thought we said . . .'

'Those were the old rules.' Jen couldn't remove the hostility from her voice. 'Chloe's alone with you five minutes and she has a dreadful accident. Where the fuck were you when she was breaking her arm, were you even paying attention?' She knew she was getting carried away, all her earlier resolutions forgotten, but anger made her irrational. 'And then to let me find out like that. How in buggery am I supposed to trust you next time?'

'Look now,' Ollie's tone hardened, 'I didn't tell you how bad it was because I didn't want you driving home upset. I knew you'd go apeshit about the scrambling . . .'

'You mean it was the *scrambling bike*?' Jen pushed her fist against her head. 'You let Chloe go *scrambling* when the ground's frozen solid?' She started pacing, holding the phone so tight her knuckles were white. 'Why didn't you just shove her into a cement post? It would probably have been less lethal.'

'I couldn't talk her out of it,' Ollie replied, raising his voice. 'We can't all be bloody perfect.'

'You're not supposed to *talk her out of it*. You're the parent. You make the rules. And what about the concert?'

'What concert?'

'The one she's supposed to play her violin in this Friday.' Jen said in a biting tone. 'The one she's lacerated her fingers for the last three months practising for.'

'Hey, it happened,' he said flatly. 'I don't need lectures from you.'

'Well you need them from somebody. I'm just curious, Ollie.' Her voice turned glacial. 'When are you going to start acting like a grown-up?'

'Maybe,' his voice matched hers in strength and ferocity, 'when you stop acting like my ninety-year-old puritan *fucking* aunt!'

'Fuck off!' She slammed the phone down.

Someone was knocking on the door. She opened it to Santa Claus clanging a bell on her doorstep. His white beard parted to reveal red lips.

'Ho ho ho,' he chortled.

'And you can fuck off too!' The door shuddered under the impact.


'It's a bloody disaster,' Aiden announced as Georgina deposited her suitcase in the hall and followed him into her home office. He had their production manager and a couple of designers to back him up, wringing their hands, their faces nervous and apologetic. Poor things dragged down to Berkshire on a Sunday. It was bad enough coming back from Devon with all the rail-service disruptions.

'Someone leaked the prelim sketches for the new Georgie Gi collection on the Internet. Brian here found out by accident. There'll be shoddy imitations showing up in the high street in a matter of days. We'll have to postpone the launch.'

Georgina felt her heart hammer, her knees go weak. Georgie Gi was her new young-fashion line, aimed at teens. They had enormous amounts of time and money invested in the project. The PR department had spent months whipping the press up into a frenzy, teasing them that the new unveiling would be big beyond belief. And now there'd be nothing to show. They couldn't make a splash with styles already on sale in bargain-basement stores. The implications were horrendous.

'How could that happen?' She threw her briefcase on her desk. 'Those sketches weren't supposed to leave this office.' She started to rattle off instructions. 'Call an emergency meeting for first thing tomorrow morning, everyone involved in Georgie Gi to attend. We need to find out how bad this is, if there's anything we can salvage, and come up with some plausible story if we need to delay. And Aiden, I want you to talk to everyone who had access to those sketches, find out who sold us out. I want their desk cleared by lunchtime.'

'Will do,' Aiden said. 'But that's not all, I'm afraid. The Heal's people aren't happy. They're being very nice about it but their chief buyer called me confidentially this morning to say that on reflection they were disappointed in the designs we presented. They were hoping for something more distinctive.'

'I told you they were substandard!' Georgina whirled on him. 'You had no business presenting that putrid mediocre crap and passing it off as Giordani.'

'I had no . . .' Aiden bit his lip, his face white with anger. 'Brian, guys, would you give us a minute alone?'

The production manager and the designers scuttled out, almost pathetically eager to flee the scene.

'To begin with,' he was visibly trying to force himself to stay calm, 'I did nothing that you . . .'

'You pushed me into it!' Georgina screamed. 'You harassed me and coerced me and called a bloody meeting with the buyers without my consent. I'm never doing that again. From now on if I don't like it it doesn't go out. You have no clue, Aiden. You can't just force creativity.'

'No, *you* have no clue,' he said with a vehemence that shocked her. 'I've been a part of Giordani from the start and you treat me as if I'm the bloody coffee boy. I'm the one who keeps this company running while you play the part of the misunderstood genius. You can't keep these big companies waiting while our one and only creative source indulges in her thirteenth nervous breakdown. There's no room for prima donna hysterics in business. It doesn't work that way.'

'Well, it certainly doesn't work *your* way, does it?' she lashed back, leaning forward, hands planted on her desk. 'I told you we were taking on too many projects, there's a limit to what I can do. And last I looked the company was still called Giordani, not Aiden Starkson. I'm the boss and don't you forget it.'

'How could I when you never let me for a second?' He paced across the room. 'Or anyone else. You've got those poor designers so petrified they're scared to lift a pencil, because anyone who submits an idea gets their head chopped off. Oh I agree no one can match you when you're on form, but when was the last time you were on form? If you can't pull it together we might as well accept one of those buyout offers, cash it all in and move to the Caribbean. Before the whole thing goes down the toilet and there's nothing left to sell.'

'Oh yes, you'd love that, wouldn't you? Bail out. Take the money and run.'

'Let me point out,' Aiden gritted his teeth, 'you haven't come up with anything you're happy with for months now. We're at a critical stage in our development, we're too high-profile to depend on a single person's creativity, especially when that one person seems to be veering between hysteria and total block. I've told you before you should focus your energies on the haute couture lines – that's the attention-grabbing stuff – and let the rest of us handle the minor shit . . .'

'It's not minor shit to me!' Georgina screeched back. 'Damn it, Aiden, if you had your way Giordani would be in the Pound Shop, flaunting cartoon duvet covers, polyester pillowcases, and a line of fluffy children's slippers.'

'At least we'd be doing something. You know damn well the Giordani name's hot right now.' Aiden wasn't backing down. 'You could scribble those initials on a tea towel and people would snap them up, but it won't last for ever. The public's fickle. They're tightening their belts right now. Businesses are going down like flies, unemployment rising as fast. If you drop the ball now, by the time you pick it up again the world will have moved on. No one will even remember Giordani once meant something. And frankly I don't know that I'll care. I'm sick of your megalomaniac attitude and the shitty way you treat people.'

'Then clear off.' Georgina jutted her chin, her voice more elevated than she'd intended, a red mist hazing her vision. 'And anyone else who doesn't like it can clear off too. I pay you all enough. I expect good service, yes, but . . .'

'It's not all about money,' he snapped. 'We've got designers on staff who would be superstars in any other company, and you act as if they're talentless lowlives. You're not only crippling yourself with your insecurities, you're crippling them too!'

'That is absolute rot!'

'It isn't. And you bloody well know it. You want me to clear off – well, fine. I'm going to the pub.'

'You can't. Not now. Aiden, get back here this instant!'

'Just watch me!' He stormed out.

What a beastly ending to a weekend that had started out so well, Georgina fretted, as she closed the door behind Brian and the others, thanking them for their trouble. It wasn't the first or even the hundredth row she'd had with Aiden. Last night on the phone they'd had a blazing fight that had left her reeling, sending her spinning out into the night virtually in tears. But recently their battles seemed to be getting worse, without the subsequent kiss and make-up that used to be a part of their passionate disagreements. She felt numb with fear that he didn't love her any more. Perhaps she clung to the control of the company because it was the only control she felt she had left?

But was it true what Aiden had said, that she treated others

329

badly, crippling them? She lay on the drawing-room sofa, sick to the pit of her stomach.

Even Nutmeg and Jennifer had said she wasn't always nice to people. How had she become so unpleasant, without realising?

Ten minutes later she was still there worrying about recent events. It was no good, this wasn't helping. Pulling herself up, she went into the kitchen, returning with a knife and a delicious-looking chocolate cake the cook had baked for them. She cut a slice and then another, eating mindlessly while doodling on a pad with a stump of broken pencil. Her thoughts drifted back to Totnes, the maze of streets, the way the light reflected off the river, the motley inhabitants with their wild eclectic outfits, the colours of the farmers' market. She fingered the silver pendant Nutmeg had persuaded her to buy with its moss-green moldavite stone, a piece of meteorite, her American friend had said, a power stone. It was Nutmeg's kind of place all right – New Age-y with its crystal healers and strange practitioners – but there was also something splendidly medieval about it all, reminiscent of court jesters, jousting knights and dancing round maypoles.

A glimmer of an idea came to her and she started sketching in earnest, her pencil flying over the page.

Jen walked across the heath still shaking from her argument with Ollie. Only six forty-five. It had been dark for over two hours, but she couldn't bear to sit miserably alone in the house, waiting. She and Ollie rarely fought openly, moody silences being more the nature of their cold war. Ollie was easy-going, Jen hated conflict. It might not mean they got all their problems aired but after his puritan aunt comment, she decided there was a lot to be said for putting on blinkers and a gag.

She blundered on, stumbling in the dark with only the moon to guide her, Feo running in the shadows, barking at things she couldn't see, eerie black silhouettes blurring in front of her.

She'd stopped to sit on a rock on the highest part of the ridge, misery sapping her energy. When her mobile rang, she snatched it out of her pocket, nearly dropping it back when she saw it was Aiden. But almost of their own accord, it seemed, her finger pressed the accept button.

'Hello? Jen?'

She was silent, unable to speak, struggling to control the sobs that were rising up from somewhere deep within her.

'Jen?'

'Aiden?' she managed. An odd snorting sound came from her nostrils and Feo trotted back to investigate. He licked her hand.

'Where are you?'

'On the ridge,' she finally managed to say.

'I'm driving over.'

'No. Don't!'

The phone went dead.

Oh God. Fumbling with frozen fingers, she tried repeatedly to call him back, but his phone went straight to voicemail. What had she done? Why had she let him hear her cry? Now she'd stopped walking, she was really cold and more than a little spooked. All alone up here at the mercy of any maniac that might happen along, and she had to wait for Aiden because he was probably in his car already and it wouldn't be fair to leave him wandering for miles looking for her or risk him turning up at the house when Ollie dropped Chloe off.

Oh well, she tried to slow her pacing heart, perhaps he'd arrive with Georgina. She'd have two friends to comfort her instead of one, two shoulders to cry on. She crossed her middle finger over her index and then slowly uncrossed them.

If she were honest, that wasn't what she wanted at all.

# Chapter 37

In the light of the full moon Aiden's tall figure strode briskly along the ridge, like Heathcliff on a brooding moor. As he drew near, she rose from her rock to greet him and shush Feo's frenzied barking. 'You didn't need to . . .'

He stopped in front of her, his eyes flashing. 'I did. Georgie and I had a huge blow-up.'

'So did I. With Ollie. Oh, Aiden, everything's so awful.' She burst into tears again. Not delicate ladylike sniffles but the all-out waterworks. Her nose was running. She could hardly see out of her swollen eyes and her body juddered with long racking sobs. She pulled out an old tissue from her pocket and blew hard, aware that she must look a complete fright but unable to do anything about it.

'Jen, don't . . .' He stared at her helplessly, his face still pale and angry, then drew her into his arms, his mouth fastening on hers in a passionate kiss. Her tears evaporated under the force of his lips. She could hardly breathe, her nose still feeling clogged, her lips bruised from the pressure of his mouth, but none of it seemed to matter. A delicious warmth spread from her toes to her stomach, flooding the very centre of her being. Jealous, Feo jumped at them in turn, hitting them with his front paws and yapping.

Finally Aiden released her, and she felt the chill of the void where his torso had been pressed into hers. His eyes searched hers, his expression tortured.

'I've wanted to do that for so long,' he said huskily. 'It's been killing me seeing you again.'

'Me too,' she confessed. She lowered her eyes, hot with shame, afraid he'd see her naked desire radiating out of them to match the feeling she saw in his.

His hand brushed a curl of wet hair from her cheek, tracing the cheekbone with his thumb.

'I shouldn't have kissed you,' he whispered, already retreating. 'I just can't stand to see you unhappy. I never could.'

Gently he kissed her nose, her forehead, then wrapped his arms around her and pulled her against his chest.

'My poor baby,' he murmured into the top of her head.

She leaned. She couldn't help it. Fell into him, arms finding their rightful place inside his embrace, wanting to be held, wanting to be his poor baby. If she'd ever needed to be cuddled, it was today, and if she'd ever needed to be cuddled by anyone it was Aiden. It didn't matter that he was Georgina's. That they would never be together again. For these few minutes she wanted to feel his arms around her, pretend that the last twenty years had never been.

After what seemed an eternity, he backed them to the boulder and sat down on it with Jen on his lap, Feo trying to push his nose between them.

'Feeling better?' He gently massaged her shoulders.

'Much,' she sniffed. 'I'm sorry, I don't know what got into me.'

'I do,' he said. Gently he brushed away a last remaining tear with the knuckle of his index finger and followed it up with a light kiss. 'And I think you do too. It's like a horrible cosmic joke but at least let's not kid ourselves it's not happening.'

'We have to.' She rubbed her eyes with the heel of her palm. 'You're married.'

'Don't think I don't regret that every single day. I made a big

333

mistake when I left you. Another when I married Georgie, convinced I'd lost you for good. She told me she never saw you. It never occurred to me I'd run into you again. I didn't even realise until I saw you at the Marlow Arms what a screw-up I'd made of my life. I wanted so badly to grab you that night, run off with you, turn back the clock. I haven't been able to think of anything since.'

'I couldn't forget you,' she whispered, wondering why his confession made her feel joyful when she ought to feel even more wicked. 'I tried for years.'

'I even – God, this sounds pathetic! – that night at the Marlow . . . I came to your room after everyone was in bed. I wanted so badly to talk to you. I was in hell. Ready to chuck it all in, ask Georgie for a divorce, throw myself on your mercy and beg you to forgive me. Even though I knew it was hopeless.'

'I heard you knock.' Her gut twisted, thinking of that night. 'I knew it was you. But I couldn't open the door. I'd just realised – at least I was almost a hundred per cent sure – that I was pregnant. I was carrying Ollie's child. And Georgina was carrying yours. You were married. What would have been the point?'

'What a bloody mess I've made of everything.' His hand continued to rub her shoulders, moving in to fondle her neck and travelling back down again. It was so soothing, hypnotic even. She felt like a stroked cat, as if she could close her eyes and fall asleep, purring.

'Do you still love me?' he asked softly.

She managed a feeble kind of smile, not answering, mesmerised by the rhythmic touch. His mouth was following his fingers now, travelling up her neck as he lifted her hair. She only turned her head a fraction but suddenly their lips met and he was kissing her and she was kissing him back, unable to stop him, not wanting to. The addiction was still there, overpowering, out of her control. He was here with her and it was amazing, a miracle, and for a brief space of time nothing else mattered, no one else existed and they were all alone at the top of the ridge, at the top of the world, lovers, soulmates and surely destined to be together. Home at last after years of being lost in the wastelands.

It was only with a monumental effort, like tearing off her own arm, she managed to break away. She wrenched herself from his knee and sat down on the cold ground, shoulders slumped, clawing at clumps of dead grass with numb fingers.

'I can't,' she said. 'This is wrong. Georgina . . .'

Aiden tilted her chin.

'Georgina'll be all right. If she's upset at losing me it'll be for the business aspect, not because she's in love with her husband.' He hesitated, clearly making up his mind whether to proceed. 'You have no idea how bad our home life is. Georgina's emotional issues are out of control. She's her own worst enemy and now her self-sabotage is affecting everyone around her.'

'What kind of emotional issues?' She finally dared to ask. A memory came to her of herself when Helen met her, painfully thin, unable to sleep, haunted by terrifying visions. If Helen hadn't befriended her, offered her a place in her flat . . . 'She's not having an affair, is she?'

'An affair?' Aiden looked startled and then his mouth twisted wryly. 'Yeah, as if she'd have the time or the inclination. She doesn't even like . . .' He rubbed his forehead irritably. 'No, it's not that. No such luck.'

Soberly he picked up Jen's hand, looking at her naked finger where the wedding ring had left a lighter band of flesh. 'She's bulimic. It hits her hardest when she's under stress but it's wreaking havoc with both our lives. I wanted to tell you before you went to Totnes but what could I say? Keep an eye on my wife for me?'

'Bulimia?' Jen thought of how rail-thin Georgie had become,

the way she'd picked at her meals in Devon. Meg saying she'd heard her vomit. 'Is she having treatment?'

'She has a therapist. He helped her the first time. I've tried making her go back, but she denies it's happening.'

He dropped Jen's hand and stared out over the ridge, his face bleak. 'She has these absurd eating binges, sometimes empties the entire freezer in a single night, packs away enough to feed a family of four and then she throws it all up. You've noticed her teeth? All that vomiting ruins the enamel, that's why she has veneers. Her two obsessions – work and her weight – and they've both ruined any chance our relationship had. Even if she wanted children and could back off from work, her body probably couldn't handle pregnancy. And she won't even admit how sick she is. She tries to hide it even from me.'

He folded his arms, hugged them to his chest and shivered as Jen stared at him in horror. He looked grim and despairing, as lonely as any Ancient Mariner.

'I guess I can understand . . . a bit anyway,' she said slowly, 'because I went through something like it. Not bulimia but severe depression. Long time back and then later after Chloe was born. I was on pills. I couldn't talk to anyone about it, either. And it didn't matter how nice my friend Helen,' she swallowed, 'or Ollie was, either. I just had to get through it.'

'Yes, well, I thought I could help Georgina but I can't. Maybe no one can. If anything I might be making it worse, just by staying with her. Becoming a codependent by covering for her all the time as she plummets on her course to self-destruction. If I left she might really have to get her act together.'

The wild elation that had filled Jen's heart just twenty minutes ago had all leaked away. Feo had wandered off. The ground was damp where she sat, the cold seeping through her jeans. She moved her arm so it couldn't accidentally brush Aiden's knee.

336

'I had no idea.' Her voice was sombre. He went to touch her hand and she snatched it away. 'Starkey, we mustn't. It would be bad enough if she were well. I can't be responsible for giving her more grief.' She looked off, blinking. 'I'd better get home. Chloe will be back any minute. Feo! Come!'

'No,' he said forcefully, fists clenched. 'I used to think that, but it's all wrong. The way I see it, all three of us can live in misery or we can face the truth and everyone has a chance at real happiness. Georgie deserves better. And so do we.' He grabbed both of Jen's hands this time, holding them so she couldn't escape. 'I'm not asking you to run away this minute or even make any decision today. But my marriage is over. And I'm here for you, any time, any place. We're meant for each other. I know it and I think you know it.'

'I don't know what I know. Except,' Jen chewed her lip, bruised from his kisses, 'yes, I still love you.'

His face was close to hers, so close she could see his eyes shining.

'That's all that matters then.' He gathered her up again, lifting her feet at least six inches off the ground as he kissed her.

And she let him because she knew this was as far as it could ever go, even if his body did seem to draw hers to his like the most powerful magnet inside the earth's core. She would have to be a monstrous person to hurt Georgina even the teensiest bit more. It had to stop right here.

But for this minute, with Aiden touching and caressing her as if he too knew that they'd have to make do with these few moments for the rest of their lives, she threw herself into kissing him heart and soul.


When Georgina had finished it was almost midnight, the chocolate cake was half gone but she was exhilarated, her body fizzing with the knowledge that what she'd done was good, maybe even great. She'd do the final touches tomorrow; get it mocked up on the computer and courier it over to Heal's before lunch. In the meantime she was too high with sugar and artistic buzz to go to bed. The house was stifling suddenly. She stepped out the back door to look at the stars, so bright and intense in the frosty night air.

There was a light still on above the former stables, now the garage apartment where Max lived. She could see his TV flickering and as she looked, he crossed to the window of the living room and stared out. Someone else not in bed yet. Perhaps he was a night owl too?

She thought again about Rowan's mother calling her high and mighty, about Jennifer and Nutmeg saying she was a snob, about Aiden saying she didn't treat people well. Was that true of Max, too? He'd never shown resentment. He was such a nice soft-spoken man. Kind eyes. On an impulse she came back into the living room, picked up the plate with the rest of the chocolate cake and walked across the yard towards the garage. Someone else might as well enjoy this. Aiden didn't care for sweet things and if she left it lying around, chances were she'd eat the whole thing herself. She shuddered. She'd already eaten far too much. It lay like a lead weight in her stomach.

The apartment was reached by a wooden staircase up the back. She climbed up, plate in hand, and tapped on the door.

# Chapter 38

'You're late.' Ollie removed his jumper from the wooden chair next to him and handed her an A5 folded programme.

'Am I?' Jen said frostily, sitting down.

'I wasn't criticising,' Ollie hissed. 'Simply surprised. You're never late. Not for years.'

'Well, I am now.' Jen stuck her handbag on the floor, then stood up as the music teacher gesticulated to the audience to rise. No point in explaining she'd let Feo out for a wee to try and prevent the 'accidents' that were becoming a feature of his stay and the little bugger had refused to come back in, running halfway down the street before she could coax him close enough to nab his collar.

A hundred-odd chairs had been set out for the carol concert, separated by a gangway down the centre. This was the big event of the school year, all classes from Years Three to Six involved. Some parents, eyes to cameras or camcorders, were forfeiting their right to a seat for a record of their child's moment of glory. The third and fourth years were lined up against a wall, waiting to be summoned, each little head adorned with a pointy green elf hat.

The choir were already in place, the music master waving his baton as he gave last-minute instructions, the orchestra making a fearsome din as they tuned their instruments. Chloe should have been with them, Jen seethed, instead of grouped in a corner to the left of the stage with her non-musical friends.

'Welcome one and all.' The head teacher wore a Santa hat and snowman-adorned woolly jumper. 'Only thirteen days till Christmas, so I'm glad you've postponed your Friday night shopping for our evening of entertainment. The first carol of the night will be "O Come All Ye Faithful", so if you'd like to join in. After three now . . .'

'And your hair looks like it's been dragged through a hedge,' Ollie whispered as a chorus of voices belted forth.

'Oh shut up!' Jen snapped. She *had* in fact gone under a hedge, trying to reach for Feo, but there was no way she'd give Ollie the satisfaction of knowing that. 'I'm here, aren't I? I had to take a last-minute phone call.'

'. . . to Be-e-th-lehem,' the man next to her sang in a loud baritone.

'Must have been a rough one,' Ollie smirked and gave a devilish grin at the woman on his right. 'Nothing beats a good old afternoon nap, does it?'

Jen's blood boiled. Was he insinuating . . .? 'Bog off!'

A mother in front turned round. Jen gave her a quick smile, then spotted Frances Hutton glancing across. She smiled at her too.

'Wonderful.' The conductor stepped up as the song ended. 'And now the steel drums will perform "Away in a Manger".' He lifted his baton high in the air. 'Take it away, Year Five.'

An odd Caribbean-sounding version of the carol began to resonate round the hall. Jen shifted in her chair, relieved not to have to talk, and instead reflected on the past days' events. What had possessed her to agree to dinner with Tom Dugan? Wasn't her life complicated enough?

He'd called twice, the first time on Sunday night when she'd returned home reeling from her encounter with Aiden, her lips

340

still swollen from the pressure of his kisses. She'd fobbed him off, pretending a cold, but on Tuesday he'd phoned again, minutes after Georgina had phoned to invite her to a dinner party to celebrate winning some contract or other.

Unable to find an excuse, terrified at the idea of being together with Georgina and Aiden in their home, she'd rashly suggested Tom join her. She'd thought he might divert attention, a human smokescreen for the ordeal this dinner was likely to be. Aching to see Aiden again, she was anxious about how she'd react in front of Georgina. If people could read her face, she was sure they'd see guilt stamped all over it. Even if all they'd done was kiss. And talk.

'Dugan?' Aiden had said when she informed him that evening. He'd taken to calling and texting daily. And she knew she should stop him but it was only harmless, she told herself, old friends sharing their worries, providing moral support. 'You're bringing the bloody English teacher?' he'd groaned. 'Oh, won't this be luvverly!'

'Georgina wouldn't let me off the hook and I thought Tom might provide a distraction, take the focus off us.'

'Well, I guess if she does insist on this do of hers, the more people the better,' Aiden acknowledged, a touch sulkily.

'I don't fancy him, you know.' Now why did she have to go and say that? It would be better for all of them if Aiden did think she fancied Dugan, and gave up hope.

'No.' He was quiet a second. 'Hey, you know at the reunion, Georgina had been worried about you and Dugan getting so cosy. Well, did anything actually happen?'

'That been bothering you?'

'No, well . . . yes, actually. It has.'

A warm tingle of pleasure curled around her spine and she'd kissed Feo, lying on the bed next to her, on his little black nose. 'Jealousy will get you everywhere, you know.' She couldn't help herself. It felt so good to flirt.

'Hope so,' Aiden growled sexily. 'Better go. I think someone's coming upstairs.'

'OK everybody.' The lights went up as teachers and parents led the youngest pupils up on the stage. 'Years Three and Four will now perform "Walking in the Air". Let's give them a lot of encouragement, shall we?'

Cameras flashed as the audience rose to dutifully clap, several people looking at their watches, losing interest now their own children's part was over.

A violin quartet played, followed by a group of Year Threes with recorders, a solo from a brave Year Six girl, then another sing-along-a-carol.

The first bars of 'Once in Royal David's City' struck up, Jen mouthing the words as her mind wandered.

Was she a bad person using Tom as a decoy? He was a nice man. If she wasn't so obsessed with Aiden she might be keen to know him better. And wasn't she being unfair to Georgina, too? Not much had happened with Aiden. Just that one moment of passion – a few kisses, that was all – but still she'd die if her friend found out. So why was she allowing this daily contact?

'Mary was that mother mild . . .' Ollie sang beside her.

What were they doing except fuelling the flames? Last night Jen had been bemoaning the fact that Chloe couldn't perform tonight when Aiden suddenly said, 'You know I love you, don't you, Titch?'

And boy, had that shut her up, because she was certain her heart was going to explode, right there in her chest.

'Who is God and Lord of all . . .'

And yet again this morning she woke to bone-crushing guilt. It was such a damn roller coaster. Just when Jen was doing her best to believe her own propaganda, convincing herself that Georgina really was a horrible self-centred witch who didn't deserve Aiden (and was only pretending to still like Jen because she suspected Aiden fancied her and there was that old adage that went 'Keep your friends close, your enemies closer'), she'd do something incredibly thoughtful. Like on Wednesday when a darling little card landed on Jen's doormat saying 'True Friends Don't Grow On Trees', with a sweet poem inside.

True friends? Jen had squirmed, wishing God would send a lightning bolt to punish her for her sins.

But then what if Georgina had sent her the card knowing it'd twist Jen's innards like spaghetti round a fork? What if she were suspicious and 'true friends' was meant as a dig – a very sly warning? And besides, if Jen couldn't persuade herself to dislike Georgie, how could she live with the guilt of falling in love with her husband?

Even though Jen had loved him first and best.

Only a few weeks ago, if Jen had been flattened by a car somewhere, she would at least have known her ticket would be marked 'Pearly Gates' and not 'Nether Regions of Hell'. She wasn't a wicked woman. She didn't steal, didn't swear (excessively), had even smiled sympathetically at the mother of a screaming baby on the plane to Greece a few years back. But now she wasn't so certain. She was morally inept. She coveted her best friend's husband.

And the worst thing? The more she spoke to Aiden the more energised she became, like a rechargeable battery. If a few hours passed without hearing from him she felt drained. She was a drug addict desperate for a fix. She loathed herself for it and yet she loathed the thought of not seeing him more.

Since their kiss she'd practically skipped to work with a silly smile plastered on her face. Even in the supermarket she wanted to prance down the aisles, kicking her heels with the joy of it all.

'How about another big hand for our talented students?' The head teacher was back at the microphone.

Jen couldn't help but glare at Ollie as the clapping faded and everyone rose to leave. After all Chloe's hard practice, it was like pouring salt on her daughter's injured arm to witness her non-performance tonight. But Chloe had insisted they both came, she couldn't let 'her' band down and besides, she'd added cutely, 'Miss said', knowing that would clinch the deal. Jen drummed into Chloe countless times, that what Miss said went.

'Mince pie, mulled wine?' Someone held out a glass as Chloe rushed to join them, and she and Ollie ambled into the corridor with all the other parents.

'Make it a double.' Jen took it from her and downed it in one.

# Chapter 39

Jen stood in front of Georgina and Aiden's front door, Tom Dugan at her side, hearing laughter from inside. Thank goodness Meg had arrived first. She was the best at filling awkward silences with her endless chatter, and Jen was betting her life there'd be a lot of such silences tonight. She'd been dreading the whole evening, and yet was strangely keyed up about it. Rather like when Chloe's birth was imminent, knowing it would involve pain, yet excited about the outcome.

Since the kiss on the ridge, six long days ago, she couldn't get Aiden out of her head. He'd invaded her thoughts, stolen her soul, captured her heart all over again. Not an hour went by without her imagining how it would be to make love with him, wake up next to him, spend the rest of their lives together. She hardly slept, barely ate. She wanted to speak his name to everybody she met – shop workers, dustbin men, bank cashiers. Well, everyone except Georgina, that is, or Meg. Ollie too, frankly.

Poor Tom, pressing the bell when she hesitated, had no idea what he was letting himself in for. He was such a gentleman, bringing her a small thoughtful gift of a rosemary bush shaped like a miniature tree, helping her on with her coat, opening her car door. The perfect escort and so delighted that she'd invited him.

Aiden answered the door. The minute she saw his handsome

face, his incredible smile directed right at her, she was dust. Had he ever looked so good?

'Hi there.' His brooding eyes fixed on hers momentarily before they turned to Tom. 'And you must be Tom.' He shook hands politely. 'Come in, make yourself at home. Let me take your jacket . . . Jen.' Thank God Tom was looking around, not catching their shared lingering stare and Aiden's hand softly squeezing Jen's when she handed over the bottle of wine she'd brought, sending tingles racing round her body.

'Jennifer, lovely to see you. Don't you look nice!' Georgina came forward to greet them and brushed her cheek against Jen's. 'And Thomas – I don't have to call you Mr Dugan, do I? – so kind of you to join us.'

'All my pleasure.' Tom leant forward and kissed her on both cheeks, which made her blush. 'Congratulations on the Heal's deal! Jen told me about it on the way over.'

'Why, thank you. Heal's deal sounds so silly, doesn't it?'

Georgina was also looking unbelievably good tonight. Last seen by Jen she'd been harrassed and upset on the Totnes platform, but the news of her business success had evidently worked wonders. Her glossy hair was styled just so, a low-cut sapphire silk dress with spaghetti straps showed off her toned hourglass figure, its fabulous ruffled hem skimming her shapely calves. Next to her Jen felt a bit self-conscious in her Giordani togs, the kick-flare jeans and lace-sleeved blouse that Georgie had given her. But then again, it wasn't a competition, was it?

'Nutmeg's already here. I gave everyone the night off.' Georgina ushered them both down the hallway. 'So if you find the service wanting and dinner a disaster, it's entirely my fault.'

'Sorry we're a bit late,' Jen began. 'My babysitter let me down and I had to ring Ollie and . . .'

'No matter,' Georgina shushed her. 'Nothing burnt.' She

escorted them both towards the drawing room. 'Champers for our guests, Aiden?' she prompted, taking charge as usual. 'We're having fizz to start, put us all in the mood.'

'Hey, Jen, Mr Dugan, sir.' Meg rose from her chair and saluted as Jen and Tom walked in. 'How are you two lovebirds?'

Jen immediately cringed but laughed to cover her embarrassment. 'If this is how she's going to be all evening, we should head home right now,' she mumbled apologetically to Tom as she took a seat on the sofa next to him.

'What a cosy foursome,' Meg said cheerfully, perching her small bottom on the arm next to Jen. 'Man, do I feel like a total gooseberry.'

They made small talk while nibbling on appetisers of bacon-wrapped dates, smoked salmon roll-ups and pâté spread on tiny crackers. Dugan answered Georgina's questions about his work, his life since leaving teaching. Georgina told them how Totnes had been the catalyst for a whole new surge of inspiration, how several looming disasters had been averted and put back on track and how she'd been designing like a maniac ever since.

'You two are my muses,' she said, hugging Jen and Meg. 'I feel like I've been given a whole new lease of life.'

She looked incredibly happy, full of smiles and affectionate touches for Aiden. Clearly one of them had bounced back from last Sunday's fight.

'Time to eat.' Georgina glanced at her delicate silver watch. 'Perhaps you'd like to lead the way through to the dining room, Nutmeg.'

'Your wish is my command.' She jumped up, but Aiden got there first. '*Entrez.*' He opened the door with a flourish.

'Get you, Mr Hosty Mosty.' Meg cheekily tweaked the back of his hair as she walked past him. 'Oh man oh man!' Jen heard her suddenly shriek.

Following behind her, Jen also stopped in shock. The

dining room was decked out in its absolute finery: table covered with a crisp linen cloth, crystal glasses, fancy napkins folded into star shapes, an exquisite hand-painted bowl with scented candles floating around inside. Everything was so welcoming, the blazing log fire, the Victorian polished-brass chandelier hanging low over the table, sultry jazz playing in the background.

What an effort Georgina had made, Jen thought with dismay. It was so sweet and considerate. All of a sudden the picture she had been trying to build up over the past few days of the bossy, domineering Georgina, neglectful of her husband, rude to people she considered inferior, a veritable slavemaster to her elderly (and overpaid) staff, shattered before her eyes. Crucified by her own deception, it took every effort not to turn on her heel, run out the door and flee the scene of her crime.

'Hey, you've really gone to town, Georgie,' she gulped, attempting to stop her mouth forming a rictus. 'You shouldn't have done.'

'Actually, it was fun.' Georgina's face flushed with pleasure. 'And, well, you know, if I can't put on a show for my *very best* friends, what can I do?'

'So you really want to quit searching for Rowan?' Meg savoured her roast tomato soup, its delicate flavours not quite enough to compensate for her disappointment.

'I didn't say that exactly,' Georgina protested. 'But unless her mother passes on the message . . .'

'But was her mum telling the truth?' Meg broke in. She knew the woman was lying. Trouble was, no one else seemed convinced.

'Look, I know you have your pact,' Jen said gently. 'But, well, I don't know what else we can do. It's been fun meeting up again and everything, but . . .' She stared at her plate, looking uncomfortable.

'Hate to say this,' Aiden added his two cents, 'but maybe it's just not meant to be.' Meg caught his cynical smile at Jen as he passed her the pepper mill, Jen's cheeks reddening.

'I tend to agree with Aiden,' Georgina said sadly. 'I really do think every avenue's been explored.'

'If I can help in any way, Meg,' Tom joined in, 'Jen can give you my number.' He rested his arm along the back of Jen's chair. 'Though I don't know what use I could be.'

Meg scrutinised him. He'd been one of the cooler teachers at Ashport, easy-going, better-looking than most and young too, which was really all it took to make him a sex symbol to overheated adolescent girls. But as Jen's new boyfriend? Was he responsible for her glowing cheeks and her distinctly girlish manner tonight?

Probably not. She'd noticed how distracted Jen seemed when Tom talked to her, the way she leaned forward to avoid that encroaching arm, finally scooting her chair towards the table so he had to move it. Why didn't she just put up a sign saying 'Not with him'? No, all Jen's sparks were flying in a completely opposite direction.

'I don't know what use you'd be either,' Meg said flatly.

'Doesn't mean we can't keep hoping,' Jen said quickly.

'Miracles do happen,' said Tom.

'They sure do,' Aiden said as he plunged a corkscrew into another bottle. 'Just when you least expect them.'

'Like angels,' Meg said. She observed Jen and Aiden trading glances again, secretive smirks. OK, now what was *that*? Some private joke? Implying she was living in la-la land? Or something else? Well, the hell with them.

'Although if Rowan's mother was telling the truth, I certainly can't find the time to visit Shanghai.' Georgina's laugh struck Meg as weird. What was up with everyone tonight?

'And we single parents sure ain't got the bucks,' Meg remarked. The lavish surroundings tonight only made the reality of her own situation hit harder. 'Talking of which, Jen, has your ex sorted out your alimony yet?'

Jen hesitated. 'Not exact figures as such . . .'

'Oh no, it has to be set in stone.' Georgina, opposite her, wagged her finger sternly. 'Your affairs are your affairs of course, but . . .'

And that was it, Georgina was off, giving her the benefit of her worldly advice, lecturing Jen on money matters, recommending firms of financial advisers, while Aiden and Tom joined in with ideas of their own.

'I know, I know.' Jen put her head in her hands. 'My friend Helen's always nagging me about how I'm ignoring all this stuff.'

As the conversation continued, Meg half listened, veering between boredom and feeling irate. Smug complacent yuppies, talking stocks and shares, property portfolios, unit trusts, while back in the Old Bear trailer park, Meg scrabbled to afford food and gas for her crummy old station wagon.

Did they have a clue? Even old Dugan had to chip in with the way the moratorium on mortgages was hurting the rental market. Had they ever experienced the panic of having to take a feverish child to the emergency room in the middle of the night, knowing what was left on your combined credit cards wouldn't cover the cost of treatment?

Had they, in their cushy National Health system, any idea how one small incident – something like Jen's daughter breaking her arm – could wipe out every dime of your hard-earned savings, leaving nothing to pay rent or bills? For the unlucky, sometimes all it took was a grim diagnosis or being smashed into by an uninsured motorist to go from prosperous middle class to homeless, jobless and bankrupt.

Welfare was a joke. For those, like Meg, with no insurance at all and no fall-back position now that Irwin had bailed . . . She shivered, feeling the cold wind of poverty whistling at her back.

'Buy-to-let investments have really gone down the pan . . .' Tom was saying.

'*The Times* says that the property market . . .' joined in Aiden.

*Buy-to-let investments. Property market.* Meg could feel the red-hot rage of frustration bubbling up inside her. How could she enrol Zeb in the public-school system? The one in her lousy neighbourhood was virtually a crack den, full of gangs and violence. And Zeb was a talented kid. If Irwin had showed a real interest instead of being a suspicious begrudging cheapskate, he'd have seen what a joy he was to be around.

She thought of Zeb tonight, most likely going over homework again with Mace so he could get to college, not that they had money for that. He'd have to rely on student loans and work to pay his way.

Whatever, it was time for them both to go home. Zeb was desperate to catch up with his friends before Christmas. But nothing was fixed yet.

If only that dumb-ass Irwin hadn't found himself a cheap little gold-digger and derailed the money train. His payments hadn't filled the fridge with champagne exactly, but they had kept the wolf from the door.

Georgina was laughing at a story Tom was telling about an incident in the Ashport Comp staffroom, Aiden was gazing into space, his mind undoubtedly elsewhere, and Jen was staring at Aiden, her plate of food almost completely untouched. So that was the way the wind was blowing. Complicated. Just as she was wondering if she could really drop a wrecking ball into their lives, it looked as though they might be ready to drop one into hers.

An hour later, the main meal had been served, a few glasses of wine had aided the flow of conversation and Jen was watching Aiden handing Tom the sauce boat.

'No, really,' Aiden laughed at some glib comment of Meg's that Jen had already forgotten because it didn't matter, because all she wanted to do was look at him and smile.

Jen loved the way he laughed, the way he ate, the way he held his cutlery, the way he sipped from his crystal glass, the way he turned his head, lifted his chin, scratched his nose, even his tiny flash of ill humour. She adored being in his company and a few times during the evening when they'd all been chattering about something, she'd glanced over at him, his eyes had locked with hers and her whole body had come out in goose pimples so large she was sure someone would notice.

She tried concentrating on the conversation, knowing she was out of control, high as a kite, insane with lust, but she couldn't help it. She loved him. She loved Aiden, he was her destiny. She wanted to bellow it from the rooftops, swing through trees like a capuchin monkey scratching at an armpit and screeching his name. Aiden, Aiden, Aiden.

So this was what life was all about. This was real joy. Aiden Kenton lovely luscious Starkson. She was so rejuvenated and happy at rediscovering the love of her life she didn't care what the future held, she simply wanted to bask in these feelings for as long as possible.

A memory popped into her head of an interview she had once watched on TV, some celebrity theorising that if people showed their true emotions then four out of eight people at a dinner party would be sobbing into their soup. Jen looked at the group round Georgina's fancy table enjoying their braised lamb with flageolet beans, a Delia recipe apparently. There was Meg, adventurous, free-spirited, yet behind the veneer harbouring secret dramas she wasn't prepared to confide; and Georgina, two places down, with her flash new contract but not realising what a misery she was making of her husband's life; Tom, pleasant, polite but perhaps a little lonely, if his persistence in asking her out were anything to go by, eyeing everyone as if he were sensing hidden undercurrents and trying to work out the dynamics of them all.

And then Jen herself, looking across the table at Aiden conversing so easily with everybody. If she showed her true emotions, she'd be throwing herself across the table and shagging him senseless at this very moment. Five out of five sobbers. That celebrity's calculations had been spot on, maybe even too optimistic.

'Ever miss teaching, Thomas?' Georgina turned to her favourite guest and handed him the jug of cream. This evening . . . well she wasn't positive if it had been a triumph exactly, but foodwise it couldn't be faulted and apart from Jennifer, who didn't seem her usual self at all, all dirty crockery had been practically licked clean. They were now on their desserts. One thing she hadn't failed to notice was how much attention Thomas had been paying to Jennifer, the way he listened to her every word, the way he looked at her admiringly, so clearly smitten. Made her feel almost envious.

'It had its moments,' he poured the cream over his lemon meringue pie, 'but no, not really. I work in computer graphics now.'

'How interesting. We're always needing technical assistance, isn't that right, Aiden?' Georgina reached for his hand, but instead of squeezing back he rather rudely extricated himself. 'I could put in a word for you if you're ever looking for a change.'

'He has a job,' Aiden said, too impatiently for Georgina's liking. What a ghastly mood he was in tonight. On more than one occasion Georgina had noticed him giving poor Thomas slant-eyed unfriendly looks. 'You didn't say you were trolling for work, did you, Tom?'

'No. But I'll bear it in mind, Aiden.' Thomas picked up his spoon and smiled at Jennifer, thankfully impervious to insult.

'Why the career switch?' asked Nutmeg rather sullenly.

And she hadn't been her usual merry self during the meal, either.

'Didn't suit,' he replied. 'Low pay, endless marking, mountains of paperwork. And maybe teaching you lot put me right off.' He laughed a little to show he was teasing.

'Couldn't take the heat? Were they such an ill-disciplined bunch then?' Aiden arched his eyebrows.

'Not so much these three,' Tom smiled at Georgina and the others, 'but some of the lads were real monsters. Of course I don't blame them, broken homes, bad parenting. Lost souls, some of them.'

'It's all changed now, anyway,' Jen said. 'School, I mean. Ofsted inspections. Smartboards instead of blackboards. Everything's interactive these days.'

'Mmm.' Georgina was thoughtful. She'd been meaning to bring it up for a while but was now the right time? She braced herself and opened her mouth, which had suddenly become extremely dry. 'Dear Nutmeg,' she reached across the table, sought out her hand and laid her own across it, 'I just want you to know, if anything ever happens to you . . . well, I, or rather we,' she glanced across at Aiden, 'will be there for Zeb.'

Meg looked startled and snatched her hand away.

'I realise I'm a poor substitute for Rowan but if you want – or rather, if anything ever happened to you, not that it will, I'd be happy to take Zeb.' She blushed and swirled her wine around her glass. 'And Chloe,' she added quickly, not wanting to leave Jennifer out, although she did have a perfectly amenable ex-husband by all accounts. 'Just the thought of any child going to an orphanage, when Aiden and I have so much, seems criminal.' She smiled brightly. There, she'd said it. Subject closed. 'Refill, anyone? I'll fetch another bottle.' She retreated to the kitchen before anyone could reply.

Some time later she was relaxing on the sofa, eyes half closed, three-quarter-empty glass of Bailey's in hand, basking in the warmth of the roaring fire while Jennifer related a recent incident concerning her daughter. Apparently her homework had been to write an adventure story and, essays not being her favourite subject, she'd put it off for ages, but for some reason once she started she really got stuck in and wrote endless pages about a cheetah and a jaguar drifting down the river on a raft, having adventures and meeting other animals. Jennifer read it and almost wept, it was so beautiful, she said, but when the teacher marked it, all he could comment on the bottom in red pen was, 'Would a tiger really be called Jerry?'

'Now that's why I home-school Zeb,' said Nutmeg. 'That's real bad, Jen.'

'I thought so too.' Jennifer snuggled her legs up into Georgina's favourite big squashy chair and accepted another top-up of Tuaca from Aiden. 'So what's your opinion, Tom, as an ex-English teacher? Am I being a pushy parent wanting to complain?'

'No, you're definitely not,' Thomas replied. 'I think her teacher was stifling her creativity. And if I'd been Chloe's dad, I'm sure I'd have felt just the same.'

Georgina noted with pleasure the way he put his hand on Jennifer's arm as he spoke. A tiny gesture, but one of support. He was so charming, Thomas. Such nice manners. She glanced across at Aiden, but he was in another world entirely.

'Yeah, and children that age, they heal incredibly fast.' Aiden suddenly threw in his pennyworth. 'Bet you in a couple of weeks, that cast is history.'

*Cast? What cast?*

'Jennifer didn't say anything about a cast.' Georgina slapped him gently on the arm. Had he had too much brandy or had she missed something? 'What *are* you jabbering on about?'

There was silence for a second while everyone seemed equally bemused, then Nutmeg piped up. 'Oh, didn't you hear, Georgina? Chloe broke her arm. I guess you were taking the

355

plates out. Poor kid skidded at the scrambling track. She's in a cast, apparently. Must make it hard for her to write, eh Jen? I tell you, once Zeb fell out of this tree . . .'

Georgina half closed her eyes again and sighed.

No, this dinner party was a great success, she smiled to herself.

A truly great success.

'Enjoy yourself?' Tom asked as he drove Jen home. He was wearing chocolate leather gloves and a big sheepskin jacket, and with his dimpled chin and green eyes he reminded Jen a bit of Ben Affleck. And she wished to goodness she could fancy him instead of Aiden. But she didn't because she was a faithful old Hector. A one-man woman. A one-man-forever woman. That's what she'd worked out tonight, that she and Ollie had always been doomed because Aiden was The One. She'd often blamed the disintegration of her marriage on their hasty wedding, their age difference, Ollie's job, the move, her reluctance to have a second child, even the post-natal depression, but now she realised it had been none of those things, it had been purely, simply because her love for Aiden had never really died.

'Yeah, very much. Lovely food.'

'And a great place – Georgina's really landed on her feet.' He pulled up at a set of traffic lights and waited for them to change. 'Handsome husband, thriving business. It's brilliant that you've all remained such good friends.'

'Mmm, yes,' she said with a weary smile, not in the mood for idle chit-chat and especially not on the subject of wonderful friendships. She just wanted to go to bed, burrow under the duvet and dream of Aiden. She wondered if he'd call her later.

'I don't think you should stop looking for Rowan,' said Tom quite unexpectedly as the lights turned to green and he pulled away.

'Why not?' Jen asked, surprised.

'Because, well, you all seem to have so much fun together. And it bonds you, gives you another reason to stay in touch.'

'Mmm, yes, I suppose you're right.' Jen thought back to the evening's events. The only odd part had been not long before they left, when she'd gone outside for some fresh air. Since 'the kiss' everything had seemed more intense, the moon brighter, stars more beautiful, air cleaner and she just wanted to experience the world and all it had to offer. It was then that she saw Meg, sitting on the garden swing seat, gently swaying. Jen smiled at her old friend and went over to join her but as Meg turned her head, Jen saw from her puffy eyes that she'd been crying.

'Are you OK?' she'd said, startled.

'Yes.' Meg sniffed into a tissue. 'Totally.'

'Do you want me to stay?'

'No, Jen,' she replied almost fiercely, staring straight ahead, as if in a trance. 'I want you to go.'

It was the amount of drink probably, or maybe she'd heard something from the hospital and still wasn't ready to 'share', but there was something in Meg's manner that made Jen retreat to the warmth of the house.

Tom finally turned into her driveway, tugged on the handbrake but left the engine running.

'Would you like to come in?' Jen asked politely, crossing her fingers that he wouldn't. She felt sure nothing would happen, even though Ollie had taken Chloe back to Saul's flat when the babysitter let her down, but she wasn't sure of the rules any more. Did coffee just mean coffee or did it automatically mean more? Dating was such a long-distant memory.

Still, it would have been so easy to kiss him, the way he was smiling at her, Frank Sinatra crooning softly in the background. It was a romantic situation; the wind had died down, it was cosy in the car and a small part of her wondered what would happen if she did just let him take her there and then. Would the chemicals or hormones or whatever inside her realign themselves, and would she start seeing him in a different way? It would solve all her problems in one fell swoop.

But it was no use, she knew, in her heart of hearts, that sleeping with Tom would be a bit like sleeping with a brother, if she had one.

'Thanks, but I don't think so.' He smiled at her. 'It's getting late and I still have a fair drive home.'

'OK,' she said, relieved. 'See you, then.'

She pecked him on the cheek and walked up the driveway feeling faintly tipsy. Even as she put her key in the lock, the mobile in her bag began to vibrate and she knew instantly it was Aiden.

# Chapter 40

'So Nobby went back then?' Enid enquired.

'Don't they always?' Mrs Cartwright cast her eyes to the shop ceiling. 'Tail between his legs.'

'Ah, well,' Walter polished some miniature china teddy bears, 'wonders'll never cease.'

'Sixty years is sixty years after all,' said Mrs Cartwright. 'Fool that he was.'

'One good thing, she'll be able to torture him till the day he dies,' Enid chuckled as she placed an orange sticker on all the items that were fifteen per cent off today.

'Which if he's lucky won't be long,' Jen heard Walter mutter as he retreated into the back room.

'So what happened?' Jen was busy putting price tags on an assortment of hardly used tennis racquets that had come in. Maybe a whole family had quit at the same time?

'Seems she couldn't make a halfway good cuppa.' Mrs Cartwright shrugged. 'And she gave him gyp all the time about leaving towels higgledy-piggledy on the rail. He never realised she was pernickety.'

'They never do.' Enid moved a bundle of clothes left in the changing room and started slotting them in their rightful places on the racks. 'Live in a cloud of fantasy, these men. Think the grass is greener.'

Jen glanced through the beaded curtain and saw Walter

staring into the mirror, lips moving, one hand forming the shape of a mouth, aping his wife as she continued speaking.

The door burst open and Jen gasped as Meg marched in.

'We need to talk.' Her voice was strangely stilted, her face white as a sheet. 'In private!'

'So what's the matter?' Jen followed a marching Meg as they strode through Huntsleigh park. The council had recently put in a new playground equipped with a wooden fort with rope-climbing nets and look-out towers as well as the usual swings, slides and roundabouts. On summer weekends it was packed, but today there was just one mother and toddler, both bundled up in winter coats.

Meg took a long slow draw of her cigarette, exhaled fiercely, then stopped and turned to her. 'OK, let's do it.' The smoke headed past Jen's right ear and some was blown by the strong wind straight into her eyes, but she didn't dare complain. The expression on Meg's face could have halted a freight train in its tracks. 'Shoot.'

'Pardon?'

'You know fucking what!' Meg fumed. 'You and Aiden. I know what you're doing.'

'What are we doing?' Jen gulped.

'You are so busted, lady.' Meg shook her head, then continued marching.

'What do you mean, me and Aiden?' Jen found herself tottering after her. 'There is no me and Aiden.' Her throat suddenly went Sahara, her stomach distinctly Delhi.

'Jesus, Jen.' Meg flung down her cigarette. 'The two of you only have to be in a room together and it's like a Fourth of July firework display. I'm surprised Georgie and Tom didn't notice – it's so frigging obvious.'

'I haven't slept with him, if that's what you're thinking.' Jen felt humble and ashamed. At least it was Meg, not Georgina, confronting her with her duplicity. But what if Meg were right? What if it had been obvious to all?

'You haven't?' There was a sarcastic twist to Meg's voice. 'Pull the other one, honey.'

'No.' Jen swallowed, willing her to understand. 'Well, I've lain on the bed at the same time as him and gazed at the ceiling and dreamed and talked. But nothing actually physical's happened.'

'Oh sure.' Meg gave a hollow laugh.

'Sure. We were in different houses, kind of hard to get up to much when you're miles apart.' A feeble attempt at lightening the tension. Feeble and pointless, because Jen could see Meg was in no mood for it, and suddenly she thought of all those people who had cybersex, text sex, phone sex and apparently got up to quite a lot. 'Listen.' She tried again. 'I admit we're close, but all we do is chat. Mostly about our day. Is that such a crime?'

'That's all that's happened?'

'Chat and text and . . . all right, one kiss up on the ridge,' she admitted.

'Where's the goddamned ridge?' Meg thundered, as if it might be some body part she hadn't heard of.

'Above the park. Next to the heath. Round the corner from the beacon.' If she kept stalling her with directions, she might be let off more lightly. 'Up there.' She pointed to a nearby hill.

'He's been driving over *here* to see you?' Now Meg looked even more shocked. 'I'm over-fucking-whelmed.'

'Only once. Well twice actually . . . well, no, three times, but the first time was dropping my phone off and the second time Georgina kind of sent him and the third . . .'

'Enough.' She curled her nose up like she'd just encountered a bad smell.

'Oh, Meg, we kissed one evening, that's all, the rest was just talking.'

'Worse than I thought,' she spat as she strode fast along the gravel path, past the flower beds so barren now in the winter cold.

'What do you mean?'

'Emotional infidelity. I hoped it was purely a sex thing, but you're in love.'

'Rubbish!' Jen snapped defensively, sorry now that she hadn't tried to deny the whole thing. 'We're old friends. It's nothing. Back off, why don't you? Give me a break.'

'Don't you get pissy with me. I'm just telling you, he's no good for you,' Meg carried on. 'Or anyone. Definitely not worth wrecking your friendship with Georgina. Even years back, when you were hooked up together, he was a scummy two-timing bastard.'

They were heading for the lake now. A pair of moorhens skittered towards the water at their approach. Jen looked at Meg in outrage.

'He was not,' she said furiously. 'Why would you say that?'

Meg kicked a stone along the path. 'All the time he was seeing you, he was still sleeping with Astrid.'

Jen stopped. She couldn't believe her ears. She'd never thought Meg would stoop that low.

'It wasn't like that,' she said, wanting to make Meg understand. 'They'd just broken up. She was still clinging to Aiden like a leech.'

'You were *so* naive, Jen. He used to bring her over to us most week nights when you were at home studying. Don't tell me they were,' she put on a mock English accent, ' "just dreaming and talking". Clover let them sleep over in the guest room and our house had thin walls. He told Herb you were "sweet but oh so young".' She took another drag of her cigarette and gave Jen a shrewd assessing look. 'You didn't really think he was staying celibate for you, did you?'

Could she believe her? Could you ever believe a thing Meg said? But she felt hollow suddenly, all her certainty drained away. 'So why didn't you say something?' she challenged angrily. 'You were meant to be my friend.'

'Maybe because I knew it wouldn't have done a darned bit of good? Sure, I was mad at him and I used to bust his balls about it, but what else could I do? You know if I said the slightest thing against him you took it as a personal insult. You'd never have believed me.'

'And I don't believe you now.' Jen whirled round and started walking back. 'You're a phoney.'

Meg ignored the insult. 'He probably knows Georgina's about to chuck him out and is trying to feather his nest somewhere else. Looking for a soft landing, he saw your cushy pad.'

It wasn't her cushy pad, she thought, and then she took in what Meg had said. 'What make you think Georgina wants to chuck him out?' Her heart kicked at the prospect.

They were attracting glances from a few dog-walkers who were congregated together chatting while their pooches scampered around. Meg gave her a look that saw right through her.

'Well, hell, I would if I were her. Face it, Jen. He was a dickweed then and he's a dickweed now.'

'I'd trust Aiden any day over you!' Jen's heart rebelled in anguish against everything she'd heard. 'You were jealous of us then and you're jealous of us now. I saw Beidelbaum's email. It's all one big web of lies with you. From that nasty bit of blackmail you've got going on to that poxy bloody angel and pretending you give a damn about me, Georgina or Rowan, when we all know that Meg Lennox only looks out for Meg Lennox!'

Meg stared at her intently again.

'*Yeah, that's right, baby,*' her voice took on a strange low husky tone. '*Do it like that. That feels so-o-o good. Yeah, baby, you're the best. Are you hot for me? Do you feel the magic?*

Jen felt the colour drain from her face, the cold sweep her entire body.

'You bitch,' she croaked. 'Stay away from me. I never want to see you again!'

# Chapter 41

The hell with that scheming bitch! Jen's throat was scorching as she stormed home, too upset to return to work. The confrontation with Meg had changed everything. No longer were her feelings for Aiden a delicious little secret she could hug to herself; Meg had made them seem cheap, tawdry, loathsome. What if she told Georgina? Knowing Meg, she was holding off until the moment of maximum impact, waiting till the revelation would create most damage or be of benefit to herself.

She threw off her coat and picked up a J-cloth, needing action to expel her fury. Half an hour later her kitchen was spotless and she was attacking the upstairs bathroom with a scourer and a bottle of Cif. The taps were gleaming, the bath whiter than white, but she couldn't erase the giant stain that had suddenly tarnished her happiness.

What right had Meg to criticise her? And why was she so angry? What skin was it off Meg's nose if she and Aiden were flirting? It couldn't be morals, everyone knew Meg had none of those. Loyalty to Georgina? Meg caring about someone other than herself? One could only wish!

She squirted the white liquid on the tile floor, scrubbing on her hands and knees in self-imposed penance. She'd spent days summoning every tiny thing that annoyed her about Georgina, so that instead of thinking of herself as a nasty piece of work slyly cheating with her best friend's husband, she could soothe her conscience by telling herself that they'd never really got along.

And what had she come up with? She rested back on her knees, reflecting. Well, Georgie had her mother's stuck-up attitudes. More than once she'd made remarks about council 'yobs' and Jen had had to remind her she used to live on a council estate. And she treated Aiden like another servant, sending him here and there. And often in their phone calls Jen could hear tap tap tap in the background and she sounded distracted, obviously still working on her laptop – even if she was the one who'd phoned. And if Jen said, 'Hey, you're busy, why don't we talk later?' Georgie would jump back with, 'No, it's fine,' but the minute Jen went back to chatting, the tapping would start up again. How was that?

Rude enough?

Annoying enough?

Reason enough to justify Jen wanting to steal her man?

Enough to cast her off as an old and valued friend?

Truth was, everyone had irritating qualities. Helen with her nagging. Anamaria with her blunt directness. Georgina with her snobbishness. Meg with her exaggerations and fabrications. And the closer you got to people, the deeper your knowledge of them, the more you discovered their weaknesses – Meg being a stunning example. Georgina probably thought Jen was unmotivated and she probably hated her style of dress or something. But would that mean the door was open for her to run off with Ollie, say, if Jen were the one still married?

What defined a friend, anyway? When did someone stop being an acquaintance or work colleague and make that transition? The first time they invited you out for a drink? Or to accompany them to a film? Did it depend on how much time you spent with them, how nice you thought they were, if they lived conveniently near you, how often they remembered your birthday or helped you through difficult situations?

For twenty-two years she'd got along fine without Georgina, and presumably vice versa, neither of them contacting each other, never even exchanging Christmas cards. What kind of best friendship was that? Was it something worth sacrificing her happiness for? Or just a childhood term that had stuck?

The floor was growing cold and hard under her knees. She stood up and wiped down the mirror, staring at her reflection. Instead of her usual sleek groomed look, her hair was shaggy and unkempt. With all the excitement she'd missed at least two hairdresser appointments, and it was in that messy in-between stage when it had passed her collar, lost its style and refused to do anything but fall in her eyes. She might have shed the middle-aged housewife veneer but golly, what a scruffbag. And yet she didn't look like an evil person, a home-wrecker. But that was what she was.

'*Yeah, baby,*' she heard Meg say. '*Are you hot for me? Do you feel the magic?*'

Unbidden and unwelcome, a parade of memories began marching round Jen's brain. Walking down Ashport high street hand in hand with Aiden and being turned 180 degrees when they saw Astrid coming the other way. The time she saw Astrid leaving the squat just as she arrived and he'd explained she'd stopped by to pick up some books. The way Aiden always opened his window and looked out when someone rang his doorbell, instead of running down to answer it. Other things that had seemed just slightly odd but were now slotting into place.

The phone was disturbingly light in her hand when she picked it up. It should have been one of those vintage black Bakelite models with circular dial, where even the receiver weighs a ton. Much more suitable for a femme fatale about to kill off her lover in true film noir fashion. She punched in the number.

'Hi, it's me,' she said, before he had a chance to speak. 'Just one question. Were you sleeping with Astrid all that time you were going out with me?'

'What?' Aiden laughed in a startled way, then recovered. 'I'm sorry, who is this?' he teased.

A shiver ran through her as she held the phone hard against her cheek, wanting to feel a different pain.

'Jen,' he said, when she failed to respond. 'What is this?' She could just see him raising his hands in disbelief, shrugging his shoulders to his ears. 'Why would you even . . .'

She pressed the red off button.

Immediately the phone rang. She knew it was Aiden but she didn't answer it. Instead she went into the sitting room and switched on the TV full volume – but nothing she watched could take her mind off things. In one ear she was hearing Georgina's voice, 'Is this piffle really on every morning?' and in the other, Meg. 'Do you think he stayed celibate for *you*? You were *so* naive.'

When the adverts came on, she rose out of the armchair and picked up the phone again.

'I'm glad you called.' Tom held the restaurant door open for Jen and guided her through with a hand lightly placed in the centre of her back. 'I was going to wait a couple more days until I phoned. The Rules, you know. Playing it cool – didn't want you to think I was overeager.'

'Who cares about rules?' Jen tossed her head as they walked past the Please Seat Yourself sign.

His hand stayed there as they weaved their way through the tables to the corner, as if without his touch she might wander in the wrong direction or – who knows – fall over. Jen felt like swatting it away or speeding up to make him run or lose contact but resisted the urge. So he had manners, holding the door for her, pulling out her chair. Was that so bad?

She might be dressed up to the nines in the marigold slinky

satin dress she'd bought with Chloe, but she was starting off the evening as a right old grouch. Better change her attitude or she might as well leave before the first course. After all, as he'd pointed out, *she'd* rung him. It wasn't his fault that all day she'd been fending off calls from Aiden, refusing to answer the phone, although every cell of her body was vibrating with desperate curiosity, yearning and yet terrified to find out what he had to say.

'So what do you think of this place?' He opened his napkin.

'Nice.' She gazed around. It was a little faux-bistro affair with vast framed posters on the wall – the Eiffel Tower, Robert Doisneau's famous couple kissing by the Hôtel de Ville, giant adverts for the Moulin Rouge and Gauloises. The tables were packed too close together, so that if she stretched out her elbow could rest on the one beside them, and there was a minuscule area set up for a band. The air should have been blue with smoke, except that of course it was banned these days.

'The food's supposed to be out of this world and they have music later. Jazz. Do you like jazz?'

'If the mood takes me.'

'Does the mood take you?'

'My mood's not worth discussing.'

'Oh?' He raised a questioning eyebrow.

'Sorry. Ignore me. I'm rotten company tonight.'

He gave a kind, fatherly smile. 'Well then, I've brought you to the right place.' He handed her the drinks menu. 'A word of warning, though. I don't know what they put in their cocktails but they're bloody lethal.'

Nor was he kidding. It was like that old joke, one tequila, two tequila, three tequila, floor, except that the drink was Long Island Iced Tea, followed by wine with dinner, and if she didn't quite hit the floor, it was only thanks to Tom's grip on her elbow when they left. Food came and went. A band started and she vaguely remembered dancing, drinking some more, then stumbling as she staggered to the car park.

The rest of the evening was a blur . . . falling through the door of Tom's bedroom, discarding clothes . . . kissing . . . making love . . . or rather having sex . . . because truthfully that's all it was.

The next thing Jen knew it was morning, and she was naked and in a strange bed in a room she'd never seen before. Her first flush of panic – where was Chloe? Had she abandoned her? – diminished when she remembered allowing her daughter to go on a sleepover, almost unheard of on a school night, but surely preferable to staying in with a mother in the state she'd been in. She rolled over, dreading what she knew she'd see.

Lying beside her on the bed, with half his body exposed to the elements, was Tom Dugan. Obviously she'd stolen all the covers. Just like Ollie always said she did. His body was good but too hairy, not like Ollie's smooth skin.

And with that thought, stricken with horror, she scrambled out of bed and into the satin dress she'd poured herself into last night, so appropriate this morning for the walk of shame she'd have to endure until she could find a taxi. She didn't want to linger, even a few moments, for the time it'd take to call a cab, in case he woke up.

Instead she found herself shivering down the road in her too-thin evening coat, hugging it to her against the biting December wind and curious stares. She could see why when she caught sight of her reflection in the taxi window. Dark smudges under her eyes, hair sticking up all over the place, there was still just enough make-up left on her face to show that last night someone had been up to no good.

Standing under the hot shower of her own bathroom, watching the soap bubbles disappear down the plug as she scrubbed viciously at every inch of skin, she was overcome with remorse.

It was like she'd deceived everybody, herself included. She thought about Aiden and his reaction, she thought about Chloe and how let down she'd be if she ever found out, but worst of all she felt bad about Ollie. All these years she'd been sleeping with him, used to his body and his ways, and now it was over and that part of her life had definitely come to a close. At least if it had been a romantic passion-filled night with Aiden, it would have been more justifiable and she would have been truer to herself. But that it had been Tom, someone she barely knew, didn't love, but who definitely hadn't deserved to be used as a form of spiteful revenge, made her feel dirty and shabby and . . . immoral.

God, she had to talk to someone. If ever she needed a friend it was today, when she'd fought with, rejected or done the dirty on everyone important in her life. Or almost everyone. She towelled her hair, staring at Feo who was sitting in front of her, staring back. He wagged his tail and dipped his body into a play bow.

'You won't believe this,' she said to him, her mouth full of toothpaste. 'We're going to do the unthinkable. We're going to visit Helen.'

# Chapter 42

It was funny how with all her mental griping about Helen, she'd forgotten one thing. When the fat hit the frying pan, her bossy interfering friend had always been there for her. Today was no exception. Instead of the expected withering response to what was admittedly a litany of ill deeds and wrong-doings, she astonished Jen with a full-on embrace.

'Poor soul,' she commiserated, as Jen's miserable recitation of woes trailed to a shaky halt. 'Sounds like you've got yourself in a real muddle.'

Jen put her tea mug down with a not quite steady hand. 'Oh I don't know,' she said wryly. 'Could be worse. I've only buggered up my life and everyone else's I've come in contact with. The original Black Spot, I am.'

'You know you and Chloe can always move in with me if you haven't found anywhere when your house completes. It'll be just like old times.' Helen smiled and placed a bottle of vodka and another of tonic on the tall circular table that formed a small island in a corner of her kitchen. 'Let's have a drink, shall we?'

'Now?' Jen glanced at the round clock above Helen's sink. 'It's not even eleven o'clock.'

'Sun has to be over the yardarm somewhere,' Helen chirped gaily. 'I won't tell if you don't.'

'I thought you'd be disgusted with me.' Jen leaned forward

on the bar-style chairs and rested her chin on her hands, her elbows on the table. 'You're always so tetchy about women who cheat with other women's husbands.'

'But you haven't cheated though, have you?' Helen reasoned as she threw ice into each glass and added a generous measure of spirit. 'And you wouldn't do anything like this unless your heart was truly involved. I know you, Jen. You'll figure out what's right. And I wouldn't pay too much attention to this Meg either. Sounds a right cow. You'd be amazed how many women loathe seeing other women happy.'

She splashed a tiny amount of tonic into each glass, took a hefty slug and sighed. 'I fell in love with a married man once. A real looker. Male model. German. Met when I was temping at his agency and bam, there was an instant connection. Anyway he was married and I was married and . . . well, we had coffee a couple of times, we even went for lunch once but that was as far as it got.'

'You didn't . . . ?' Jen let the question trail away.

'Not even once. I was gaga over him, couldn't think of anything else – but in the end we took the high road. It all felt very noble at the time, but six months later that bastard husband of mine ran off with his floozie. I 'spose I've often regretted I never went for it.'

'I thought you were so against that sort of thing,' Jen said, dumbfounded. 'Solidarity of sisterhood, etc.'

'I was. Still am really. I don't ever want to do to some poor soul what that mercenary bitch did to me when she walked off with Roger. But fact is both our marriages broke up without any help from me, and all these years later I'm still the one left sleeping alone. That's where hifalutin' principles got me.' Her mouth drooped cynically.

'So what happened to the German in the end?' It was a relief to focus on someone else's story for a change.

'He found someone else, fortnight after I told him no. A

Polish girl. Swept her off to paradise instead. They ended up getting married and moving back to Munich. I guess he wasn't lying when he said his marriage was on the rocks.' She stirred the ice in her glass noisily and gave a rueful grin at Jen. 'Probably a narrow escape if I could be replaced that easily. My number one rule – never go out with a man who looks better than you do.'

'Should have been one of mine,' Jen grimaced.

'Nonsense,' Helen said stoutly. 'I don't know why you say those things. Men swoon over you, always have. You're very attractive, Jen.' She took a second glance at her jogging bottoms, lack of make-up and scraped-back hair. 'Well, not today, of course.'

It was so Helen that Jen had to laugh. Alas, it was short-lived. Helen leaned forward, mouth pursed, to deliver the kind of news that makes killing the messenger seem a reasonable, even enlightened, act.

'By the way, I saw your ex-hubby the other day. Apparently that Frances Hutton has suggested that they visit Euro Disney with the kids.'

'Euro Disney? Ollie and Frances?' Suddenly all the breath was squeezed out of Jen's lungs.

'Yes, well, Chloe and her daughter seem to have hit it off and besides, they are both single.' Helen sucked on her piece of lemon and nodded to emphasise the point, apparently unaware of the hurt she was inflicting. 'Frances has free tickets. Some promotional thing through her company.'

'But he can't,' she said, incensed. 'What about Chloe's passport? When? Why didn't he tell me? Leaving the country? Can he do that without my permission? Flying her off without asking me?'

'Oh come on, Jen calm down.' Helen tutted soothingly. 'It's not like he's going to abscond with her. It's only France, not Fetihye, for Christ's sake. And do you even need passports for the EEC any more? They may even be taking the Eurostar for all you and I know.'

'Well, Chloe's got football practice after school tonight. I'll ask him when he drops her off.'

'Oh no, don't,' Helen looked dismayed. 'He'll know I told you. Wait till he mentions it.'

'Helen. How did you find all this out? Do you have a spy camera in their walls or what? You've never taken an interest in Ollie before. It's always been "Oh, Ollie's there, is he? I'll come over some other time." I thought you couldn't stand him.'

Helen had the grace to look a little embarrassed as she primped her hair fussily, eyes flicking away.

'Probably didn't want to intrude. Oh maybe we've had our ups and downs but, well, of course I only ever cared that you were happy.'

This was so far from Jen's recollection of past history that she had to stop and think about it. Had Helen's dislike of Ollie been all in her imagination, then? Or had her recitation to Helen in the early days of the small everyday quibbles, trivialities really, her relationship doubts, petty miseries, idle complaints about men's impossible nature, been responsible for tainting her friend's attitude towards her husband? Either way this was such a turnaround that her head spun.

'And besides,' Helen continued, while she was still digesting this, 'I was having real trouble finding a gas fitter. Worst time of year, it seems.'

Jen frowned, baffled. 'What's that to do with Ollie?'

'Well, he's living with one, isn't he?'

'He is?' She'd forgotten what Saul did when he wasn't running up and down the football sidelines. She always thought of him as the kids' coach and one of Ollie's gang of pals from the pub, but now she thought about it, of course he had that big white van with the blue-flame logo on the side.

'Yeah. Saul. Anyway I'd gone through local papers,

Thomson's, Talking Pages and whatnot and then I mentioned it to the cashier in the newsagent and she had his card in the window. Small world as they say.'

'Unbelievable!' Jen was stunned.

'Saul and I got on like a house on fire,' she laughed loudly, throwing back her head, 'to coin a phrase. Told me I could drop in any time. I might at that. He's dead nice. A few years younger than me but who's counting?'

Had the world gone crazy? Had she fallen into an alternative galaxy? Jen stared at her friend in amazement. Helen was going to be dropping in on Ollie and Saul where Jen dared not tread? Helen was going after a younger man after all those years of implying Jen had robbed the cradle?

'I thought he was engaged?'

'It didn't work out. She finished with him a few weeks ago. Ah, well, one woman's reject is another woman's dream date.'

It was all too much, Jen thought, rattling her ice cubes. Bad enough her ex-husband had a whole other life without her. Unreasonable as it might seem, fresh from the bed of a semi-stranger, she had the very strong conviction he ought to be shoved into cyberfreeze, only to be thawed out for parenting and babysitting duties. Ollie and Frances at Euro Disney, whirling together in the teacups, snuggling through the Haunted House and Pirates of the Caribbean . . . it was shocking how much it hurt.

Almost as much as her head, now that the hair of the dog seemed to have viciously turned on her. How could she object to Euro Disney when she herself was canoodling with one man and shagging another?

Nor could she exactly accuse Helen of disloyalty for consorting with the enemy and the enemy's new flatmate, when she'd spent the last hour admitting her urge to steal her oldest friend's husband. She couldn't even articulate her inner surprise that Helen, so keen on doctors and solicitors, would be interested in a gas fitter, because then she'd be revealing that she was as big a snob as Georgina.

In one respect Helen was dead right. She was in a real muddle. Perhaps the best thing would be to retreat to her own house, crawl into bed, pull the blankets over her head and not emerge until at least tomorrow.

'Helen,' she kissed her at the door, 'you're such a good friend. A real lifesaver.'

'Hmm, not sure about that,' Helen replied. 'But I read somewhere that you can't have more than seven friends in life – real friends, I mean, lifetime ones, not casual acquaintances. Friends who'll stick by you no matter what. Well, Jen, I've always thought of you as one of my seven and I hope you can count me as one of yours.'

She felt like she'd been beaten with a hundred birch brooms by the time she made it home, hung up her keys and collapsed on to the couch, Feo jumping on her and licking her face. When the bell rang, without thinking she answered the door.

'I lost you once.' He stood there on her doorstep, hands in pockets, white-faced. 'I'm not going to do it again. Why didn't you answer my messages? What have I done wrong?'

'Ask Meg, Starkey,' she replied coldly, turning on her heel. She should have slammed the door, she thought, but instead she left it ajar. 'Ask Meg.'

'Let me get this straight.' Aiden sat with his head in his hands, his wavy hair spilling through his fingers. He'd followed her into the living room, listened to her without interruption and now he looked completely bemused. 'You don't think it'll work out between us because of something that happened when we were both silly young kids. It doesn't make sense.' He raised his gaze, his eyes looking haunted. 'Are you sure that's all Meg said?'

'She told me you were screwing Astrid when you were with me.' Jen stuck out her chin. 'Why, what else was there?'

Across the room Feo was busy killing a small stuffed penguin that Chloe had bought him. He'd already removed its shiny black eyes. Now he was throwing it in the air, catching it and shaking it, growling. On any other day his antics might even have been entertaining.

'Nothing,' Aiden met her gaze levelly, 'but it'd be just like Meg to fill your mind with poison.' He crossed over to the sofa next to Jen, reaching for her hand. 'Don't be like this, please. The whole thing was so juvenile. I was a jerk, maybe. I did love you, hopelessly, but I hated to hurt Astrid.'

Furious, Jen pulled her hand away, but Aiden held her shoulders, forcing her to face him. 'Hear me out. After I finished with her, right when I started seeing you, she came crying back, desperate, wouldn't leave me alone. And I was weak, I hated seeing her upset, so, well, like an idiot I let her in.' He released her, wearily rubbing his temples as if they were throbbing. 'Then as we got serious I knew I had to cut her out of my life, but I kept putting off the evil day. I handled it badly, I admit, but it wasn't because I wanted to two-time you.' His brows drew together darkly. 'I imagine Meg tells it differently.'

'Not really.' Jen was torn between empathising with his pain, mirroring her own, and feeling wholly let down with the disappointments and shocks of the last twenty-four hours. 'It's only . . . I thought we had this incredible love. It's like it's been the one shining beacon I've built my life around. That for a short time, at least, you loved me and me alone. And all the while you were . . . cheating.' She could hardly say the word.

'It wasn't *all the while*.' He sounded the faintest bit frustrated as Feo, heedless of the atmosphere, dropped the penguin at his feet and waited expectantly for him to throw it. 'It was just at the beginning. What else can I say? You're talking about events that happened when I was nineteen. I can't turn back the clock, but I loved you then and I love you now, you know I do.'

'All right then, while we're being honest, cards on the table, I have another question. Did you sleep with Meg?'

'Did she say I did?' He frowned again.

Her mind flashed back to the park, to those horrid sounds that Meg made, the words she'd used.

'No. But she knows . . . things.'

He stared into her eyes and gave a huge heartfelt sigh. Expecting him to deny it, she knew, when he got up and walked around, what his answer would be.

'Yes, I did.' He picked up Feo's penguin and slung it across the room, to the dog's delight. 'Another mistake. I admit it.'

'And how did that happen?' she said snippily.

'How do you think?' He met her eyes. 'Broken heart. Too much brandy. Wrong girl. It's hardly original.'

'You mean you slept with her at the Marlow Arms?' Now she was confused. Was that worse or better – that it was Georgina he'd betrayed with Meg, Georgina who'd been lied to and turned into a fool?

'I told you about that night. Some of it, anyway. Meg, Irwin Beidlebaum and I had been in her room, knocking back a bottle of brandy he bought somewhere, shooting the breeze. Irwin left and I went to your room. I was in shock from seeing you again. I was ready to leave Georgina that very night. To run away with you. Make up for all the lost time. I was also smashed out of my skull. But you didn't answer.' He was walking towards her, his burning dark eyes locked on hers. She couldn't look away. 'I stumbled back down the corridor, feeling like my life had ended, and as I passed her room Meg opened the door. She was pretty drunk too. She started off comforting me and we ended up in bed together. It meant nothing to either of us. Nothing meant anything. I knew I'd lost you.'

'I always wondered . . .' her voice cracked, 'what would have happened if I'd opened the door that night.' Would he really have left Georgina?

He said what she was thinking.

'We wasted so many years.' He came and sat beside her, put his arm around her, pulling her in towards him.

But then she'd been pregnant with Chloe.

'I was still so angry with you . . . for vanishing like that . . .' Shit. She was struggling to keep some composure but her voice was choking up and they'd only done ten minutes of the first round. '. . . I was so crushed . . .'

'I know, baby.' He kissed her on her hair, squeezing her harder. 'I know. I'm so *so* sorry.'

She pushed him away and sat up. 'Yes, but you see it affects everything. Not just Meg but Astrid too. You must think I'm a pathetic moron but, well, if I feel this bad about things that happened all those years ago, can't you see how terrible it would be for Georgina? She's *married* to you, for Christ's sake. And to have one of her supposedly best friends cheat on her and the other one steal her husband – it doesn't get any worse.'

Irritably, he stood up again, flinging his arms about as if they were loose fire hoses gushing impatience. His hair looked wild, his piercing eyes glowing embers above those perfect cheekbones.

'Georgina! It's always about Georgina. I'm sick of it. Sick of kowtowing to her delicate nerves. Sick of being treated like a second-class being. Sick of being her nanny and her caretaker and her dogsbody. I would have left her years ago if I hadn't worried she might do something terrible to herself. If it might tip her over the edge. But it's like the Astrid thing,' he said bitterly, 'you try to avoid hurting one person and your whole life goes to pot because of it. I'm realising my wife is a lot stronger than she likes to let on. You saw her on Saturday. She bounces back. Crushed one minute. Cloud nine the next. But I'm done sacrificing.'

'Your decision.' Jen wiped her cheeks, tilting her head up to stare fixedly at the curtain rail. 'But I won't be part of the reason you leave. I can't bear thinking about Georgina suffering if she discovers we've been sneaking about behind her back. Who knows – if Meg hadn't told me . . . Sod it, I don't know who I'm angriest at. Meg or you or myself. It's as if I've stepped into a lovely scented bubble bath to find the water's freezing cold.'

'This is about you and me,' Aiden said softly. 'Two people in love. Not Georgina. Not Astrid. And certainly not Meg.' Feo was nudging him insistently with his toy. He bent and threw the penguin across the room again and the little dog skittered after it, barking joyfully.

'Maybe not, but I wish to hell Meg had warned me Georgina was married to you before I went to the Marlow Arms. I wish I'd never seen you again.'

'You can't possibly mean that.' Aiden looked aghast.

Jen clasped her tissue tighter in her fist. 'I'm sorry,' she said quietly, 'but I do.'

For a second he stared at her, every line of his body tense and rigid, until perceptibly the fight went out of him, his body and attitude softening. He returned to sit back down beside her.

'Let's not fight,' he said, taking her hand in his and squeezing it. 'I only want you to be happy. That's all I've ever wanted. OK, maybe it can't work for us, maybe it never will, but you'll always be my one great love. You've given me back something that's been missing for years, a part of myself. After I leave Georgina . . . when I'm in my own place . . . we can still be friends, can't we?'

'Distant friends. Very distant. Like Timbuktu distant.' She managed a watery smile. 'Oh Starkey, it's all so difficult. Being in love is far too painful. Painful when it starts, painful when it ends. And it always ends. Always. However much you believe in it. I never thought it would end with you the first time, or with Ollie either for that matter. We're all so sure at the beginning, aren't we? And then it all goes wrong.'

'What will you do?' he said, stroking her neck, so lightly it made her shiver.

She nestled into his shoulder, exhausted by the outpouring of emotion. 'I don't know. If I didn't have Chloe to worry about, I'd probably move somewhere remote, like Cornwall, bury my head in books and slushy films.'

Feo stood on his hind legs, trying to push his nose between them, and whined, all interest in his penguin hunt diverted by macho jealousy.

'You're a kind, sweet, lovely, beautiful person.' He kissed her cheek, placed another softly on her nose and then gently turned her chin up to face him, his lips finding hers. They began to kiss, slowly at first but with increasing passion, sinking into each other's arms. Feo jumped into the space beside her on the sofa and curled into a ball, sulking.

She should pull away, she really should. But her head was swimming in cotton wool, her legs rubber. She couldn't fight it, all willpower and sense had evaporated under his touch.

'Not here,' Aiden whispered. He took her hand and led her towards the stairs. She was a mute servant, following him obediently, slavishly willing.

Her feet were on the first step when her landline rang. And stopped. Rang again. Stopped. And rang. Breaking her out of her trance.

A shiver went down Jen's spine, freezing her in her tracks. It was their code. Their SOS. She had to answer it.

'Won't be a minute.' She jerked her hand from Aiden's, Feo jumping and barking, excited by her burst of speed.

'Wait!' Her master's voice had no effect now, the spell was broken. She'd already picked up.

# Chapter 43

'What are you doing, Jennifer? Now? Right this minute?' It was Georgina. Brisker than ever.

Jen thought quickly. 'I'm about to have some lunch.' *After shagging your husband.*

'This is critical. Will you come to London?'

'When?'

'ASAP. Trafalgar Square. By Nelson's Column. I've no time to talk.'

When Jen put down the receiver, Aiden was staring at her. Waiting for an explanation.

'It was Georgina.'

'Georgina?'

'Your wife,' Jen said sternly.

'What did she want?' He took her hand again but she pulled it away.

'She didn't say. But I have to go. I've arranged to meet her.'

'You can't.' He stepped in front of her, blocking her path, every inch the tortured hero. 'Ring her back and tell her no. Tell her you're busy. Don't go. Please, Jen. Not now. If you care anything for us at all, please not now.'

'You'd better leave.' She shook her head, backing away from him. 'And Aiden, don't call for a while. I'll be in touch, I promise. But I need time to think.'

\*

Georgina was waiting underneath Nelson's Column, checking her watch impatiently and stamping her feet against the cold. She glanced up as Jen approached, waved, and started walking towards her. Suddenly it clicked. Meg was right behind her, looking sheepish.

'OK, right.' Jen stood frozen, feeling like a shroud had fallen over her head. 'I know what this is about and I . . .'

'You don't.' Meg threw her a diamond-cutting glare. 'You *really* don't.'

Georgina's eyes darted from Jen's to Meg's and then back again. 'Come on, both of you. I haven't long. Look sharp now.'

She headed off at a hefty pace and they ended up trotting behind her like a couple of carriage dogs.

'Don't say anything,' hissed Meg when a distance opened up. 'I'd hate her to . . .'

'Screw you!' Jen bared her teeth. It was a smile, but the kind that Dracula gave before he drew blood.

They stopped outside a grey concrete building, with a sign that read Klingman's Fine Art above the door. Walking in, Georgina picked up brochures from a pile stacked on a table in the entrance. They climbed up two flights of steel and glass spiral stairs and followed Georgina as she marched through a large gallery with polished oak floors, up a ramp, left down a passageway, right into a smaller room with black-framed photographs mounted on white board, and through into an even tinier space. After passing a weird construction which looked like wooden blocks leading up to a basketball net, she suddenly jerked to a halt in front of a blue painting. It showed a raging sea painted with big swirly circles for waves. On one of several billowing thunderclouds sat a small black cat. It was entitled *Secrets*.

'Look at the bottom left corner,' whispered Georgina.

*Dyllis Bedlow.*

There was no mistaking it. The painting was definitely Rowan's.

'She used my maiden name,' Jen said in a hushed voice.

'I only came in because I was visiting a client nearby and thought I'd browse around, just in case.' Georgina's eyes shone. 'It is her, isn't it? I'm not mistaken, am I?'

They all looked up at the painting in awe, like religious devotees standing before a statue of the Messiah.

'Has to be. What's the odds against it – the surname, someone coming up with exactly her old style, sticking in her signature cat?'

'And she had an aunt called Dyllis,' Meg said solemnly.

'Her mum told us she'd given up.' Jen peered at the painting from another angle.

Meg scrutinised the tiny scribble below the artist's name. 'Her mom's a fruitcake. Anyway it's got this year's date.'

'Wait here.' Georgina left them standing in front of the painting as she headed down the stairs.

Meg and Jen glowered at each other, but they didn't speak, couldn't speak. Too much had been said between them already.

Five minutes later Georgina returned. 'Apparently the artist brought it in a couple of months ago, but they've also sold other works of hers. They won't give out her details but I've left a note and card with the owner asking her to contact me. He says the exhibitors only usually visit when they've something new to display. But he promised to pass the message along. Let's hope that this time we've finally struck gold!'

It must have been obvious to Georgina there'd been some tension between Meg and Jen, but she didn't bring it up that afternoon, nor when she telephoned Jen the day after their gallery visit and asked to meet her and Meg later that morning in a small café near her office. She wouldn't say what it was about, but she sounded cheerful. Not like someone who'd discovered her husband loved elsewhere.

No reason then to worry. No reason at all. So Jen kept telling herself. Nevertheless she crossed her fingers as she ambled up the cobbled hill. She'd never felt so confused about her feelings, so dreadful about her actions. If Georgie hadn't interrupted them yesterday she would have ended up upstairs, making love with Aiden in her and Ollie's bed. That it hadn't happened was by pure chance, not any merit on her part. Impossible to pretend to herself any more that their relationship could stay innocent.

So now she was traipsing off to see her lover's wife, the very picture of duplicity, the very worst sort of person who would cheat on a friend. She was feverish, veering between elation and despair. Aiden loved her. She loved him. She ached for him. But what would happen – could they really run off together, build the life she'd dreamed about for so long? If she saw him again she was sure she couldn't resist. Perhaps it was wiser not to see him again. Yes, that would be the smart choice. Forget him. Find a nice man like Tom and move on. But she'd tried that strategy already and had had no luck. And in the meantime she had to face Georgina, pretend that all that was on her mind was looking for Rowan, and pray that Meg didn't choose today to drop her in it.

'I've called this meeting here because . . .' Georgina paused and a knowing smile lit up her face. Not that it needed lighting up. Georgina seemed to be blooming these days. Perhaps Aiden was right, perhaps she was unusually resilient, the kind of woman who could bounce back from marital stress, even divorce. At the dinner party it had seemed as if something had released inside her, springing her free from the coiled, barely contained tension that Jen had noticed ever since Guy Fawkes Night, when Georgina had opened the door to this whole adventure. Today she was dressed in a tailored midnight-blue trouser suit, with just the right amount of accessories and make-up, looking glamorous and smart while Meg and Jen were both in jeans and warm-but-nothing-to-write-home-about woolly sweaters.

The waitress was walking over with their caffè lattes and cappuccino. They waited, unspeaking, while she placed the cups in front of them.

It was remarkably quiet for the time of morning, but then again it was a weekday and a bit too early for office workers to get their lunch. Plus this place was a bit of a heap, not Georgina's style at all, you would have thought. Tatty old paper chains everywhere – fake green plastic Christmas tree in corner. Weary-looking waitress with reindeer horns on, attempting to look jolly.

Through the window they could see an Eastern European-looking singer, doing a jiggy type of song on a fiddle with other musicians behind, and people around him putting money in his hat and dancing together.

'Gerron with it,' Jen urged. She made herself add some levity. 'Keeping us all in suspenders.'

'Because, because . . . I received a message from Rowan.'

'What!' gasped Meg.

Georgina passed her mobile over to Meg. 'I could have told you over the phone, but I wanted you to hear it for yourselves. Our first decent success.'

Jen waited while Meg listened attentively and her eyes slowly enlarged to saucers.

'Unfortunately the number's withheld. Seems like a Rowan trait. Your turn, Jennifer.' Georgina took her mobile from Meg and pressed some buttons before passing it over to Jen.

*'Hi, it's Rowan . . . listen I'm sorry, but . . . I got your messages and I just . . . I just don't have time to get together with anyone right now. I've a full life, plenty of mates and . . . I – I don't see the point of rehashing history. If I change my mind though, I've got your numbers. All right, bye.'*

'Christ!' said Jen. Almost by accident, she caught Meg's eye and the American girl gave a faint shrugging movement, her downturned lips expressing equal disappointment. Instinctively

Jen knew they'd both called a truce – for the moment, anyway.

'Iceberg or what!' Meg remarked, when Jen had finished listening. 'And to think I was going to leave Zeb with her.'

Jen gave the phone back to Georgina. 'You call that a decent success?'

'Well all right, I know it's not an actual decent success as such, but you know what I meant, it's an answer and that's really what we wanted, isn't it?'

Was it? Jen's brain frizzled as the message sank in and she thought of those wasted hours of searching, asking around and chasing dreams. Was this it then, the end of the rainbow? So all those imagined rapturous reunions with Rowan – the four of them skipping down the street arm in arm, singing 'Girls Just Want To Have Fun' – were merely a fantasy, reality a million miles away. There was Jen sneaking around with Georgina's husband, she and Meg were barely on speaking terms and Rowan didn't want to know a single one of them anyway.

What a mess.

On Saturday night at dinner Georgina had said, leaning over and patting her hand, that Jen was a 'good egg'. But she wasn't a good egg. She was a stinking smelly rancid egg, that's what she was. It was like that article she'd read in the shop, all those weeks ago. When good friends go bad. Well, she had gone bad. Very bad. Disgustingly bad. On a level with Meg who, let's face it, had slept with Starkey when Georgina was pregnant and at her most vulnerable. What a pair they were.

Suddenly guilt overwhelmed Jen as an isolated memory pushed its lonely way to the front of her up-till-now blissfully ignorant mind. All the girls from 4L were in the changing room having showers and she remembered mentioning to Rowan, who was struggling to get her Aertex shirt off and her school blouse on without revealing her 32AA bra, that Murgatroyd, the young colt they'd been jointly taking care of, was being gelded that morning.

'What's gelded?' Rowan had asked, bemused.

'It means he's going to have his testicles cut off.'

'But if they're cut off, how will he be able to wee?'

Jen stared at her in amazement. 'But Rowan, his testicles are . . .' Then she stopped. Now, a true friend would have pulled her to one side and said, 'Look, Rowan, the testicles are the balls behind the willy, which have nothing to do with the wee coming out but hold the sperm,' but instead she went guffawing round the changing room, doubled over, crossing her arms over her tummy and shouting, 'Guess what Rowan said? You'll wet, you'll wet,' and everyone had laughed nastily at Rowan.

Why did she do that? And Rowan never held it against her.

Or maybe she did . . .

Jen was about to relate an edited version of this to the others when Georgina suddenly came out with, 'I bullied her once. Told her I'd send her to Coventry if she didn't come to the school discotheque with me. You were off sick, Jennifer, and Nutmeg into serious snogging with Gregory Henshaw, and when she said she'd prefer going to drama club, I didn't speak to her and she kept saying, "Please Georgina, please talk to me. Why won't you talk to me?" Poor lamb.'

'She probably couldn't figure out what Coventry meant, either,' Jen said. 'Never the brightest button in the box.'

Georgina stared into the middle distance. 'I can hear those pitiful pleadings now. Her mother was right when she implied I made her timid.'

'And I stole Gregory Henshaw from her.' Meg looked even more depressed than Georgina. 'Darn.'

'Don't worry, I think it's me she doesn't want to see,' Jen told them. 'First Gwyneth, then Rowan. My reputation has finally caught up with me. I knew I'd be punished for my sins one day.'

'But why?'

'Because I was a telltale bitch who humiliated her in public.' Though she was far too ashamed to go into precise details about the Murgatroyd thing.

'No wonder she doesn't want to see us then,' said Georgina. 'The bitch, the bully and the tart. Fine bosom buddies we turned out to be!'

There was something wrong. Very wrong, thought Jen. In fact, there were so many elements in her life verging on pure disaster that she was sure every planet in her astrological chart had to be whizzing backwards, Pluto colliding with Uranus, Venus giving Mars the cold shoulder, the entire heavens in an uproar.

The feeling, however, that kept her awake at three a.m. thinking, wondering, was pure dread. And not for herself, she was sure of that – though she was ready to kiss the Angel Gabriel himself if he ensured that Meg continued to be discreet – but dread for Rowan.

Why didn't she want to see them? And why, all those years ago, had she asked to meet and then failed to show?

The whole thing didn't make sense. Could Rowan still be holding grudges against them all? People did – Gwyneth Minksheath, for example – and Helen seemingly had only just pardoned Ollie for suggesting she was Jen's mother all those years ago.

Rowan wasn't like that, though. She'd never seemed to mind being teased. She had a sort of forgive and forget quality about her that was almost saintly. Even if she'd said explicitly that she didn't want to see them, they couldn't leave it at that, they just couldn't. If nothing else Jen *had* to find out why.

Enough of moping, analysing, wallowing in self-pity. It was time to act.

# Chapter 44

Thursday morning, eight thirty-five. Having dropped Chloe off at her school breakfast club, Jen now sat on the morning train to Victoria, dressed in a smart and stylish Giordani skirt suit, with a scalding hot cup of cappuccino in one hand and Feo's lead in the other. By nine fifteen she was back at Klingman's Fine Art only to discover it didn't open till nine thirty and she had to pace the pavement, waiting.

'Can I help you?'

A tall elegant woman in black gloves and a coat with a fur collar had stepped out of a taxi and towards the door, keys in hand. The fur looked real, fox probably. Maybe even two foxes. Her legs were sheathed in black tights, her make-up immaculate down to the smoky eyelids and burgundy lipstick.

'I need to get in touch with one of the exhibitors.' Jen's throat was dry. 'It's a matter of immense urgency.'

She was about to add 'life and death', but it reminded her too much of Meg and her lies. From now on, she, Jen Bedlow, was wedded to the truth. Or some of it, at least. She would try not to fib her way out of trouble unless it was absolutely essential.

The fox trembled as its owner's head produced an emphatic no. 'Against company policy to give out personal information. We do have meet-the-artist receptions quite frequently, usually at the opening of a show. Otherwise the artists don't tend to be in here often and most of them like their privacy. And may I add, you can't let that dog in here.' She unlocked the door.

'I wasn't going in. I've been already.' Quickly Jen tied Feo's lead to the railings, following the woman through the door.

'You could however leave a note. May I ask which particular artist interested you?' She'd stripped off her coat and gloves, revealing long manicured nails, a classic navy knee-length tunic dress topped off by a gold brooch and a tiny nearly transparent cardigan.

'Dyllis Bedlow. Top floor. Next to the three wooden blocks and basketball-net structure.'

'A netball net actually. That's why it's named *Netball Net*,' she said, a bit too pompously for Jen's liking, as she hung her things in a closet. 'Miss Bedlow?' She stepped behind her computer, which was perched on a desk close to the table with brochures. 'Fine choice. So dynamic, full of passion. We've sold quite a few of her pieces over the years and the price keeps rising. An excellent investment if you're contemplating one. Are you considering purchasing?' She gave a wide professional smile, fingers clearly itching to write up invoices.

'Well, no, actually, I'm her . . .' Sister? But then they'd never looked alike and the gallery owner might have met Rowan and know she had no siblings '. . . mother. I'm so terribly sorry, but I'm in a frightful tizzy.'

There went her commitment to the truth; it had never been more than a short ill-fated engagement. Jen patted at her hair, smoothing it down in what she imagined was a fussy-mother kind of way. 'I was supposed to be meeting her for a shopping trip but my train was delayed and I mislaid her mobile number and my battery's died, damn charger, so now we've lost each other. She could be anywhere in London by now, pounding the streets, searching for me.' She contorted her face into a worried frown. It must have worked because the woman arched her left eyebrow, disdainful expression giving way to a more human kind of puzzlement. 'And then we were going to visit her father . . . my husband, in hospital. Oh please, you have to help me.'

'How strange. Then I'm sure you know Ms Bedlow rarely travels to London. I was led to believe she's rather reclusive, refuses all publicity. I've only met her fleetingly myself, when she drops off her paintings, but I must say you don't look old enough to be her mother. No resemblance at all in fact.'

Scratch puzzlement. Make that blatant suspicion.

'Why thank you.' Jen found her voice becoming falsetto, more posh, her back straighter. In a minute she'd be standing on tippy-toes as she tried to out-Sloane the Sloane. 'So kind. That's because it's um . . . er . . . true. I'm not her *real* mother, no, I'm her stepmother. But we're so close and I treat her like my own. My husband's in his seventies, severely ill with emphysema, but a very fine-looking man nevertheless.'

'Would you by any chance have some sort of identification? A driving licence perhaps?'

Jen rifled through her handbag, gratified to see a tiny flicker of reaction when the woman studied an old Holmes Place membership card and extended her talons to give it back. Luckily it was almost ten years old, and therefore in her maiden name. Beside her, Feo was straining at the lead, anxious to investigate his new surroundings.

'We're not supposed to reveal clients' details, security, you see.' She was already tapping at the computer keyboard. Then she frowned. 'But it hasn't got a phone number. There's only her address. I'm sorry.'

'But . . .' *Think, Jen, think.* 'Now hopefully you have her new one.'

'New one? I can assure you we keep clients' records up to date.'

'But she moved recently. Can I . . . er . . . see?'

'I'm afraid not.' Her voice had turned frosty again. 'It has a note: Extremely Confidential. Since it can't help you phone your daughter, I really don't see the point.' She clicked out of the document.

'Well, thank you anyway.' Jen's eyes swept helplessly across the desk. They were obviously in the middle of mailing their Christmas cards. A pile were in envelopes with sticky address labels waiting for stamps, more envelopes and blank cards were in another stack. If only she could get her hands on that list. Or even . . .

'I know it's a terrific nerve, but you wouldn't by any chance have a glass of water and an aspirin please?' She gave a weak smile. 'All this running around . . .'

'Maybe in the main office. Just one minute.'

As soon as she left the entry area, Jen rifled through the sealed envelopes. Just as she hoped, Bedlow was one of the first. She grabbed it up, pushed it in her pocket. She'd just save them the cost of posting it.

The receptionist, manager, owner – whatever she was – came back with a tumbler and two paracetamol. Jen thanked her profusely, gulped the tablets down and left with Feo, walking away as fast as she could. She kept expecting to hear a shout and see the woman running after her, outraged. As soon as she was sure she'd got away with it, she yanked the envelope from her pocket.

Bryn Du Farm, she read, scanning the address and the postcode.

Wales. Rowan was in Wales.

Jen caught the Tube and train home, dug a soft tubular sports bag out from the murkier depths of the understairs cupboard and started to pull clothes from drawers.

Hastening into the bathroom, she picked up her toothbrush and toothpaste, throwing lipstick, foundation, eyeshadow after her moisturiser, taking them out again because why would you need them on a Welsh farm and dropping them back in because you never knew and why not?

Still there might not be central heating so she took out the nice sweater she'd packed and replaced it with an overstretched bobbly thing that Ollie had left behind in the laundry basket, and for good measure went to the hall cupboard again and pulled out an old raincoat, found a lead and a bag of dog food for Feo.

While the directions were printing from multi-map she glanced at the clock, twenty-five to twelve. In a few hours she was supposed to be collecting Chloe from school. One last thing to do.

She took a deep breath and began dialling.

'Hi.' Ollie's voice sounded so familiar and yet odd, as if he were receding from her down a very long tunnel. 'Strange. I was just dialling your number.'

'Oh yes?'

'I was thinking of taking Chloe away this weekend.'

'This weekend?'

'Yes. It's . . . er . . .' He laughed, almost nervously. 'Someone I know's got us tickets to . . .'

'Don't tell me,' she said, disgusted. 'Euro Disney. You're going to Euro Disney this weekend?'

'You knew about it?' She'd taken him completely by surprise.

'Helen told me. And Saul told her. Seems like I'm the last person in Huntsleigh to hear the news.'

'Helen?' He sounded flabbergasted.'Might have guessed. Those two could be a dangerous combination.'

'Well, I think you should have asked me first!' She was outraged. 'I am still Chloe's mother. Don't you think I should know when my daughter goes abroad? What if something happened and I needed to contact you?' *Especially after what happened the last weekend you had her* – she bit her tongue to stop herself saying it.

'Yes, well, I'm asking you now.' He sounded maddeningly

394

unruffled. 'But I wasn't sure if I was definitely going until today. I didn't want to get Chloe's hopes up.'

'But it's Thursday. When were you going to decide?' she fumed. 'When you set foot on the Eurostar? Doesn't Frances Hutton need to make reservations? Or does she own shares in Eurostar and the Disney hotels too?'

'Look, if you're so dead set against it,' Ollie began, 'we won't . . .'

A little too late she remembered the reason she was calling him. Anger and sarcasm weren't perhaps the best tactics to use.

'No, that's all right. Go off with your girlfriend. Only next time I'd appreciate some advance warning. It so happens that I'm away too this weekend. And I wondered if you could pick Chloe up tonight instead of tomorrow?'

'Oh, *you're* going away, are you? Again? And don't you think you should have asked *me*?' he echoed her practically word for word. 'You are her mother. What if I needed to contact you?' He was trying to piss her off, she could tell. Only she wouldn't let him.

'You'd call my mobile, I assume. I'm only off to Wales. What difference does it make when you're in France?'

'And who are you going with this time? That English teacher of yours? What was his name? Dugan?'

'What bloody business of yours is it who I go with or what his name is?' Her temper flared again. 'And who told you about Tom Dugan anyway?'

'Chloe said you went on a date. And Helen told Saul who with.'

Oh Christ, what else did old blabbermouth spill? About the one-night stand? Was it too much to hope for that her friend had been even marginally discreet?

'Yes, well,' Jen felt flustered suddenly, anxious to end the call, 'if you could fetch Chloe, that would be a huge favour. I'm rushing out the door and since it's so last-minute . . . Her passport's in the top drawer of the bedroom.'

'No problem. I've still got a key.'

'Oh. Yes. Of course you have.'

'Which I can always give you back, you know, if you need it for anybody?'

'Who would I need it for?' Was he suggesting . . . 'Don't bother, I can always get another cut. And anyway hopefully we'll be shot of it soon. The house, I mean.'

'So why *are* you heading off to Wales?'

'It's to do with Rowan. Look, I've got to run, Ollie. Talk to you later, OK?' She hung up hurriedly before he could ask her anything else.

She picked up the sports bag by the handles, slung the strap over her shoulder and at the last minute found a fleece hat and opened the zip of a front pocket to shove it in. Something gleamed in the darkness. She poked her index finger into the fluff in the corner and something slipped over her nail. Disbelievingly, she put down the bag – the very one, she now remembered, they'd taken on their honeymoon – and held up her hand. Halfway between her nail and her knuckle rested the simple gold band: Ollie's missing wedding ring.

# Chapter 45

On the way to the motorway, Jen pulled on to the A322. There was one more thing she had to do, and she had her fingers crossed he wouldn't be home. Call her a coward but her plan was to check the coast was clear, sneak up to the front door, drop her hastily scrawled note in the letter box and be on the road before it had a chance to hit the mat. No embarrassing conversations. No tortuous excuses.

With this in mind she parked a good hundred yards from his house, gestured to Feo to stay in the car, then edged along the pavement as close to the hedge as possible. She was inconspicuous, she hoped, without being so noticeably doubled up as to set off alarms with the Neighbourhood Watch.

The last hedge ended at the door of Tom's flat. She ducked down, poking her head round the leafy bush, and just as quickly jerked it back.

Damn. Tom was in the driveway, standing beside his rusty Toyota which had the bonnet up. A man in overalls was leaning over, bottom in the air, fiddling about in the entrails of the engine. Tom was slapping his arms against the cold, talking to him.

She didn't think Tom had seen her but then suddenly there he was, standing on the pavement looking down as she rested on her heels, planning her next move. He put out a hand to help her up and shamefaced, feeling like a bumbling fool, she took it.

'Just tying my bootlace. Slippery out here.'

'What a nice surprise!' He seemed really pleased to see her, unfazed by her spying. 'What are you doing here?'

'I came to give you this note.' There was no easy way to say it. She held out an envelope.

'What can it be?' He started opening it with a happy smile. 'Don't tell me, a Christmas card. Could be my only one this year. I'm not great at staying in touch.'

'No!' She put out a hand to stop him. 'Not yet. Wait till I'm gone.' Hugging her arms to her ribs, her body twisted into one big awkward squirm. 'It's a Dear John letter. Well, in your case, Dear Tom.'

'Oh.' He paused, with only a small corner ripped, his green eyes arresting hers. 'I see.' Thoughtfully he tapped the envelope against his jeans. 'Why don't you come in? Let's talk.'

'No, it's definitely over,' she said gently, shaking her head. 'I thought you should know. It was selfish and wrong sleeping with you, not that it's your fault or anything, and I'm sorry about the morning, slinking off like a stoat, and I, well, I wanted to say sorry all round. For everything.'

'No need to be sorry,' he said softly, touching the back of his hand lightly against her cheek.

'No, you see, I don't want you to think you've been used. I like you . . . very much, but, well, don't feel bad about this, it's not you, it's me. And . . . well . . . it's not the right time for me now. There's no future in it for us.'

'You're a darling, Jen. Did you know that?' He squeezed her hand, then leant forward to kiss the top of her head.

'Oh, I'm not as nice as you think I am,' she said wryly, relieved he was taking it so well. 'Look, you'll find someone special again. I just know you will.'

There was a forced silence as the mechanic bore down on

them, wiping his hands on a greasy rag. A middle-aged man with a large belly, he gave Jen an up and down once-over with yellow jaundiced eyes before shoving back his cap and scratching his head.

'I don't have the right part with me,' he told Tom. 'We should have one in the yard but if we don't I'll have to make some calls. It might take me an hour or two to track it down but we should have her up and running before the end of the day.'

'Great, thanks.' As the mechanic lumbered away Tom turned back to Jen. 'It was thoughtful of you to come all this way, just to tell me this,' he smiled sweetly.

'It's not that far out of the way.' She fidgeted, her tension decreasing a notch now the worst was over, but still itching to get out of there. Only it seemed rude to bolt when he was being so nice. 'I need to take this road for the motorway.'

'Off somewhere good?'

'Wales.'

'Wales! What is it – a weekend break?' He moved over to the car and dropped the still propped-open bonnet.

She couldn't hold back any longer. 'I think I may have found Rowan, you see,' she said excitedly. 'Only she's not called Rowan now, she goes under the name of Dyllis – at least that's her artistic pseudonym. She's living in a place called Bryn Du Farm near Carderistwyth and oh God, Tom, I can't wait to find out if she has children, if she's married, divorced, widowed. My life's a mess right now, but today for the first time in months something's gone my way. And she's used my maiden name. Mine. Not Dyllis Carrington, nor Dyllis Lennox, but Dyllis Bedlow, and it makes me so proud. Like I was incredibly important in her life.'

'I'm sure you were.' Tom was laughing at her enthusiasm, his fingers turning purple with cold now. 'Dyllis Bedlow. You must have been her top favourite friend,' he said as if that settled the popularity question. 'Drive safe, don't speed.' He was already backing towards his front door, holding the blighted letter in his hands, reversing out of her life. Which reminded her – she patted her pockets, rummaged through the stuff on the passenger seat for the gallery Christmas card. Damn, she'd left it at the house. Oh well, Bryn Du Farm, Carderistwyth. How hard could it be to find?

When she drove past his driveway, he hadn't made it past the doorstep. He raised his hand and she smiled as she waved back, seeing him through the car mirror turn and walk in.

It had ended well, a good smooth finish. People should always end one-night stands with good smooth finishes. Give some closure, as Meg would say, to the whole affair. It would make the world a so much better, more wholesome place in which to live.

Three p.m. and Jen was knocking at the door of a ramshackle old farmhouse, Feo beside her held tightly by the leash. It had taken her nearly three hours. Three long hours of being on her own, with only an old Neil Young CD to listen to.

It took ages before she heard steps in her direction and the door opened just a crack, big enough for someone to peep out. An old woman, maybe, but she couldn't make her out.

'Hi.' Jen shuffled her feet, shivering with cold. 'I'm looking for a Dyllis Bedlow. I'm a friend of hers, Jennifer Bedlow.'

'I know who you are.' The crack widened to six inches. No old woman. Rowan's Aunt Dyllis, she was sure. Much younger than she'd expected. There was a definite family resemblance, though the face was round and chubby-cheeked, all hint of bone structure buried under fat.

Her niece, last seen, had waist-length raven locks; this woman possessed a bird's nest of paint-spattered iron-grey straggles held up unsuccessfully with what looked like a wooden peg amongst a mass of hair pins. Face weather-beaten, clothed in a man's lumberjack shirt, baggy stained combat trousers and mud-spattered wellies, she was of similar height to the beautiful fragile Rowan, with eyes the same riveting violet, but the genetic blueprint stopped there. No wonder Rowan had contemplated passing her kids to a flaky, lying, even schizophrenic American – if any of Meg's story were remotely true. What a choice otherwise – Ma Howard or Cold Comfort Farm!

'Aunt Dyllis? I'm looking for Rowan?'

'Are you now?' A hint of a familiar smile flickered across the woman's face, the voice uncannily identical to their old schoolfriend's.

It was only then that the truth infiltrated Jen's brain.

Bloody hell.

Bloody bloody hell.

'Rowan?'


'So can I come in?'

Jen still stood on the doorstep, bag in hand. Whatever reception she'd expected, it certainly wasn't this.

'Go home, Jen.' The door closed back to a three-inch gap.

'Rowan, please,' she jammed her foot there to stop herself being barred completely, 'we've been looking for you for months. Your mum told us you were moving to Shanghai and had been in Beijing, or Peking as she calls it. And why the name change? Yours, not Peking's.' Jen braced against the pressure on her foot. 'Not ashamed of your paintings, are you? They're fabulous, as always.'

'I told Georgina on the phone,' Rowan peeked through, 'I'm not into all that nostalgia. What's the point in raking over what's past?'

'Raking over?' Jen shook her head. 'But why . . . Are you cross with us? Did we do something wrong?'

'You wouldn't understand my problems.' She began to push the door in earnest. 'I just want some peace. Now if you don't mind.'

'No . . . no . . . Er, I have problems too. Terrible huge whopping problems, that's why I came to see you.' *Good thinking, Jen, swoop on her kind nature, play with it a little, make a friend of it.* 'You're the only one that can help.'

'What sort of help?' The door opened a fraction. 'What's happened?'

'Well,' she thought briefly of going through her mess-up of a life, but then again she'd be at the door all night, 'truth is, Rowan, we've been looking for you for months and everything's gone wrong in my life lately, and all I want is for one thing to work out. Just one tiny thing.'

'What's it to do with me?'

'Well, maybe nothing,' she sighed. 'But, please, Rowan, I've been driving here for over three hours, I'm tired, I need a cup of water or something. Please let me in.'

She heard Rowan take a long deep breath, then the door began slowly opening.

'Thanks so much,' Jen said as she walked through. 'It's so good to finally find you. Wait till Meg and Georgie hear . . .'

'No!' Rowan's response was whiplash-sharp. 'Don't tell them. Only you.'

Not the bully or the tart? So Rowan *had* liked her best, after all. Funny how even after more than two decades that could give her a little glow.

Inside was old and dishevelled with low raftered ceilings, the front door leading straight into a sitting room – if you could call it a sitting room. There was a fireplace, responsible for the room's coating of soot and ash, a pile of broken sticks taking up much of the hearth, easels and paint tubes all over the place, mixing palettes on sideboards, half-finished paintings hanging from above, leaning against every available surface. At the same time, though, there was a cosiness about it, herbs on the windowsill, a couple of tatty but comfy-looking armchairs.

402

'*Dach chi isio panad,*' Rowan said, apparently forgetting Jen didn't speak Welsh.

'*Dach chi isio panad,*' Jen repeated, assuming it was a greeting.

Rowan gave her a funny look. 'I was asking if you'd like a cuppa rather than water.' She led the way into the kitchen. 'The kettle's boiling.'

True enough, it sat on the blackened surface of an old Aga, simmering gently, the whole room permeated with the warmth of the wood-burning stove. Rowan pulled down two cups from hooks on an ancient Welsh dresser and took out tea bags from a scratched yellowing canister. The light was bright in this room, thanks to huge glass panels that had replaced the original windows, clearly to benefit the giant easel taking up all available space in the centre of the room and adding its own rich odours of oil paint and turpentine to the olfactory stew.

Poking out from behind a screen in a corner, Jen noticed the rounded end of a cast-iron claw-foot bath, probably installed by the original occupants.

She wandered over to investigate, running her fingers along its pitted enamel.

'This is nice. What is it – an antique? You could get a fortune for it, I bet. I'm surprised you have it in the kitchen, though.'

Rowan snorted. 'And where else would I be having it? The taps on the sink are gravity-fed from the spring but I still have to fill the thing. And if the spring dries up I'm after hauling buckets from the well.'

'Oh.'

Jen had passed the well on the way in. She'd thought it was a quaint touch to an already rustic scene, the perfect addition to the falling-down barn, the three cows behind a rickety fence and the dilapidated structure that looked like an historic old privy or outhouse, frosted with ice. It had never occurred to her that these things were in actual use.

But that didn't mean . . . did it?

Surely nobody, outside the most primitive campsites, still used . . . *Ugh!*

'What about electricity?' She looked up and saw a bulb dangling from a wire.

'I have that all right. And if I want to phone anyone, the Sheepshearer pub up the road's got a landline.'

Jen strolled back towards the easel, feeling out of sorts. She needed to use the loo – it had been a long drive with no stops – but apparently there wasn't one, except for that rundown outhouse privy. It was enough to make anyone a little grumpy.

As scalding water poured from the heavy kettle's spout, Jen examined her companion out of the corner of her eye while pretending to study the masterpiece in progress.

A few things were becoming crystal clear.

It was definitely Rowan.

She didn't want to see them.

It wasn't just her crazy mother who'd gone prematurely grey. She looked at least ten years older than the rest of them.

Georgina was by no means the most altered after all.


'So why all the mystery?' Jen asked, two cups of tea and three scones later. They were seated side by side on the distressed leather sofa, so distressed it had a rip down its back. 'What's going on, Rowan?'

'Another scone?' She fed one to a cloudy-eyed deformed-looking sausage dog that Feo was beside himself to meet. Jen had tied him to the sofa, not trusting her grip on the lead as he panted madly.

Jen put up her hand in refusal. 'I'm full, thanks.' She hesitated, not sure how to continue her questioning. Shrieking, 'Rowan, what in God's name happened to you?' hardly seemed diplomatic.

'It's so beautiful out here,' she started. 'Wild and, well, isolated, but don't you find it a touch remote? No plumbing, no shops, no neighbours. What if you slipped and cracked your head and no one found you?'

'Leave it out, will you? I'm not worried. The village is only a couple of miles away, if you walk it. Road's much further, it has to go round the mountain. And Jones the Post usually stops by on his rounds to say hello, share a brew. Besides, I like the quiet of the countryside.' She crossed her swollen ankles. 'I'm a right hermit. I like to paint, listen to the birds in the morning as I milk the cows, feed the badgers and foxes at night. It suits me. I've peace, tranquillity and five acres all to myself.'

'So you became a farmer as well as an artist? I can't wait to tell the others.'

'You can't.'

'But why not, Rowan?' Jen asked, perplexed. 'And why was it so hard to find you? Why were you such an elusive butterfly?'

'Because . . . because . . .' Suddenly her eyes began to fill and her heavy chest heaved up and down at an alarming rate. 'I can't say.'

'But you must. Please, Rowan. Is it because you're annoyed with us?'

'No.' She shook her head.

'Is it because you're not into nostalgia?'

'No.'

'Then what's the matter? Just tell me. Then I'll leave.'

'Did you ever stop to think, Jen, the reason I might not want finding is because I'm terrified. Sodding bloody terrified.' A lone tear trickled down her fat cheek.

# Chapter 46

'Of all things, *that* didn't cross my mind.' Jen put her arm around Rowan's big wide shoulder. 'But why? Terrified of what?'

'Because . . . I've memories . . .' Racking great sobs shuddered through her as she leant her weight against Jen.

'Shhh, shhh. It's all right. We all have memories,' she clucked gently. 'Each and every one of us. Surely yours aren't that bad?'

'Right enough, they are. I – I . . . things went on.'

'What type of things?'

'Can't say.' She dropped her head like a child and stared into her lap.

'Can't or won't?'

'It's too awful.'

'Hey, nothing can be that awful,' Jen soothed. 'I've been in terrible dilemmas over the years. Look, here's the deal,' she said, sounding like Meg, 'you tell me what you've done and I'll tell you what I was about to do the other . . .'

'*I've* done?' She suddenly jumped in, incensed, lifting her head and glaring into Jen's eyes. '*I've* done nothing.'

'Who, then? Come on, Rowan, better out than in as my dad would say.' Jen tried to sound jovial and encouraging, sensing she was getting near the truth.

'My ex-husband,' Rowan said flatly. She took a deep breath

and then started to speak in a quiet shaky voice. 'It was me mam's fault. She'd stuck me in that immersion school with teachers as barmy as herself, bunch of raving nationalists, detentions for speaking English, lamenting the loss of the birch rod, raging about Londoners buying their land. I was never so heartsick and lonely. And he was, too. He managed to get mail to me through my friend Gwyneth. It was the only glimmer of light in those dark days. I thought he was my saviour.' Her heavy shoulders slumped. 'And so we eloped.'

'Carry on,' Jen urged gently, afraid that the wrong word or inflection would stop her in her tracks, hardly able to believe the tale her friend was spinning.

'He was superb in the beginning, you know, soft, sweet, caring, would do anything for me, run me baths, buy me flowers, get the shopping. Even learned me to cook . . .' She started to sob.

'Phew, that's a relief, you were always rubbish at domestic science.' Jen rubbed her back, hoping to encourage her to continue, but Rowan wasn't smiling.

She took another breath. 'He was jealous, but then so was I a bit in the beginning. A handsome devil he was and I thought, stupid cow, that his jealousy just proved how much he loved me. As time went on though he got worse, never wanted to let me out of his sight, not even to go shopping. I couldn't talk to another person without him going off on one. Seemed like whenever I made new friends and wanted to meet them, just for coffee like, he'd sell up and we'd go and live somewhere else.'

She got to her feet, moving around the room restlessly. Jen didn't dare say a word as she continued talking.

'I lost touch with me mam, everyone, until it wasn't worth making friends any more. He was rude as well. If people came visiting, he'd just sit scowling at them. It was embarrassing for them and for me.' She got down on her knees and began to build up newspapers and kindling for a fire. 'Slowly he chipped away my confidence, wouldn't allow me to dress nice, wear make-up, nothing, tried to stop me going out alone. It was like he wanted us in our own little bubble – no else around. *Where are you going? What were you saying to that man? Who was that you were speaking to?*' She gulped. 'If I so much as asked the paper lad how his nan was doing, he'd think I was arranging to meet him later.'

'Couldn't you just up sticks and leave?'

'How? I had no money of my own, you see.' Rowan's voice was loaded with emotion. 'No savings. No job. He had complete control of the finances. It was his money that paid the bills, he always reminded me, his wages that covered the mortgage, his name on the deeds.'

'You couldn't have found a job yourself?' Jen said gently.

'I wanted to but without any skills or training . . . Anyway he was dead against it, said no wife of his was going to work. He was that worried I'd run off with someone and when he sensed me distancing myself from him, that's when things got tougher. He took my door key from me, unplugged the phone and locked it away.' Rowan fiddled around, making a perfect cage with her kindling, and reached for a matchbox, sliding it open.

'I was a prisoner practically. I told him we couldn't go on like this. That we needed counselling. That it weren't healthy and we shouldn't just live in each other's pockets, not seeing other folk, but he just got angry, said he'd kill himself if I left or if I ever took up with another man. And that's when it became physical.'

'He hit you?' Jen could feel her fists tighten in anger.

Tears welled in her eyes. 'The occasional kicks and a slap or two. Once he even threw me mam's sugar bowl at me, missed but that weren't the worst of it.'

'Did you call the police?'

'Which time?'

'When he threw the sugar bowl?' Jen picked on the biggest instance of abuse.

'No.' Rowan touched a match to the paper, which burst into flames. 'I was too ashamed of the way I was, of how I'd caused the situation.' She blew on the conflagration, sending sparks shooting up the chimney. 'I felt it must have been me, you see, because I encouraged him in the first place. I was as much to blame. And really there were a few bruises, where he'd grabbed my arm or something, but nothing that would stand up in court.' Her voice was bitter. 'It weren't real wife-battering or nothing. No broken bones. They'd never have given me round-the-clock protection.'

'They could have helped, though.'

'Nah.' She shook her head and another loose strand fell down. 'I went to this drop-in centre once. They were very pleasant, friendly like, but the lady said if I really wanted to leave, I should just go. She said he was manipulating me and people who threatened suicide rarely did it.'

She turned brimming blue eyes to Jen. 'But she didn't really understand. Didn't know how low I felt, how little strength I had to fight. All she went on about was occupational orders and injunctions and where I could find lawyers, but I had no money. So I left with piles of leaflets and that was that. I managed to get away a few times, hitched back to Mam's, but each time he came round, promising to change, weeping, telling me how he only lived for me, and I always felt so guilty. Rowan Howard is a coward, that's what they used to chant at school. And they were right, I was, I am.'

'That's not true.' Jen got a tissue from her bag and passed it to her. 'You were brave and sweet and . . .'

'No, Jen,' she said evenly. '*You* were brave, *Meg* was brave, even Georgina could be brave occasionally. I weren't. I was Rowan Howard the coward.'

'What about when you called asking us to meet? In Wiltshire?'

Rowan sat back on the hearth, a smudge of soot on her cheek. 'That was when I finally left. I had it planned out. I saw him spying on me when I went into the phone booth to call all of you, I knew he'd follow me wherever I went and so he did, all the way to Warminster. So when I went into the hotel . . .'

'You were there?' Jen gasped. She racked her brain, trying to remember who else she'd seen at the inn. Definitely not her friend.

'I saw you arrive. And Meg. I was hiding in the hallway to the toilets when you checked in. But I made sure you didn't see me. He'd be wondering who I was meeting, probably imagining it was a man. If he saw you I knew he'd think we were all scheming a big escape, that I was inside, pouring out my woes and troubles, that we'd be there ages chatting and if he didn't stop me on the way out, he could at least follow until he had his chance to find me alone.'

'So near to us,' Jen said in a whisper, picturing the scene as she described it. All the time they'd been hoping and waiting and excited about seeing Rowan, looking up each time the door opened, wondering what had happened, she'd been down the corridor from them.

'I so wanted to be normal like, to talk with you and the others and have a laugh, catch up on news. But I knew it was impossible, that it was my last chance. And I weren't normal, I'd made a muck-up of my life, nothing to be proud of. So when you and Meg went into the bar,' she continued, 'I slid out the back and raced to the train station. All I had was an overnight bag and I was so scared my heart was ready to burst out of my chest, indeed it was.' She shook her head. 'He probably sat there all night watching you through that window. The glass was so dark you could only see shapes.'

'If you could have got a message to us somehow . . .' Jen shook her head with the maddening frustration of it all. They could have smuggled her out, maybe. One of them could have set up a false trail to lure away Rowan's abusive husband. Georgina could have taken Meg out the front door with a blanket over her head so the bastard would give chase, and Jen would have sneaked away with Rowan as soon as the coast was clear.

Rowan poked at the fire with a stick before answering, sending sparks flying. 'It was easier my way. If you knew where I was . . .' She stretched out her legs and yawned, a sleepy lumberjack in her blanket-sized checked shirt, firelight flickering over her face. 'Let's be realistic, the three of you never could keep a secret. Georgina would have blurted it out somewhere or Meg would have just had to tell someone or . . . well, never mind, it was too big a chance to take. I didn't want to involve you.'

But she had involved them, Jen thought, vaguely indignant. At least she could have pretended she didn't want to get them hurt, instead of implying they were useless dimwits. Rowan always used to be so sweet. What had that brute done to her?

'We were your friends. We could have helped you.'

'No one could have helped me.'

'We really missed you.' Jen reached out her hand to touch Rowan's. She waited for an 'I missed you back', but instead Rowan pulled her hand away.

'So how did you end up in Wales? Or were you there all along?' It was Jen's turn to stand up and give the fire a poke. A cat walked across the back of the sofa, unnoticed by Feo, who was lying where Jen's feet had been.

'No, but Wales was the last place he'd look. I'd vowed I'd never go back after my ordeal at that awful school. So I found this village. Changed my name, took on a new identity and swore me mam to secrecy. But I needed money so I had to start painting again.' She gave a loud sigh. 'If only I'd taken dressmaking instead of English in fourth year.'

'English was compulsory.' Jen pursed her lips, thinking

maybe she too could have been a seamstress. Why didn't they teach you practical things? 'They say there's two people you need in a controlling relationship. One a bully and the other an enabler, which is a person who'll allow the bully to let it happen.'

Rowan slowly began nodding. 'They're wise words, you know. Did you become a therapist or something?'

'No,' Jen grinned, 'I saw it on the Trisha Goddard show.'

Rowan began smiling a little. 'I'd forgotten how you always made me laugh.' She took Jen's hand between her own. Rowan's were rough and cracked from working in the soil, weather-beaten like her face. Jen doubted if either had seen a lick of moisturiser in their lifetime.

'It took me years to escape him but finally I did, and now I'm so happy and content here without the worry of him ever finding me. Maybe I'm being paranoid, and he won't come after me any more. It's been almost ten years now. Perhaps he's even forgotten all about me.'

'I'm sure he has.'

'You know something, Jen,' she blew into her tissue again, 'having you around to put things in perspective, well, I'd sort of put a line through the past, blocked it all out. But in blocking out all the sad memories, I seem to have blocked out all the happy memories too. I think I'm glad you came here.'

'I'm glad I came here too,' Jen smiled.

Rowan ignored her, staring into space. 'And what is a name, after all? Rowan Howard/Rowan Dugan/Dyllis Bedlow. They're all just names.'

'Dugan? Rowan *Dugan*?' Jen stammered, aghast.

'You must remember him. He was our English teacher and he taught drama after school.'

'Tom?' Jen spluttered. 'Hairy-backed Tom?' She felt chilly suddenly and panicky.

'Hairy-backed? How did you know that?' Rowan looked

alarmed. 'He didn't sleep with you as well, did he? I thought it was only me and Linda Petroski?'

'No. I mean . . . he never made a pass at me at school. It's . . . so it was true about him and Linda?' She hardly knew what she was saying, her mind whirling like a rat in a cage, the hairs on her arms and neck standing up in dread.

What should she do? Her brain quickly scrambled for answers.

'Who knows?' Rowan shrugged. 'She always were a big fat liar, so she was.'

Jen's panic rose. She'd told him Rowan's bloody address. Or as near as dammit. 'I remember seeing you and Tom . . . I mean Mr Dugan . . . huddled together in the playground once. You told us you were interested in drama.'

'I was. But our big plays became little plays, then tiny weeny plays, just the two of us, and it went further and of course we couldn't let anyone know because they'd have given him the sack, he could even have gone to jail. We were terrified Hawkeye Hawkins suspected. And even though he left the school the same year we did, old Hawkins gave him a terrible reference and he couldn't get work teaching again.'

Come to think of it, Jen now realised who the white-haired old man at the reunion was, the one who'd been giving Dugan the evil eye. Hawkeye Hawkins, their old headmaster. So that was why Dugan was clinging to Jen all night. All the time she'd thought *she* was using *Dugan*, *Dugan* was using *her*!

'Maybe I've been hiding away too long. For all I know Tom could have died or emigrated. I could be like those Japanese living on Pacific islands not knowing the war's over.'

'On the other hand, maybe the war's still raging.' Jen hated bursting her small bubble of hope, but she had to fess up some time. Already she was starting to look around nervously. As the light faded the farmhouse seemed full of shadows, and she kept imagining she heard the whine of a car engine.

'What do you mean?' Rowan said, perplexed.

'I told him where you live.'

'What! When? How?' She sprang up, looking like a rabbit about to run.

'I wasn't to know. I'm *so* sorry, Rowan.' Jen put her head in her hands, not wanting to see the terror and accusation in Rowan's eyes. 'He came to the reunion. He implied he'd never married. I didn't connect the two of you. How would I? It seems like Georgina, Meg and I might have stirred up a hornet's nest.' Well, she sure as billy-o wasn't going down alone.

Rowan chewed nervously at her lip, her eyes buggy with fear. 'What do we do? What do we do now?'

'Grab some things. I'll get you out of here.'

It was lighter outside than it had been in the house, the last lingering hint of dusk turning everything to a flat shade of grey. They were rushing towards Jen's car when Rowan clutched her arm.

'Look!' She pointed.

The passenger-side tyre was flat. Not just a little; the steel rim was almost touching the ground, the rubber pancaked around it. In her haste Jen hadn't noticed the rotten plank with three-inch nails she'd run over.

'We'll have to take yours.'

'I haven't got one any more.' Rowan looked miserable and terrified. 'Just a bike. And it'll be pitch black before we can walk to the Sheepshearer. What if he's there, waiting for us? What are you doing?' She watched as Jen pressed buttons on her mobile.

'Dialling 999.' From a shed behind them a cow gave a mournful low. Jen almost jumped out of her skin.

'There's no signal. You have to climb up that hill there to get one.' Rowan pointed at a cone-shaped mountain towering over the back of the farm. 'But the police won't help. We don't even know he's coming tonight. And besides, I can't leave.' She

414

looked around wildly, as if only now realising. 'I've three cats, a dog and goats needing feeding, the cow to milk in the morning. And then I'll just be running again. I might as well stay here,' her face crumpled in defeat, 'let him find me. I knew it couldn't last.'

'No,' Jen said forcefully. 'That's plain wrong. You can't just give in.' Light bulbs exploded in her head. 'I know what we need to do.' Her voice sounded odd, even to herself.

'What?'

'Whenever we had trouble, ever since we met at school, what was our greatest defence?'

'Um . . . I don't know, running away, telling a prefect?'

'No.' Jen was already tightening her boot laces, ready to tackle a ruddy great mountain in the dark. 'The four of us. Standing together, shoulder to shoulder. Come what may.'

# Chapter 47

'Talk to me, Nutmeg. I'm tense. Tell me a joke.'

'You know you won't get it.'

'Please,' Georgina begged. 'I'm starting to feel my body rising like I'm floating and I might not be in control and I might swerve into a motorbike or something and . . .'

'You won't swerve into a motorbike, honey,' Meg soothed. She'd been trying to placate her friend all through the three hours of driving, cursing the luck that had placed her in this situation. She'd taken the train to London hoping to find Aiden in the Giordani offices and confront him at last. Instead she'd found only Georgina, packing up for the night. She was improvising some story about wanting to see where all the action took place just as they heard the SOS signal ring on Georgina's cell.

'Bring Meg and tell no one,' Jen had instructed down the crackly line, sounding as if a hurricane were blowing by her. 'It's crucial. Life and death.'

Too bad Georgina had seemed more nervous about an uninsured Meg driving her plush car than she was about her own motorway phobia, until now – when it was too late to turn back.

'Oh shit!' Meg cried out as Georgina did a kind of S maneouvre. 'Cool it, G.'

'I can't cool it. I'm taking off. Like an aeroplane on a runway.

416

Look at my hands, I'm clutching the wheel so hard they've gone numb.'

'Unclutch them then.'

'Oh goblins, what was that?'

'Thirty-ton truck gone by on our inside.'

'Oh no, oh no.'

'Hey, look now.' Meg grabbed the wheel as the car swerved into the fast lane. 'Maybe you better swing over to the right, I mean left,' she quickly corrected herself. 'When it's clear, of course.'

'What if my tyre explodes?'

'What if what?'

'My tyre. What if it explodes?'

'It won't, Jeez. You get your car regularly serviced, don't you?'

'Max does. God, I hate motorways.'

'Well you shouldn't. They're just like normal roads but a shitload faster. Far less accidents.'

'Yes but when the accidents happen they're unbelievably humungous.'

'Talking about unbelievable,' Meg swiftly changed the subject, 'how the hell do you think Jen found Rowan?'

'And why didn't she take us down there with her?' Georgina found that if she took slow pants of breath, she could keep relatively calm. 'After all our searching, deciding to go it alone. She's been acting very strangely recently.'

'Maybe she wanted all the glory, huh?' Meg said cynically. 'Abandoning us at the final hurdle. She actually said urgent, then? Life and death?'

'And not to tell anyone. Oh, oh, I'm going again.'

'Deep breaths.' Meg began panicking. Georgina's nervousness was rubbing off on her now.

'I'm rising again . . .'

Meg checked the map. 'Only one more junction and we're off. Think of something else.'

417

'What?'

'Shoot, I don't know. Something comforting, a beach, lapping waves.'

'OK.' She seemed to calm down. 'I'm thinking, I'm thinking.'

A few seconds went by. Meg looked across at Georgina. She was quiet . . . too quiet . . . much too quiet . . . Maybe she was rising again or had fallen asleep or . . .

'Georgie!' she yelled fiercely.

'Yes!' Georgina yelled back. 'I was just thinking of the nice thing.'

'Well stop, and . . . um . . . sing instead. Sing out loud. It might help.'

Georgina warbled something Meg couldn't quite recognise.

'Good, good. I can see the three-hundred-yard sign. Now indicate and get ready to move across. That's it.' Meg breathed a huge sigh of relief as they moved into the slip lane and began to slow down. Despite her frazzled nerves, she smiled – Georgie's singing voice had always been atrocious.

Twenty minutes later Georgina had calmed down and was now listening to Magic radio.

'Sorry. I'm sure you must despise me for this ridiculous phobia of mine.'

'Not in the slightest, Georgie. In fact . . . I admire you.'

Georgina was startled. 'Me? *You* admire *me*? You're teasing, right?'

'Why would I be? Internationally famous design genius. Gorgeous husband. Rich as billy-o. You got it made, girl.'

'Yes, but what does it all mean? I have money and business success, granted, my husband . . .' She let the thought trail away. 'But aren't there more important things in life? Like friends? Children? Hobbies, even?'

'Jen and I are your friends – your work *is* your hobby and as

418

for kids . . .' Meg paused. 'Somehow I got the idea you didn't want any. After you lost the first one.'

'I couldn't anyway.' Georgina felt tears spring to her eyes. 'I got sterilised.'

'Oh?' Meg looked shocked briefly, then recovered. 'Well you probably made the right choice, Georgie. Motherhood's a tough road. Take it from someone who knows.'

'It seemed the only thing to do.' Maybe she shouldn't be telling Nutmeg but dash it all, she was tired of all the secrets between them. 'Aiden fell apart when I got pregnant, just when I needed him most. He started sleeping around. Going out at night like a prowling tomcat, coming in stinking of other women. He never wanted the baby, the idea of being a father terrified him. And I was beside myself with worry and stress. The miscarriage devastated me, but it wasn't surprising, not really. And I didn't want to risk the same thing happening again. I had to face the fact I already had one child on my hands, I couldn't have coped with another. I loved Aiden. I didn't want to lose him.' She took a deep breath, relieved at getting it out. 'Please don't tell Jen.'

'I wouldn't. But why not?'

'Because she still . . . admires Aiden. It'll shatter her illusions. You know, Meg,' Georgina turned for a second to her friend, 'I've never said this before, but I like you.'

'You do? Hang a left here.'

'Yes, I mean we were always friends and everything. But I wasn't always sure whether I actually *liked* you. But I do. Underneath all that kick-ass attitude, I think you're, well, tremendous, really. A tremendous original true-to-yourself type of person.' She felt a surge of emotion rise up inside her.

'And you are too, Georgie,' Meg replied, leaning over to squeeze her hand. 'But why are we telling each other now?'

'Just in case I crash,' Georgina muttered as she headed for a sharp bend.

*

There were loud insistent raps at the door.

'Shush your noise,' hissed Rowan sharply. 'It might be him.'

'No.' Jen peered through the window, frying pan at the ready. 'Quick, open it. I recognise the car. It's Georgie's.' Thank God for that. They'd been cut off just after she gave the address. She wasn't sure if they'd heard enough to find the place.

'Rowan!' Georgina burst through the door and rushed towards Rowan for a hug.

'Da da!' Meg followed close behind and opened her arms wide, then wider still, as she realised Rowan's size. 'Shit, is that you, Rowan? After all these frigging years?'

'What are you doing?' Georgina asked Jen as she began busily locking the doors behind them.

'Safety measures. You haven't heard the worst.'

As fast as she could, Jen enlightened her appalled friends about Tom's antics. They took turns watching the window while the discussion raged about what they would do if – when – he showed up.

'Any chance he might have followed you?' Georgina asked, back in her role of commander.

'No,' Jen said, 'his car was getting repaired. But I told him the name of the farm. And the town.'

Rowan sank on to a chair. 'He's definitely coming then.'

'I had no idea,' Jen mourned. 'To think I slept with him. I feel so used.'

'You slept with him?' All three heads whipped round to stare at her.

'Only once,' she said guiltily. 'It didn't mean anything.' Then she remembered that was what Aiden had said about Meg. But this was different. Wasn't it?

'None of us knew,' Meg consoled her. 'He was using us all, giving us ideas like Gwyneth and Totnes, so that we'd track Rowan down and lead him to her.'

'Bastard,' said Georgina, her face grim.

'What car's he got?' Meg pulled back the grubby net curtains.

'Red Toyota.'

'Oh goodness!' Georgina's mouth flew open before she smacked it shut.

'What?'

'I saw a red Toyota on the hard shoulder, round about Junction 28.'

'I didn't see him,' Meg said, astonished.

'You were busy map-reading. But now I think of it, he had Dugan's kind of hair, though his back was to the road. He was on one of those motorway phones, smoke coming from his bonnet.'

'That settles it,' Jen said decisively. 'He's definitely on his way. Have you anything we can use as a weapon?' she asked Rowan.

'Maybe a shotgun?' Meg suggested. 'A rifle? Or even a pitchfork?'

Rowan shivered. 'Only a nail file up in the bedroom.'

'Run and fetch it then,' Georgina ordered. 'You can stick it up your sleeve and if he gets violent . . .'

'He wouldn't be violent. He's never physically attacked me before.'

Jen gave a meaningful look at Georgina. If kicking and slapping wasn't physical, she didn't know what was.

'Doesn't mean it won't start.' Meg crossed her arms, looking like a Comanche warrior. 'He's been thwarted a long time – you've never been missing this long before. People get killed by their lovers all the time, driven insane by jealous passion. I remember once in Vegas . . .'

'Meg!' Jen and Georgina snapped simultaneously and Meg clammed up under their glares.

There was a moment's silence as the frightened-rabbit look

421

came over Rowan's face again. She raced up the narrow stairs to the only other room in the house, a tiny attic-style bedroom with sloping ceiling, and came back down with a pathetically small nail file.

A log fell off the fire and they all jumped, nerves on edge, acknowledging the seriousness of the situation. A madman was coming to find Rowan. And Meg was right. He could turn nasty. Murderous. Ten years of pent-up frustration and they were miles from anywhere, no telephone connection, no way of calling for help.

Meg raised a tentative finger. 'Can I just say one thing? He's hardly likely to kill . . .'

'Shut up!' This time three voices drowned her out.

Jen looked at the faces of her friends, tense and nervous. 'It's all my fault, Rowan.'

'Can't be helped, Jen, bach,' she answered. 'He's a charmer.'

'Shit. Shit.' Meg started jiggling suddenly.

'What's up?'

'I'm dying to pee. But I don't want to go out there.'

'What about a bucket?' Jen suggested.

'It's in the cowshed,' Rowan said. 'And we're using the only mugs.'

'I'm not going in a mug anyway,' Meg said decisively. 'I can hold it. Quick, someone, distract me.'

'Um . . . um . . . what happened at the reunion?' Rowan tried to oblige. 'Did Yvonne Spitz turn up?'

'Oh yes,' Georgina beamed, and began to tell Rowan all about Yvonne and her Hong Kong counterfeit dress.

Rowan laughed. 'She came up to me on my first morning, called me a les and I didn't know what it meant. Shows how naive I was then.'

'You weren't naive!' Jen patted her arm.

'Oh I was. When it came to sex I didn't get half the things you were talking about.'

'Nor did I, Rowan. Nor did I,' Georgina empathised. 'But I was a good bluffer.'

Meg gasped, crossing her legs and bouncing. 'It's not working, who the fuck lives in a house without a bathroom?'

'What about that pony we used to look after, Murgatroyd?' Jen carefully tried to sandwich the subject between the other distractions. 'Do you remember what I did to you, Rowan? Told everyone about your ignorance of testicles.'

'Testicles? Whose testicles?'

Jen had to fill her in and she laughed. 'Let's face it, Jen, teenage girls can be right bitches.'

Meg's eyes were watering now. Suddenly she screamed, 'Crap! I gotta go!' and bolted out the front door.

They were still staring after her, frozen in shock, when the lights flickered and then went off.

Meg burst back in seconds later and slammed the door behind her. 'It's gone totally – and I mean totally – black out there. Why are we in the dark?'

'It's him, isn't it?' Georgina whispered hoarsely. 'He's snipping wires.'

'Probably a power cut,' Rowan said, sounding only slightly shaky. 'It's always happening. Here, I'll go and get candles.'


Half an hour later Georgina had taken her place on watch, and across the other side of the room Rowan was threatening to pace a furrow into the cold stone floor, veering off to check the window every third circuit.

The crackling fire had now burnt down to embers and there was a draught from a broken window, which was sending a sub-zero wind throughout the downstairs rooms.

'I'm freezing.' Meg acknowledged what the others were thinking.

'We need logs.' Rowan shivered. 'They're out back.'

Everybody suddenly started looking occupied, loath to volunteer.

'I've an idea.' Rowan opened an antique sideboard and pulled out a flask. 'Single malt. Surely that should warm everyone up.'

Though the drink went down well, they were no warmer.

'Maybe we can burn something else instead?' suggested Meg.

'Like what, the furniture?' said Georgina.

'How about,' Rowan looked around and picked up a pile of sketches, 'these?'

'What are they?' asked Jen.

'Just old stuff, ideas.'

Georgina walked over, began skimming through, then through again. 'Rowan, these are fabulous.'

'Thanks but . . . they're no use to anyone.' She began to tear at one.

'No.' Georgina stopped her. 'They're top stuff. You can't waste them.'

'Oh let her,' said Meg, shaking and flinging the sausage dog's blanket round her shoulders.

'No, I'm keeping them. Can I?' Georgina pleaded.

'Wait!' Meg was back at the window. 'Car headlights. He's here. He's really here.'

They all raced around the room and huddled in the shadows. Lucky, Jen reflected, that Meg had thought to ask Georgina to move her car and throw an old tarp over Jen's. Extra vehicles in the lane might have given the game away.

Jen grabbed her frying pan again, her hands sweating so much she could hardly hold it. She positioned herself behind the door as Rowan fumbled in a kitchen drawer for candles, Meg and Georgina clutching each other, eyes globe-like in the dying glow of the fireplace. Meg had the nail file, Jen noticed.

'This is ridiculous, I feel like we're in *Curse of the Rabid Zombies*. Or playing sardines in Georgina's basement,' whispered Meg. She stuffed her fist in her mouth to stifle a nervous giggle.

'And there's four against one,' Jen whispered back, trying to sound braver than she felt. 'We can handle him all right.'

'But Tom's a big man and he's, well a man,' pointed out Georgina.

'Shh.'

What were they thinking of? How could they ever imagine they could handle this?

Tyres screeched to a halt by the gate. Footsteps crunched along the frosty path. 'Jen? Rowan?' The man's voice was almost blown away by the wind. No secrecy, then. He probably guessed they were still there. Wanted them to know he knew. Amp up the terror. There was an imperious knock on the door and then the doorknob turned and the latch shook.

'Jen bolted it, didn't she?' Meg hissed to Rowan as the footsteps moved away.

'The front door, yes,' nodded Rowan.

'You mean there's a back?' Jen raced to the other door just as the man stepped through. She lunged, bringing the frying pan down hard on the first bit she could hit, which was his shoulder. Georgina and Meg jumped, screeching, at the intruder, Meg stabbing randomly with the blunt nail file, Georgina pulling wildly at his hair. The din was deafening, everything chaos. Feo was barking hysterically, jumping into the fray, savaging the stranger's trouser leg, the sausage dog yapping in unison. Rowan had found a small milk pan and was hitting Dugan on the head as he raised one hand against the onslaught, his shoulders bowed, Jen going for the belly and shins now, attacking with gusto.

For a moment it looked inevitable he would go down but then suddenly it all went horribly wrong. He shook his ankle and Feo flew across the room, taking the sausage dog with him. The man grabbed the frying pan from Jen and sent it clattering across the floor, stood up and with a shrug of his muscular shoulders raised his arms and the other three women went tumbling to the ground. His strong hand had both Jen's wrists pinned, her friends lay helplessly looking up.

'Of all the effing . . .' he cursed, brushing off Feo who'd returned for more. His voice was deep and husky, not a bit like Dugan's come to think of it.

Jen felt a sob catch in the middle of her throat.

It was Ollie.

# Chapter 48

'Tell me something,' Ollie said, cautiously touching his scalp and examining his bruises by the light of a candle. 'Do I have *any* hair left?' Gingerly he lowered his body into the nearest armchair.

Georgina surreptitiously brushed a few blond strands from her jacket.

'Ollie, I'm sorry,' Jen said for about the fourth time. 'How could we know? You're supposed to be on the teacups at Euro Disney. What the bloody hell are you doing here?'

'Saving you.' He rubbed ruefully at his stomach where she'd nailed him with the frying pan. 'Chloe needed some things from the house so while I was waiting I happened to google Dugan.' He looked slightly abashed. 'Idle curiosity, I suppose. Anyway I pulled up this newspaper article from years back. All about a non-molestation order against some creep and, guess what, his wife had been a student at Ashport Comp and the stalker's name was one Thomas E. Dugan.'

'That's impossible.' Jen looked at the others. Meg's eyes were large as saucers, Georgina seemed mesmerised, her whole body tilting towards Ollie as if she were a magnet and he was true north. Only Rowan sat like a Buddha, stroking the cat that had sought refuge in her lap. 'We did hundreds of searches on Rowan Howard.' Jen frowned, thinking it over. 'Why didn't we see it?'

'They never mentioned Rowan by name. The court order was for her mother. I guess her aunt had to take one out too. Is that right, Rowan?'

'Right enough, boyo.' Rowan nodded sagely.

'But how did you find this place?' Meg's suddenly dulcet tones were dripping with admiration. Jen didn't like the way she was looking at Ollie; as if he were a giant steak and she a hungry hyena.

'Wasn't too difficult.' He turned to Jen. 'You left the Christmas card addressed to Dyllis Bedlow on the table.' Rowan's head jerked up. 'All I had to do was drop Chloe with Helen and hit the road.' His eyes fixed on Feo lying at her feet. 'Is *that* the "darling little puppy"?'

'Yes.' She bent down to pat the unfortunate mongrel, avoiding her Welsh friend's accusatory glare. 'Why? What about him?' she asked defensively.

'Nothing.' He stretched out his legs, amused.

'Enough of that.' Jen stood up briskly, 'Dugan might be here any minute. Even if the AA have to tow him. Did you pass a red Toyota?'

'Didn't notice.'

'What are we going to do?' Georgina seemed relieved to hand the problem to a higher authority.

'I have an idea.' Ollie flexed a fist thoughtfully. He looked happy at the prospect of it connecting with flesh and bone.

'No!' Rowan stood up, tipping the cat off her lap. 'You mustn't injure him.' She stared wide-eyed at the others. 'It's not his fault. He can't help himself. He's a victim too, in a way, poor dab.'

'Now hang on a sec.' Ollie ruffled his hair, clearly not believing his ears. 'You all hurt *me*. I thought I was under attack by a pack of wild dogs.' He bent down to show the hem of his jeans, ripped by Feo's sharp teeth. 'I suppose I should be glad that wasn't my ankles.'

428

'We were scared stiff,' Rowan said simply. 'But now you're here. And you're a lot younger and stronger than he is.'

'Stop . . . wait.' Jen jumped in as Ollie tried digesting that, the logic baffling to a man of action. She placed herself in front of Ollie, hand up like a traffic cop.

'It was very nice of you to come,' she addressed him. 'But you're not necessary. We can handle this.'

'Too bad,' he said, crossing his ankles and looking immovable. 'Because I'm staying.'

'No, if you scare Dugan off he'll only wait until you're not around and come back. Don't you see, Rowan will be running for ever. Nothing will have changed. She's got to confront him herself. Show him she means it.'

'That's very wise, Jen.' A faint smile flickered over his lips. 'Not the Trisha Goddard show?'

'No. I thought of it myself.' She glanced out the window into the blackness. 'And now I've got a plan.'

'So now there's only . . .' Georgina stopped and motioned everyone to silence. 'I think I hear another car.'

'Is it stopping?' asked Meg nervously.

Georgina peeked over the windowsill. 'Yes. It's him.'

'Quick, into your places!' Jen ordered.

Moments later, there was a knock on the door.

'Georgina?' Rowan whispered.

'Check.'

'Meg?'

'Check.'

'Jen?'

'Checkmate,' Jen said.

Another knock. A loud creak of an opening door. They heard footsteps walk in, then stop.

'Fox is in the lair,' Rowan whispered.

The footsteps started again. It seemed impossible he

429

wouldn't hear the hammering of their hearts even from beneath the bedroom floorboards.

'Shhh!' hissed Georgina. 'He's coming up the stairs.'

What seemed like a terrifying age later, the bedroom door slowly opened and the shape lying under the covers stirred a little.

'Rowan?' Dugan said in the unlit gloom.

The figure under the blankets moved a little more.

'Rowan?' He began pulling back the covers.

'What, what is it?' Rowan sat up and rubbed her eyes. 'Who's there?'

'It's me. Your husband,' he said coldly. He stood legs apart, a sliver of moonlight streaked across his face, leaving half in shadow. His lips were tightly pressed together.

'*Ex*-husband. What are you doing here?' Rowan's voice was trembling.

'You don't know how long . . . how much . . .' he began.

'I left you. I want you out of my life,' she said, gripping hold of the bedsheet, pulling it to her chin.

'I told you I'd find you. You can never leave me. I won't let you. Can't you see, fate has brought us together again. We were never meant to be apart.' He took a step closer to her, hand reaching out imploringly.

'We should never have been together, you mean,' she said shakily. 'Can't you realise I'm happy without you?'

'Don't fool yourself. We need each other. I made mistakes but I'm here to make it up to you. I want to take care of you, Rowan.'

Jen watched through a tiny crack. Rowan was whiter than the sheet she was clutching, her eyes wide with horror as he sat down on the edge of the bed.

'You can't get away from me, you know.' His voice softened, coaxing. 'Give in, you love me, I love you. You can't fight it.'

'Don't come near me!' She backed away, huddled against the bedstead, her face stricken.

'There's no one to hear you,' Dugan said ominously, his manner now changed. He moved his hand towards the sheet.

'I said don't come any nearer. Don't . . . Help!'

Suddenly Georgina rose up from behind an armchair. 'Leave her alone.'

'What . . . what are you doing here?' Dugan spluttered.

Meg stepped out from the heavy wooden shutters and Jen emerged from her hiding place, stretching out her arms, which were aching badly from being squashed to her sides in a tiny cupboard.

'Leave her alone!' Georgina repeated forcefully, placing herself between Dugan and Rowan.

Dugan's eyes swivelled towards Jen. 'I thought you'd have left by now.'

'Well, you thought wrong, didn't you?'

'She's told us everything,' said Georgina. 'What you did, how you treated her.'

'She's got it all wrong. You mustn't believe her. I've only ever wanted to love her. To cherish her.'

'We're not listening to your bullshit, Dugan,' Meg growled.

'And if you set foot near Rowan ever again,' Georgina joined in, 'we'll make sure everyone knows the truth of what you did. That you're a predator. She was only a child when you seduced her, a schoolgirl. Your reputation will be ruined.'

'You deserve to fry,' Meg sneered threateningly. 'Or at least suffer the way you've made her suffer. One false move and you can bet you'll get what's coming to you.'

He glared at them. 'You're pathetic, all of you. Do you think you can scare me away? You can't do a thing to me.'

'Try us.' Georgina fixed him with her haughtiest look. *You . . . scoundrel.*

'I'll have you up for slander.' Dugan's voice was scornful, confident. 'Think of the scandal. The press'll have a field day. You wouldn't want your precious Giordani dragged through the courts.'

Jen looked across at Rowan, who'd used their distraction to slide out of bed, fully dressed, and was cowering in a dark corner. Jen thought she could see her friend's body shaking. Dugan was more menacing than they'd thought.

Georgina stepped forward, raising the frying pan. 'OK then, why don't we just make it assault?' She looked imposing, a warrior queen, another Boadicea. Involuntarily Dugan retreated a pace.

Meg lit a candle, holding it up. 'I'll testify. I've got nothing to lose.'

Dugan sneered, his lip curling. 'No one would believe you after that fake paternity suit. I googled you and guess what came up?'

Meg shrugged as they stared at her illuminated face.

'It's true,' she admitted. 'God knows who leaked it. Irwin the Schmuck was paying child support for Zeb.'

'Irwin Beidlebaum?' Georgina gasped.

'He called me the day after the Marlow Arms. Escorted me around for a few weeks until he traded me for some other actress. I thought he was the dad, the timing was right. And Irwin was OK with having a son, not that the cheapskate ever went out of his way to be part of his life, sent us some measly payments, stopped by to see us about every two years – until he married that bimbo and discovered all his Oompa-Loompas were swimming upstream.' She told the story with a world-weary lack of passion. 'He totally wigged out, made us get DNA tests but it didn't go to court.'

'But we thought . . . what about the Vegas bull rider?' Jen asked.

'Pregnant when we hooked up. Only it hadn't started to

432

show. He had no interest in being a father either.' Her gaze met Georgina's.

'And before you chip in,' Dugan turned glowing eyes to Jen, 'you're not the most credible witness. An aggrieved one-night stand, bitter because I failed to repeat the performance. Who'd listen to a pair of slags like you two?'

Jen flinched, wondering if Ollie, down in the kitchen with Feo, glass to the ceiling, could hear everything. She almost expected him to race upstairs and punch out their ex-teacher – or perhaps just walk out and never speak to her again. Fury overtook her. Dugan thought he had them cowed.

'Go on then,' she said. 'Grab him, girls!'

A minor scuffle later, Dugan was perched on the bed, clothes line tied around his waist and arms.

'You've got to be joking.' He pushed against his bonds and slumped back. 'I'll have you all arrested for unlawful imprisonment. This is a criminal offence.'

'They'll laugh you out of court,' Georgina scoffed. 'Besides, we'll deny it.'

'Yeah, just like you denied you tormented Rowan, asshole,' Meg said. 'Now let's hear you say it: I'll never bother Rowan again.'

He shook his head. 'No.'

'Go on, Rowan,' Meg urged. 'Give him a gelding. Get your nail file out and hack off his testicles.'

'They're the two little balls behind the willy,' Jen added helpfully.

Rowan was standing in the shadows, head bowed. Jen had the uneasy feeling she was crying.

'OK then.' Meg brandished a penknife Jen recognised as one she'd once given Ollie. 'I'll do it. Unless you prefer jail.'

'What for?' Dugan cast his head around, looking from one to the other.

'Child abuse!' Meg said defiantly. 'You're going down,

433

dipshit. I hear prisoners reserve special treatment for molesters.'

'Rowan was sixteen,' he said hoarsely.

'But Linda Petroski wasn't, and she'd love nothing more than to testify against you.' It was a gamble, but even big fat liars sometimes told the truth.

'And Yvonne Spitz,' Jen added, crossing her fingers. Well, Linda and Yvonne used to do most things together.

'You couldn't!' He sounded desperate now, the tough nut beginning to crack. 'She can't. I'm innocent. I didn't lay a finger on her. Linda cornered me after class one day in fourth year, holding a measuring tape, and asked me to measure her bosoms. I was stoned and I thought it was hysterically funny. I remember Yvonne took a picture. It was stupid, juvenile nonsense, but that was all there was to it, I swear.'

'Yes, but we have the photo,' Georgina said authoritatively. 'And Linda will swear in court that you then removed her clothes and had sex with her behind the stage in the assembly hall. She always was a big fat liar. That's enough to condemn you these days. And Yvonne Spitz will do anything for a lifetime of Giordani. I'm sure they'll both be delighted to confess to underage sex in a good cause. Fourth year, you say? How many years do you think that's worth?'

'You'd be sending an innocent man to prison.'

'Not so innocent,' Jen said, still smarting from the slag comment. To think she'd actually felt sorry for this bastard. And why wasn't it her holding Ollie's penknife? When had he given it to Meg? 'You abused your position of trust. Seducing Rowan.'

'If you ever go near her again, or contact her or harass her, we're right there on your case,' Georgina chipped in. 'You'll be arrested and you can think yourself jolly fortunate we haven't emasculated you already.'

'OK. OK.' Dugan's whole body slumped suddenly, all bravado visibly evaporating. 'Now untie me, *please*.'

'Why should we?'

'Look, it's over,' he said, defeated. 'I promise. Please, I'll leave Rowan in peace. You have to believe me. Let me go. I've got claustrophobia. I can't stand being tied.' Suddenly his bottom lip began wobbling, his face contorting and twisting in strange ways, and then without warning he made a coughing noise.

It took Jen a moment to realise that he was actually crying. Not just crying but weeping in a sort of coughing, spluttering way. Up till now she'd managed to stay reasonably detached, barring a slight contempt, shock at his brazen manipulative ways and a sneaking desire to knee him in the nuts for the insults and selling her out to Ollie. But now looking at him so crumpled and crushed and alone, Jen couldn't suppress a tinge of pity. Everything he'd done had been wrong, very wrong. And bullying Rowan was unforgivable, but all the same . . .

'I loved her. That's all I'm guilty of. Loving Rowan too much. Please, Rowan, please?' He stared towards her shadow, his eyes desperate.

But then love was such a powerful emotion. Made vicars run off with their congregations – or members of them, anyway – doctors get struck off after years of hard study, caused long-held marriages to be cast aside like yesterday's newspapers, doting fathers to lose their kids, all in the name of that four-letter word. When it struck it was a power virtually impossible to harness. And sometimes it made people do idiotic irrational things as it crashed over them, knocking every obstacle in its path out of the way. She knew she was gawping at Dugan while she was thinking this, but she also knew that he didn't realise because he was staring into the darkness, trying to focus on Rowan.

Suddenly Rowan stepped forward and allowed her eyes to meet his. Just as she did so, there was a sparking sound and the lights came back on. It was the perfect dramatic moment. Jen saw Dugan jerk as he took in the shock of his ex-wife's appearance. No wonder Rowan hadn't bothered with prettying herself up for the last decade. Who on earth would want to be a raving beauty if it attracted madness like this? Worse than being a superstar and having paparazzi chase you down the street. They'd all been a little bit in love with Rowan. And where had it ever got her?

'What have they done to you?' he whispered.

'*They've* done nothing. It's what *you've* done. I've had enough of your weasel words and crocodile tears, so you can stop that now,' Rowan rasped. She turned to her old classmates. 'He can switch them on and off like a tap. They don't mean anything, and they don't do anything for me. Not any more.' She stared stony-faced at the man before her, hands planted on her ample hips. 'You've wasted twenty-two years of my life, turned it into an arid desert, full of fear and paranoia. I've nothing but contempt for you. And for myself.' She shook her head, sending her straggly hair falling about her pudgy cheeks.

Dugan shrugged and immediately the tears dried. 'I promise it's the end,' he said, defeated, his eyes scanning her up and down, left and right. 'You look . . . you look . . . I never meant it to be this way.'

Georgina hesitated a moment, then spoke. 'Well, we'll have to trust him now. What else are we to do? I think Rowan's strong enough to show him the door if he comes knocking again. Besides we can't keep him here for ever. Come on, let him loose.' She stood back while Rowan and Meg untied him.

'Now beat it!' Georgina raised one fist high into the air as he wriggled free and the clothes line dropped to the floor.

'And never darken Rowan's doorstep again!' Meg sneered theatrically before adding, 'Or you'll have *all* of us to deal with.'

He headed quickly down the stairs, feet hardly touching wood, followed by the women.

'Tom. Wait!' Jen called out after him as he opened the door.

436

He stopped and turned. 'What? What is it?'

'Were you ever in Quebec?'

'Er, no?' he said nervously.

'Launching timber on the deck, where ya break a bleeding neck riding on a donkey.' She couldn't help it. It just tumbled off her tongue.

# Chapter 49

As Dugan's Toyota rattled away the jubilation was noisy and intense. The four women grabbed at each other, hollering and jumping in a group hug as Ollie burst through from the kitchen laughing, with Feo in hot pursuit.

'You ladies are terrifying,' he said. 'I'd have run for cover too.' His blue eyes, veiled by long sooty eyelashes, met Jen's. 'You were right. You didn't need me.'

'I wouldn't say that,' she muttered, cheeks scorching. She bent down, nuzzling into Feo's neck as an absurd shyness swept over her.

'I definitely wouldn't either.' Meg linked her arm through Ollie's. 'Hey, let's go drink to our victory. Coming, Ollie?'

Ollie was still observing Jen. She didn't know what to make of his expression. It was clear as her bright red ears he'd overheard Dugan mention their one-night stand. Was he disgusted? Furious? Or had the knowledge just confirmed what a massive mistake he'd made in his marriage and how lucky his timely escape was, almost as fortunate as Rowan's?

With diplomatic ease Ollie extricated his sleeve from Meg's grasp, found his jacket and pulled out his car keys. 'I can't stick around.' He looked from one to the other of them, each of Jen's three friends melting under his gaze. 'I've got to get home, rescue poor Chloe from her "Auntie" Helen's tender care. Anyway the four of you have a lot of catching up to do, I'm sure.'

Meg handed him his penknife, closed the door behind him and then giggled as she leaned her back against it.

'That was the stud boy?' she marvelled. 'You said he was hot but, oh boy.' She blew on her bent fingers and waved them up and down as if they'd been scorched. 'How could you let that babe get away?'

'Just like the Lone Ranger,' Georgina sighed. 'Coming to the rescue and then galloping away.'

'Yes, but who was he?' Rowan looked baffled. 'What's a stud boy? And who's Chloe?'

'You've been living in Wales too long. Chloe's my daughter.' Jen sat down suddenly on the sofa again. 'And that was my ex.'

'Oh.' Rowan sat beside her, the sofa sagging under her weight. 'Funny. All these years I always imagined you married to that boyfriend of yours – what was his name – Sparkey or . . . ?'

Jen caught Georgina's eye as Meg said, 'Starkey. Yeah, that is funny, isn't it?' and perched herself on the other side of Rowan.

'No,' said Georgina, '*I* made that particular mistake,' and sat down on the hearth in her now rather crumpled suit. 'Can you imagine Aiden rushing all this way to rescue me? I don't think so.'

'Oh I'm sure he would,' Jen said loyally. Though whether she was being loyal to her ex-boyfriend or reassuring Georgina she wasn't sure.

'Doubt it.' Georgina looked quite miserable. 'He doesn't feel that way about me and I'm not sure I still feel that way about him. Sometimes I think he's never going to grow up. He's like the apple tree at the bottom of the garden that I overpruned one year and I've been waiting each summer for the apples to appear and drop off, but they never have. Aiden has never produced anything either. And it seems like I've been under his tree for ever, standing holding out my frilly fucking apron waiting to catch whatever he deigns to offer me. Your Ollie's more of a man than him any day.'

'My Ollie,' Jen said quietly. And something pricked her heart. 'Only he's not my Ollie any more. And, quite frankly, he probably only drove down here to make sure Chloe didn't lose a mother, however awful I may be.'

'I say we move this conversation to the pub. We might just manage to get one in before last orders,' Meg proposed, eyeing the clock. 'Because I'm in the mood to celebrate and listening to you two sad sacks is bringing me down.' She held her nose and shook her head horizontally, pretending to sink to the bottom of an imaginary ocean. 'Way, way down.'

It felt so good, the four of them being together again. So natural, so balanced.

'You know what's remarkable,' Jen said, as they were sitting in the Sheepshearer reliving the excitement of the confrontation and Dugan's downfall. 'We actually achieved something tonight. Your angel was right, Meg. Rowan *was* in trouble.' She put a bottle of beer to her lips.

'Meg has an angel?' Rowan gasped. 'Now there's posh.'

'Too right,' Meg agreed happily.

Georgina smiled. 'She told Meg to come over from the States because of your pact.'

'Pact?'

'You know,' Georgina carried on, 'the one with you and Meg leaving your children to each other if you died.'

Rowan looked bemused. 'We said what?'

'There was no pact, was there?' The truth suddenly dawned on Jen.

Meg looked suitably embarrassed. 'Hey now, it worked out for the best, didn't it?'

'What else were you lying about, Meg?' Jen shook her head. The girl was worse than Linda Petroski. 'Let's have it all.'

'OK, OK, while I'm coming clean, there was no lump either.'

'No lump!' gasped Georgina.

'Well actually there was,' Meg quickly backtracked as she registered Georgina's expression of distaste. 'But it was four years ago and benign, thank God.' She crossed herself. 'So it wasn't an outright lie cos I thought it could be cancer, for a while . . . until they checked . . .'

'Well thank goodness for that at least,' Georgina sighed, relieved at the result.

'And the angel?' Jen probed.

'The angel's real, definitely.' Meg ducked as Jen threw a beer mat at her. 'Cross my heart.'

'I think I've missed something here,' said Rowan.

'Oh, it was only Meg looking for attention as usual,' Jen explained, 'Hasn't changed. But at least you don't have to hide away any more,' she told Rowan, her mind busy making plans. 'You could leave the farm and move in with me and Chloe, if you like. I'm going to be buying a new house, it'd be fun to have you as a lodger.' She hesitated, wondering how to phrase this. 'You could have a normal life again. A place with indoor plumbing.'

'Yes,' agreed Georgina. 'You don't have to be . . .' she gestured, 'you know . . . quite so . . .' The word off-putting trembled on her lips. 'We could spiff you up a bit, bring you back to your old self. I have oodles of Giordani samples I could give you.'

'I'm great at colouring hair.' Meg's eyes were gleaming. 'And I know the most fab facial products including this yoghurt-based mask that's to die for. I bet a few weeks with those and . . .'

'Wait a minute,' Rowan interrupted, and started to laugh so loudly that several old men in the corner playing bar billiards glanced over. 'What makes you think I want to go anywhere? This is my home. Now Tom's been sent packing, I'm finally free to enjoy it. I love my little cottage and my painting and my "isolation" as you call it. And what do you mean, spiff me up?'

She gestured at her outfit, her hair tumbling down her back as the last hairpins broke free 'Are you suggesting this is all a *disguise* of some sort?'

'Hell, no.' Meg and Georgina tried to dig themselves out of their well-intentioned hole, though Rowan was wiping her eyes with mirth.

'Just you were always the most beautiful of us all,' Jen said gently. 'You cared the most about your appearance, and with Dugan hounding you, I can understand why you might . . .'

'Realise that all that prettying yourself up for men is so unimportant,' Rowan finished her sentence. 'You used to think so too, Jen-o. When did *you* change?'

Probably when I married a younger man, Jen thought. Started comparing myself to all those girls his age.

'Think I'll just stay the way I am, right enough,' Rowan said, slapping her broad thighs. 'Who gives a hoot anyway? If I want to eat a doughnut, I'll eat a doughnut. Or a pizza. Or two pizzas if I feel like it. And not worry about my hair greying or care if I get wrinkles from being outside in all weathers. I've earned this face. And thanks for the offer, Georgie, but except for the occasional trip to the gallery, *this* is my big night out.' She gestured around the pub. 'I think the Giordani garb would be wasted here, don't you?'

'You're right, we're sorry.' They all started apologising together, Meg and Georgina shooting Jen you-started-this looks.

'I've seen your shop in Covent Garden, though,' Rowan told Georgina. 'You're incredibly talented.'

'You think so?' Georgina went pink with delight. 'We thought your paintings were terrific. I'm going to start collecting some. And if you ever want a job . . .'

'I don't think she does, somehow,' Jen smiled as she lifted her drink to her lips.

'Here's to Rowan.' Meg raised her glass in a toast. 'The nicest, sweetest and most together of us all.'

Rowan laughed again and waved her hand dismissively. 'Away with you,' she said. 'I didn't go running across country to save *you*, did I? You're better friends than I've ever been. And believe me, no angels are visiting *me*.'

A shadow loomed over them. A short dark man, wringing his hands nervously.

'Rowan, bach, can I be getting you and your friends another round?'

She nodded graciously. 'That you can, Jones the Post.'

Damn, Jen thought. The girl still had it.

'Thing is . . .' Jen was swigging on her fourth bottle, 'the thing is . . . I always felt I trapped Ollie into marriage. If I hadn't got pregnant . . .' she turned unfocused eyes to the others. 'I found out that night we met in the Marlow Arms. When I saw you, Georgina, I suddenly realised . . . my periods were never late. He was so young. Only twenty.' She shook her head violently from side to side. 'It wasn't fair.'

'Hogwash.' Meg squinted across the table. 'You didn't intend getting knocked up, did you? You didn't force him to put a ring on your finger.' She laid her cheek against her knuckles and closed her eyes. 'Well, then, kiddo. You didn't trap him.'

'Sounds like, if anything, you trapped yourself.' Georgina's words rang out clearly, her voice bell-like, belying the vast amounts of alcohol she'd drunk. Perhaps it was infantile consumption of gripe water doled out by nanny, or early exposure to all those Martinis, but somehow she was the only one of them who seemed entirely sober. She looked as if she could go on and drink a whole fleet of sailors under the table. 'You weren't quite ready for marriage and motherhood. No one could blame you for that.'

'No, but . . . once I'd decided . . . I could have made the best of it. Instead of always wishing . . . wondering . . .' Jen took a few deep breaths, trying to suck oxygen into her poor beleaguered brain. 'Don't you think, if I was going to steal his youth, his freedom, I could at least have put my heart into it? But I didn't, did I?'

She rubbed a hand over her face, which was feeling alarmingly numb. 'I focused on all the things which were wrong with us instead of all his great qualities, and all the things which were so incredibly right.' Tears prickled the corners of her eyes as she felt swamped with remorse. 'Bitch, bitch, bitch. I turned into a tetchy strait-laced flannelette-pyjama-wearing old moaner. Obsessed with cleanness and tidying. Made him feel bad about dropping crumbs and tracking in mud. No wonder he wanted rid of me. It was all my fault.'

'I'm sure it wasn't, Jen, bach,' Rowan slurred as she put a heavy arm around her. 'You poor dab, you.'

'Obviously it wasn't your fault, Jen.' Georgina squeezed her other shoulder. 'It's always the men's. Ghastly, ignorant creatures. Peter Pan has a lot to answer for, if you want my take on it.'

'You can lead a horse to frigging water, dude.' Meg lifted her head and with extreme effort opened one eye. 'But he's still got to stick his muzzle in and suck.'

'Now, Rowan, Nutmeg, Jennifer.' Georgina rose to her feet. 'Talking of horses, time to saddle up and head off to the ranch. Otherwise we're going to be too tiddly to walk back.'

At four in the morning, from her place on the floor in front of the fire, Jen opened a bleary eye to see a moonlit Georgina sitting down to a giant sandwich.

She crawled out of her sleeping bag and wrapped a blanket around her shoulders as she staggered about in search of water for her aching head.

'Sorry,' Georgina whispered. 'I was starving. Did I wake you?'

'No.' Jen kept her voice low too. 'Dehydration did. Too

444

much booze. Georgie, I just wanted to say . . .' She faltered. What could she say? Sorry for falling for your husband? Sorry for being such a selfish ratbag? 'Sorry.'

Georgina patted her hand. 'Don't worry. We'll be fine. Whatever it is.'

'But are *you* fine? Really?' Jen felt emotional again. Georgina had been so brave, so incredible tonight with Dugan, she couldn't remember when she had last admired someone so much.

Both their eyes turned to the sandwich. 'Aiden told you,' Georgina said. It wasn't a question. 'About the bulimia.'

Jen nodded slowly. 'Isn't there something you can do?'

Georgina stared at the bread and cheese in her hand and then took a thoughtful bite.

'It's not as bad as he makes out,' she said quietly. 'I did have bulimia. Happened after I lost the baby, but I got counselling. I had a bit of a setback when I was fretting about the Heal's thing and a blip in Devon. Visited an all-night café. It's when I get overstressed. But that's all in the past. And I'm determined that it's going to stay there. If I put on a few pounds, so what. Look at Rowan, so comfortable with who she is.'

'You're right,' Jen said. 'Really, we're so much more than our age or what we look like or the state of our house or our clothes. I guess we needed Rowan to remind us of that.'

'I guess we did.'

'Georgina, I have to tell you something . . . about Aiden.'

'About you and Aiden, you mean,' she smiled knowingly.

'Nothing happened, you know.'

'Look, even if it did, I don't want to know. I just don't want you to be hurt.'

'*Me* hurt?'

'He'd never leave me, Jen, he has too much to lose. It's my money, my house, my business. He knows it and I know it. He toys with the idea but it never goes anywhere.'

'Never? You mean . . .'

'He's had endless affairs. Women fall at his feet. I don't blame you being tempted. I truly don't. You have all that history together and he has this endearing way about him, makes you feel so special inside.'

'Endless affairs?' Jen was shaken. 'But then . . . how, why do you stay? How can you be so forgiving? Why don't you leave?'

'I've wanted to, Jennifer, many times, but it's complicated. I suppose, like Rowan and Thomas, I've always felt he needed me. To support him, mother him, slap his hand when he's a naughty boy, kiss his knee when he gets a graze. And I need him, because you know, inside I've always been the insecure, bossy, chubby-chops little girl, grateful for a boyfriend, grateful that someone as attractive and appealing as Aiden Starkson could want someone as ugly and plump as me, Chubby Carrington.'

'But you're not Chubby Carrington any more. You're Gorgeous Giordani Carrington, Magnificent Giordani Carrington, Courageous Giordani Carrington.'

'Courageous Carrington, now I like the sound of that.' Georgina cheered up. 'Then you must be Bravissima Bedlow and Nutmeg could be the Legendary Lennox, Marvellous Meg.'

'Shh.' Jen put her finger to her mouth. 'For God's sake don't let her hear you say it. Her head's big enough as it is.'

Three days later Jen took off her gloves, settled herself on her regular rock and checked her watch. Monday. Eleven a.m. 22nd December. Right on time he arrived.

'Hi there.' He sat down and gently took her hand in his.

'I'm glad you could come.'

'Well of course I did.' He looked nervous, nervous but sweet and so very very handsome.

She smiled at him wistfully and he laughed. 'Come on, you're making me uneasy. What did you decide?'

'I decided yes, Starkey. Yes. If you want to be with me, I want to be with you.'

'You do?' Relief flooded his face. He wrapped his arms around her, nuzzling into her neck. 'Baby, that's wonderful. I was so worried.'

'So was I, but I know it'll work out all right,' she mumbled, smothered by his coat, then pulled her head back. 'Now come on, no time to lose. You go home and tell Georgina and I'll go home and tell Chloe. No more sneaking around. Pack your bags this afternoon.'

'Hang on.' He looked startled. 'Where's the fire? You're being rather hasty, aren't you? I can't just change my life at the drop of a hat. Why today?'

'I just thought,' she looked at their linked hands, 'no point in putting it off. We've wasted so much time already. I can't go on pretending another minute. We might as well start searching for flats as well. Come new year, I'll have to leave my house and obviously Georgina will be living in yours as her grandmother's money paid for it.'

'How do you know that?' His eyes flickered.

'Girl talk,' Jen sighed, adding, 'no secrets between friends. Apart from our little one of course, which I suppose is rather a big one. It's going to be a struggle at first, financially, I imagine. I mean obviously Ollie will shell out for Chloe, but if we're living together that's the end of my maintenance. For a start my pride wouldn't allow it. We'll both be looking for work too, I suppose, though with my skills it'll probably be stacking supermarket shelves. I'm afraid you'll have to support us, darling, but at least you'll be able to finish that novel. Oh Starkey,' she clasped her hands in rapture, 'it's going to be heaven.'

He'd risen to his feet, a frown creasing his brow.

'Wait, wait,' he held up his hand, 'you're going much too fast. I have a job. At Giordani's. I can't quit in five seconds flat. The whole company depends on me.'

'Oh?' Jen bit her lip. 'I just assumed Georgie would kick you out once she finds out about us. We have to be realistic. We'll probably be broke for ages, or until you write that best-seller, but what does that matter when we're in love and sharing our lives?'

Aiden was pacing now, his face pale. Somehow she didn't think it was all from cold. Twenty-two years she'd pined for this man, her thoughts continually drawn to him the way you probe a hole in your mouth where a tooth has been extracted, as crazy in her longing and romantic fantasies as Dugan had been over Rowan. Now she got to see what he was truly made of.

'Yes, yes, great,' he said impatiently. 'Can't you hush a minute. I've got to think. You know Georgina's in a fragile state. I'm not sure this is the moment . . .'

'Forget Georgie!' she retorted. 'I'm sick of hearing about her. What about *us*, our happiness? Besides, you should have seen her this weekend, she's a lot more together than you imagine. I've been checking the housing market,' she continued, watching him walk in perturbed circles. 'We can't afford this area, far too expensive, but I've had a quick browse through *Loot*, and we could probably find a two-bed flat in East Croydon, the area near the railway station. We'll need the extra room for Chloe.'

'Chloe?' He stopped his circling and stared at her.

'She'll be at home with us seventy-five per cent of the time at least. Ollie won't want the expense of a big custody battle but he'll get one if he kicks up a fuss. It will be such fun, all three of us, six if you count the rabbit and gerbil and Feo, until Anamaria comes back from Spain, that is. We'll be a real family.'

The harrowed look wasn't leaving his face. She stood up and threw her arms around him, snuggling into his warmth.

'Oh, baby, you'll love getting to know her. She's a sweetheart when she's not throwing pre-teen tantrums or showing off to all those friends of hers that arrive on our doorstep demanding sleepovers.' She fussed with the collar of his coat, turning it up to protect his neck. 'But heck, that's kids for you.'

'Yes, well, tantrums aren't my forte.' He stepped away, returning his coat collar to its rightful position. 'Except throwing them myself maybe.' He tried to smile. 'Isn't it unfair to bung Chloe straight in with your new lover? Shouldn't there be some time . . . a lot of time . . . in between? Let her get used to the idea?'

'But darling,' she looked surprised, 'you'll be her stepfather once we marry. And as you told me, children adapt. I was even thinking we might have a little sister or brother for her. Cement our union.'

'Sounds like you've been doing a bloody sight too much thinking,' he blurted angrily. Their eyes locked. She saw in his widening pupils realisation dawn of what she was doing.

His hand went back to brush a wave of dark hair off his forehead, clearly planning his next move. Then he spread out his arms, smiling in a charming, helpless way. A hollow reed bending with the slightest breeze.

'OK,' he said, 'you've got me. Fact is I'm not sure.'

'Not sure about what?' She pinned him with her stare, daring him to speak the truth.

'I'm not sure I can go through with this,' he said finally. 'I'm not sure this is what I want.'

She looked at him dispassionately. This man she'd cried so much over. Dreamed about. Painted in her mind as everything that was romantic, perfect and ideal.

'You know, Starkey,' she crossed her arms and sighed, 'somehow that's exactly what I thought you'd say.'

# Chapter 50

'I do apologise, Jennifer.' Georgina's voice crackled down her mobile the next morning. 'I tried getting away, but ended up caught in a meeting. I'll be there in ten minutes, tops. Promise. Look, there's a key under the snowdrops pot. Just let yourself in and make yourself a brew.'

Which was the snowdrops pot? What did it look like? Jen spent five minutes searching fruitlessly for a snowdrops pot amongst the many tubs, barrels and troughs that Georgina's gardener had placed outside the front of her house. Finally she found the key, hidden under a container of compost with a bundle of little green shoots sticking just above the surface.

It felt odd being here again on her own. No one offering her drinks, plumping up the cushions behind her back or throwing out fresh suggestions for finding Rowan.

Aiden had gone away for a few days, according to Georgina, seeming moody and out of sorts and saying he needed a break to get his head together. She wandered towards his study, the presumed centre of all their clandestine phone calls. It wasn't like the door was closed or anything, and half of her only wanted to check what the view was like from his window. Or at least that's what the other half – the devil in her right ear – told her. It was a nice view too, finely mowed lawns, assortment of conifers. She spent all of thirty seconds admiring it before the devil spurred her on, focusing her attention on the contents of his office. She glanced across at his filing cabinet, up at his books neatly displayed on solid beech shelves. Then she opened a drawer of his leather-topped desk and then another drawer, followed by a third and a fourth, and there, underneath a manila folder, lay a manuscript. Her eyes scanned the first pages.

She was so absorbed that she didn't hear the key turning in the lock, the footsteps down the hallway, the opening of the study door. All Jen heard was; 'Found what you're looking for?'

She whirled around. Georgina was standing in the doorway, briefcase in one hand, coat over her arm.

'I'm sorry,' Jen said, flustered, quickly shoving the manuscript away and shutting the drawer. 'I wasn't snooping.'

She gave a curious smile. 'Oh yes you were.'

'Well OK, maybe I was,' Jen admitted timidly.

'Have you read it? Aiden's novel?'

'Parts. I skimmed through.'

'And what do you think?'

'Excellent. Really highbrow. Should make the Booker.'

'Honest?'

'Honest.'

'Poppycock!' Georgina stepped forward, throwing her briefcase and coat on the couch. 'Come on, let's have it out. Let's play the truth game, shall we? One last time.'

'Look . . . I only . . .'

'No, come on. Right here, right now. You and me, Jennifer.'

Jen took a deep breath. 'All right, you asked for it. Aiden's book . . . what I've read . . . and maybe I'm missing something because I'm certainly no judge. But . . . it's drivel. Absolute, mindless, incomprehensible drivel. He's completely up his own arse. I never thought I'd say that about anything creative, because who am I to spout forth my big fat self-important opinion, but I'm sorry, Georgie, I think it's the worst heap of rubbish I've ever read in my whole life.'

'I do so agree,' she tittered gleefully. 'And so do the

publishers he's sent excerpts to. You know, sometimes when I'm feeling low and needy and insecure and he's being beastly, pretentious and aloof, I come in here and read a few pages and I think yes, Aiden Starkson, you're not God's Precious Gift to All Mankind or whatever you like to imagine. You have many faults. And this is a delicious example.' She pulled open the drawer Jen had just closed and tapped her index finger hard onto the manuscript.

'But I thought you'd be offended. Considering you're his wife.'

'Exactly. Who would know better than his wife – alas? Anyway, it's the truth.' She closed the drawer again. 'And you have to play the truth in the truth game, don't you, Jennifer? Nobody's black or white. We're all shades of grey, good and bad. We each have our little idiosyncrasies.'

Georgina led the way out of the office and through to the kitchen, where she switched on the kettle.

'Miss Dandridge took the day off, her sciatica's been bothering her.' She pulled out cups and saucers from a glass-fronted cabinet. 'Frankly it's a relief to be honest at last.' She took a deep breath. 'I always fancied Aiden, you know, even before you went out with him. Of course I knew it was one of those impossible crushes that schoolgirls get on their friends' boyfriends. I'd never have done anything about it, just like you'd never do anything horrible to me. But even when fate threw us together, all those years later, I always felt second-best to you, Jennifer, and to be quite truthful my heart practically stopped when I heard Nutmeg had contacted you again. I just knew Aiden would target you. Why wouldn't he? You were his first, maybe his only love.'

'Men, huh! So predictable.' Jen sighed heavily. 'I thought for years that Starkey was my one true love, I had this stupid romantic notion of it all, the great tragedy of our parting kind of crap. I even bought into it a bit when we met again, but you know what, Georgie, it was all bollocks. We were kids living a hormonal teenage dreamlife. Aiden doesn't love me. Not in a real way. And I don't love him. It was all a fantastic illusion, both of us wanting to recapture something that probably never was. I only wish I'd realised it years ago. All through my marriage, whenever I had problems with Ollie I had this handy image of the wonderful Aiden Starkson to compare him with. But everyday life can't be about thrills and uncertainty and excitement. And I almost lost something just as precious to me – your friendship – because I didn't want to wake up.'

'I know – only too well.' Georgina walked over and gave her a one-armed squeeze. 'It's so much easier to close your eyes sometimes and just pretend. Refuse to look at your dreadful marriage and cheating husband.' She gave a kind of shiver, visibly returning to her hostess self. 'What kind of tea would you like? Earl Grey? Ceylon? Lapsang souchong? Oolong?' Her fingers ranged along a row of canisters. Her kitchen was a gourmet's paradise, with a six-burner hob and gleaming copper pans.

'Any PG Tips?' Jen found herself a stool and sat down. 'You know, I've given it a lot of thought and I've decided that so much of my yearning for Aiden wasn't the man himself but what he represented – being that age when you feel everything so keenly, when you've just discovered sex and it's the most amazing thing on earth. At sixteen everything was so intense, all those emotions brand new. It was as if we were living our lives in Technicolor and as an adult it gradually faded back to shades of sepia. And much as I wouldn't want to go back to being a teenager, somehow I mixed Starkey up with those feelings, that zest for life which I'd absolutely lost.'

For a moment Georgina looked quite crestfallen. The kettle boiled and she stared hard at it, apparently forgetting why she'd switched it on. 'You know, Jennifer, with this whole searching for Rowan saga, it's almost as if she was like the Holy Grail for us all. We worshipped and envied her at the same time. You had this thing about her being beautiful, even though you're so attractive yourself. I always felt that she had all the talent, even though Giordani is a great success. And Nutmeg told me, in confidence, that she'd always wished she could be as nice as Rowan.' She poured the water into the teapot. 'That she knew she could be selfish and controlling, and Rowan was always so generous and self-sacrificing it made her feel even crummier in comparison. And then we find out Rowan's not all that – she's just, well, human, I guess. Flawed, like the rest of us.'

Jen laughed, accepting the cup and saucer offered her. 'That's funny. I was thinking it was like *The Wizard of Oz*. You, the timid one looking for courage. Me, the shiny perfectionist looking for love. And Meg . . .'

'Must be looking for her brain,' Georgina joked gently, sipping tea. 'In a cloud of marijuana and chemical haze.'

'Exactly. Only don't let her hear you say that. Actually, I think she's a lot smarter than both of us probably. She likes to play the dippy hippy but that mind's always working, calculating the angles.'

'Or angels,' Georgina chuckled.

Jen smiled. 'Maybe I'm the one looking for my brain and she's looking for her heart. In fact, last night I decided I'm going back to college to study photography. I've always wanted to.'

'Good for you,' Georgina encouraged. 'I do wonder, though, what will become of Nutmeg. After everything we've been through together I hate to see her go.'

'Go? Go where?' Jen said, alarmed.

'Oh, drat. I'm not meant to say anything until tomorrow. She's leaving this morning. Hates goodbyes she says, so didn't want anyone seeing her off or anything. Heading back to Oregon. Said she'd write.'

'What time's her flight?'

'Around three I think.'

Jen glanced at her watch. Noon.

'Georgina. You *have* to help me.'

Meg watched the guy opposite, his eyes jerking weirdly left and right as they attempted to focus on the passing station. Zeb sat beside her playing on his PSP, their suitcases taking up most of the aisle to the annoyance of people trying to squeeze past.

You'd have thought Mace would be thrilled to get rid of her after two months taking up his spare room, but he'd actually seemed sad to see her go. Hugged her and Zeb, told them to visit any time. Maybe they did have a fucking relationship in spite of everything.

And for the rest of her schemes? Nothing had worked out the way she'd expected. There wouldn't be another dime from Irwin, that was for sure, although they had had one last lunch together in which he expressed a sort of regret, offered her tickets for his latest Broadway show, and implied that the new bride was pulling the strings. That other idea – well, for all kinds of reasons, she'd decided it wasn't to be. Or rather she wasn't going to pursue it. She grinned a little, sucking some candy that Zeb had given her. Maybe a little of Rowan's saintliness had rubbed off on her, after all. Whatever – they'd get by. She was a survivor, always had been.

And as for the whole Rowan adventure – what a wild ride that had been. The totally awesome thing was that her angel had turned out to be right – even if none of the others believed in his existence. Rowan *had* needed them – but who would have guessed they'd needed her just as much? And that they'd rediscover the closeness that had shattered the day Starkey came on the scene. Georgina had almost been in tears when they'd said goodbye. She felt bad not calling Jen, but she still wasn't sure that she'd entirely forgiven her for all the things she'd said to her in the park. Maybe she'd send a postcard from Oregon.

Jen jogged along the travelator at Gatwick, checking her watch as she went and cursing the fact that her fitness schedule had been so curtailed this past couple of months. Georgina had been a whirlwind of motion, researching the baffling number of airlines that had connecting flights to Portland, arguing over passenger confidentiality, finally tracking down Mace's office and winnowing the information from him. North West Airlines. Via Houston. Only trouble was, she glanced at her watch again, skin clammy under her layers from all this running, she was more than likely too late. Déjà vu all over again. Another feature of her old life that seemed to have haunted her recently.

She just managed to scrape into the lift to the second floor, alongside a mother with a double buggy and a couple of kids. Looking desperately around, Jen tried to focus her eyes on the big yellow South Terminal International Departures signs as she wiped sweat from her brow. Once in the main hall, she frantically searched the left-hand side of the blue screen that she'd stopped in front of for Meg's flight number.

There it was, North West Airlines. NW43. Her eyes scanned along – Boarding Gate. Damn it. No delays, take-off at five past three, Gate 27. She checked her watch again. Shit! Even if she knew which zone, it wouldn't matter. She'd be bound to have checked in already. And she would definitely have gone through security, since you had to check in two and a half hours before departure. It was hopeless.

Oh well, she made her way back through the throngs of thousands. Silly idea anyway. It was just . . . she really wanted to see her off.

Jen spooned the froth from her cappuccino. No rush to get back. Chloe was off school now, finished for the Christmas holidays and out at the park with her friend Sophie and her mum.

She watched as a plane, probably Meg's, North West Airlines at least, taxied down the runway, imagining she could see her from the window, with her little angel on her shoulder.

Gulping down her coffee, Jen stood up, and that was when she saw Meg's doppelgänger flicking through a magazine. The double they said everyone had somewhere in the world. Long red hair, aquamarine beanie hat, calf-length purple skirt and Ugg boots.

It couldn't be. Georgina had said . . . But it was. For once the great, 'I might not always be right but I'm never wrong' Giordani Carrington had definitely been wrong.

Jen skipped over and tapped Meg on the shoulder, looking past her as she did, realising she wasn't alone. Leafing through a comic was a boy around Chloe's age. He was wearing a rucksack, his hair dark brown and cropped short. He looked nothing like Meg.

The American woman did a double take, then shrieked and hugged her.

'I thought you were on your way to Portland.' Jen grinned.

'Change of plans.' Meg grinned back. 'Talked to Herb this morning. We lucked out. He sent me a ticket to Bangkok. Might as well get some sun before we head back to that damp Oregon winter. Zeb,' she steered his shoulders so he was facing Jen, 'this is Jen. She was my best friend at school. Say hi.'

'Hi, Jen,' he said in a twangy American accent. He held out his hand and shook hers solemnly. Jen was arrested by his eyes. Unmistakably familiar. So dark they were almost black.

'Here, honey.' Meg emptied her purse with shaking hands on to the table. 'Do me a favour, go check out the souvenir section. Pick up something nice for Poppa and Imee. Oh and get yourself some gum.'

'Sure, Mom.' He jogged obligingly away.

'And he's supposed to be Irwin Beidlebaum's son? Yeah, right.'

457

Meg pursed her lips, a faraway look in her green eyes. 'He could have been. I wanted him to be. So did Irwin at first. If the old toerag hadn't got hitched again, we'd all still be happy campers. I don't ever want Georgina to know. You gotta promise me!'

'I promise.' Jen's head was reeling. 'Was it that night? In the Marlow Arms?'

She nodded. 'It only happened once. Way too much booze, not a single functioning brain cell to tell me it was a real bad idea.' Meg twirled a strand of long red hair around a finger, casting her eyes ruefully to the heavens. 'Now you see why I was loathe for you guys to meet? It wasn't so obvious at first but as he's gotten older . . .'

'Are you a hundred per cent certain?'

Her mouth quirked. 'Well there might be a few other contenders, I wasn't exactly locked at the knees back then, but no one else is in the front running. Take a look, you tell me.' She hitched her carry-on bag over her shoulder as they both glanced across at her son, being served by a cashier. 'I don't have definite proof. I could push for tests but well, shoot . . .' She sighed and then resumed. 'For a while there I was kind of thinking . . . the bank of Irwin has run dry, and until I get my healing practice going – if ever – the only money coming in is what I earn as a lousy waitress. There wasn't exactly a line-up of eager candidates wanting to pay Zeb's living expenses, health insurance, college tuition, and Giordani's undoubtedly worth a mint. But looks like Mace wants to step into the uncle role – he's keen that Zeb should go to a good school. And, hey, now I think about it the resemblance isn't that strong. You know, appearances can be deceiving.'

'Yes, they can.' Jen nodded, watching Zeb weave his way back through the crowded kiosk.

'No point in speculating about things that we'll never know for sure.' Meg followed her gaze.

'No point at all.' Jen felt choked. 'How's your angel? Still sitting on your shoulder?'

'Actually he's standing behind you, honey. He has a message for you.'

'He does?' Jen turned around but of course all she could see was a teenage girl reading *Cosmo*. Zeb skidded to a halt beside them, his hands full of plastic bags.

'Yes.' Meg put her arm around him. 'He says don't worry, man, the show ain't over till the fat lady sings.'

Zeb grinned. Jen gawped, then laughed so hard she almost knocked over a stand of postcards.

'That's a message?' she said, wiping her eyes.

'From my lips to God's ear.' Meg touched the crystal around her neck. 'You don't hate me, do you, Jen?'

'No, Meg,' Jen gave her a hug, 'I could never hate you. You'll always be my heroine for life.'

'Heroine for life? Where did that spring from?'

'The first morning we met. My first impression of you. I looked it up recently. Here, I wrote it down.' She pulled a piece of paper from her pocket. 'According to Wikipedia, heroine refers to characters that in the face of danger and adversity or from a *position of weakness*,' she emphasised the last three words, 'display courage and the will for self-sacrifice – that is, heroism – for some greater good, originally of martial courage or excellence but extended to more general moral excellence.'

'Moral excellence?' Meg smiled ruefully.

'When the chips were down, Meg, you were there for us. Standing up to Dugan. Not telling Georgina about my silliness with Aiden. And now,' she gestured toward Zeb, 'sacrificing potential child support for Georgina's happiness. Hey, now that's a true heroine.'

'Well then you're mine, dude.' Meg squeezed her back. 'You're mine too.'

# Chapter 51

'You're ready to exchange contracts, Mrs Stoneman. All you need do is sign the documents and send them back to the office. We already have Mr Stoneman's signature and the courier could be there in ten minutes if you're not going out.'

'I'm in all morning.'

So, all those insurmountable problems with the Radcliffes had suddenly resolved themselves and they were now all set to go. Today would mark the end of her and Ollie owning this house, 36 Woburn Close. It was an odd feeling. Not quite sad, but something close. On one hand she was glad to get shot of it. She'd never loved the house. Their lives had taken a down-hill turn from the moment they'd moved in. On the other hand it wasn't to blame. There'd been joyful moments too, celebrations, laughter, family evenings with all three of them watching Disney films by the fake-log gas fire. And thankfully the new buyers thought it was perfect. But still it was the end of an era. And the new one ahead of her looked hazy and a little bereft.

She switched on the radio. The announcer was twittering on about the weather. 'Moderate snow likely in the afternoon . . . High of minus two degrees Celsius . . . Wind east-south-east around fifteen knots, gusting to twenty knots. After several false starts, looks like we may have a white Christmas in spite of everything. Coral have cut the odds by . . .'

She was packing books in boxes when the doorbell rang. Jen

grabbed a pen from a kitchen drawer and answered it. Instead of the courier she'd been expecting, it was Ollie standing on the doorstep holding a large thin rectangular package.

'Early Christmas present,' he said, holding it out.

'Coffee?' Jen moved aside to let him in. 'Kettle's just boiled.'

'I've got a better idea.' He brought his other hand out from behind his back with a bottle of Moët.

'At eleven?' She looked at the clock. This was getting to be a habit. First Helen, now Ollie.

'What better time? It's a big day.'

Jen was bringing out a couple of champagne flutes when the bell rang again.

'I'll get it.' Ollie jumped up, speeding for the door. He joined her in the kitchen moments later. 'It's a courier from the solicitor's office. He's waiting outside.'

'Contracts arrived?'

'Guess so.' He handed her a brown envelope. 'You need to put your signature there, next to mine, and he'll take it right back. They can exchange this afternoon apparently.'

'I know.' She placed the papers on the table and leafed through to the appropriate pages for signature. 'Now we really do have something to celebrate, don't we?'

'Don't we just?' He pulled his chair close, his forearms inches away from her own, eyeing her as if she was a time bomb and he had to decide between the red and blue wires.

'I heard you missed me.' She couldn't resist a sidelong peek even as she initialled pages.

Ollie grinned and took a sip of champagne. 'Said who?'

'Saul told Helen. Helen told me.'

'Big mouths,' he swallowed, Adam's apple bobbing as he put his glass down. 'I knew they'd blab.'

Jen sat down, pen poised, then hesitated. 'But if that's true – why couldn't you just tell me that yourself?'

'Are you serious?' His youthful face sparkled – or not so

461

youthful, she realised now. He seemed different, or maybe she hadn't really looked at him for a while. A man, not a kid. He was thirty, after all. 'After the way you attacked that poor bugger in Wales?' he teased. 'I'm treading very carefully around you from now on.'

'Like you were ever scared of anything.'

'Maybe I thought you'd get even more big-headed than you are already.' He went back to her question, still grinning. 'All these men pursuing you madly the minute I'm out of the picture.'

'Ha bloody ha.' She felt wretched suddenly. What must he think of her? First Aiden, then Dugan. At least she'd broken her perfect-housewife image. Next thing she'd be traipsing around Huntsleigh high street in leather miniskirts and fishnet stockings. And maybe collagen lips, puffed up to look like a grouper. Or a groupie. A groupie grouper.

Ollie's face turned grave. 'What happened to us, Jen?'

'Life, I suppose.' Jen put the pen down again and looked up to meet his so very blue eyes. 'Great expectations, as Charles Dickens might say. Too great to live up to. I used to miss you so much when you went away to work even though I knew that was part of the deal, that you were doing it for us.' She made a face, uncomfortable with her own mawkishness. 'Perhaps all the time, subconsciously, I thought you were going to get off with a camel. Or find yourself taken hostage in some stupid terrorist situation and cost me a small ransom.'

He smiled. 'I have to say, Saul might be more knowledgeable than you about football, cars and cooking but he doesn't have your sweet way with words.' He put his hand over hers and she could feel a strange flutter. 'You know, you were my best friend, Jen.'

'And you were mine, Ollie.'

She could smell his familiar spicy aftershave as he let go. She picked up the pen again, the pen that would allow them to lose this house, untie their ship, set Jen forever adrift into the big wide world.

And in microseconds her mind flashed back to all the wonderful and tragic things that had happened through their marriage. Like when Jen and Ollie played in the parents versus kids football match and Jen took a ferocious kick at the goal, only to have the ball bounce off the post and hit Ollie in the face. And the time Chloe played in her first concert with the school orchestra and she dropped her bow and the audience gasped while she quickly picked it up and she and Ollie were instantly on their feet, applauding wildly in a standing ovation. And sitting up all night together by Chloe's bed when she was in hospital with suspected meningitis. And burying her hamster Bucky in a torrential downpour because Chloe was grief-stricken and Ollie due to fly out at dawn the next day. And the way Ollie held her hand when she was giving birth to Chloe and wouldn't let go, even though he had deep gouges in his fist from her clawing nails. And their wedding day when they both got the giggles over a pimple on the registrar's nose and almost couldn't get out their vows from falling about in hysterics.

She felt as if she was drowning, her entire marriage appearing before her eyes as she sank for the third time. Life as she knew it was ending. For good or bad.

A few discreet coughs from the doorway reminded them that the courier was still waiting.

'We mustn't disappoint the Radcliffes,' Ollie said, 'they've waited a long time for this.' He handed her the pen and she signed her name for the last time and took the papers down the hall to the courier.

'I've never liked this place,' he said, staring around. 'I know you were in love with it but . . .'

'Me?' Jen glared at him. 'You picked it if I remember correctly.'

'You wanted to live in Huntsleigh.'

'You said it was modern and easy to keep clean,' she reminded him indignantly.

'Little did I know,' he said. 'Open your present.'

It was a painting. Big swirly clouds and a whirling sun over a landscape of wheatfields and crop circles and a tumbledown cottage. On the doorstep sat a little black cat. The brass plate on the frame read *Freedom*.

'An original Bedlow,' he said. 'Should be worth a fortune some day.'

'It's lovely, Ollie,' she kissed his cheek. 'That reminds me, I've got something for you.' Jen rose to her feet, went over to a drawer and picked out a six-inch-square red leather box. 'Look inside.'

Ollie opened the lid and poked around. 'Green tissue paper?' He raised his eyebrows.

'Inside the green tissue paper. That was the smallest box we had.'

Carefully he removed the wrappings, to reveal his wedding ring. She took it out and placed it in his palm.

He turned it around in his fingers. 'You found it?' His face was almost awestruck, staring at the small item as if mesmerised.

'Well I didn't get it remade, if that's what you're imagining. It was in your old sports bag. Weird timing, eh?'

'Very weird.' There was a long pause and then they both spoke at once.

'Look . . .'

'I was thinking . . .'

'You first.'

'No, you.'

'All right,' Ollie sighed. 'You know, Jen, I've missed you. Your face. Your smile. Your laugh. The way you sing a song, saying the words before you sing them. The maniacal way you clean the table before we've finished eating. The way you chase after me and Chloe with your dustpan, your madness and eccentricity.'

'Hey stop, stop,' she laughed. 'It started well but now you're making me sound like I'm some type of nutcase.'

'Well, you know, I'd given up on us. It seemed that whatever I did I couldn't make you happy. But, lately, well, maybe since you met up with those friends of yours . . . it's like you're back to the funny, bright, off-the-wall girl I fell in love with. And I'm having real trouble letting her go.'

'What about Hot Lips Hutton?' She couldn't contain herself.

'Frances? She's a nice lady,' he said. 'But she was only ever a friend, whatever Saul and Helen dreamed up. I wasn't ready to get involved again so soon. Besides,' he looked at her guilelessly, 'I'm not even sure she thought about me in that way.'

Jen laughed, she couldn't help it. The day suddenly seemed twenty degrees sunnier. 'Oh Ollie,' she said, 'even despite Euro Disney? That's *exactly* why I love you.'

'You love me?'

'Yes.' She nodded vigorously. 'Yes, I bloody do.'

They snuggled up together in the sitting room on the beige cotton sofa.

'And this is the first thing I'm getting rid of.' Ollie wriggled uncomfortably, leaning into its ungiving back.

'We haven't got anywhere to put it anyway,' Jen reminded him. 'We've sold the house.'

'Good riddance,' he said. 'We'll get a new one. I mean an old one. A new old one. Maybe a farmhouse like Rowan's, only, you know, with less dry and wet rot and a solid foundation and even some plaster on the stone walls.'

'Now you're getting awfully picky.' She felt giddy with happiness. 'Can we have acreage? Only there was a notice in the Sheepshearer pub, someone selling their whole alpaca herd and equipment in a divorce sale, and we could do some farming. Besides my photography I always wanted to be a farmer.'

'You can have your alpacas,' Ollie promised, 'Chloe can have a baby lamb and I'll have my organic market garden.'

'Organic market garden?'

'Why not? I've always wanted to. If it's good enough for Prince Charles, it's good enough for me. Maybe it's time we discovered our roots again.'

'Yeah.' Jen tilted her head forward, examining her unbleached parting in the reflection of the window opposite her. 'I've been thinking about those . . . Hey, this'll be great.' She turned to him, enthused. 'We'll find a smallholding, some place with character, where we can put up Chloe's drawings and it won't look odd and the paint peeling off the walls will look quite natural because it's ethnic and old and we can have filthy floors and feel cool about them.'

'Filthy floors?' Ollie laughed at her. 'Wow, how lucky am I!'

'I've got to say one thing first,' She was suddenly sober, 'About you and me. And Aiden.'

'You don't need to . . .'

'No, I do. Wait. Ollie, I never told anyone this before, but something terrible happened that night I waited for him. You know, when he was supposed to visit me and stood me up instead. He didn't show up at the station and I waited and waited in case he'd missed the train and was coming in on a later one, and it got dark and it was raining and my dad's boss, Mr Farber . . . he came along on the last train and he offered me a lift and . . .' She broke off, biting her lip. 'Anyway, he was disgusting. Been drinking at a Christmas party. I shouldn't have got in, he smelt so bad, stale whisky and stinky wet wool but he was friends with my dad, he used to come to our house a lot. He parked up in a dark wood and I . . . I had to fight him off. If it hadn't been for a woman passing with a dog . . .'

'It's OK.' Ollie held her as she started to shake. 'It's all in the past now. It can't hurt you.'

She took a deep breath and forged on. So many years she hadn't wanted to talk about it, now it all came spilling out.

'I managed to get a lift home from her, but in spite of her

466

begging me to call the police, I couldn't. And I couldn't tell my dad either, it would have killed him to feel he hadn't protected me, he would have lost his job, everything, and it would have been my word against Mr Farber's. So I took off to London, telling Dad that I had a bunch of parties to go to, making up friends I didn't have, telephoning him weekly, saying what a great time I was having, that I'd found a wonderful job and flat. In reality, I spent Christmas in a dingy hostel surrounded by drunks and druggies. My only real friends, Rowan, Meg and Georgie, were all spread out, Georgie in Switzerland, Meg back in the States and Rowan in Wales. Could have been worse, I guess, could have been the soup kitchen, on the streets.'

Ollie stroked her hair; she leaned against him, cuddling into his protective arm.

'I spent my seventeenth birthday staying in some graffiti-strewn short-term high-rise flat, where you could hear everything through the walls, every terrifying bang and shout through the night. It was the most miserable, loneliest time of my life. I could see Brent Cross shopping centre from my window, all the people arriving with their money, parking, going to the sales. I ended up on antidepressants, the only thing I had going for me was work. I managed to get an office job and then I met Helen. She saved me. Literally. I was almost suicidal, not knowing which way to go. I wasn't eating, could barely afford my rent and she took me in. She was like a mum to me. Mum, landlady, interfering friend. She's the only one who knows the whole of it. That's why she's so protective of me.' She turned her head to look up at Ollie. 'I know you've not always got along.'

'Nah, she's not so bad,' Ollie smiled. 'I've got to know her better recently. We're almost, I hesitate to say, friends.'

She laughed, suddenly feeling about five stone lighter. It was such a relief to unburden herself, as if she could finally let go of the weight she'd carried for so many years. 'But after all that, boy did I have a real sour attitude towards men. And I still felt that way until I met you, Ollie. You were so funny, kind and sunny, that I . . .'

'Shh,' he stopped her with a kiss. 'You're all right now.'

'Anyway,' she said, when she came up for air, 'it made it hard for me to trust people. Even when I was happy I felt deep down inside it wasn't going to last. That it wasn't meant for me, I wasn't worthy somehow. I think with us getting divorced and meeting Aiden again, well it all became complicated, like I was caught up in going back to an earlier time when everything felt simpler. I never meant to be such an awful wife. No wonder your friends thought I was a naggy old drag. Maybe I didn't show it or even appreciate it myself sometimes, but I always really . . .'

He kissed her again. 'You weren't such an awful wife. I bet we had the cleanest house in Huntsleigh.'

'I'm trying to tell you I love you, you jerk.' She broke free and punched him with a cushion. 'I've always loved you and always will.'

'Does that mean we should get married again?' Ollie mused when he'd wrestled it from her. 'For Chloe's sake? Or do you have strong feelings about living in sin?'

'I don't know.' She pretended to ponder. 'I like my freedom.' She took his hand and pulled him to his feet. 'Now I'm divorced, I can shag anyone I want,' she added flirtily, climbing the stairs and sashaying her hips in a way that would have made Anamaria proud.

'Is that a fact?' He grabbed her from behind, whizzing her off her feet and over the threshold into the bedroom. 'And might I ask if you have a victim in mind?'

And this time there was no Helen glaring at her.

'You, Ollie,' she said meekly as he threw her on the bed and kick-closed the door. 'Only you.'

468

# Epilogue

Jen let go of Walter's waistband and collapsed on to her new black leather couch, waving off Enid's request for her to rejoin the conga.

'No, I've had enough,' she laughed, watching the line of people dance around her lounge, shuffling their feet then kicking alternate legs at every third beat as they filed past and into the hall. Enid was leading then Anamaria, followed by her new boyfriend, Nemesio, whom she'd brought back from Madrid to live with her. Squashed between him and Walter, who was at the back now Jen had left the line, was Chloe, her face beaming.

'Come on, Daddy,' she yelled as she spotted her father trying to sneak past with an empty tray. 'Join in.'

'Not again,' groaned Ollie. 'Helen needs a hand in the kitchen.'

'*I'll* help Helen.' Jen stood up and manoeuvred him towards the conga tail. 'You amuse our guests.'

After a short time of being ordered around by Chef Helen and her deputy and chief Brussels-sprout-scorer, Saul, Jen had sneaked off to her bedroom with Anamaria to fill her in on all that had happened since she'd been away. Just in case she put her big Barcelonian foot in it.

'So you will remarry your Ollie, yes?' Anamaria smiled.

'Who knows?' Jen scratched Feo, who immediately turned on his back and stuck his little legs in the air in rapturous delight. 'At the moment, it's just fabulous the way it is. Ollie's moved back in with us and Chloe's thrilled and we're scouring the Internet for a new house to buy, but if we don't find one by our completion date, heigh ho, we'll just rent or whatever.'

'Your face, it is sparkling.'

Jen laughed. 'You know, Anamaria, even though Ollie and I have had to go through all this, I truly think it's all been for the best. It's like we're in the honeymoon phase. The sort of honeymoon we should have had. Now here,' Jen reached under her bed and brought out a large thin wrapped box, 'your present.'

'A present? For me? *Maravilloso!*'

'You might not think so when you open it,' Jen said as Anamaria greedily ripped off the paper. 'It's a photo jigsaw of your dog. Custom-made.'

'I love it!' Anamaria squealed. 'All thousand pieces. But,' she frowned, 'he is not *my* dog.'

'It is Feo. Look.' Jen pointed at the picture on the lid. 'Same moustache, same wispy fur, same blood-red tongue. I sent them in a photograph.'

'No, I mean he is *your* dog now. See the way he looks at you?'

'But . . .'

'Besides, my Nemesio, he is allergic, so,' she shrugged, 'it is, how you say, a done deal.'

'Well, thanks.' Now she had to break it to Ollie. But the truth was the three of them had grown fond of the ugly mutt.

The bell rang for the umpteenth time, and seconds later Chloe stepped into the bedroom and sighed dramatically. 'More visitors, Mummy.'

Jen was shocked by the surprise – but most welcome – guest.

'Georgina!' Jen looked behind her quickly. Thankfully on her own.

'Merry Christmas!' They greeted each other with a warm hug as Anamaria ushered Chloe back to the party.

'So you came alone?'

'Yes,' she sighed. 'These past few months – everything that

happened – you, Meg, Rowan, well it's finally given me the courage to call it quits. Aiden. England. Even Giordani. A short sabbatical of sorts. Flying out in two days. Heading for Bora Bora, would you believe. Max will . . .'

'I know.' Jen nodded. 'Max will drive you to the airport.'

'No, actually, I was going to say Max will be coming with me. It was his idea.'

'Max? Your chauffeur? Your right-hand man?' She felt her jaw sag, caught completely by surprise by the tell-tale sparkle in Georgina's eyes.

'His left hand's not bad either.' She gave a little chuckle.

'Georgina! You hussy!' Jen laughed, astonished and amused.

'It was while I was driving on that dashed awful motorway, Meg told me to think of something calming. Well, the only person that keeps me calm, sane, even – is Max. We've spent hours talking on all those car trips, and I started to see that the man outside the chauffeur's cap is even more than I ever imagined. He's had a fascinating life. Stunt driver. Bodyguard. Lived in Japan. And so smart. You wouldn't believe his bookshelf. Don't worry, Aiden will do all right. He has his Giordani shares and he'll get a decent divorce settlement. More than he deserves anyhow.'

They walked arm in arm down the hall as Georgina babbled on with her plans. 'Aiden was right in one respect. I've hired all those very talented employees, so let them run the show for a change. Call it recharging the creative batteries.'

'Call it recharging the old love juices more like, you cheeky minx,' Jen teased gently as she opened the kitchen door. 'Come on through and meet everybody.'

Georgina seemed amazed at the number of people crowding round Helen, who was showing everyone how to make the perfect stuffing, giving them all the benefit of her worldly advice.

'This is Helen, my dearest friend, and Saul, Ollie's ex-landlord and best mate. And Anamaria . . .' She went through the introductions.

'*Hola. Feliz Navidad.* Happy Christmas, Georgina.' Anamaria swapped double kisses with her before Georgina spotted Ollie and ran towards him, flinging her arms around his neck. 'Oliver. So brilliant to see you again.'

'Oy, oy, hands off the head, please.' Ollie backed away laughing, pretending to be scared. 'I'd like to keep my hair as long as possible, thank you.'

The bell rang once more, which set Feo barking again. Enid went to answer it and came back with a chubby-cheeked rosy-faced woman, multicoloured poncho around her large shoulders, and a pair of what Enid considered might be chopsticks in her piled-up greying hair.

'Someone to see you.'

'Rowan, you made it!' Jen's eyes lit up when she saw her. 'Everyone, I'd like you to meet my old friend Rowan.'

'Quick.' Georgina came over, mobile in hand, and pulled Rowan to one side. 'Guess who I'm on the phone to – here, I'll put her on loudspeaker.'

'Merry Christmas!' Meg's voiced boomed out.

'Merry Christmas!' they all yelled back.

Walter turned to Jen and whispered, 'To think we were worried about you. Enid and me and Anamaria. We thought you were unhappy, hated Huntsleigh and had no friends.'

'Did you now?' Jen looked across at Helen, chatting animatedly to Anamaria, and Enid beside them, who'd stooped down to baste the turkey while being licked to death by Feo. Saul and Ollie discussing football scores. Rowan with her arm around Georgina, two heads stuck together as they tried to chat to Meg over the noise of music and laughter. New friends, old friends, even bad relationships turned good.

'I thought so too at one time.' She smiled and kissed Walter's cheek. 'But I was wrong. I might not deserve it but I have the best friends in the world.'

# Acknowledgements

First of all, thanks to our terrific editor, Emma Rose, whose insights dramatically improved this book and all the Arrow team, especially Laura Mell, our publicist, who survived working with us on *Sisters*. Thanks too to our terrific agent, Caroline Hardman at the Marsh Agency, and to Camilla and Annina for our foreign rights sales.

Many people including Jeni (LBC), Phil (BBC Radio Wales), *Times* Online Alpha-Mummy, Laura (*Daily Express*) and other journalists and radio interviewers, made the launch of our first novel special. Carol Smith threw us a great party and she and Fiona Walker took time from writing their own fabulous novels to review ours. Teri at Bookworms and Dawn organised the Pavilion do along with Sheila, Paul, Eleanor, Lesley and Kay. Waterstone's, Redhill gave us our first book signing where terrified shoppers fled from our pink 'champagne'. Thanks to you all.

Special thanks to our husbands (and BFs), Ian and Gary, and our ever-supportive families. Also to Pam's New Year friends for everything (we must meet more often!), fellow badminton partners (especially Angela for the photo), Sue and John (I told you I was rubbish at netball), Kim and the co-bike riding challengers (see you in Paris), Chris and Mike (for endless cuppas), Ana and Amanda for their worldly advice, friends who live afar but who I know are always there when needed – Irv, Mary, Ced, Deanna, Ginny, Tim and, as ever, Ness.

Hooray for Koni, Debbie and Christine, Lorraine's surrogate sisters; Kaitlyn who always brushes her hair nicely; Xanthe and Michelle; partners-in-hilarity, and their partners, Dana and Scott; also the fun-loving crew of the *It'll Do*: Tommy, Liz, Cheri, George, Mary Kay, Guy, Rod, Christina, Barb, Evan; all our great Boulder buddies including Charlotte, Firuzeh, Navid, Kate, John, Jean, David, Bonnie, Kat, etc. Thanks to the "horsey" pals, Lyn, Joan, Jodi, Julie and all Sue's gang; also Bob, Sophie, Aunt Pat and neglected London friends like Clare, John, Rose, Gaynor, Richard, Megan and Nancy – I think of you even if we've lost touch.

We fondly remember the old friends in Bognor (especially Guv) who helped us survive our school years. And send everlasting gratitude to all neighbours, friends and colleagues at East Surrey College, the Y, and in the UK and the US who bought *Sisters*, came to the Pavilion or otherwise encouraged us. You're all the best!

And please feel free to contact us at www.elliecampbell books.com